Maelstrom of Malice

KAREN TAYLOR

Karen

Published in the UK 2025
Copyright Karen Taylor 2025
ISBN T/C

Copy Editor: Sophie Brownlow
Cover illustration: Janine Wing
Cover layout: Cavan Convery

Karen Taylor has asserted her right to be identified as the author of this Work in accordance with the CPDA 1988.

Printed and bound by Imprint Academic, Devon.

For Alec and Maureen Taylor

Are you not you moved, when all the sway of earth
Shakes like a thing unfirm? …
I have seen tempests when the scolding winds
Have rived the knotty oaks, and I have seen
Th' ambitious ocean swell and rage and foam
To be exalted with the threat'ning clouds;
But never till tonight, never till now,
Did I go through a tempest dropping fire.
Either there is a civil strife in heaven,
Or else the world, too saucy with the gods,
Incenses them to send destruction.

Casca to Cicero, Julius Caesar, Act 1, Scene 3.
William Shakespeare.

1

February 27, 2022

Rachel

The sky went black as the Great Western pulled out of St Erth Station. It was just five in the afternoon, but the clouds were having none of it.

Rachel Matthews glanced up from her phone screen which had moved to night mode. The storm which had been brewing since Exeter had arrived. It had been raining hard for most of the day. But that could well have been the warm-up. Having lived in Penzance most of her 35 years, Rachel was used to the changeable weather. But today she wanted to meander into town unobtrusively, not drenched and battered by torrential conditions. Her mother Lizzie had threatened to meet her at the station. Would she have enough good sense to either stay at home or bring a brolly? Rachel started to tap into her phone to warn her off, just as a streak of lightening emblazoned the sky. A clap of thunder started the terrier in the basket in front barking.

A young guy with dreadlocks was at the window across the aisle taking photos with his phone. 'Armageddon,' he murmured, one hand reaching for the back of his chair as the train jolted.

Rachel got up from her seat and moved to the empty one behind him. For an artist it was too good a spectacle to miss. She wiped the condensation off the window with the sleeve of her cardigan, but the rain made it hard to see anything but a thin streak of light between sea and sky. The carriage rocked again. The guy in the dreadlocks sat back down and started talking into his phone. 'Gotta be Gale Force 9 out there, man.'

Too wild for surfing. Too wild for sailing. Too wild for … a massive wave smashed down on the carriage as the train took the bend past St Michael's Mount and into the home stretch to Penzance station. The coastal path was flooded. Beyond it waves were rising. Rachel hadn't seen anything like it. Her phone battery was low, but she kept on clicking and wiping the window. A shaft of biblical light shone through the clouds onto the angry sea. Rachel glided her finger to video mode, just as the carriage lights went out and she was thrust forward, her hands outstretched to break her fall, one still gripping her phone. The dog had stopped barking. But a baby was wailing and there was a cacophony of voices and gasps.

'It's tilting. I think it's going over,' a man was shouting. 'We hit something. A fallen tree?'

Rachel went to turn, but she couldn't move. The seat behind was rammed up against her back. Her legs were trapped beneath the chair in front. She could still move her head. She took a deep breath to steady her rising panic and turned to the window and the sea. A wave was building. She prepared for its onslaught, one hand holding her phone, the other wiping the glass.

There was someone out there. By the metal fence which divided the coastal path from the railway line. Click. She saw another shadowy figure, clambering up from the tracks and mounting the fencing. Click. Click. Then her phone went black.

2

Brandon

Detective Inspector Brandon Hammett was taking a call from his office landline at Penzance Station. It had been a quiet, wet day, full of foreboding. A major storm had been forecast. Storm Ida, a violent beast which was hurtling over from the Scilly Isles, fresh from the Caribbean.

'What?' Brandon said into the receiver, feeling in his pocket for his vibrating mobile. 'I take it the fire brigade are on their way?' he said into the landline, glancing down at his mobile. Lizzie Matthews was calling him. Rachel Matthew's mother. He took the call: 'Lizzie. Can you just wait one minute?'

'I'll get along to the train station,' he said into the landline. 'Lizzie? Everything okay?'

Detective Sergeant Jo Menhenrick had rushed into the room, so he put Lizzie on speaker.

'Rachel's on that train. That train!' Lizzie was hysterical.

'The Fire Brigade will be there any minute.' The sound of sirens was coming through the phone. 'Where are you, Lizzie?' He was trying to sound calm. But years of training and practical experience couldn't steady his pounding heart.

'I'm at the station.' He could barely hear her over the commotion. 'Rachel's on that train. They're saying something was on the tracks.'

'Where is the train, Lizzie?' Brandon said, nodding at Jo and pulling his jacket off the back of his chair.

'It's outside of the station. The front carriages are off the rails. She hasn't called me. Rachel would have called me if she was okay. She knew I was coming out to meet her. Brandon, I'm going to her.'

'Lizzie, don't,' he said, feeling for his car keys. 'The Fire Brigade are there. I'm on my way. Jo and I will be with you in no time.'

Jo had her coat on and the door open.

* * * * *

In a bright yellow fisherman's cagoule, matching hat and wellington boots, Lizzie Matthews stood out like a beacon at the far end of the crowded platform. Firefighters and police were on the tracks and mounting the train. The carriages were still upright, but some looked in danger of rolling over. Lifting and cutting equipment was already being employed, with the emphasis on getting the passengers out. Brandon hurried down the platform to Lizzie.

Her face was wet with rain and tears.

'They're bringing them out,' she said, waving an arm at a group of passengers walking down the tracks, wrapped in blankets. 'Not Rachel. She hasn't called. Brandon, she hasn't called.'

Brandon took her outstretched hand. 'That doesn't mean anything, Lizzie. She could have lost her mobile in the ...' He didn't know how to describe it. Collision? Electricity black out? Flooding? The waves were crashing over the coastal wall and fencing onto the carriages.

'Or her battery may have died,' Jo said, smiling sympathetically.

Lizzie tutted. 'That would be typical of Rachel.'

Brandon's mobile was ringing. He took the call, brushing back his fringe from his eyes. 'You are kidding?'

'Rachel? Is it, Rachel?' Lizzie was tugging at his sleeve like a child.

Brandon put a finger to his mouth, then whispered. 'No.' He clicked off the phone and turned to Jo. 'As if this isn't enough, there's a distressed yacht just beyond the harbour. It's been heeling since the storm broke. The RNLI are there but aren't getting any response from the yacht. They keep trying to board, but the waves are pushing them back.'

Jo gave him an exasperated look, brushing aside sodden strands of hair. 'We'll have to leave them to it?'

'Of course,' Brandon said. 'Nothing we can do there. But I'm going to see if I can help on the tracks.'

'I'll come too,' Jo said.

Brandon nodded at Lizzie and the other wet and forlorn characters on the platform and coming up the tracks. 'You'll be better here. I may be able to do some heavy lifting.' He lowered his voice as he said those last words. He hadn't had to deal with a scene like this before, but it didn't take a leap of imagination to envisage what to expect inside the carriages. The ones at the back had been concertinaed.

Brandon braced himself as he strode towards the end of the platform and down the brick steps onto the rails. The storm wasn't easing. Born in Texas and raised in the southern states of America, he had seen some wild weather in his time and this was comparable. It was difficult to walk, especially as he was having to navigate a way through the stream of passengers being helped off the train. Some were relatively spritely, others the walking wounded. Rachel wasn't among them. His heart rate began to quicken. The firefighters were doing the logical thing – getting passengers off the most endangered carriages. The front one was teetering and looked set to topple. Was she in the end carriage? Probably not. She'd have gone second class, they usually seated them in the middle.

Brandon walked along the row of carriages, past the first one that was swarming with firefighters, pulling people out, cutting through the jammed doors. He stepped into the second carriage. Catering. Food and equipment were scattered all over the place. The third was empty apart from strewn luggage, laptops and rubbish. Where was she? He could see activity through the windows to the adjoining carriage. He went to the door, but it was jammed shut. Brandon didn't have the muscle to kick it in, so he went back through the door the firefighters had cut open and along the tracks to Carriage D. Even from outside he could see this was one of the worst hit – right in the middle, it was proper squeezed – propelled forward and shunted from behind.

It was pretty much impossible to see through the windows. Rain, condensation, and firefighters were blocking his view. So, he got on board. A firefighter at the door stretched out a hand to block his way. Brandon drew his badge.

The firefighter wasn't impressed. 'We've got this covered, Detective.'

Brandon brushed him aside and looked around. A young guy with long-matted hair and a bloody nose was being helped out of his seat, one arm hung limp at his side. A young woman with a baby was being seen by a paramedic. Two firefighters were struggling to pull back a seat in front of a woman. Brandon caught sight of a crown of dark blonde hair and held his breath. It moved and he exhaled.

'Rachel?' he said, the words softer than intended, but all he could muster.

A hand appeared above the head and waved.

Brandon sighed and pushed forward. 'Can I assist here?' he said, coming alongside the firefighter who was shoving the seat in front of Rachel forward, a colleague holding back the one behind, giving her space. She hadn't moved her body. Apart from that one arm.

'Can you feel anything?' The paramedic had moved alongside her chair, as the woman and baby exited the other way. It was the question on his lips. He was glad he didn't have to ask it.

Rachel gave a weak grimace. 'Yes. I ache all over. Particularly my back, head and right foot.'

The paramedic crouched down, the firefighter securing the seat in front to give them room.

Rachel stretched out her legs. 'Ouch.'

'Can you feel this?' the paramedic said, touching her ankle.

'Yes. But it really hurts. Is it broken?' Rachel said, flexing her right hand, the one that had waved to him. That was working okay.

'We'll have it looked at.' The paramedic nodded at the firefighters. 'I think ...'

'Rachel,' Rachel offered.

'Rachel needs an ambulance.'

Brandon watched a burly firefighter gently lift her out of her seat. He moved aside as the man edged forward with Rachel in his arms.

'Hi Brandon,' she said, smiling weakly. 'Thanks for coming. But I have a ride.'

He smiled and touched her briefly on the shoulder. 'Hi. Make sure you do as you're told in A&E.'

'Who do you take me for, detective inspector?' The mischief was still there in her eyes.

'Rachel Matthews,' he said, smiling softly.

He followed as she was carried down the aisle – one of the last to get out of Carriage D.

'Brandon,' Rachel said, catching his eye over the firefighter's shoulder. 'Take a look for my phone. I dropped it – must be on the floor somewhere near the seat. iPhone, green case.'

'Everyone needs to get off the train now,' said an officious sounding voice.

Rachel raised her voice. 'It's important.'

3

Brandon

'Can you give Lizzie a lift back in the car,' Brandon asked Jo, as they watched the ambulance speed off with Rachel and other wounded passengers. Most of the passengers were off now, thirty minutes after the derailment. There were casualties. Fifteen at last count. But it was February, and the train was far from full. The survivor stories were coming through. A trolley attendant doing his rounds had escaped death, but a passenger making his way to the toilets at the same time had been less fortunate. A Yorkshire terrier had been catapulted to safety, landing on a duvet coat five seats up the carriage.

Lizzie had rallied at the sight of her daughter. 'An exit fit for a Drama Queen,' she had crowed, as Rachel went by in the arms of the firefighter.

'You staying here, Boss?' Jo said, Lizzie by her side, eager to get home.

'I'm going to take a wander down to the harbour. See what all the fuss is about with the yacht.'

'Last I heard they hadn't managed to board it,' Jo said, steering Lizzie away.

Brandon walked with them down the platform. It was still crowded – with the emergency services and worried relatives and friends – but progress had been made. Work was switching to the track and righting the train.

'Who would go out on the sea on a day like this?' Brandon said, as they turned left at the end of the platform and past the ticket office to the exit.

'Madness,' Jo agreed.

* * * * *

There was an ambulance and police car in the carpark which fronted the Penzance Sailing Club. Brandon walked alongside the harbour towards the club house, the anchored boats rocking violently, gulls circling and crying above.

A group of people, including a uniform from the station, were looking out to sea from the viewing gallery on the first floor of the two-story build. Brandon pushed open the front door, headed up the stairs, and through the bar to join them. He knew a few of the sailors, and one of them, Cal, looked over his shoulder to greet him. The others couldn't tear their eyes from the capsized yacht – a beautiful 52ft classic pilot cutter – and the two rescue RIBs. A couple of men on one of the RIBs were attaching ropes to the yacht's stern.

'They're towing her in,' said one of the onlookers. Brandon knew him vaguely. A pleasant guy called Martin – mid-forties, long wiry hair tied back in a ponytail.

'Couldn't get on board?'

'No,' Martin replied. 'They've been trying for nearly an hour. Only had the one RIB to start, but they called in another.'

'Do we know who's on the boat?'

Martin turned to face him. 'No. It's quite the mystery. The yacht isn't one of ours and it didn't set sail from Penzance harbour. No one was sailing out of the harbour today.'

One of the other men turned around – Bert, a man in his mid-sixties. 'It sailed in from the east around an hour before the storm broke. Just sat there in the ocean. We thought they'd laid anchor. But, after a while, it started to drift and then, when the wind picked up, it was all over the shop. There was no movement on deck. The vessel was at the mercy of the elements. No Mayday calls. No radio—'

'They've secured it,' a younger woman at the front said,

her hair covered in a nautical snood. 'They're bringing her in.'

'Who's on the deck, Thea?' Martin said. There was someone in heavy duty waterproofs attempting to get into the yacht's cabin. He was slipping and sliding and grappling with the door. It was a perilous task, with the boat on its side, waves lashing the deck.

'Looks like Jason Pascoe,' Thea said, her eyes on the yacht. 'Newlyn fisherman. Best person for the job.'

They watched as he pushed at the cabin door only to be thrown back as a mighty wave crashed onto the deck. The boat plummeted and bounced back; the top of the mask snapping like a toothpick.

'Any more hits like that and the hull will crack in two.' Martin wiped a hand across his mouth. 'They need to step on the gas.'

Brandon could see that was easier said than done, with the yacht lying low in the water, taking the full force of the thirty-foot waves. The ropes were holding though and the RIBs, even at this funereal pace, were approaching the harbour mouth and the safety of the ancient wall that formed a barrier to the wider sea.

'Jason oughta give up on that door before he gets tossed in the water,' Martin said.

It looked like Jason had the same idea. He raised his arms in an exaggerated shrug before slipping down and resting his back against the cabin.

Brandon lit a cigarette and took a long drag. So, the captain was still incommunicado. Heart attack? Martin ran a hand through his hair, probably going through the same likely scenarios as the yacht turned the corner into the harbour, dragging behind what was left of its sails.

4

Rachel

Emergency services had been impressive; the Triage system concentrating on the serious injuries, while fast-tracking minor ones. Within half an hour Rachel was resting her sprained right ankle on an applique cushion on one of her mother's poufs. Her left wrist was strapped to a bag of frozen peas – on the medic's advice. Her bruised forehead was turning yellow last time she looked. Or when Lizzie updated her.

'Stop grumbling, darling. You got off very lightly,' Lizzie said coming into her living room with a tray of food.

'I haven't said a word,' Rachel replied, trying to raise an eyebrow. 'Ouch.'

'There you go! Grumbling again. You're lucky. Nothing broken. They've had to put that poor dog down, you know.'

'How do you know?' Rachel was astounded by her mother's knowledge of local news and gossip.

'Gisela told me. It's all over X.'

Rachel winced at the name. 'Gisela whose luggage is taking up the—' she stopped herself saying "my room". 'The back bedroom?'

'Yes, darling.' Lizzie plonked the tray down on Rachel's lap. Glutinous liquid slopped over the side of a bowl. Rachel recognised it as one from Lizzie's chipped collection that gathered dust on the kitchen shelf. She hoped, but doubted, she'd rinsed it. Rachel dipped in a spoon and raised it to her lips. The soup was lukewarm. Lizzie's culinary skills hadn't improved.

Rachel picked up a slice of bread and took a nibble before asking: 'So Gisela's moving in?'

'Yes,' Lizzie replied. 'Don't you want your soup?'

'I'm not hungry right now. Maybe I'll microwave it later.' Rachel lifted the tray off her lap and placed it on the floor. The effort made her muscles jangle. 'Mum. Why didn't you tell me Gisela was moving in? I would have made other arrangements.'

'Darling, you wouldn't have come. And you needed to. London wasn't right for you. And that … man you've been living with—' Lizzie ran a palm down the length of her slender neck. 'You're better off out of there.'

'For goodness' sake, Mum. I came here to look after you.' Lizzie had shown signs of a mild form of dementia. Her doctor had advised Rachel to be mindful.

'If you say so.' Lizzie moved over to her settee and sat down.

The two women sat in silence, appraising each other.

Rachel spoke first. 'So why is Gisela moving in?'

'I told you!'

Rachel raised both eyebrows, even though it hurt to do so. 'You didn't, Mum. I thought I'd be staying here for a while until … well, until.'

'Exactly,' Lizzie cut in. 'It wouldn't work. I've already asked Julia if you can move into Hartington Hall. She's rattling around in that ancient pile and, as you know, she will be grateful of the company.'

Rachel reached down for a mug of tea on the tray. It was almost stone cold, but it gave her a moment to reflect. It would be so much better to stay with Julia – her best friend and the place would give her all the space she needed. There was an artist's studio too. But this new development – Gisela

– concerned her. Lizzie seemed captivated by the woman, and she was blossoming under her influence. Her Art Therapy classes had added a new dimension to her life. Purpose and friendship. Although Lizzie had been using art as therapy before Gisela von Schoenburg had pitched up in Penzance with her online qualifications and Wellbeing Arts Centre.

Rachel put aside her mug. 'So how long is she staying?'

Lizzie sniffed. 'Oh, not so long, I'm sure. Her tenancy has just ended, and this will be temporary. She will be no trouble at all.'

Rachel wasn't convinced, but she was willing to give the woman a chance. She had, after all, offered Rachel a temporary role as a tutor at her Centre. Rachel had checked her out and she appeared to be on the level. Her qualification was gained in Bremen, Germany. She had some glowing testimonials – mainly from German students, who endorsed the Centre's slogan, Die Kunst des Lebens, *The Art of Living*.

'Is she moving in straightaway?'

'Well, she was.' Lizzie was adjusting the improvised scrunchie tying back her long grey and blue tipped hair. Rachel recognised it as an old floral face mask. 'But, when I said you were coming and after the awful accident, she insisted on moving into the Premier Inn.'

'Okay,' Rachel said watching her carefully. 'For how long?'

'For as long as it takes for you to … feel comfortable about moving to Julia's.'

Rachel was tempted to book an Uber there and then. But remembered her manners and, also, that they didn't have Uber in Penzance. 'I guess the sooner the better. No point offloading what luggage of mine they've salvaged here. And, also, Julia will have things that I can wear.'

Lizzie frowned. 'Are you the same size?'

'I'm not looking for an haute couture fitting. A jumper. A pair of jeans. A coat. That will be fine for now or until I get down to Peacocks on the high street.'

'We'll have to get you some more appropriate clothes for the classes,' Lizzie said. 'Gisela is very keen to encourage her students and staff to dress vibrantly. There has been so much doom and gloom of late. She wants to radiate a sunny atmosphere.'

'I'll buy orange then.' Rachel shifted in her seat.

'Are you uncomfortable, darling?' Lizzie was leaning forward, her brow creased.

'Just a little. I'm sure it will pass … with the right therapy.'

'That's the spirit!' Lizzie had taken the barbed comment at face value. She was such an innocent, in many respects. It was a worry.

5

Brandon

Jason Pascoe was crouched on the bow of *The Seagull*, doing his best to help ease its passage into the crowded harbour. The RIBs were dragging the stricken vessel to the walkway where Martin and Bert, and other club members were waiting with ropes to tug it upright. Crowds had formed at the harbour and on the adjacent Ross Bridge and seafront. The yacht lolled listlessly like a dying swan as five sailors waded into the water to right it.

Pascoe hopped off the boat and onto the walkway as Brandon approached.

'Want to look inside, Detective Inspector?' Jason flicked his head towards the boat but kept his eyes on Brandon. A fug of melancholia hung over the fisherman.

'Sure. I reckon we can open that door,' Brandon said, watching the boat being heaved back upright with ropes and the brute force in the water.

The soles of Brandon's shoes were wearing thin – he never did find time to pop into the Arcade Cobbler – and he stepped carefully along the wet walkway to join the others just as the boat was righted. From what he could see, the cabin door was still shut fast. He would have thought the movement and correction might have jolted it open.

'Okay,' Brandon said, 'Let me see if I can't open up. God knows I've had enough practice.'

Bert managed a smirk and let him pass.

The wind had calmed, and the boat was rocking like a

cradle. Brandon put one tentative foot on the deck, and then the other, reaching for the cabin roof to steady himself. He looked around for something to smash open the door and decided the anchor and chain by his foot would make a great wrecking ball. But when he looked through the cabin window, he saw a crate blocking the door. Better to bash that along. 'How about we use one of the dinghy masts as a battering ram?' Brandon shouted over his shoulder.

'I wouldn't argue with that,' Bert said, glancing around.

'Use mine,' Martin said, 'it's resting ready in *The Flying Fish*'.

Brandon crouched down to get a better look in the cabin. It was pitch black in there. A proper *Mary Celeste*. No captain. No crew. No light. The crate was on its side – would have tipped when the boat capsized. He could make out shapes on the floor by it.

'We're ready when you are.' Martin was on the walkway holding the top end of the mast, Bert and two others were holding the rest.

'Let's get this over with.' Brandon moved to the cabin door and took the top end of the mast from Martin, who had come on board. Bert and Cal joined him.

With the mast tucked under their arms and their hands gripping it, they prepared to ram the door.

'In all my born days, I ain't ever seen this done before,' Bert said.

'After the count of three pull back and push forward with the mast.' Brandon had plenty of experience with battering rams. He figured Martin's would be enough.

The door budged a fraction with the first hit. And then further with the second. The ram was doing its job, pushing the crate back into the cabin.

When the door had been forced opened three or so feet, Brandon turned to the men. 'We're good for now. I'm going in.'

He felt for a light switch on the wall by the entrance. There was a switch. But no electrics.

His mobile phone torch would have to do. Pressing it on Brandon pointed it at the crate. He could already smell what was in it, now he could see what was in it. Fish. Dead ones. The scales shimmered in the torchlight.

Two oblongs jutted out from the far side of the box. Brandon edged round to take a closer look. They were legs dressed in grey flannel – and they were attached to a body. Brandon inhaled sharply and turned his head to face the cabin door and the men beyond.

'Can someone get a lamp in here asap? And can someone alert the ambulance crew.'

'I have a torch, Brandon,' Martin said, passing it over the crate.

The light was fierce, throwing shadows at the polished mahogany. Fish scales gleamed in the beam – as did the metal curve of a hook which penetrated the gaping mouth of a man's head, its glassy eyes wide with horror.

A charge of shock made Brandon lurch forward and grab the edge of the crate, the fish skittering over the dead man's chest. Brandon pulled out a crumpled mask from the Covid days. He placed it over his nose and mouth to block the foul smell of decaying fish and as an instinctive form of protection from the horror before him. The corpse looked fresh enough, though. The man looked to have been dragged on board, probably this very day.

'What do you make of it?' Jason had joined Martin at the entrance of the cabin.

'Not natural causes.' Brandon paused. 'Jason, I'm going to have to ask you to leave the boat now. We have a crime scene here.'

Jason stepped back. 'I'm assuming you'll want me to make a statement?'

Brandon nodded and turned back to the crate. He moved the torch beam slowly around the interior until he came to an item of clothing among the herrings, and sole, and other rotting fish. On closer examination he could see it was a black woollen beret.

It was a bizarre set of images. A beret. Rotting fish. And a dead man in an expensive grey flannel suit, shiny leather brogues and a fishhook through the roof of his mouth. By no stretch of the imagination was this man intending to go either sailing or fishing in Gale Force 9 conditions.

6

Jo Menhenrick sat alone in the station interview room. Brandon was at the harbour with chief Crime Scene Investigator Al Chapman. She was waiting for Jason Pascoe, the fisherman who had boarded *The Seagull,* to come in and give a routine statement.

Jo was pleased to have an easy job. Today's events had taken the wind out of her. Brandon hadn't spared her the gory details and it had brought back the trauma of the summer of 2019 and the Sleeping Beauty serial killer case. Her world – the world – had changed dramatically since then. Covid, the stealth killer, was a different department's responsibility. The scientists and politicians had taken charge, and crime had slipped into the shadows. Fewer people on the streets, less visible crime, cleaner air, bluer skies. It had given her time to heal. She hadn't realised she'd needed to. But something was brewing. She could almost smell the stench Brandon had described on the yacht. It was a horrific murder. And seemed symbolic. On the surface it had factors that suggested an attack on the French – or at least their politicians. The stinking fish they were fighting over in UK waters. The smart Savile Row suit, but with the iconic French beret. The fishhook through the mouth. Jo shuddered. She hadn't had much time to discuss it with Brandon, but she could imagine what he would make of it. 'Bit Cluedo?' He'd want the body identified before coming to any assumptions. He was right. Impetuosity was for cubs. Jo was nearly 32 – almost as old as Brandon when he took on the Sleeping Beauty Killings. Was this her time to shine? To get the big case under her belt? She'd had her share of gruesome experience now, like her boss. Brandon would say adversity helps focus the mind. But he couldn't deny the demons waiting to disturb it.

'DS Menhenrick?'

Jo looked up sharply to see a man at the door. Dark hair, with a dark, almost swarthy complexion, he was dressed in waterproofs, and looked to be five foot ten, or eleven.

'Who let you in?' Jo pulled herself upright.

'Your plod on the desk. He said I should knock.'

'Why didn't you, then?'

'I did. Twice. When I opened the door, you seemed miles away.'

He was right. And it annoyed her. 'Jason Pascoe?'

He nodded.

'Take a seat.'

He rested his arms on the table and lent forward, watching her as she opened her notebook.

Jo picked up a pen and met his eye. 'You boarded the yacht *The Seagull* at around 6pm this evening?'

'That's right.' Pascoe maintained his leaning position.

'Did you have any idea what you might find on board the vessel?'

Pascoe paused for a moment. 'I figured it would be a man – and maybe one other crew. And I reckoned … because we couldn't get radio contact – that they were—' he struggled to find the right word. 'Incapacitated? Maybe knocked out, because of the turbulence. Or the radio was down. I didn't give it too much thought. I'm a RNLI volunteer, and we're trained to save people in all conditions.'

Jo gave a sympathetic nod. She had great respect for their

work. 'When you got on board did anything strike you as odd?'

Pascoe pulled away from the table, before looking to the side. 'It stank of fish. Rotting fish. Which was odd. This was a beautiful pilot cutter not a trawler.'

'Did you manage to see into the cabin?'

'It was right dark in there and I was concentrating on staying on board. *The Seagull* was being tossed all over the shop.' He paused and returned his arms to the table. 'I got a look through the cabin window when we came into harbour. I saw the box and glint of fish scales. But I didn't see the body.' He looked her straight in the eye. 'Until I saw it over Martin Brady's shoulder.'

'Did it surprise you?' Jo leant forward.

'No. Well, yes and no. No, a dead body didn't surprise me. Could have been an old geezer going out for a joy ride, which he couldn't handle. Or a suicide trip.' He fixed Jo with his deep-set brown eyes. They were close together and gave him an injured expression.

'And yes?'

'I don't think anyone would expect to see a man harpooned like a shark.'

'A shark?' Jo was intrigued. 'He was wearing a grey flannel suit and brogues.'

'Detective Sergeant Menhenrick, I ain't too fancy with words. But shark came to mind. Might have been the grey of the suit. Or the shine on those shoes. But that's what struck me at the time.'

Jo decided not to mention the beret. He wouldn't have seen that. She'd save it for later.

7

Brandon

The Seagull was rocking again. CSI Al Chapman reached out to the wall to steady himself.

'The sooner we get the body off the boat, the better,' Al said, feeling in his pocket for a tissue and wiping his brow.

'You okay?' Brandon said.

'I've felt better. These … conditions aren't the best for a detailed analysis. And the fish aren't helping.'

Brandon raised an eyebrow over his mask and turned to go. Al followed him, ducking under the cabin door frame and onto the deck. Brandon was already off the boat, his mask below his chin.

Al inspected the wide gap between the boat and the side of the walkway. 'How'd you do that, detective inspector?'

'Long legs,' Brandon said, folding his arms and watching Al prepare to jump. 'And a misspent youth on the waterways of Alabama with my pop and his drinking buddies. If I didn't make it across back then, I'd have to drag myself out of the drink.'

Al made the leap, grabbing hold of Brandon's jacket sleeve. 'Surprised you survived,' he said.

DC Stewart Bland was waiting for them as they walked towards the top of the slip. 'Just got word that *The Seagull* was rented for the weekend by a Roberta Bevan. She'd forwarded all the right credentials. Grade 5 Sailing. Best this and that in a stack of regattas,' he said.

'Have you managed to get hold of Bevan?' Brandon said.

'I left some messages. I'll let you know when she gets back to me.'

'Who owns the boat?'

'A syndicate of four sailors. Fairweather, I'm told by Martin. Ex-bankers who like the look of the boat on their Insta feed more than they like sailing her.'

'Contact them, Stew.'

'I have, Boss.'

'Good work.'

Stew smiled broadly.

Brandon walked Al to the car park where he'd parked his Toyota Prius, leaving the Scene of Crime Officers (SOCOs) to do their business. He was jangling his keys. Looked keen to head off.

Brandon stopped by the car and rested his hand on the roof. 'When do you think the report will be ready?'

'Couple of days. It's late on a stormy Sunday night. But I'll pressure the lab. Try and get some good timings, despite the cold weather.'

'That would be helpful.'

Al nodded and beeped his car open, Brandon moving away from the door to let him get in.

'Brandon,' he said, as he settled into the driver seat and started the engine. 'What do you think? It has the whiff of a mafioso killing. Fish heads instead of a horse's.'

Brandon grimaced. 'We'll have a better idea of motive when we find out exactly who the man is.'

'Brandon! Brandon!' Nadia McGowan, one of the SOCOs, was charging across the car park towards them. 'I found this a few feet from the body.' She brandished a business card in her blue gloved hand.

'Let me see?' Brandon said.

Nadia held it up for him to read.

'Alain Boucher. Fine Arts, Marlow, Buckinghamshire. An art dealer?' Brandon looked from the card to Nadia and then to Al, who was out of his car.

'More money in art than fish,' Al said.

'True,' Brandon agreed. 'Roberta Bevan may enlighten us further.'

8

It was 9.30pm and Jo was hunched over her laptop in her one-bedroom conversion flat in Penzance's Belgravia Street. Brandon had phoned through the details, including the name of the sailor who had chartered *The Seagull*. Roberta Bevan. Trouble was, Roberta Bevan had died two years ago in a skiing accident in Val d'Isère. Jo had already alerted Falmouth Harbour, where the yacht set sail, of the identity fraud and was waiting for the local police to issue witness statements and CCTV images. Brandon had told her to leave it for the night. Get some rest. But she doubted he would, and her own mind was racing.

She walked over to the compact fridge freezer in her galley kitchen and opened the top drawer. She took out a neatly labelled Tupperware box of fish pie and put it in the microwave. Returning to the fridge she took out a bottle of elderberry juice and poured herself a glass, before sitting down to watch the box revolve on its plate.

A wired weariness hung over her. She knew she should be excited by this new case; it offered myriad opportunities to prove her worth. But there were too many questions and all she could think about right now was the look in Jason Pascoe's eyes. They radiated the same powerless exasperation that she was feeling. He'd put his life on the line to save a stranger on *The Seagull* for what?

The microwave pinged and Jo took out her supper. She went back to the table and ate the pie straight from the box, not bothering to add vegetables. A flyer about a new Wellbeing Arts Centre in St Ives caught her eye on the fridge. Brandon's teenage daughter Chelsea had come round with it and pinned it on the door with a fridge magnet. 'You have just gotta come along. It's so cool. They'll totally tear down your style and allow you to rebuild it with no preconceptions. Awesome. And you can wear what you like. Or nothing at all.' Chelsea had a mischievous smile on her face when she said that.

'Nothing at all?'

'There's a life drawing room. A nudie one,' Chelsea had replied.

'And you've been in there?' Chelsea was 18. But she still had a childlike naivety about her.

'No! But you might!'

Jo had blushed at that. At 32 she also had too much naivety.

She peered at the flyer over the top of her glass. Her curiosity had been whetted. Brandon's artist friend Rachel Matthews was meant to be running some classes. Jo was uneasy about Rachel's return to Penzance. It dated from when Jo had had a crush on Brandon, and he seemed fixated by her. But that was in the past, Jo told herself. She was over him. Her secret love had gone down with the ship. Brandon just didn't – and would never – see her in a romantic light. Rachel Matthews still irked her, though. She seemed a person of contradictions – exuberant at times, prudish at others. Jo couldn't imagine her stripping off and going all avant-garde in the nude room. That was more Gisela von Schoenburg, the German woman she'd seen around Penzance wearing flowing robes and mad hats. But if Chelsea recognised her need to 'let rip', maybe she needed something more than Zoom Pilates.

Jo got up from her chair and went into the sitting room;

opened her laptop and shut it. The meal hadn't dulled her nervous energy. She reached for her notepad and flicked through to the page where she'd taken down Jason Pascoe's number.

Pascoe picked up the call after two rings. 'Hi.'

'DS Menhenrick.'

'Yes, I know.'

Jo paused as she processed this. 'How did you know it was me?'

'Recognised your voice.'

'I wanted to share something with you.' God that sounded awful. Unprofessional, but she didn't want to mention the beret, particularly as she couldn't see the relevance now the profession of the victim had been identified.

'Tonight?' He had a soft spoken, deep voice.

Jo glanced at the time on her ironic cuckoo clock. A holiday souvenir from Stew. 9.45. She was hyper and wouldn't get to sleep for hours.

'If that suits you?'

'Yes.'

Her default caution resurfaced. 'Maybe we should wait until tomorrow?'

'Do you want me to come to you? Or we could meet at The Dock Inn if that's cool.'

The Dock Inn by the quay in Penzance was a ten-minute walk. There would still be plenty of people around. It was a safe option – but she'd text her whereabouts to Brandon regardless.

'I'll be there in 10 minutes,' Jo said, clicking off the call, before she'd the chance to change her mind.

*****

Jason Pascoe was sitting at a table to the right of the door when she entered, two glasses of red wine at the ready.

'It was last orders. I took the liberty,' he said, getting up as she came over.

'Well,' Jo said, unbuttoning her coat, 'What made you think I'd want alcohol?'

'I took a gamble. And there's a jug of tap water on the counter.' He nodded towards the bar.

Jo sat down, eying the glass like a recovering alcoholic.

Jason took a sip from his own. 'You wanted to share some information with me?'

'Yes.' Jo remembered why she was there and the fact that it was her idea. He wasn't a random date who might spike her drink. Through the window she could see the lights from the harbour reflected in the mirror of a parked car. She was on safe ground. 'Just a small thing.' Jo picked up her glass and took a sip of wine. 'They found a beret in the cabin. Did you notice it when you were on board?'

'No. It was dark. I didn't even notice the body, just the fish – and that was mainly due to the stench.'

Jo was going to leave it there. The beret could have belonged to the woman who was posing as Roberta Bevan. Or something the syndicate owners had left on board.

'Are you suggesting the beret was symbolic? Like the fish-hook? A French connection?' Jason said, watching for her reaction.

Jo looked down at her glass before returning his gaze. 'It's a long shot. I just wondered if there had been any antagonism with the French fishermen.'

Jason lowered his eyes and shook his head gently. 'Nothing that we haven't learnt to live with and deal with for many years.' He looked back up at her. 'This isn't about fishing rights. It's not our way. Next question?'

Jo smiled. 'I have wasted your time.'

'Not at all,' Jason said lifting his glass and clinking the side of hers. 'I really needed an excuse to come out for a drink tonight. It's been quite a day.'

Jo put down her glass and rested her hands on the table. 'Yes.'

He reached over and turned her hands to reveal her palms. 'Let me foretell your future. You are about to embark on a journey with an average-size, dark stranger. It won't be all plain sailing … but you will reach safe shores.' He was smiling a sweet, soft smile and she felt heat rising from her neck to her cheeks.

Jo left the hand he was analysing on the table and picked up her glass with the other. 'Where did you learn the dark arts?' She was teasing and hoped he recognised that.

'In my ma's kitchen. She was the wise woman of Newlyn, famed for her forecasts and love potions.'

'Love potions!' Jo took another sip of wine, her hand still in his, his thumb softly kneading its heel.

'What do you think I'm rubbing in right now?'

'That has got to be the best line I've heard for … ever.' Jo couldn't help smiling.

'I'll take note,' he said, gently dropping her hand and leaning against the back of the wooden bench.

People were leaving the pub, and the bar manager was making noises. Jo started to fuss with her coat.

'Can I walk you home?'

'No, I'm good,' she said, rising from her chair.

'I can see that.'

The wind had picked up outside, and he took off his scarf and wrapped it around her neck. 'See you for coffee? Or tea.

I can read the leaves.'

'I will probably be quite busy ...'

'Make time,' he said, looking at her. 'Call me. We can discuss that beret. You never did tell me what colour it was.'

9

February 28, 2022

Brandon

Brandon was nursing a cup of coffee at the communal table in the incidents room when Jo turned up, a good ten minutes late.

'I didn't get much sleep,' she said, flashing him a quick look before putting down her rucksack the other side of the table and unravelling what looked like a new scarf.

'Me neither. This is an odd case. Any news from Falmouth?'

'No. I've been checking my phone every time it beeps. Nothing so far. It is Monday morning and they're still clearing up after the storm.'

'Figures,' Brandon said, glancing down at his phone which was vibrating by his coffee cup.

'Rachel, hi,' he said, getting up from the table and walking towards the window at the back of the room. 'There were quite a few phones on the train. You'll need to come in to identify yours. How are you otherwise? Good, good. See you in a bit.'

'Rachel,' he said, looking over at Jo. 'She's feeling a lot better but is keen to get her phone back.'

'Any particular reason she called here?' Jo was looking out of sorts. 'Couldn't she have called the desk sergeant?'

'She did, Jo. And obviously everyone wants their phones back. She says she took some shots just after the train crashed which may be of interest … to our inquiry.'

'Oh, yes?'

'A few people near the tracks – one climbing back over the fence onto the coastal path. It could be nothing. But worth looking into.'

Jo was looking far from impressed.

'They found a tree trunk on the tracks, Jo.'

'I'm sorry, Boss, I'm just a bit tired, that's all.'

'Well, that information came in late. So don't beat yourself up about it. But there aren't any trees lining the tracks between St Erth and Penzance Station. It would have taken the hand of God to toss that piece of wood onto the approach to Penzance.'

'Or a couple of pairs of human ones?'

'Quite possibly.' Brandon opened a manila file on the table and took out two photographs of a tree on the tracks. He passed them to Jo. 'What do you make of these?'

Jo picked up the first photo and studied it. 'Do we have any close-ups of the markings on the trunk?'

Brandon took his phone and went into photos. He tapped an image and stretched it before handing his mobile to Jo.

'I'm no expert, but the markings look like something from the occult. A spell?'

'Or a warning,' Brandon said, looking over her shoulder at the image. 'Do you know of any wise women or witches' covens?' Brandon was smiling as he voiced the question.

Jo continued to look at the photos. 'Maybe.'

'Maybe?'

Brandon tilted his head. 'Enlighten me. What else did that storm blow into town?'

'I think Jason Pascoe's mum is a little more established than that. She was the wise woman of Newlyn, apparently.'

'You got that in an informal witness statement?'

Jo's eyes were boring into the photos. She picked one up and drew it close. 'We could ask him if his mum could look at these? Maybe get her along to the actual tree trunk?'

Brandon stroked his chin. 'Why not. It won't be the first time the police have used psychics and mystics to help solve mysteries. Do you want me to phone Jason Pascoe?' Brandon was watching her carefully. He sensed a shift in her energy which, he suspected, was down to tiredness. Had he given her too much work?

'No. I'll call him,' Jo said, looking past him and out of the window.

* * * * *

Fifteen minutes later Brandon's mobile was vibrating and announcing Rachel Matthews. 'You found it?' Brandon said, taking the call.

'I went through the basket with Stew. I'm in reception now. Do you want to see the photos?'

'Of course. Come in.'

Jo was on her mobile when Rachel entered the room. She looked at Brandon and clicked off the call. 'I think it might be an idea if I go straight to Falmouth.'

Brandon turned to her. 'Any developments?'

Jo shook her head and turned her attention to Rachel. 'How are you? Shouldn't you be resting up?'

'I'm okay, Jo, thanks. Just a bit sore but surviving. It's my first day at work so I had to drag myself out of bed. And don't worry, I know you are really busy, so this will be a flying visit,' Rachel said. 'I thought you might like to have a look at the shots of the tracks just after the train crashed.'

Brandon smiled at her. 'Let's have a look.' He ushered Jo

over. 'This won't take a minute and then you can get going, Jo.'

Rachel tapped her phone, enlarged an image, and handed it to Brandon.

He squinted, before holding the phone away from his face. 'It would be difficult to identity this guy in a line up. But it's an interesting shot all the same. He looks in a hurry to get off the tracks.'

'The other one's a bit more blurred. Swipe left.'

Brandon smiled and did as he was told. There was a shadowy figure on the other side of the fence looking directly at camera. 'Was this the first shot you took?'

Rachel nodded. 'Just after the train crashed. I also have some video, which I took of the storm. No figures – but it was further down the tracks. These shots were taken at the point of impact.'

'Rachel, can I pass this to Jo?'

'Of course.'

Jo touched the screen, swiped through the images and looked back at Brandon. 'Wow.'

'I think we're going to need an evidence bag for your phone, Rachel.'

'I guess you couldn't lend me a burner, detective inspector? Remember, I start my new job today.'

Brandon regarded the flowery flared trousers she was wearing and the bright orange t-shirt under the purple fun fur coat. 'You've got a job as a children's entertainer?'

Rachel shrugged. 'You are in the right ballpark. Lizzie lent me these to cheer up my students.'

Brandon shook his head lightly. 'At the school?' He was referring to St Piran's secondary where Rachel had worked for a short time as a Learning Support Assistant. His daughter

Chelsea had been one of her pupils.

Jo looked up from labelling a plastic bag. 'Rachel's going to work at the new Wellbeing Arts Centre in St Ives. Chelsea goes there.'

'Does she?' Rachel asked Jo. 'Well, that's made my day. And you didn't know, Brandon?'

Brandon shifted some papers on the desk. He couldn't keep up with all of Chelsea's fads. She was eighteen, after all. 'She did say something about art classes. I didn't know it was therapy.'

'It's not like she's in rehab, Brandon,' Rachel said, smiling. 'Well, at least I hope not! I'll find out later.'

'You don't know?' Jo said, her back to Rachel and Brandon. She had her hands in the metal cabinet at the back of the room and pulled out a Perspex box of phones and chargers.

'I have a good idea,' Rachel said grimacing. 'It's light-hearted, immersive art therapy. Or that was the brief I was given by mum and the woman who runs the centre.'

'Gisela von Schoenburg?' Jo said, bringing the box over. 'Will a Nokia do?'

'Do they still make them?'

'The stalwart of the burner industry.' Brandon chose one for her. 'This is one of the better ones. We'll return your phone asap.'

Rachel picked up the phone and its charger. 'Look, I'll let you get on. I'll sort this at work. You can call me at Julia's if you need me.'

'Julia's?' Brandon sucked in a breath. 'I thought you'd be staying with your mom?'

'It's a long story. And you're busy, Brandon. But I'll be holed up at Julia's for a while.' She slipped the phone and charger into her rucksack. 'It will be a bit like old times. Me teaching again and getting under Julia's feet.'

'Rubbish, she'll be glad of the company. We all will.'

Jo was rustling behind him, getting her things together.

He turned around. 'Hang on a minute,' he said, 'Rachel's leaving now. No state secrets will be divulged.'

'Ah, shucks, my cunning plan failed,' Rachel said, swinging her rucksack over her shoulder. 'See you soon.'

Maybe sooner than she thinks, Brandon thought as he watched her walk towards the door. He'd been seeing a lot of Julia since the easing of Covid restrictions. The pandemic had nipped in the bud what had been the promise of romance after her crisis in 2019. He'd taken his time with her, not knowing that social time in 2020 was facing a severe shortage.

'Penny for them,' Jo said drawing close.

He smiled. 'Save your cash for bigger reveals. Now, before you go off to Falmouth to binge watch CCTV footage, want to give Jason Pascoe a call? That piece of timber's looking more intriguing.'

10

Rachel

Rachel parked her Fiat 500 outside a converted barn on the outskirts of St Ives. The spacious glass and stone buildings were holiday lets, which made them ideal for Gisela's venture. She pressed the doorbell at the side of the massive wooden door and heard it ring out into the hollow space beyond. After a minute she rang again. Silence. Was it the wrong day? She itched to check her phone. Felt powerless without it. The sooner she could fire up the burner the better. Heat was creeping up her neck and she unbuttoned the ridiculous fur coat Lizzie had lent her. She'd been led to expect an exuberant welcome. But it was a big place, the inmates – why did she think of them as that? – could be in any of the assortment of buildings. Perhaps they hadn't got any bookings? It was Monday. Maybe the centre was closed on a Monday, like the restaurants in Penzance.

Rachel moved away from the door and looked up. No sign of life. She'd check the back, before leaving. She found herself tiptoeing along the gravel path which skirted the wall of the main building. There was an eerie quiet – even the gulls were toning it down. But they were there to greet her when she got to the back of the building, cruising the sky over the turquoise and green sea. The garden had the wow factor. A verdant lawn, not quite camomile, but sprinkled with early spring crocuses and bordered by tufts of dwarf daffodils, sloped down to a low slate wall and gate. To her left was a porcelain paved patio, with wooden tables and easels stacked against the far wall. Bifold windows ran its width. Rachel walked over and peered into a kitchen diner. Dirty dishes idled by the sink. From last night? Or this morning? Perhaps the group had gone for a walk by the sea for a spot of plein air painting. She turned and strolled across the lawn to the gate. It was bolted but not padlocked; the grass beyond wild and festooned with pink thrift dipped dramatically to the cliff edge. Rachel stopped at the wooden warning sign: 'Danger, Sharp Drop'. As she anticipated, there was a rough pathway of steps to the small cove below. Rocks jutted out of the restless sea.

'Rachel.'

The voice made her jump, and she spun around, grabbing the arm of the woman before her. The wind had strengthened, and the woman's hair flew away from the face she recognised as Gisela von Schoenburg's.

'Gisela? I did ring the front door. No one answered, so I came looking for you.'

'We saw.' Gisela turned her head towards the glass doors, which were now open. A young woman was walking across the grass, pointing a camcorder at them; others started to follow.

'Well, why—'

Gisela cut in. 'Everyone is unique. Everyone has their way of approaching a new adventure. We wanted to observe you.'

Rachel placed her hands on her hips, the wind pushing her from behind, shoving her towards the open arms of the imposing German. She side-stepped the embrace.

'An interesting introduction,' Rachel said, biting back her irritation.

Gisela took her arm and started to walk with her towards the others. Rachel could see Chelsea lurking at the back of the small group. She was mouthing something at her and rolling her eyes. It was good to have an ally in camp.

'Let's go inside and have some coffee,' Gisela said, her arm still annoyingly linked in hers. A splash of rain fell on her free hand.

'I would have called to let you know what time I was coming.' Rachel couldn't think of a better way to start up a conversation. 'But my phone went missing in the train crash.'

'Never mind.' Gisela released her arm when they reached the patio. 'I knew you would come. You were a little late, but Lizzie said you'd be calling in at the police station.'

Lizzie. She couldn't be relied upon to keep quiet about anything. That said, what did it matter. She'd lost her phone. She went to find it.

'Did you get any good shots of the train crash?' Gisela said, walking in through the bifold doors. 'That must have been dramatic.'

'My phone died,' Rachel replied.

'Shame,' Gisela said, fixing her with steel grey eyes.

There were around ten of them in the kitchen diner-cum-studio. The young woman with the camcorder started to make drinks for them – camomile teas, soymilk lattes, Earl Grey and a cappuccino for Rachel. She needed its frothy, milky warmth. By the time she'd finished it was drizzling, and clouds were gathering. Gisela strode over to the bifolds and snapped them shut.

She turned to the room. 'Feel the energy the storm has bestowed on us. Use this gift to release your creativity?' Gisela was off, her long brown hair swept back from her impressive brow, her arms outstretched, her fingers glancing Rachel as she sat perched on a high stool by the breakfast bar. In her colourful clothes Rachel felt like a mute parrot. In contrast,

Gisela looked like an eagle in her sharp grey trouser suit. Her only concession to vibrancy was the blood red colour of her lips and matching mules. How could Lizzie have done this to her? She often wondered if her mother didn't have a perverse sense of humour after all, lurking within that scatterbrain.

Chelsea was grinning at her from a seat by the windows. She was wearing a pink T-shirt with a large yellow smiley face. It cheered her. Rachel thought she recognised the goth to Chelsea's left from her time as a Learning Support Teacher at St Piran's Secondary. Making her presence known in the middle of the room was a middle-aged woman, with a mass of wiry grey hair atop an elaborately textured kaftan shift and electric blue satin slacks.

In the far corner, two places from Chelsea, was the only man in the group. Slim, tousle-haired and wearing grey jeans and a battered biker's jacket, he looked like he'd just stepped out of his garret.

'Rachel.' Gisela was addressing her. The woman looked to have a knack for catching her off guard. 'Rachel Matthews is our artist in residence. She has an extraordinary talent – but the daughter of Lawence and Elizabeth Matthews is no Nepo facsimile. Rachel has a style entirely her own. How many people can say that? Let's throw off the chains of conventionality. Ditch derivatives. Die Kunst des Lebens.' Gisela's guttural German accent shaped the slogan nicely, her voice softening for the translation. '*The Art of Living* is all about finding your own style and your best self.' She paused to survey the room, before breaking into a full-beam smile. 'I am excited to invite Rachel Matthews to our family!'

Rachel looked into the mists of her cappuccino for inspiration, before raising her eyes to the room. 'This is going to be fun,' she said to the sea of expectant faces.

11

Brandon

Alain Boucher lay prone on the mortuary slab, his mouth minus the fishhook but still gaping like a carp, rigor mortis well set in. Al Chapman's own lips parted, ready to give his verdict.

'The victim died of a massive loss of blood caused by a deep cut to the main arterial vein in the neck.'

'Not the fishhook, then?' Brandon was standing next to Al.

'No. It would have taken some feat to kill the victim using such primitive weaponry. Particularly as he put up quite a fight. Cuts to his hands and to the right side of the face,' Al indicated the area with a gloved hand, 'suggest he was killed and then *styled*.'

'How long had he been dead before the makeover?' Brandon stepped back from the table and turned to Al.

'Difficult to say because of the cold weather – up to 24 hours.' Al moved away from the table, allowing a lab technician to cover the corpse with a sheet.

'So,' Brandon said as they left the viewing room. 'Boucher could have been killed the night before the storm and been on the boat as it set sail?'

Al took off his glasses and gave them a quick wipe on a cloth he kept in his lab coat pocket. 'It's a real possibility.'

Brandon's phone was vibrating in his pocket. Jo. 'I'll get back to you,' he said, returning to Al.

'Anything interesting?' Al was a nosey sod. But he'd earnt the privilege. Few forensics had his tenacity and expertise.

'Jo's at Falmouth. May well have some timings. Thanks, Al. Your speed is really appreciated,' Brandon said, taking the phone from his pocket and calling Jo as he walked down the white-walled corridor and out into the windswept day. Two more storms were lining up for an encore. It was like being back in hometown Alabama.

He headed for his BMW. Sometimes he missed his old Skoda, but Chelsea was delighted when the station upgraded his motor. Brandon beeped the door open, slid onto the leather seat and hunched over his mobile, Jo's face beaming at him.

'You got something,' he said.

'Alain Boucher was unknown to the Falmouth Sailing Club. Roberta Bevan had signed her guests in as Piers Jardine, an art dealer based in London, and a woman called Sophie Bryatt-Jones. Another fake ID. However, Roberta Bevan did visit the club on Friday night with a woman. Piers Jardine didn't show. Cried off, maybe because of the weather.'

'Do we know what his association was with Alain Boucher?'

'I'm working on it. But they were clearly both in the same business.'

'What have you got on CCTV?'

'A lot. But not sure how much will be relevant. I'll bring back print outs.'

'Thanks, Jo.'

Brandon closed the call and rested back in his chair. Piers Jardine. The name rang a bell.

12

Jo placed the file of CCTV print outs on the back seat of her Skoda. The car she'd inherited from Brandon when he got his upgrade. She was still finding empty sweet wrappers and cracked CD cases in the oddest places. It made her smile. As had one of the CCTV images of a short woman with long blonde hair in a black beret. It had to be 'the beret', surely? The woman, who was identified as 'Roberta Bevan', was also wearing big glasses and a stripey t-shirt – like *Where's Wally*. Mostly, she was caught on CCTV alone. Sophie Bryatt-Jones didn't feature until later, when a shadowy figure was seen meeting Bevan in the carpark on the Saturday night. A man, likely to be Alain Boucher, joined them at the harbour. Jo had sent the image to the Major Crime Investigation Team (MCIT) in Newquay for face and body recognition. There was another shot of a tall woman, with short dark hair and a hoodie leaving the harbour at 8pm. The club staff didn't recognise her, so she was of interest.

Jo turned on the ignition and took a deep breath. She was pleased with her morning's work. Although they hadn't got a prime suspect, she'd narrowed the field. It was a box ticked. Sometimes she wondered if her life was a succession of ticked boxes. The next on the list was a call to Jason Pascoe. Her heart quickened. Would he think her an idiot to come up with another flimsy line of inquiry? Markings on a log. And yet? She had to shake off her dismissive reaction to Rachel's suggestion. It had possibilities.

Jo pulled out of the harbour car park onto the main drag out of town. She put a call through to Pascoe as she passed the hospital. Her finger hovered over the off button on the fifth ring.

'Jo?' His voice sounded tired.

'Yes. You're not working?'

'Not my shift today. And it's still choppy out there?'

'Always my shift.'

'Don't sound so happy.'

'Sorry, forgot to smile into the phone.' When did she become so cynical? 'I have another question for you?'

'Oh, yes?' He'd perked up.

'Don't get your hopes up … it's another long shot. But—' She lost the line as they passed The Cornwall Fire and Rescue Centre. 'You're back? Good. There were some markings on the tree trunk which derailed the train. Do you think your mum would know what they signify?'

'That's a rum one.' She thought she heard him stifle a chuckle. 'I know I said she was a wise woman. Not sure she's much of a linguist.'

He read into her silence. 'I didn't mean to belittle your enquiry. Do you have any images?'

'Yes.' Jo pulled up at the lights and slipped the gears into neutral. 'You understand I can't send them to you. Can we meet in, say, twenty minutes?'

'Sure. At the station?'

Jo hesitated. 'I can come to you. If that's easier. It won't take long.'

'Eden Place, Newlyn. The White Door.'

* * * * *

Jo parked the car a few streets away and walked to the small terrace by Newlyn Harbour. Jason opened the door before she'd knocked on it. It was a small place which wrapped itself around him.

'Coffee?' he said, an amused look in his eyes. 'Instant? Or Instant plus?'

'Instant will do,' Jo smiled. 'Although I am intrigued by Instant plus. Does it involve wizardry?'

Jason's smile spread to his lips. 'Trade secret.'

He walked through to his kitchenette and pulled out a wonky wooden chair for her. Jo pulled out her phone and fiddled with it as he sorted the coffee – just two feet away.

He turned to her with two mugs of steaming coffee. 'Milk?'

'A touch,' Jo said, watching him turn and reach down to the fridge.

'Everything at my fingertips,' he said, drawing out a carton of semi-skimmed. 'Could well be in the cabin of my boat.'

'A trawler?' Jo said, pouring herself a dribble of milk.

'No. A bit better than that.' He sat down opposite her at the small Formica table. 'I'll take you out on her if you like.'

Jo looked down. She could feel her cheeks reddening. 'I'm not much of a sailor.'

'No? I'll teach you.'

'I don't get the time.'

'Make it.'

She caught his eye, as she placed her bag on the table. Feeling for the right file, she pulled out two photos of the trunk with close-ups of the inscriptions.

'Can I?' he said.

Jo passed the photos across.

'Some coincidence for these markings to be on the tree that crashed that train.' Jason raised his eyes to her.

'We thought they could be significant. Do you know what they might mean?'

'A warning.' He looked down at the photos. Picked one up. 'More than that. This is a curse. We don't need Ma to tell us that. But she is due a visit. Fancy coming?'

His eyes looked like two halves of a triangle, separated by the bridge of his nose. The Newlyn Triangle. She'd have to stop herself from being sucked in.

'Fancy coming,' he repeated, leaning in. 'I know it's a little early to introduce you to my ma. But she may well have pre-ordained your coming.'

'She's that good?' Jo shot him a look.

'Do I take that as a yes?'

Jo nodded and started to gather her things together.

He remained seated as she rose. 'We'll take *Crest of the Wave* out.'

'Your boat?'

'Yes. Ma lives in The Lizard. We can moor in Polpeor Cove.'

'When?' Was this a waste of time when she already knew what the markings meant?

'Now if you want – though it's still a bit choppy.'

'I've got to get back to the station,' Jo said her eyes cast down, one hand fiddling with the strap of her bag.

'Why. Phone your boss. Tell him about the curse. Say you want to confirm it from the witch's mouth.'

Jo frowned. 'I need to drop the files off at the station.'

'I'll pick you up at Penzance Harbour, then.' He was grinning now. The two half triangles twinkling. 'At two.'

13

Rachel

Rachel hesitated before picking up the call. 'I'm at work, Mum.'

'Gisela won't mind, darling. I just had to tell you—'

'What?' Rachel was standing over a diminutive woman's self-portrait, which depicted her as even smaller than she was.

'The fishhook man,' Lizzie said.

'Hmm?' Rachel lent down to the tiny woman and whispered 'Bigger. You are bigger than that.' She was getting into the lingo.

'He was a friend – well associate – of Pier's. Piers just called to tell me. He's in town. Almost went on that sailing trip himself. But you know how Piers hates water at the best of times—'

Rachel cut in: 'Mum. Thanks for letting me know, but I must get on.'

'Isn't it extraordinary! He was so lucky. Roberta Bevan had been badgering him to go on the trip and promising to place a huge order at his gallery. It makes me shudder to think—'

'Don't worry yourself, Mum. But do phone Brandon. And send my love to Piers. Got to go. I'll drop by later.' Gisela was walking towards her with a formidable smile on her face. 'Lizzie. You know how she is.'

'No boundaries.'

'Which is a good thing?' Rachel said, still testing the water. Gisela's lips stretched into a thin line. 'Mostly.'

Rachel held her gaze. 'Mostly?'

'I like to think of boundaries as elastic bands – you can

stretch them. Reach out. Bounce off them. But ultimately, they are our harnesses.'

Rachel nodded in a wise way; she hoped. Gisela wasn't someone she'd like to bounce into on a regular basis.

The small woman was meticulously erasing the fine lines on her sketch pad with a rubber

'Rip it up!' boomed Gisela. 'That person doesn't exist.' She turned and started to unravel paper from a roll on the nearby work surface. She tore off a long strip and handed it to the astonished woman. 'Now show us what you're made of,' Gisela said, smiling beatifically, before marching on.

'I'm sorry, I didn't catch your name earlier,' Rachel said as she pegged the paper onto the woman's easel.

'Dot,' she almost whispered. 'Although Gisela likes to call me Dorothea.'

'What do you like being called?' Rachel said, standing back from the easel.

'Neither.'

'Parental choices.' Rachel tilted her head. 'If there was ever a time to change your name it's here and now.'

'Beatrice,' she said in her quiet voice. 'But please call me Bea.'

'Suits you,' Rachel said her attention turning to the woman with the statement kaftan who was standing back from her easel and admiring her work. As Rachel approached, she scraped some paint off her palette with a knife and swiped it across her canvas.

Her self-portrait was what her father Lawrence would have called accidental art and owed little to portraiture. Rachel made a fist of her hand, tucked a thumb under her chin and peered in. 'Great colours—.'

'Aren't they just. We haven't been introduced.' She looked

over at look at Gisela and rolled her eyes. 'I'm Jackie,' she said, applying a thick layer of blue and chopping it impasto style.

Chelsea's head popped up from behind her easel at the back of the class and Rachel headed over, glancing at the other work en route. It was a mixed bunch – some canvases a riot of colour, others overworked, some not more than a few pencil marks. She stopped in front of Chelsea's easel, not knowing what to expect. Rachel had tutored her when she was younger and didn't consider her a natural talent. Her drawings and paintings had been naïve and contained – the work of a little girl trying to impress. Rachel had put it down to arrested development, stemming from the death of her mother. Jess, Brandon's late wife, had died when Chelsea was just ten.

'She won't bite you,' Chelsea said from the other side of the canvas, her usual effervescence under wraps. Rachel caught a waft of posh perfume and moved swiftly to the other side of the easel before Gisela joined them. She was amazed by the transformation in Chelsea's work – her self-portrait was mostly two-dimensional, not unlike her naive figures of old – but they possessed an unrecognisable quality and weight. And a dark, melancholic air

'What do you think of the new me?' Chelsea was gnawing her top lip.

'Fabulous!' Gisela said, drawing close. 'This portrait speaks to me.'

'Screams at you. Like Munsch?' Chelsea quipped, reasserting herself.

Rachel burst out laughing. There was something of *The Scream* in the muted grey and purple palette, the swirling lines of the body and over-sized head.

The goth gave it a sidewards glance. 'Cool.' In contrast, her portrait was bright pop art.

'Do you like it?' Chelsea had lowered her voice, her eyes on Rachel. She wasn't wearing her thick lens glasses. Was she painting blind or wearing contacts?

'It's so different. And quite stunning. Haunting even.'

Chelsea looked back at the painting and gave a small, stiff nod of the head.

'Let's take a look at Jethro's,' Gisela said, striding towards his easel in the far-left hand corner. He twisted the easel towards them as they approached.

His biker jacket took up three quarters of his canvas. There was no head or body: all energy had gone into the worn leather, which was pocked with tears, markings, and badges.

'What an incredible image,' Rachel said.

'Thanks,' he said. 'Every jacket tells a story.'

'How very creative. Maybe you could use your jacket as your canvas next time,' Gisela said. He was still wearing it, and Gisela ran a hand down the length of his arm. 'If you can bear to take it off.' Her hand lingered on the red silk lining, which protruded from the sleeve.

Jethro was unmoved. 'But what would keep me warm?'

There was heat in the slate grey eyes that washed over him. 'Use your fertile imagination.'

The moment was interrupted by the buzzing of Chelsea's phone.

'Get your dad. Now!' Someone was shouting on the other end.

'Oh my God, Oh my God!' The colour drained from Chelsea's face, as she stared into the screen. She held it up so Rachel could see a blur of images, the voice more urgent. 'Help me. Phone the police. Now! Now!' The voice was unmistakeably Damien Kane's, Chelsea's boyfriend and a former student of Rachel's.

Chelsea was tapping her phone with trembling fingers. 'I'm recording this, Damien. Rachel, phone dad. Damien's in deep trouble. He's being chased. Quick. Quick.'

Rachel drew out her phone and scrolled down for Brandon's number, all the while listening to Chelsea's distressed questioning.

'Where are you! Damien, where are you?' She flashed her phone at Rachel, images jumped up and down as Damien ran, and then they stopped as the phone switched direction, the camera trained on two guys in hoodies. Chelsea snatched the phone back, her voice shaking. 'Where did you say, love? The harbour. Newlyn? Penzance? Where, Damien? Where?' Then she stopped talking and stared at her mobile, with its sparkly pink cover and yellow flowers. 'He's gone, Rachel. The line's dead.'

Chelsea was sobbing as Rachel passed her phone to her. 'I've got your dad on the line, Chelsea.'

'Dad?' She was having difficulty speaking, tears streamed down her face, her lips and voice shaking. 'Damien's at Newlyn Harbour, where the warehouses are. The – you know – the disused ones. He's being attacked, Dad. You need to get there, now. Before it's too late!'

14

Brandon

Brandon jumped out of the BMW at the far end of Newlyn Harbour, Stew behind him, another cop car pulling up by the fish market, the sound of sirens in the air. The place was deserted, apart from a few people hanging around outside the fishmongers. Every now and then a car would pass along the sea road out of town.

Brandon ran a hand through his hair. 'Let's check with the shopkeepers, find out if they heard anything. Chelsea said Damien was crying out, as if his life depended on it.'

An ambulance pulled up as they crossed the road to Stevensons, one of the major shops.

A middle-aged man in a white coat was serving a woman in a red head scarf, who looked and sounded like a local. 'No plaice today, most of the boats didn't go out this morning. Too choppy,' said the man, who Brandon recognised as the manager Ned Riley.

The storm had left its mark. The roads were littered with debris – seaweed and stones and bits of driftwood.

Riley turned his attention to Brandon, looking over his customer's shoulder as she perused the fish counter. 'Detective Inspector, how can I help you?'

'We're following up on a distress call. A young man was being chased along here. Did you see or hear anything?'

Riley tapped his brow with a gloved finger. 'Nothing that stood out, particularly. We often hear a bit of shouting – usually banter from the Fish Market.'

'You didn't see anything?' The shop had massive glass

windows – it would have been difficult to have missed a chase.

'No.'

'And you were here around noon?'

'It was lunchtime. I shut the shop for a 15-minute break. Business isn't exactly brisk today.' Ned shrugged. 'Did you see anything Liz?'

'Nothing that struck me as unusual. But I only got off the bus five minutes ago,' Liz replied.

'Well, if you hear anything from your other customers, please let me know asap, Ned. It's important.'

Brandon hurried out of the shop, surveying the street as he did so.

'Go down to the beach, Stew. I'll look in the warehouses. If you find the kid, do what you can, and let the ambulance know.'

Brandon left PC McShane to do the door-to-door enquiries and got in his car for the brief journey to the end of the road. If this was more than a false alarm or prank – which Chelsea seemed to think it was – time was of the essence. He pulled up, leaving his car at an angle, as he beeped it shut and strode across to the metal doors of one of the outlier builds. It had been a while since the place had been put to any use. An open padlock hung limply from the door latch. He pushed the door open, feeling for his taser. Warehouses made him wary at the best of times – too much cover for people to lurk.

'Anyone there?' He shouted into the shadows. He heard a noise – low and furtive – as he moved into the space, past empty sacks, one on its side spilling its contents, others stacked.

'Damien?' The name echoed in the void.

'It's DI Hammett. Make yourself known.'

Thump!

Brandon swung around to see the door had slammed shut.

The scant light in the warehouse snuffed out. He switched on his phone torch and walked back to the door, looking all around, moving his taser from side to side.

When his phone started to ring, he almost dropped it. 'Fuck!'

'You okay?' Stew's face lit up the screen. 'It's pitch black. Where the hell are you?'

'The big warehouse at the end of—'

Stew cut in: 'Brandon. We've found your boy. At the bottom of the steps by the market.'

'Is he okay?' With his left-hand Brandon felt the handle of the door. He rattled it, pulled down hard, but the door didn't budge. He'd walked into a trap. 'Is he alive?'

'Barely.'

Brandon took a breath and exhaled slowly. 'The medics with him?'

Stew was looking away. 'Yes. They're just getting him in the ambulance now. It's looking bad, Brandon.'

'He's in the best possible hands now. Go with him, Stew. Keep talking to him. But get someone along here, fast. I've been locked in.' He clicked off but kept the phone in his hand. Chelsea. How was he going to tell Chelsea? And, in some ways, Damien had been like a son to him. More importantly, he'd been a male role model for the kid. Or thought he had. Brandon felt sick to his core and lashed out at the metal door, tearing at the handle, throwing the full force of his shoulders at it, before he backed away and took stock. It was then he saw the film of liquid oozing beneath the door, travelling towards him, carrying the strong smell of paraffin.

Brandon's heart was pounding, his eyes searching for another exit, or battering ram, as the first flames crept under the door.

He tapped Stew's number. 'The place is on fire. Get the fire brigade. Now!'

In the flickering light Brandon could make out shapes in the room – fly tip garbage. A rusty propeller on the floor to his right rested against a pile of broken greenhouse windows. There was a chest of drawers and broken dishwasher to his left, a wonky shopping trolley poking out behind. Brandon walked over and crouched by the washer, grabbing each side before rising steadily and jerking it up against his chest. Sweat poured from his brow as he staggered towards the trolley. His arms trembling under the weight, he lowered the metal box slowly into the trolley, praying it would take its weight. The flames were getting higher as Brandon grabbed the vehicle's handles and rushed the trolley at the door, bashing it open, the trolley's legs buckling and colliding with a paraffin bottle, sending it rattling into the gutter, a rolled-up piece of paper falling out. Brandon felt in his pocket for gloves and put them on before picking up the paper.

'If you're reading this you've been lucky, DI Hammett. Luck tends to run out.' Brandon bit down hard on his bottom lip and looked back at the warehouse, the flames taking hold as two fire engines screeched to a halt beside him.

15

He was standing on the jetty, togged out in waterproofs, a rucksack in his arms, his eyes on her. She couldn't remember when she'd ever commanded this sort of attention. Her cheeks were reddening, and she let some loose locks of hair flap over her face.

'Is that you in there, DS Menhenrick?' he said when she joined him. He pushed back her long red hair. 'Oh yes. Undeniably. You can't hide from me. Not now that I've found you.'

Jo flashed him a fiery look. 'Found me. Plu-ease. Have you been reading the tea leaves again or drinking something stronger?'

Jason stepped back and grinned. 'I'm more of an Americano guy. But let's see what my ma has to say, eh?'

'We're not going there for a reading, Jason. This is Police business.'

'Of course,' he said, watching her closely. 'I brought you some proper clothes for the trip. Although I can see you've made an effort.' Jo was wearing Millets waterproofs. 'Here,' he said, handing her the rucksack. You can use the Sailing Club changing room. 'Tell them Jason sent you. Or flash your badge.'

Jo rolled her eyes. 'You have it all worked out.'

'Yep,' he said, a smile forming below those watchful eyes.

Jo came back out of the club ten minutes later and ten inches fatter. If she'd felt hot ten minutes ago, she was sweltering now in the oil skin layers.

Jason slipped a life jacket over her head, and adjusted the straps, clicking in the fasteners as if she were a child. He wiggled a helmet onto her head and tightened the chin strap, so it fitted snuggly. 'There,' he said, standing back. 'You are safe and seaworthy. You also have your own personal RNLI saviour.'

'Nice,' Jo said, waddling behind him to his boat, which was moored off the harbour walkway by *The Seagull*. The yacht looked haunted as it creaked and rolled, crime scene tape rustling on the breeze.

'Shall we take a selfie,' Jason said, smiling at her, as she stood by his boat.

'This isn't a pleasure cruise, Jason.' Jo was seriously thinking of backing out. But there was nothing else to do right now at the station. Brandon and Stew were investigating both the Yacht murder and the attack on Damien Kane. Not much she could add to that. This other strand – potential sabotage – was something she could follow up. She wouldn't spend too much time on it – half a day. Max. Just so she could eliminate it from her inquiries.

'Cheese,' Jason said, putting his cheek next to hers and clicking his phone in an outstretched hand. 'Lovely,' he said, admiring the photo. 'You have a faraway look in your eye, DS Menhenrick. Wistful, even.' He passed his phone to her.

She did look enigmatic. Thinking about murder suited her. She deleted the photo.

'Hey!' he said.

'No photos,' Jo said, returning his phone.

Jason took his phone with one hand, and took her hand with his other, helping her onto the boat. It was in a beautiful condition – the deck wood polished, the sails clean and tidy.

'So, you have no experience of sailing?' Jason was tightening the ropes of the main sail and attaching the rudder.

'Correct,' Jo said.

'I figure you for a quick learner,' he said, pulling up the fenders and pushing the boat away from the walkway and into the harbour, a south-east wind escorting them to the Harbour mouth and open sea.

It was beautiful on the ocean. Rippling waves sparkled in the afternoon sun, belying their ferocity just 24 hours ago. The wind was still there but turned down and perfect for sailing. Jason had given her some ropes to control the main sail and called over instructions. 'Pull it in now', 'Tighter', 'Let her out.' She seemed to be getting it right. Which was a pleasant surprise. If she'd known she was going on a sailing trip she would have spent last night swotting up on techniques. As it was, she'd been on YouTube over lunch. She'd even refreshed her knots knowledge. *Be Prepared*. Once a scout always a scout.

'You're smiling,' Jason said, coming up beside her.

'Aren't you meant to be at the back steering this thing?'

'*This thing* knows I won't leave her for long. Besides she's in capable hands.'

He reached out a hand to touch hers. 'Pull the sail in tight here, let's gets some speed up.'

The boat leapt over the waves like salmon, Jo's hair streaming back below her crash helmet.

'So, you're enjoying yourself?' Jason said, crouching down beside her.

'Yes,' Jo admitted. 'I'm not sure I would have on my own.'

'You're a natural. But you're right, there's a lot to learn.' He got up and moved back to tighten the main sail, and they sailed on in companionable silence, broken only by brief instructions and the chatter of gulls.

* * * * *

They moored the boat in Polpeor Cove and clambered up the slip, past the old lifeboat station, and onto the footpath through the fields to The Lizard village. Rowena Pascoe lived in a small, terraced house in a tiny street that skirted the main road. Directly in front of her house was a potter's.

'Ma sells a few things in there,' Jason said, looking at the shop window. 'Runes and stuff.'

Jo peered in. The place was a hotchpotch of ceramics – some cutesy, some grotesque, nothing to her taste.

'Come on, let's see what's brewing in Ma's kitchen.'

Jason rapped the large brass knocker twice and they waited as heavy footsteps made their way along the hall to the door.

'Jason, my lover!' Rowena Pascoe was a big woman with a big smile. 'And who is this delightful young lady?'

'I'm Jo.' She stood stiffly in the hallway, wondering whether to shake hands. Rowena had no such reservations and flung her arms around her and kissed her cheek.

'Covid wouldn't dare cross my door, my lover. So pleased you found time to visit. I've been waiting for you.'

Jo felt the hairs on the back of her neck prickle. She hated how responsive her skin was to any shift in atmosphere and disguised her discomfort by making a show of observing the display of little figurines and bells on the shelf over the hall radiator. Rowena noticed. 'All my work – they sell well in the shop.' She reached over and picked one up. 'Here take this one, my lover. He's made for you.'

'Thank you—' Jo took the ornament and turned it in her palm. 'Is there any folklore attached to this little chap?'

'There is indeed,' Rowena said. 'He's a witch's familiar. An imp who safeguards his mistress. Keep him close.'

'Ma, don't freak Jo out before she's had a sip of tea and your magical walnut cake.' Jason put the emphasis on magical and winked at Jo.

'What am I thinking. Come in Josephine, the tea's brewing, my cake's cooling on the rack.'

Josephine. No one called her that. And if they took a stab at her full name, they usually picked Joanna. Rowena either had supernatural powers or a good grasp of Google. Psychics, she'd heard, always did their homework.

Jo followed Jason through to the small living room, Rowena veering off right to the kitchen.

'Impressed by the coven?' Jason said, as Jo surveyed the room.

'There's a lot to take in.' Weathered books lined bookshelves on one wall. A heavy wood coffee table was weighed down with more books and boxes. Ornaments – much the same as the imp in her hand but bigger – peered out from everywhere. It was a witch's emporium. A saucer of sour milk on the floor by the sofa was just waiting for a black cat to turn its nose up at. Partially drawn tasselled red curtains gave a glimpse of an antechamber.

'Does your mother do readings?' Jo said, taking the seat Jason had placed beside her.

'On rare occasions. For special reasons,' Rowena said, coming into the room with the tea tray.

Jason did the honours, giving Jo time to acclimatise. She imagined this is how you might feel when invited to The Queen's for tea and observed the protocols. Her phone remained on silent, and she looked to the grandmother clock in the corner for the time. They'd been a few vibrations – but for now any messages could wait.

The walnuts wedged into the cake's vanilla icing made her think of imp brains. She played with her slice like an actress wary of calories.

'Eat up, my lover,' Rowena said, 'There's plenty more if you want to take some home with you. You don't have little-uns? Otherwise, I'd warn you about the walnuts – poor mites might choke on them.'

Jason took the remainder of Jo's cake. 'In the interests of health and safety,' he said smiling at Jo.

'Now, Josephine, what was it you wanted to show me?' Rowena said, pushing aside her plate.

Jo wiped her hands on a linen napkin and unzipped her rucksack. At last.

'I'll take these through, Ma,' Jason said, clearing the coffee table. 'Lovely tea and cake as always. Well worth the sail.'

'You'd be in that boat of yours and over here for a bag of crisps,' Rowena said, reaching out to stroke his arm as he went by.

'Jason thought you might be able to … interpret these markings on the tree trunk.' Jo placed three photos before her.

Rowena put on heavy-framed reading glasses, which, to her surprise, Jo found disappointing. She'd expected an exuberant Prue Leigh pair.

'Well, I never. I ain't seen markings like these for many a year.' Rowena took off her glasses and looked at Jo. 'You say the trunk derailed the train?'

'Yes.'

'Pure evil, isn't it.' Rowena put her glasses back on and picked up the photo with the clearest shot of the markings. 'They're a warning. There's been a lot of unrest about strangers coming into town since Covid. Spreading disease. Local people don't like it.'

'Only some local people, Ma.' Jason came back into the room and sat down beside her.

'Those with dark hearts.'

'So—' Jo didn't know whether to call her Mrs Pascoe.

'Rowena, my lover, we're all family here. You being Cornish, Josephine.'

'So,' Jo continued. 'The markings are warning off strangers. But, derailing a train – with loss of life, is more than a warning.'

Rowena reached for Jo's hand across the coffee table. 'These warnings. They aren't about territory. They're personal.'

'What makes you think that?' Jo's arm brushed the other photos she'd brought, scattering them across the table.

'Initials. In old Kernow. When you read downwards, you can see them right as rain. H. M.' Her eyes shifted to one of the photos by Jo's elbow. 'What have you got there, my child?'

'Some shots of people by the tracks when the train crashed.' Jo had hoped to pick a time to show her them but passed them over.

Rowena studied them carefully before returning them to Jo.

'Do you recognise anyone? I know it's hard to see – but stances, body weight, clothing?'

'No,' Rowena said, 'Too dark. Much too dark. But I feel them.'

'You okay, Ma?' Jason came in from the kitchen and put a hand on her shoulder. 'You're trembling.'

'You best go now, my lovers. Go, before the night draws in.'

'Any chance of a slice of cake for the journey?' Jason said, trying to lighten the mood.

'Go now.' Rowena picked up a knife and plunged it in the

cake, splintering the walnuts and catching the top of a finger. The blood ran down her hand as she got up from the table.

'Ma, wrap your hand in this.' Jason offered her a napkin.

'Don't worry about me. Just go, now. Before the storm breaks.'

'Storm?' Jo sat up in her chair. 'There wasn't one forecast.'

'The spirit world is troubled. Something's brewing.'

'Come on, Jo.' Jason was getting on his coat. 'When Ma gets one of her premonitions best to heed it.'

'We'll leave the boat moored and get the bus back to Penzance,' Jason said at the door.

Rowena nodded. 'You forgot this,' she said, handing Jo the imp figurine. 'Keep him close.'

16

Rachel

Rachel parked her car on the gravel forecourt of Hartington Hall, got out and walked to the portico entrance. Paint was peeling on one of the columns. It was unlike Julia to let the façade crumble. Rachel felt a pang of nerves – as if she was visiting the big house for a job interview. The last time she was at The Hall was at Julia's Golden Age of Film Ball in July 2019. So much had happened since then. Their deep friendship had survived via FaceTime chats during Covid and, the odd visit, but would they be able to reignite their sisterly bond? Julia was seeing Brandon now. How would she fit in?

She could hear Julia coming down the stairs, chatting to someone, probably on the mobile. Brandon would be at work. And he didn't live at The Hall. Yet. Surely, she wasn't jealous. She wasn't the jealous type. But anyone can say that until loyalties and love are threatened.

A chain rattled on the other side of the door. That was new. Julia had always been tight on security, but a door chain when she had CCTV?

Rachel composed her face; hoped she didn't look as shattered as she felt after her strange first day at *The Art of Living*.

The door opened and Julia stood before her in expensive loungewear. She looked Rachel up and down before smiling broadly. 'What the hell are you wearing?'

'My—' Rachel pulled a face and spread her arms wide, 'vibrant work uniform. It's going back to the store.'

Julia wrinkled her nose: 'Lizzie's store?'

Rachel nodded.

'Come here,' Julia said, enveloping her in two silky arms. Rachel nestled into them while glancing over her shoulder. The entrance hall was empty, apart from the portrait of her late son Oliver which still hung in the stairwell. The sight made her heart lurch.

Julia pulled back and looked at her: 'You okay?'

'Yes. Just a hard day. It's lovely to be here. To see you. To see you both.' Rachel sucked in her top lip.

Julia let her go and turned to the portrait of Rachel's son, Oliver, who'd died in a swimming accident eight years ago. 'I'm taking good care of him. He's going nowhere, until you say so.'

'Thanks, Julia. Thanks for looking after both of us.'

Julia crinkled her brow. 'We all need a bit of looking after, don't we? Let me get you a stiff drink. I think you're going to need one. Do you want to bring your luggage in?' Julia glanced at the Fiat.

'It's just a rucksack. It can wait. Was that Brandon on the phone?'

Julia tilted her head.

'I heard you talking to someone as you came to the door.'

Julia moved aside to let her in. 'Yes. It was Brandon. Bad news ... again. Let me get you that drink.'

* * * * *

'Oh My God,' Rachel said, taking a gulp of Malbec. They were sitting in the main salon. That alone had alerted Rachel to the importance of the news.

'But you say Damien's alive?'

'He's in a coma on life support.' Julia was sitting perched

on the edge of the sofa opposite Rachel, a coffee table between them.

'But why? I mean, I thought Damien was a reformed character. He wasn't getting into trouble anymore?'

Julia picked up her glass from the table. 'Well, yes. But.'

'Poor Damien and poor Chelsea.' Rachel fumbled in her pocket for a hanky.

Julia pushed over a box of tissues in an ornate art deco dispenser.

'Thanks,' Rachel said, taking one and blowing her nose.

'I know you were very fond of him, Rachel.'

'Well – he gave me grief at the school. But, yes, I was fond of him.' Rachel picked up her glass. 'Will he pull through? Has ... Brandon given any indication?'

'Too early to say, I think. He was badly beaten. Left for dead and thrown over the sea wall at Newlyn Harbour. Just terrible. No one deserves that.'

'No,' Rachel said taking a gulp of wine. 'Whatever could he have done? I thought he was clean. Going to college and doing a tech course. He was brilliant at tech.'

'I have no idea.'

'Old scores?'

Julia ran a palm down the soft sheen of her joggers. 'Brandon will have a better idea once he's interviewed his mother and friends.'

'Of course.' Rachel felt out of the loop. Which she was. You can't go off to live in London for two years during a pandemic and come back expecting to be everyone's best pal and confidante.

Julia wiggled on the sofa and reached for her glass. 'How was your first day as an art therapist tutor? Better than teaching special needs children at St Piran's?'

'Different needs,' Rachel said, 'But easier. So far.'

'So far?' Julia's bright blue eyes were questioning.

'I don't know. Just a sense. Gisela von Schoenburg – the centre's founder – is a weird fish.'

'Gisela? I've met her. Lizzie introduced us at the Gallery.'

'Oh, she didn't say.'

'Not important.' Julia pulled a tissue out of the box and used it to wipe a smear on the glass top. 'Gisela was looking at possible joint ventures with The Arthouse.'

'You aren't interested?'

'Not yet. She needs to prove herself first. You can be my spy in the camp!' Julia clapped her hands together.

'I'm surprised I got the job.'

'Lizzie is giving her a roof over her head.' Julia put down her glass and leant forward. 'So – what are the students like?'

'Reasonably normal,' Rachel said.

'Reasonably?'

'I was joking. They're roughly what you'd expect. Mainly mature women with a little time on their hands. Chelsea and her goth friend Summer who make the average age group plummet. And a youngish man … in an air force jacket.'

'Is the jacket relevant?'

'It was today. He painted it as his "self-portrait" and Gisela started flirting with it.'

Julia burst out laughing. 'Rachel, your day's been more fun than mine! How old is The Jacket?'

'Early '30s, I'd say.'

'Good looking?'

'In a pale and interesting way.'

'Hmm,' Julia said, picking up her glass and running a manicured fingertip around its rim. 'Can I enrol?'

Rachel gave a short laugh. 'More than likely. Gisela will be looking to get the numbers up. But you are kidding? And you have Brandon!'

Julia looked to the side. She picked up a tissue and blew her nose gently before returning her gaze to Rachel. 'Of course. I adore Brandon. But you know what poor taste I have. And I'm not sure we're totally suited.'

Rachel reached across the table and took Julia's hand. 'Brandon is worth ten of any pale poseurs.'

'But in the Kingdom of the Blind the one-eyed man is King.'

'I'm sure *The Jacket* will have a few in the group fighting over him. Gisela's already got him marked and Summer was throwing him some looks. But Julia don't go there. You don't need to.'

'And you, Rachel?'

'He doesn't do it for me.'

'Yet,' Julia said, letting go of Rachel's hand. 'It is your first day.'

17

Brandon

Chelsea was sitting hunched over a mug of hot chocolate on the living room sofa, Brandon next to her, his arm resting above her shoulders.

'Shouldn't we be having this conversation in the incident room, Dad?' Chelsea said, some of her old cheek returning. She'd been crying since the news came in. At the hospital and in the car home. Hot chocolate was always some sort of solution for Chelsea.

He let his hand fall softly to the top of her head and stroked her hair. 'You can talk to me any time you like, darlin'.' His hand stopped for a second. 'It's hard to stop you usually.'

Chelsea spluttered a small laugh and dug him in the ribs

'Did Damien have any new mates? Or spiteful old ones?' Brandon said, continuing the stroking.

'No.' Chelsea blew into her steaming chocolate. 'Damien didn't really have any mates. Apart from me. He was quite the loner.'

'But he liked a smoke?'

'Yes. But he got that, mainly, from his mum. And—' Chelsea picked a film of chocolate off the top of her drink and popped it in her mouth. 'And ... he wasn't even smoking weed much anymore. Never with me.'

'Really?'

'Yes. I'd never lie to you, Dad. Never. I don't take drugs. You drummed that into me. I hardly drink alcohol. Chocolate is my weakness!'

Brandon ruffled her hair. 'You are not alone there, dar-lin'.' Brandon rested back into the cushions. 'So, Damien was enjoying his time at college? Was he working hard? Talking about it? Mentioning names?'

'He's not the chatty type, Dad.' Chelsea took a long last sup of chocolate. 'But I could tell he was enjoying the classes. He was top of the class! So good at IT. And I should know. Every time I have an issue – he fixes it. Immediately.'

'I never knew you had computer problems?'

'Duh! Why would you. I go straight to Damien. Horses for courses, Dad.'

Brandon smiled. 'I'm not so bad with tech.'

'But you're not so good, Dad. No offence.'

'No offence taken. I am more than happy to outsource skills to my betters.'

Chelsea put down her mug and snuggled against him. 'Do you think he'll make it?'

Brandon gave a long sigh and pulled her close. 'I hope so. I sincerely hope so.' His phone started to ring, and he switched it off.

'Dad, take it. It could be important.'

He tilted his head and looked at her.

'I'm okay. I'll get through this.'

Brandon didn't want her to have to get through anything else in her early years on the planet. But she was right.

'If you say so, Boss,' he said, getting up from the sofa and studying her.

'I do.'

She'd been forged in fire and would make a good cop. That, he would keep to himself. For the time being a pleasant career in the Arts seemed her best option.

Brandon turned his phone back on. They'd been two

missed calls from Jo. He clicked on her name.

'Where are you?' Jo sounded like she was in a wind tunnel.

'Traipsing along the A3083 towards Penhale.'

'Aha?'

'I've been to The Lizard. By sailboat.'

'Monday is a working day, Jo.'

'I've been working hard. Believe me.'

'Why are you whispering?'

'I'm with Jason Pascoe – he's walking up ahead to the bus stop to check the times back to Penzance.'

'For crissake, Menhenrick. Have you taken leave of your senses? I'll get a patrol car out to pick you up.'

'Jason did phone the local cabbie, but he isn't answering.' She sounded defensive.

'Jo, when I put the phone down, call for a patrol car. Tell them you have my authority. No point me calling, as only you know how far down the road you are.'

'That sounds ominous, Boss. A bit like my conversation with Jason's mum.'

'Interesting. What did she have to say about the photos?'

'The markings are warnings – like Jason suggested. But, also, she picked out some letters – an H and M.'

'My surname starts with an H and yours with an M.'

'It had occurred to me,' Jo said.

'I had a more direct warning this afternoon in Newlyn Harbour.'

'Damien too. But his initials are different.'

'True. But his attack could be unrelated.'

'Got to go, Jason's coming back.'

'Don't give too much away.'

'I won't. I'll call for the car. But one thing.' She lowered her voice further. 'His mum seemed freaked by the photos on the tracks.'

'Did she recognise anyone?'

'She said no. It was too dark. But she sensed evil.'

'Sure. Of course, those guys were up to no good. Where are you?'

'I'm coming for you, now.'

'Why?'

'Keep your phone on and keep your wits about you.'

* * * * *

It was dark when he hit the main drag towards Helston and The Lizard. A long old journey, so he turned on the sirens and put his foot down. It wasn't just witches who had instincts. Maybe some of the old voodoo rife in the Alabama of his childhood had rubbed off on him. He'd learnt to listen to his instincts, although they'd never govern him. Cold facts would always trump. But there was an atmosphere of menace – and it felt personal. Rachel's train was derailed. A butchered art dealer who knew Piers Jardine – a friend of Lizzie's. Damien, Chelsea's boyfriend left for dead. And they'd had a good go at him today too. Jo took a risk going out on that boat today.

Brandon weaved through the roadworks on the A30 and hit the A394 at 6.30pm.

'Where are you now?' Brandon was keeping constant contact with Jo on the carcoms.

'We're still trudging along the A3083, approaching Cross Lanes.'

'I won't be long – just coming into Helston now. Wait at Flambards Theme Park if you get there before me. Plenty of light.'

'Will do, Boss. But I reckon you'll be there before us.'

There were few cars on the road and Brandon stepped on

the gas. He could picture Jo and Jason walking along, chatting, oblivious to any lurking danger. Jo had been acting strange lately. Dropping her guard – at the exact same time she needed it.

What the hell. Something shot across the road in front of him. A rabbit or badger; the creature's eyes bright in his head lights. Brandon slowed just as a hefty vehicle came over the ridge, its lights on full beam blinding him. The Ford Ranger was hurtling towards him in the middle of the road, forcing him to veer to the left into a hedgerow.

'Fucking idiot!' Brandon shouted as the Ranger blasted its horn and careered past.

Brandon turned off the ignition and then started it again, handbrake off, the gears in first, the wheels spinning as they failed to get traction. It was gonna be back breaking pushing the BMW out of the ditch. But the ditch was shallow, and it could be done.

Brandon got out of the car, just as another light appeared at the top of the ridge. It was small, like a bike lamp. Another one shone behind it and the two of them approached in single file on the left-hand side of the road.

'Who goes there?' He sounded like a night watchman.

Brandon felt for his phone torch, but his mobile had fallen off the dash when he hit the hedge.

'Make yourself known.' Brandon's hands were on the holster of his taser. It seemed extreme, but today's events had made him twitchy. 'Who fucking goes there!'

'Brandon!' He recognised Jo's voice immediately.

'What the hell!'

'You did tell me to walk towards you, Boss.' Jo was just metres from him now. He could see the whites of her eyes.

'Brandon, do you need a hand getting this beauty out of

the ditch?' Jason Pascoe walked past Jo and rested a hand on the car roof.

'That's mighty kind of you. Let's get her back on the road before we cause another accident.'

*****

Brandon had hoped to grill Jason Pascoe on the journey back, but the fisherman wasn't having any of it. He was as slippery as a conga, fending off any intrusive questions with a quip or non-committal answer. Brandon wasn't fazed. As psychopaths go, the guy didn't fit the profile.

'I think you did the right thing, leaving the boat moored,' Brandon said as they approached Marazion on the A303. Although these roads can be lethal at night. Did you see the Ranger fly past?

'Yes,' Jason said. 'Rear view. We were walking on the right, facing on-coming traffic.'

Brandon gave a small nod. The man was sensible. As was Jo. Shame about her potential mother-in-law, he thought a secret smile forming.

'Did you get the reg?' Brandon asked. He hadn't had a chance, blinded by the headlights, and preoccupied flinging the BMW into a hedge.

'I took a photo,' Jo said. 'He was well over the speed limit.'

'Was it a man?' Brandon caught her eye in the rear view mirror. It irked him that she had let Pascoe clamber in up front.

'I'm not sure. They were wearing hoodies.'

'I have an aversion to people who wear hoodies in cars,' Jason said.

On that they had something in common.

18

March 1, 2022

Rachel

Rachel turned up for work the next day in a pair of Julia's jeans and one of her stylish grey sweats. She'd leave the colour to her paint palette. She tried the front door, but, when it didn't open, went around the back.

Gisela was in the kitchen wearing a verdant green jumpsuit; a canary yellow twisted hairband swept her hair back. Numbers were up on yesterday. An androgenous thirty-something woman in khaki vest, sweat, and yoga pants was new. As was a silver fox in his late '40s or early '50s. The sort of man they use in mature dating site ads. Chelsea had taken the day off and was nestling under a duvet at home until she could get to the hospital to see Damien.

'Now Rachel is here, we can get started,' Gisela said, clapping her hands. 'Yesterday you did self-portraits. We got an idea of how you view yourselves. Today I want you to start afresh and present yourself how you'd like to be seen. Be honest. Don't hide your true colours. Your ambitions. Dreams. We all have them. Or did. You may think yours are crushed and forgotten – withered to nothing like burnt out fireworks.' Gisela paused and glanced around the room, her eyes resting on Bea. 'But all things are possible here. No one is judging you—'

Gisela was interrupted by a knock on the bifolds. The room turned to see who it was.

'Magda?' Gisela said, putting aside the paint brush she'd

been waving around.

'Yes. Magda Pethick.'

'No surnames, here Magda.'

Magda's expression remained unchanged. 'Where do you want me?' she said, coming into the room. Magda (no surname) Pethick seemed an unlikely artist. She had a no-nonsense, practical air about her. She was short, like her conversation. And she was solid; her round face make-up free, her wiry grey hair pinned back with black hair grips.

'There's an easel here, in the corner,' Gisela said, pointing to it. 'We are asking you –'

'I heard you,' Magda cut in. 'I was standing outside, waiting for you to finish, before I knocked.'

'Very thoughtful of you, Magda.'

Magda smiled revealing a line of small, discoloured teeth.

'So! Paint brushes at the ready. Paint Yourself a Better Person!'

Rachel went around the room checking that everyone had the right materials, before heading to the coffee machine at the back. She'd shared a bottle and a half of wine with Julia the night before and her head felt fuzzy. She slipped a café au lait pod into the machine and turned to face the room. Jethro was in the far corner, his jacket on the back of his chair, slender arms protruding from a white t-shirt. He looked up from his easel and caught her eye. Rachel looked away quickly. He was not her type. And she was on a break … from men, sex and romance generally. No can do, she thought, turning back to the coffee machine and picking up her mug.

It was warmer today and Summer, the goth, had taken off her oversized black hoodie to reveal an undersized black t-shirt with a tattoo design to complement her own tattoos.

The Silver Fox was trying to fix the strings of an artists'

apron around his back.

'Let me help you.' Gisela crossed the room and wrapped her arms around him, taking the strings from the back and tying them across his abdomen. 'It's easier like this,' she said, smiling and moving back to admire her handiwork.

'Thank you,' he said, rewarding her with a smile which reached his pale blue eyes. He looked happy. Rachel wondered how he planned to paint himself better.

'Could you help me adjust my easel please?' Rachel turned to see Bea by her side. She was wearing a flowered pinafore, with matching hair slides.

'Of course.' Rachel followed her across the room to her chosen space. Although the course was designed to promote the breaking down of boundaries the students had already marked out their territory. Bea was heading for All Man's Land, having positioned herself to the right of Jethro and left of Silver Fox.

Rachel moved awkwardly between them and lowered the easel to Bea's height. 'Okay?' she said moving back.

Bea smiled. 'Thank you, Rachel.'

'Good luck,' Rachel said, and then wanted to kick herself. She wasn't going on a journey – well only metaphorically if you adopted the course's premise.

'Can you adjust my easel too?' Silver Fox was watching her, his arms folded above his apron strings.

The cliché 'get a room' flitted through her mind. And she smiled thinking of the Life Drawings room, which Chelsea said was upstairs under the eaves.

'Did I say something to amuse you?' Silver Fox's eyes were twinkling.

'Sorry, I was miles away,' Rachel lied. 'Let me show you?' Gisela was watching them from the other side of the room.

'Higher?' Rachel said.

'Please, Rachel. I'm Duncan. Nice to meet you.'

'Nice to meet you, Duncan.'

Rachel went to walk away.

'Where are you going?' Jethro piped up.

'To check if anyone else needs help.' Rachel's tone was testy. There was something if not sinister – too harsh a word – not quite right about him. He always seemed to be observing everyone but still managed to produce good work.

'Good. I wanted to ask you if we have Schmincke Mussini cobalt turquoise and Schmincke's Payne's grey.'

'We only supply the standard oils, Jethro. You can mix your own tones.' Rachel turned to leave again.

'I particularly wanted those colours. They are hard to replicate. Can you help me?'

He was living up to early expectations. 'If you can show me the shades you want on your phone, I'll see what I can do.'

Jethro took out his phone. 'Here.'

Rachel stretched her lips into a supercilious smirk. 'I'll do my Rembrandt best,' she said, catching Bea's eye and a low chuckle from Duncan.

'Will this do,' Rachel said, stepping away from the materials table with its paints, palettes, and brushes.

'Better than, Rembrandt,' he said lightly. 'It's a Matthews.'

'It's a turquoise, Jethro,' Rachel said. 'Let's see what you can make of it.'

'And the grey?'

'The Payne's grey? How could I possibly forget?' Rachel squirted out a big blob of black and an equal measure of white and whipped it into a mass of light grey.'

'Thanks, Rachel,' he said as she moved away, knocking into Bea's easel as she went. *Damn!* When she turned to right it, she saw Jethro adding black to his grey.

*****

Rachel went back to the coffee machine and made herself another cup. Expresso this time.

'Heavy night?' Gisela said, coming up beside her.

'Not unduly.' Rachel added some milk. 'How are you settling in at Lizzie's?'

'Wonderfully.' Gisela gazed into the gardens. 'Your mother is a remarkable woman. She has no boundaries but is so grounded. A unique combination.'

'She is unique,' Rachel agreed. 'I am glad it's working out for you.'

'She inspires me.' Gisela turned to face her. 'All she's been through and yet her essence is undimmed. I have asked her to do a masterclass here towards the end of the course.'

'What a good idea.' Lizzie would be in her element. Her painting at the moment was extraordinary. Her portrait of Oliver. Her portrait of herself. Lizzie's personality not only coloured her portraits, it enhanced them. She really did paint people better. Rachel took a sip of coffee.

'I'd like you, Rachel, to take the life drawings class tomorrow.'

'Tomorrow?' The coffee burnt her tongue.

'Yes.'

'I haven't seen the room yet.'

'Be my guest. We have a few minutes while the students get some paint on their canvases.' Gisela was gazing into the middle distance again.

'Do we have a model?'

'We usually take one or two from the group. This is an

opportunity for the students to bare all – strip themselves of all inhibitions.'

'But you can't force them to take off their clothes?' Rachel had a vision of the students walking naked into the room like political prisoners.

Gisela turned her neck slowly and rested her eyes on Rachel. 'Absolutely not. Everything here is voluntary. But the course is about renewal. Being happy in one's skin. And being at one with others. This is the ultimate challenge for the group.'

'But if they—'

Gisela waved a hand. 'There are always some who can't wait to get their kit off. Believe me – word of mouth draws these people in. I usually turn them down for the course. This isn't about exhibitionism. Or voyeurism. I want to encourage people to take new – possibly difficult – steps and make progress.'

'Okay.' Rachel could see Jackie's hand waving over the other side of the room. 'Shall I go and see what Jackie wants?'

'No. Leave her to me. Go to the room. Acclimatise. See for yourself what a safe environment we have here.'

'O—kay.' Where was this leading?

'You may have to be the model if we don't get any volunteers.' Gisela spoke quietly, but she'd made herself heard. Rachel felt the beating wings of butterflies in her stomach. It would be hard to teach a class if they'd all seen and painted her in the buff. Or maybe that was a boundary she needed to cross? Rachel shook her head lightly, fixed her eyes ahead, like a harassed waitress not wanting to engage, and left the kitchen.

* * * * *

When she opened the attic room door, she was on the threshold of a Parisien brothel. Rachel inhaled sharply. This she didn't expect – the louvre windows in the eaves were draped to exclude light rather than invite it. There were animal skin rugs on the floor, sumptuous deep pile velvet chairs and two chaise longues. A full-size suit of armour – the sort you'd expect to see in a castle – stood in the corner. Small metal cages hung from the ceiling, some with stuffed birds. One with a live canary, which was chirping noisily. At the back of the room was a stack of easels. So work was expected. Rachel walked to them, rested against their solid structure, and surveyed the room. It was pure theatre. A platform for the students to enact their fantasies, act their literal pants off, or hide in the shadows. Bravo, Gisela.

Rachel heard a sound outside, like a quiet cough. She took this as her cue to exit, stage left.

19

Brandon

H M. Brandon had written the letters on the white board in the incident room. It was all he had on all three of his new inquiries. Just the warnings and the initials carved into the tree trunk which derailed the train three days ago.

'What do you make of it?' Brandon addressed Stew, who was looking pensive.

'Dunno. As you say, Boss. Your surname begins with an H and Jo's with an M. Happily my initial isn't carved into that trunk, being Bland.' Stew rubbed his chin thoughtfully and raised an eyebrow. 'Maybe it will be on the next trunk.'

Brandon sighed. 'So, DC Bland, if you think these initials refer to Jo and me, why?'

'Because you've both done something to piss off some snarky perps?'

'That's one theory.' Turning back to the board he wrote revenge.

'Any others? Jo?'

'Could be the initials of the actual perpetrators. Or Her Majesty?

Brandon winced. 'Nothing, concrete then.'

'As yet,' Jo added.

'Nothing on the two hoodies by the tracks?'

'There were two guys in hoodies hurtling down the A3083 the other night. I put a check on the Reg. The Ranger was stolen. Found dumped in Helston.'

Brandon shot her a look. 'That is something, Jo. Well done. Get the forensics to sweep the car.' Brandon walked back to the table and rested against it. 'Talking of which, I've got an appointment at the Morgue in –' he glanced at the clock. 'twenty minutes.'

'Alain Boucher's widow,' Stew said.

'Yep.'

'Do you want me to go?'

Brandon looked at him carefully. He was improving, but ...

'I take it that's a no?' Stew said.

'Next time. It's gonna be a hell of a meet. Run through the CCTV, Stew. See if you can't find some better images of those hoodies.'

Stew nodded. 'I'm on it.'

'Jo, can you check the hospital? See if Damien's conscious? He could have some answers.'

'Of course. I'll do it now.'

'And Jo.'

She looked up from her bag.

'Ensure security is tight around his room. Who's on duty today?'

'Will do, Boss. PC Rhydian Hocking is on duty again today,' she said, gathering her things.

20

Rachel

There was a hum of anxious activity in the garden room studio. The group had been at it for over an hour and things were expected of them. Jethro and Chelsea had set the standard the day before and there was a competitive energy. Rachel was curious to see what Duncan had to deliver. He was such a suit. But so are Gilbert & George. Artists came in all guises.

'This can be an eye opener,' Gisela whispered as Rachel joined her at the breakfast bar. 'If they are being truthful.'

'Isn't that what we encourage?' Rachel looked up at her.

'Of course.' Gisela grimaced and lowered her voice. 'But human nature being what it is ... Besides,' Gisela was whispering right into her ear. 'Creative tension is essential for progress.'

'Hmm,' Rachel said, wondering when it would be appropriate to wipe away the spittle.

Gisela stepped forward and clapped her hands: 'Turn your easels!'

There was scuffling and scraping.

'All of you.' Gisela's eyes were on the back of the room where Duncan was helping Bea turn her easel and Jethro continued to paint.

'Let's have a look,' Gisela said striding across the room, nodding at the efforts in the front row and reaching Jethro just as he turned his easel.

'Another inanimate object,' Rachel heard Gisela say.

'It's delicate. Quite a departure,' Rachel said, referring to

Jackie's ballerina.

Jackie gave a small nod. 'I was always too big, as a child. But it was my dream.'

'There's always Zumba,' said Magda, who'd painted an Indian Squaw.

The arrow hit its mark. 'Not my thing,' Jackie said, picking up a palate knife and chopping into the pool of light at her dancer's feet.

Fryda, the young woman who'd pitched up that morning, had painted a radiant Joan of Arc, walking away from the stake with fire in the palms of her hands. It was impressive but Rachel kept quiet. This was about self-discovery, not The Portrait Artist Of The Year heats.

'You are the stone?' Gisela was asking Jethro. 'Your dream is to be a stone? And not a leather jacket?'

Rachel walked over. So that's why he wanted the Schmincke's Payne's grey and the Schmincke Mussini cobalt turquoise, which was splashed over it.

He raised his eyes to Rachel. 'Do you like it?'

'It's a tidy composition.' Was he taking the piss?

Gisela seemed to think so. 'Perhaps you are already the stone?'

'No,' Jethro said, 'I aspire to be the rock.'

'Ah.' Gisela was looking happier. 'The steadfast rock?'

'A rock, yes.'

Gisela smiled enigmatically.

She turned to Bea. 'Lovely,' she said glancing at her portrait of a Queen Bee, resplendent on a cushion of pollen, but clearly taken by the painting next to it.

Duncan stood back from his epic seascape; a small figure captured mid-flight diving from a cliff into a pool of the deepest blue.

'Interesting,' Gisela said standing in front of it. 'And beautiful.'

He glanced at Rachel.

'Is it you taking the plunge?' Rachel said softly.

'I wish,' he replied.

'Progress indeed.' Gisela tossed her hair back and returned to the breakfast bar. 'We'll take a break for lunch and—' she pulled out her phone which was ringing. 'It's Chelsea. She's asking for you, Rachel.'

Of course, Chelsea wouldn't have her burner number.

Rachel took the phone. 'Hi Chelsea. Everything okay?'

'I'm at the hospital. Damien's coming round. He was asking for you, Rachel? Kept saying your name.'

Odd. She hadn't been in touch with Damien for years. 'Anything else?'

'No. He was looking distressed, and the nurses asked me to leave. I'm in the waiting room, right now.'

'Good news that he's talking.'

'Yes. But why you Rachel?'

She had no answer for that. 'Have you told your Dad, Chelsea?'

'Not yet.'

'You should. If Damien's gaining consciousness, he could have something on the …' Rachel gave Gisela a quick look and walked away with the phone. 'He might have something on the attack. Names. Descriptions.'

'I know,' Chelsea said. 'I'm the detective's daughter. But he looks so fragile. I don't want him bothered.'

'Your dad wouldn't put him under any sort of strain.'

'I know. But—'

Rachel could hear her muffled sobs. 'Maybe I could come along after work. It won't be for a few hours.'

'That would be great, Rachel. Just to hear your voice. Damien did like you at school. And he's a bit afraid of Dad.'

Rachel smiled. 'Surely not?'

'I know! But he can't see beyond the badge.'

'Better go. I have Gisela's phone and a class gawping at me.'

Chelsea sniffed. 'Okay. Tell Gisela I'll try and make it for tomorrow. For the Life Drawing Class.'

'You want to come along to that?'

'Of course … if Damien is okay. It'll take my mind off things.'

The things Rachel wanted to take her mind off were stacking up. She returned Gisela's phone and pull a call through to the station on the burner. 'Jo, it's Rachel.'

* * * * *

Jo was sitting in the hospital café when Rachel pitched up at 4.30.

'How's he doing?' Rachel said drawing up a chair.

'He was sleeping when I went in 20 minutes ago. But the nurses say he is pulling through.'

'Has he said anything else?'

'No.'

'Have you told, Brandon?'

'Of course.' Jo took a sip of coffee. 'It was a good idea getting me along. Brandon has his work cut out now.'

Their eyes met. 'Yes. I think it could be a long-drawn out process – Damien's recovery and getting any information from him,' Rachel said.

'True,' Jo agreed, 'But any details he can provide now are key.'

Jo drained her cup. 'Let's go back in together. Your voice might rally him.'

Rachel followed Jo out of the open plan café area and to the lifts. The stark whiteness of the place made her feel light-headed. Hospitals had that effect on her. Which was a good thing. She'd needed the psychological anaesthetic. Jo, in contrast, was bristling with energy, eyes everywhere, checking. A trolley went past with a pale face and arm visible above the white sheet, a drip feed pushed by an orderly behind. Jo's eyes frisked the patient as he was wheeled into the lift opposite, the arrow pointing down.

They waited in silence until the arrow on the second lift pointed up. Jo pressed the button for Intensive Care. The doors opened onto an active scene. More trolleys. More orderlies in white, surgeons in blue, more doors with buttons to press.

It took a while before the nurse opened the main doors to the ward.

'Damien's in a private room at the end,' Jo said, leading the way past the cubicles with their bedside screens and the hushed conversations behind them.

'He's not there!' Jo said as they reached the end of the ward and faced a row of doors.

'Damien?'

'The police guard.'

Jo's head swivelled. 'Nurse,' she shouted. 'Nurse!'

A nurse stirred at the central workstation.

'Now!' Jo yelled, pushing open the door to Damien's room. 'Christ!'

'Calm down,' said the nurse who had joined her, 'This is Intensive Care.'

'Where's PC Hocking and where's the patient?' Jo's eyes were blazing.

'The patient was taken down to X-Ray five minutes ago. PC Snellers left for a convenience break.'

'PC who?'

'PC Snellers.'

'I've never heard of him. What station? And he's not back yet?'

The nurse pulled herself up to her full five foot. 'No. It's only been five minutes. I think PC Snellers said Falmouth. He was seconded.'

'You're sure about that? We were told PC Hocking was on duty this afternoon.' Jo walked to the window and looked out into the busy carpark. Felt in her bag. Emptied it on the table by Damien's empty bed. 'It's gone. My phone's gone.' Jo ran a hand through her hair. 'Someone must have lifted it at the café.'

She rushed to the door, her head oscillating as she scanned the ward. 'Phone Brandon, Rachel. I've got a bad feeling.'

21

'I'm so sorry, Boss. I should have checked PC Snellers' credentials when I got to the hospital. You told me to be tight on security. I feel so bad.' Jo couldn't meet Brandon's soulful blue eyes which were radiating the understanding she didn't deserve.

'DS Menhenrick,' Brandon said.

Jo kept her eyes on his shoes. 'No excuses.'

'No excuses. But you did check on security yesterday. PC Snellers only pitched up this afternoon. He had a badge and a plausible story for the hospital. If anything, they should have phoned us to check.'

Jo nodded and gave Brandon a quick look. 'True. Thanks, Brandon. But I feel so bad. How the hell is Damien going to survive out of intensive care? Where is PC Hocking? This is madness.'

'Agreed.' Brandon touched her shoulder gently. 'And just on cue—'

Stew walked in with a tray of coffee and biscuits. 'I come bearing gifts.'

He placed the tray on the incident room table with a flourish and got to the point.

'They've found an empty ambulance on the B3304 to Porthleven. We have CCTV of a patient who fits the description of Damien Kane being lifted off a trolley into said ambulance at 4.40pm this afternoon. A police officer boarded with him.'

'So, we know how he got out. But that's a lonely road. No

cameras there to track the second leg of his journey.'

'Sadly no.' Stew picked up a chocolate chip cookie. 'Rome wasn't built in a day, Boss.' He offered the plate to Brandon, who waved it aside. 'Put out some signs on the road asking for witnesses. And we need to get this across media asap.'

Stew nodded. 'I'm on it.'

'Any news on Rhydian Hocking?'

'His wife is having a meltdown.'

Jo jerked up her head. 'Poor woman.'

'Yep,' Stew replied looking uncharacteristically concerned. 'This all took Jan by complete surprise, as you can imagine.' Stew put down his biscuit. 'Rhyd went out in the morning. And he hasn't returned. His phone is dead.'

Brandon took a deep breath. 'The patrols are out?'

'Yes.' Stew picked up his biscuit and examined it. 'CCTV is being sifted through by hospital security. It's just a matter of time—' The distant bells of St Mary's church could be heard striking the first of seven chimes. It was getting late, but no one wanted to make a move.

'I wonder where Snellers got the ID and uniform?' Brandon was leaning over the table, both hands on it.

'The Dark Web. An old friend in the force? Someone good at photoshop?' Jo said.

Brandon narrowed his eyes. 'We had a bent copper here at Penzance a few years back. Got slung out of the force for aiding and abetting smugglers.'

'Philips,' Jo said, meeting his eye.

'That would be he.' Brandon pulled himself up straight. 'Where did he go?'

'I got a postcard from Thailand during Covid. He was rather pleased with himself for getting off *plague island*,' Stew said, picking up another biscuit.

'You would have had to have been on Mars to avoid the virus. Phillips wasn't a well man at the best of times. Can you check his whereabouts, Stew? It's a long shot, I know. The world is full of bent coppers with uniforms in their closets.'

Brandon turned back to Jo. 'Shall we go and see Damien's mum?'

Jo furrowed her brow. 'Why don't you let me do it with Stew. You have the Piers Jardine interview and Chelsea to deal with.'

Brandon felt in his pocket and pulled out his car keys. 'Indeed. Look he's not dead yet. I know it looks bad, but the boy is young and resilient.'

'Is that the spin you want on it?' Stew said, his hands in his pockets ready to go.

'I'm just asking you to use a little tact and compassion.' Brandon shot him a look which would have floored a more sensitive soul.

'My middle names, Boss.' Stew turned on his heels. 'Shall we go?

Jo was already at the door.

22

Brandon

Brandon glanced up at the clock. Piers Jardine was already ten minutes late – he was wasting his time before he'd even entered the room. He checked himself. There was no need to be irritated with the man. It wasn't his fault that someone got murdered in his name and he appears baffled to the reason why. Perhaps he'd be more forthcoming when they met face to face.

Brandon could hear laughter and chatter in the corridor outside. PC Gupta opened the door with a smile on her face. 'Mr Jardine, Detective Inspector.'

Brandon nodded. 'Thank you, Saira.'

Piers held out his hand, beaming. 'You keep such charming company, Brandon.'

Brandon had met the guy a few times. Years ago. He'd saved his skin after a break-in related to stolen artwork. Did he attract trouble? Standing there with his bouffant white hair, purple chinos, pink linen jacket and flowered shirt, he could have walked off the set of the Antiques Roadshow.

Piers' smile was faltering under Brandon's steady gaze. 'I will do my best to help you, Detective Inspector.'

Brandon gestured for Piers to take a seat at the interview table. He fancied a cigarette. Maybe because Jardine looked like he'd stepped off a 1960s film set where smoking was the culture. But he settled for a swig of water. 'Mr Jardine, how well did you know the deceased Alain Boucher?'

'Extremely well. We often did business together.' Piers

paused, 'Do you mind if I hang my jacket up – I have an appointment later?' He was looking at the clothes hanger on the back of the door. Brandon nodded.

'Was he involved in the smuggling back in 2019? That had a European connection.'

Piers gave a short laugh. 'No. Alain is as English as me.'

Brandon's eyes washed over him.

'Well. Maybe he doesn't have my *pronounced* English eccentricity. But he's lived – he lived—' Piers grimaced and looked at his manicured hands. 'in England all of his life.'

'In Marlow?'

'In the Home Counties – but Marlow for some considerable time. Maybe 15 years or more.'

'Why do you think he was killed?'

Piers edged his chair back and rested his arms on his legs. 'Mistaken identity.'

'You think they were after you?'

'Yes.'

'Does that scare you?'

'Shitless, Detective Inspector.'

Brandon was surprised at the expletive but could understand the sentiment.

Piers, still hunched over, raised his head slowly to meet Brandon's eye. 'I have been waiting for this interview. To express my fear for my life. Is there any way you can provide protection? Witness protection, perhaps?'

Brandon wiped a hand across his mouth. 'You haven't witnessed anything Mr Jardine.'

'No. But, I have theories. And, obviously, there is a connection. I should have been on that boat. Alain took up my invitation. We dined together the night before.'

'What did you talk about?' Brandon rocked back and studied him.

'Business mainly. I have some nice pieces he was interested in. In fact, that was why Roberta Bevan invited me on the voyage.'

'What were the pieces?'

Piers pulled himself up right and met Brandon's gaze. 'Five Lawrence Matthews. Late work which is considered some of his finest.'

'Tell me more.' The connections were stacking up. Rachel's father's paintings. The break-in in 2019 had been at her mother's place.

Piers blew out and moved his chair closer. 'I have nothing concrete. Just a feeling that there is a connection. The perps are still behind bars?'

'Yes,' Brandon said, adding. 'I checked when your name came up. I don't like coincidences.'

'Me neither.' Piers rolled his eyes.

'Had you met Roberta Bevan before the planned trip?'

'Briefly. On Zoom. She bought a Lawrence Matthews signed edition print during the second lockdown in December 2021. A birthday present for a loved one, she said.'

'Where did you send it?'

'To a private house in Algiers.'

'Really?'

'Yes. We get some interesting and exotic addresses.'

'But she came back to you. Recently?'

'A few months ago. We had some Zooms and she was looking to take my whole collection. Five paintings.'

'Worth?' Brandon unscrewed the water bottle.

'£450,000-500,000. We were still talking details. I presumed the trip was a sweetener.'

Brandon regarded the water bottle. 'You're a lucky man.'

'Indeed. Brandon, is there anything you can do?'

'Do you have a holiday home in Algiers – or any other far-away place you could disappear to for a while?'

'I have a place, yes.'

Brandon fiddled with the bottle top. 'Where?'

Piers paused.

'I'm not going to divulge your bolthole. Just need to know how secure it is. And how to reach you. You'll need to be contactable.'

'Am I a person of interest, Brandon?' Piers' signature blue eyes were on full beam.

'No. Your alibi is tight and no prints or CCTV to incriminate you. But it's in your own interest to be at the end of a phone.'

Piers exhaled a long slow breath. 'Of course. I have a place in Provence.'

Then I suggest you go there. Asap. And lock up those paintings.'

Piers went to get up.

'But not quite yet.

'Before you start packing can you take a look at these?' Brandon took some photos out of a file and passed them over.

'It looks like Bevan. Same big hair and athletic build.'

'Reckon that hair's real?'

Piers launched into a mock cockney accent. 'Nah. A right Joan Collins.'

Brandon laughed. 'Any other observations?'

'Mid-fifties. Meticulously made up. Big, metal framed glasses and Gucci scarves. She purred privilege. Who would have thought she bore such claws?'

'And a vicious fishhook.'

Piers raised an eyebrow. 'I'll book my flight.'

23

Rachel

The last thing Rachel wanted after yesterday's drama was a challenge in the Nude Room, as it was affectionately known. She'd worn some loose-fitting layers just in case she was persuaded to disrobe. The thought made her cringe. She scanned the room to identify fellow refuseniks. Sadly, their faces were as enigmatic as a Modigliani muse.

A huge jug of orange juice sat on the breakfast bar.

'Something to get the creative juices flowing,' Gisela said, popping open a bottle of prosecco and pouring it in. Dutch courage more like it. Gisela poured a flute for Rachel.

'No thanks.' Rachel shooed the glass away, almost sending it flying.

'I thought you liked a drink?' Gisela brought the glass back to within an inch of her mouth.

'Not at 10.30 in the morning.'

'Buzz's Fizz is perfect for a morning get me up.' Gisela leaned in. 'I would have thought you needed one after last night.'

'Coffee's fine.' Rachel turned to the machine.

'Would anyone else like to join me in celebration of another day on this wonderful planet.'

Bea put up a hand. 'That would be lovely.'

'I'd like a latte,' Magda said. Dressed in light brown slacks and a matching top she merged with the easels at the back of the room.

Gisela ignored her. 'Now, artists. We are going to have five minutes to get our kit together for the life class upstairs. Please help yourself to Buzz's Fizz or coffee. Rachel and I will be arranging the room. It is a delightful, welcoming space, designed to make you shed your inhibitions. You will not need to bring your easels.'

Jethro took off his jacket and hung it on his.

Rachel surreptitiously studied the students. They all seemed to be doing the same – furtive glances ricocheted around the room.

Gisela stood at the door with a flute in her hand and gave a small motion of her head.

'I'll be along shortly. Just making a cappuccino,' Rachel said, turning away.

Duncan was ahead of her making an Americano. 'Looking forward to this?'

'Not sure.' Rachel picked a pod in readiness. 'But I am a woman of the world.'

'I gather. You've spent some time in London?'

'Yes.'

Duncan moved aside to let her use the machine. 'But you're back.'

'Yes.'

'To find yourself?' he said, and she couldn't decide whether Duncan's expression was ironic or genuine.

'I found myself a long time ago. It's what I lost that still draws me back.'

Duncan was watching her carefully. 'Do you want to—'

'No. No. This isn't really the place for heart to hearts.'

'I thought it was exactly the place. Isn't this what the course is all about,' Jethro said, joining them. He grabbed hold of the prosecco and poured himself a full flute.

'Steady on,' Jackie said, empty flute in hand.

'There's plenty of booze in the fridge.' Jethro opened the door. 'And plenty of teetotallers.'

'No one said you could help yourself, Rock.' Rachel flashed him a dagger look, picked up the open bottle and poured Jackie a glass. 'Anyone else fancy some fizz?'

'I'll have some,' Summer said. 'No juice.'

There was a flurry at the bar and Rachel opened a second bottle. She assumed Gisela had budgeted for it.

'Shall I be Mum?' Duncan said, smiling with his mouth closed.

'Not a bad idea.' Rachel was warming to him. With Chelsea gone, she needed allies in this strange set-up. 'I'll see you upstairs in about five.'

* * * * *

Rachel walked slowly up the white wooden staircase, careful not to spill her coffee. The stairwell was an empty white space. The aroma of incense drifted from the attic studio, mingling with the heavy smell of oils and acrylics. Rachel knocked on the door.

'Come in.' Gisela had lowered the pitch of her voice. Was she going to be naked? Happily, not. When Rachel entered, Gisela was lounging on a chaise longue, resplendent in flowing gown and a silk turban, in the style of a 1920s salon matron.

She held a lighted cigarette in a long holder. 'Just an affection. Forgive me. I'll stub it out before they come in. The incense will mask the smell. You know, I get a little nervous too.' Before Rachel had a chance to react, Gisela added. 'But that is all part of the process. Nerves are essential for growth and action.'

The chatter from the kitchen was getting louder. Like play-time at school.

'How are they?' Gisela got up from the chaise longue. 'Are they ready?'

'What for?'

'To progress.'

'I would have thought so. Isn't that what they're here for?'

'We shall see. There is negativity in some quarters, don't you think.'

'Maybe cynicism?'

'Could be.'

'But there is also huge optimism. Bea and Jackie.' Rachel paused as she heard feet on the stairs.

'Ah, here they come. My protégés. Climbing the stairway to heaven.'

Was that weed in her roll-up. Gisela took a long drag before flinging open the door. 'Welcome to the Art of Living!'

The group strolled around the room, flutes and coffee cups in their hands like people at a Private View.

'Love it!' Jackie exclaimed. 'Inspirational.'

Magda ran a finger along the edge of one of the sofas inspecting it for dust. Jethro went straight to the easels and selected one. Bea trailed Duncan who was wearing his small, amused smile.

'Welcome to the house of fun,' Duncan whispered to Rachel as he passed. The set up did remind her of the Madness song. It was nutty.

'I am going to leave you for a short while with Rachel. Decide who will model first between you.' Gisela glanced at Jethro. 'Rock, Paper Scissors, if you like. Choose your weaponry.'

'She means materials,' Bea said quietly to Duncan.

'Let's see what you're made of. I'll leave you in Rachel's capable hands.' At that Gisela glided from the room, her cigarette holder out front very much alight.

24

'What are you doing here?'

Jason Pascoe stood at the door of Jo's apartment, a bunch of snowdrops in his hand.

'I stole these from the Morrab Gardens. Will you arrest me?'

Jo gave an uneasy smile. 'It's not that easy to get my attention. I warn you.'

'Under caution?'

'If they die on the premises.' Jo took the flowers, went to the kitchen and turned on the tap. Jason followed her in. She stretched up to the kitchen cupboard and took out a jug; could smell his aftershave as she did so. When she turned, he was inches away and she ducked quickly around him.

'What's the matter?' he said, as she fussed with the snowdrops.

'Nothing—'

'Nothing?'

'I don't know you. You come into my home with—'

'My heart on my sleeve.'

Jo's head shot up. 'That's a cliché.'

'All the best lines are. How else would you describe this? Me? Here? With a bunch of the only flowers in town. Trying to win over its fairest damsel?'

Jo smiled. 'Brazen cheek.'

Jason's smile stretched to his soulful eyes. 'This is our third date. Or haven't you been counting?'

'Oh, come on!' Jo walked into her living room and slumped down on the sofa. The tension left the room in that small puff of a move.

'Okay, I picked up the flowers en route as they were nice. And I thought you'd like them. But I'm here because I wanted to see you. I wanted to know if you fancied bringing the boat back from Polpeor cove with me. Today. Tomorrow. Whenever you're free. I want to see the wind in your hair again and the fine trace of salt on your cheek. I just want to see you.'

Jo's heart was thumping. The audacity of the man. She thought she'd been professional. Civil. She'd given him absolutely no encouragement. She looked up. Met his eye. Let him reach down and hold her hand and pull her up from the sofa and cradle her in his arms.

'This afternoon's good,' she said as he stroked her hair and leant down to plant a tender kiss on her forehead.

'How about tomorrow morning?' he said, pulling her back down onto the sofa.

25

Rachel

The door to the Nude Room opened hesitantly and Chelsea's head peered in.

'Rachel. Can I have a word.' Her voice was quiet and altered. Even in the clatter of easels being lugged out and props being sorted, her words had impact. Heads turned to the door and Rachel made for it.

Rachel shut the door behind her and followed Chelsea to the far corner of the landing.

'What is it?'

Chelsea's lips were trembling. Her eyes were streaming, and she wiped them roughly with the sleeve of her sweater. 'He's called me.'

'Damien?'

Chelsea lowered her voice, so it was barely a squeak. 'Yes.'

Rachel stretched out a hand to the banister to steady herself. 'He can speak? Are you sure it was him?' It seemed incredible.

'It was him. He phoned from his mobile.'

'The one that's missing?' There was a noise downstairs and Rachel pulled away from the banister.

'Yes. He just said, really slowly—' Chelsea stopped to catch her breath, the palm of her right hand flat against her chest. 'He said, I'm to tell no one, but you. They want money. £250,000. Or they—' Chelsea looked away, rubbed her nose, 'Or they kill him.'

'Everything all right up there?' Gisela was stirring below.

'I've got to go, Rachel. But I'll be at The Hall later. On some excuse. We need to sort this. Soon. Before—'

'You must tell your—'

'No!' Chelsea's eyes were pleading. 'They said on no account. He can't be told.'

'Chelsea, go to the station or home right now. Look, wait a minute and I'll drive you.'

'No, Rachel. Tonight. I'll see you tonight at The Hall. Don't tell anyone. Promise.'

Rachel sighed. 'I—'

'Promise?'

It was so hard to be an adult sometimes. Her brain screamed tell Brandon. But her instinct said hold off. For now. 'Okay.'

The jingle of ice in glass broke their silence. Gisela was on the middle landing, making her way up with a tray.

'A top up,' she said as she took the final flight. 'Well don't look so pleased,' she added when she reached them.

'I'll take a glass,' Rachel said, picking off a flute as Chelsea mumbled her excuses and hurried down the stairs.

* * * * *

Rachel struggled to be in the moment. Despite the moment being quite something. Jethro stood centre stage stark naked, apart from strips of art paper covering his privates, his arms hung limp over a metal lampstand, which rested on his slender shoulders. Jesus Christ. The symbolism was stark.

Gisela was lost for words. For a full five seconds. 'Excellent, excellent. But how long will you be able to hold that pose?'

'How long was our Lord Jesus Christ nailed to the cross?'

Gisela's mouth opened, but nothing came out.

'I'll manage,' he assured her.

Gisela regained her composure. 'Everybody, please, make the most of this opportunity. It is a wonderful pose. But, as you can imagine, a difficult one to sustain. Jethro is only human, after all.' Gisela turned to Rachel and rolled her eyes. 'Although he may believe he is the son of God,' she hissed in her ear.

Rachel was finding it hard to focus on what would otherwise have been an interesting class. Bea had stripped off to a stripey swimsuit and nestled close to Duncan who was in cords and a blue linen shirt. Jackie hovered naked behind her easel. Magda had also stripped, her solid beige body, not so different from her daywear, with its neat bulges and curves. Summer had, if anything, more layers on today – she lurked at the back, like another piece of furniture. Jackie was smearing her naked body in lurid yellow and purple paint.

Rachel drained her flute and put it on a tall wooden candle stick. She didn't know where to start. Her brain was fogging up with thoughts.

She said: 'I am going to leave you for a few minutes to make what you will of this *arresting* pose. Imprint your own ideas and personality on it. And then we will move on to our next model. You can create a scene or do solo portraits. Make it your own vision.'

Rachel walked swiftly away, giving Gisela a polite glance as she left the room.

'And don't forget to embrace the moment. Enjoy yourselves.' Rachel could hear Gisela saying as the door slammed shut and she raced down the stairs to the garden room.

* * * * *

'Jo?' It took an age for Jo to pick up her phone.

'Rachel?' Jo's voice sounded sleepy.

'Have you got a moment?' Rachel could hear her moving around and the small thud of her feet as they found the floor.

'What is it?' Jo said, her tone sharp, concentration back.

'Nothing important.' She couldn't confide in Jo, she was police. She just wanted some sort of steer. Some support – if only subliminal.

'Well?'

'I was wondering about how long—' She was going to say how long you need to keep a suspect on the line before you can trace their whereabouts. But that was a dead giveaway. 'It took you to … sail to The Lizard?'

'Er?'

Rachel could visualise Jo circulating a finger at her head.

'Silly question. And sorry to bother you. But one of our students asked as he is thinking of going there—' Rachel was rambling. But good. Let her incompetence be confirmed in Jo's analytical mind. 'And I'd heard you'd been there recently. Was it long?'

'Well, around three hours – and that was in quite good weather. Anything else?' She sounded testy.

'No. That was it. Thanks for filling me in. And sorry for bothering you at work.' There was a silence and Rachel added. 'Won't happen again.'

She'd have to Google the call duration. But what good would it do, really. By the time she'd delivered the cash, if she could get it, the captors would be well away. Rachel hit her head with the palm of her hand. She needed to think. Where the hell was she going to get 250k? And why that number. Because it was just about doable, by the time she'd flogged every asset she had – or Lizzie had – and taken out loans?

Rachel could hear Gisela's feet on the stairs. It was going to be difficult having a private conversation with Lizzie at Seabird Cottage with her around. She was breaking into a sweat and pushed open the bifolds.

'You okay?' Gisela came out onto the patio to join her.

'Yes. Just needed a bit of air. It is quite stuffy up there.'

'Intense. Yes.'

Rachel walked back into the room and over to the breakfast bar, helping herself to an americano pod.

'Drinking a lot of coffee this morning?' Gisela said, watching her carefully.

26

'What was that all about?' Jason was sitting up in bed, his hands behind his head.

'Just a bit of police business.'

Jason didn't look convinced. 'Well, if it's just a *bit* of business. Why don't we pick up where we left off.' He patted the mattress and Jo walked over and sat on the edge of the bed, twisting her body towards him.

He reached for her hand. 'I take it that's a no?'

Jo smiled and squeezed his hand. 'You know the old cliché?'

'Of course, I'm full of 'em,' Jason said, edging closer to her.

'About police always being on duty?'

Jason wrapped his arms around her. 'Can you wear your uniform next time?'

Jo laughed and let him hug her. 'I'm a detective. Not a plod.'

'Too right, nothing plodding about you DS Menhenrick.'

Jo sighed. 'I was a sprinter at school.'

'Bet that comes in handy.' He was kissing her now and she found it hard to break away.

'I have got to go … back to the station.'

'You still on for the boat trip tomorrow?'

Jo was wriggling into her trousers.

'Let's see if I can spare the time.' It was odd Rachel phoning to ask about the trip. She hoped she hadn't been gossiping about it. Jo picked her blouse off the dressing table chair, smiling as she remembered, even in her haste, carefully placing it there.

'I'll call you,' she said, getting her things together. He was still lounging in her bed, and she didn't want to leave him there.

He read her mind and pushed back the sheets, revealing a muscular chest, covered in merman curls.

'I'm keeping you,' he said, picking his clothes off the floor and tugging them on.

'Speedy.'

'I'm used to doing this in all kinds of conditions.' He smiled at her. 'At sea.'

'You have everything?' Jo said as they stood at the door.

'For now.' He pulled her to him and kissed her hard on the lips.

27

Rachel

Jethro was just stepping down as Rachel opened the door to the Nude Room. As he walked into the light coming from the landing, she noticed some markings on his legs. They looked like the tattooed scribbles she'd seen on others. Words and symbols were trending now.

He caught her staring. 'Want a closer look.'

Before she could answer he was in front of her. 'You'll have to bend down to read the inscriptions.'

Bend down and look right up his paper nappy. Not likely. But, on the other hand ... they could be relevant.

Rachel switched on the charm. 'They look fascinating. Do you mind if I sketch them?' She would have preferred to photograph them and ping them to Brandon, but discretion is the best part of valour.

'If you desire. At lunchtime.' He nodded towards Magda who was sitting cross-legged like Buddha on a velvet pouf. 'First we have another *religious* icon to capture.'

'Lunch would be good. If that's okay with you?'

'I rarely eat at lunch.' Or any other mealtime, by the look of him.

'Cool,' Rachel said. 'We can stay here when the others go down.'

'Cool.' He gathered up his unravelling loin cloth and waddled to his easel, a piece of loose blue paper sticking to his buttocks. Rachel wanted to laugh but remembered she had more important things on her mind. Like finding a way of securing £250k. Her stomach churned buck's fizz and black coffee.

She pulled herself up straight and surveyed the room. The students were beginning to get going on Magda, some using the same canvas, like Duncan, others starting afresh.

Duncan was rolling up his sleeves as Rachel approached. 'This,' he said in his soft Edinburgh lilt, is as naked as I get … today.'

'So not plunging in then?' Rachel smiled weakly.

'No.' He tilted his head and looked at her. 'You, okay?'

Rachel sighed. It was at times like this that she wished for a Covid mask to hide behind. 'Just a few—' she was going to say money problems but stopped short. 'Issues to deal with.'

'Ah, issues. They can be a bastard.'

'So, this tiny figure is Jethro?' Duncan had drawn him as small as a crucifix on a chain.

'To be fair, I portrayed myself as tiny yesterday.' Duncan turned away from his canvas to look at her.

'True. Is your work in celebration of small men?'

'Could be,' he said, 'I never did make six foot.'

Rachel smiled and moved on to review the other attempts, her attention never far from her phone.

* * * * *

Rachel made a show of tidying up the room, while the class filed away for lunch.

'I'll be down in a minute,' she said breezily as Gisela passed.

'Don't be long or the sandwiches will be gone.' Gisela turned to Jethro. 'You too?'

'Just finishing off my portrait. I don't do lunch, Gisela.'

'So where do you want me,' Jethro said as soon as

Gisela had left.

'On the chaise longue. Left leg revealing your tattoos.'

He moved away from his easel and reclined on the sofa, right leg out straight, left one bent at the knee, a hand resting on it.

'Perfect,' Rachel said, adding: 'Do you mind if I take a photo so I can finish it later? Gisela has got the stopwatch on me.' She felt for her phone.

'I do mind. Why are you afraid of her?'

'I'm not.'

He shrugged. 'That's what it looks like.'

'I also eat lunch. And I'm hungry. So … I'll get started.'

28

Rachel

Chelsea was lurking behind the magnolia tree when Rachel drove onto The Hall forecourt. She parked the Fiat and walked over.

'Any news?'

'No. I think they'll call you, Rachel.'

Chelsea seemed calmer, as if relieved to share the load.

'There's quite a gathering in the living room,' Chelsea said, as Rachel turned the front door key. The portrait of Oliver was there as always, and she felt a pang of love and sorrow. There was something about her child's open, knowing expression that not only reassured her, but crystallised her thoughts. It was the first painting she could sell. It was hers, after all. No matter how much it pained her, it was a sacrifice that needed to be made. She had lost her son; she could help another.

The Hall drawing room was like a doctor's waiting room. Brandon and Julia on one sofa, Nick, Julia's 18-year-old son, on the other. No one looked happy.

Brandon got up and poured Rachel a glass of red. 'Look like you need this, gal.'

'Thanks.' Rachel took the glass and sat down next to Nick. She could hear the clock ticking in the hall. 'Are you staying for supper, Brandon?' she said, breaking the silence.

'No. I just dropped Chelsea off. She wanted to catch-up with you about class tomorrow.'

'Oh, you're coming?' Rachel glanced over at Chelsea who was loitering in the doorway looking at her phone.

'Yeah,' Chelsea said, putting away her phone and crossing the room to sit beside her. 'It's not doing my chakras any good mooching at home.'

Brandon gave Chelsea a look.

'My energies, Dad! I need them all … We've got to get Damien back.'

Brandon nodded gently. 'Can you tell me where I can get myself a chakra.'

Chelsea bounced off her sofa and went to the back of his and began kneading his shoulders.

'Your wheels of energy are rusting, Dad.'

'Thanks for the vote of confidence,' he said, reaching out to stop her hand.

'You'll find him Dad. I know you will.'

'Darn right, gal.' Brandon sprung up from the sofa.

'I've put some chili con carne in a container for you,' Julia said, getting up to see them out.

'That's mighty kind of you, Julia.'

Rachel also got up – she was looking for a chance to get to her room, or the studio. Somewhere she could take a private call. And make a few.

'Jo said you mentioned the trip to The Lizard,' Brandon said, as Rachel met him at the drawing room door.

'It was just a random conversation I had with a student.'

Brandon was regarding her carefully. 'Everything okay?'

She looked down. 'Yes. In the circumstances.'

He was still looking at her.

'The circumstances we all find ourselves in. Damien's disappearance. The murder.' She couldn't meet his eye. He read her so well.

'I'm glad you're staying here,' he said. 'It's safer.'

'Yep.'

They stood there. Neither making the move to go.

'If you need to talk to me about anything. You have my number,' Brandon said, his hand on the door frame.

She looked into his eyes. 'Thank you, Brandon. I will.'

'Promise.'

'Promise.'

* * * * *

As soon as Brandon was out of the door and Julia occupied in the kitchen, Rachel headed for her room. Within moments there was a quiet knock.

'Can I come in?' Chelsea said.

'Okay. But I need to make some calls.'

Chelsea's mouth fell open.

'I'll be able to see if they're trying to get through. But I need to get money.'

Chelsea grimaced. 'I'm sorry, Rachel. We'll get the money back. Dad will get the money back.'

Rachel wasn't so sure. But a refund wasn't upper most in her thoughts. She sat down on the edge of her bed and scrolled through her contacts until she found Piers Jardine.

He answered after five rings. 'Hello?' She could hear laughter and the clinking of glasses and cutlery.

'Piers, um …'

'Rachel, darling.'

'Is this a bad time?'

'Aperitifs, darling. Farewell party. I'm off tomorrow. But lovely to hear from you.'

'Piers, I don't want to alarm you – and please don't speak to Lizzie … yet. But I need to get hold of some cash. Quickly.'

'Oh?' Pier's tone hardened.

'I want to sell Lizzie's portrait of Oliver. And her one of me – I have that in London. And—' she took a deep breath. 'The ones you're safekeeping for my mother. The Lawrence Matthews.' Her father's paintings. She named him to give them more weight. He was, though, still very much in demand. Or so she hoped.

'Rachel, are you in trouble?' Pier had lowered his voice.

'No. But I need the money. Piers, please, no questions for now.'

Someone called out in the background. Piers shushed them.

'You will need to speak to your mother.'

'I know,' Rachel said. 'I wanted to give you a heads up so you can … think about options.'

'There are some collectors.' Piers could be counted on. 'Rachel, darling. How much are you looking to secure.'

'Two hundred and fifty thousand pounds.'

Piers exhaled loudly. 'Well, I'm not sure if we can manage a sum like that without going to auction—'

An unknown *WhatsApp* number appeared on her phone. 'Just see what you can do, Piers. Part payment, maybe? I've got to go. Now.'

Rachel heard the exasperation in Pier's voice before she hung up and accepted the call.

An electronically distorted voice said: 'Have you got the money?'

Rachel's heart was thumping, but she controlled her own voice. 'No. But I'll get it.'

'Be quick, Matthews,' the sinister voice said. 'The toe rag's life rests in your hands. He's not strong.'

'Can I speak to Damien?'

'After the first payment? Your reward.'

'I need to speak to him now. Your proof.'

'He's not well.'

'Then return him to hospital. If he dies, there's blood on your hands.'

The caller made some dreadful cackling noises. 'If you must waste his breath ...' The line went quiet. Rachel noted the time. 45 seconds.

There was a creaking sound – his trolley, or wheelchair.

'Rachel,' said Damien's quiet voice. Even when he was in the best of health it was little more than a whisper. 'Do as they say.'

'Are they treating you well?'

'£100,000 by Friday.' The line went dead. 60 seconds.

'How did he sound?' Chelsea was sitting on the floor by her feet, hugging her knees.

'Like Damien. Quiet, but alert.'

'Frightened?'

'Tense. But he often is.'

Chelsea pulled herself up. 'Yes. He had a shit childhood. Made him guarded.' She looked at Rachel. 'What doesn't kill you makes you stronger.'

'I don't know if I agree with that.' Rachel reached for her rucksack and dropped in her phone. 'I've got to go out.'

'Before supper?'

'I'll get some later.'

'Are you going to your mum's?'

Rachel got up and walked to the door. 'If you need me, just call.

* * * * *

The Fiat's petrol gauge was touching red. Rachel wouldn't get paid until the end of March. And here she was, running on empty, on a mission to raise £250,000.

She hadn't warned Lizzie about the visit. Sometimes it was best to get her unprepared. But how much should she tell her? Lizzie was a generous woman – had applied to take in Ukrainian refugees – but had given her spare room to Gisela instead.

Rachel turned off the ignition and headlights when she got to the top of the lane which led to Seabird Cottage. Maybe a *version* of the truth would be best. She got out of the car, locked it, and started to walk, a warm glow from the cottage lighting her path.

'Gisela not in?' Rachel said as Lizzie led her into the living room.

'No, darling. She's out tonight. She goes out quite a bit … which is nice.'

'Oh?'

'No *oh*, about it, Rachel. Gisela is good company. But, sometimes, we all need a little time alone.'

Lizzie was looking tired. She was 77 and poured herself into many activities, so it was reassuring to hear she enjoyed a quiet evening to recharge.

'I'm not ready for the scrap heap yet!' Lizzie said, reading Rachel. 'In fact, I have my book group in less than half an hour.'

'Here?'

'Zoom, darling. So much more convenient when it gets yarda yarda.'

Rachel sat down on the small sofa. 'I won't keep you long.'

Lizzie perched on the armchair opposite. 'As long as you need, darling. It's always lovely to see you … even when you look like that doom monger Chris Nitty.'

'Whitty. You still remember him?'

Lizzie picked at a loose thread on her cardigan. 'Not really, darling.' She looked up at Rachel expectantly.

'How to put this.'

'Next slide please!' Lizzie chortled.

'Oh, Mum!' Rachel put her head in her hands. 'If only it was that simple.'

Lizzie reached across and touched her hand. 'Come on. Whatever it is, you can tell your mother.'

'I need £250,000.' Rachel couldn't look at her.

'Is that all!'

Rachel's head shot up. 'Yes. But can you lend it to me?'

Lizzie's eyes were drilling into her. 'What for? Are you in some sort of trouble? Or do you need it for a down payment?'

Rachel looked over her head at the Lawrence Matthews painting above the mantlepiece. 'Neither. I need the money to help a friend. It's crucial they have it as soon as possible.'

'Is your friend in trouble, Rachel?' Lizzie was still looking at her, but her gaze had softened.

'Severe danger. That's why I can't say anymore, right now. Trust me.'

'I always trust you, Rachel. It will take a little while to get that sort of sum.'

'Can Piers arrange a bridging loan? If he were to sell Dad's paintings, we'd have enough, wouldn't we?'

Lizzie lowered her eyes. 'Yes. That really is the only way. I don't have savings.'

'Mum.' Rachel reached out and took her hand. 'This is so good of you. I know you had plans for the money from Dad's paintings. The refurbishment.'

Lizzie waved her other hand. 'It can wait. Or might never happen. A lick of paint will do. Why do I want a big extension? I'll only be persuaded to take in more lodgers!'

Rachel smiled. 'Can you call Piers tonight? I believe he's leaving the country.'

'Oh?'

Rachel gripped Lizzie's hand harder. 'Why don't you go with him?'

'I can't, Rachel! He mightn't want me and, also, I have Gisela here.'

'She's not here now, though. I worry for you, Mum.'

Lizzie pulled back and tugged at her cardigan. 'I'm not going anywhere.'

'Well, speak to Piers anyway. See what he has to say.' Rachel got up from the sofa.

'Are you going already?' Lizzie's eyes widened.

Rachel had seen that look before. The terrors. Mainly Lizzie suffered little more than what the Americans call 'friendly dementia', but several years ago she'd experienced hallucinations and paranoia, triggered by the death of her husband Lawrence and grandson Oliver. Although this hadn't reoccurred, Rachel was always watchful and sought to reassure her. 'You can come with me. There are plenty of rooms at The Hall.'

'I can see you're already treating it like it's *your* home!' Lizzie's eyes narrowed and balance was restored.

'I know Julia wouldn't mind … in the circumstances.'

'Why do you need the money, Rachel?' Lizzie rose to her full five foot four inches.

Rachel held her gaze. 'I can't …'

'Is it a ransom for that young boy. Dominic? He's still missing, isn't he?'

Her intuition was uncanny.

'Damien. Yes, and yes.'

'I'll do what I can as fast as I can. And, Rachel, don't worry.

I won't tell anyone.'

'Not even Piers.'

'Especially not Piers. Such a loose tongue.'

'Now you understand why I want you to leave? Maybe go to London? Or the Hall.'

'Batten down the hatches?'

'For a while.'

A car could be heard slowing down at the end of the lane. Then the slam of a door and footsteps. Rachel went to the window.

'Gisela?' Lizzie said.

'Yes.' Rachel had hoped to leave before she returned. 'Whatever you do, don't breathe a word to her.'

'What do you take me for?'

An open, trusting person. Rachel left the words unspoken and left.

* * * * *

'What are you doing?' Julia had walked out of the kitchen as Rachel was taking a photo of Oliver's portrait. A measuring tape was in her other hand.

'I'm taking a photo.'

'I can see that. But why?'

Rachel sighed and slipped the phone and tape into her pocket. 'Because … Just because.'

'What the hell is going on, Rachel?'

'I'm so tired. Can this wait until the morning.'

'No!' Julia had crossed her arms – an early warning sign Rachel had come to recognise.

'Okay.' Rachel nodded towards the kitchen and Julia followed her in.

Rachel's half empty wine glass was on the island, and she picked it up and drained it.

Julia topped up her own and sat at the island, her hands cupping her face, her eyes on Rachel. 'When you're ready.'

Rachel took a breath. 'I need the money. I thought I could sell the portrait on eBay.'

'What???' Julia reached for her glass. 'Are you crazy?' She took a slug of wine. 'I'll buy the portrait. It's not leaving that wall … unless you take it home with you.'

'I don't have a home.'

Julia shook her head. 'You know what I mean.'

Rachel picked up a flyer for Julia's gallery from a pile on the marble top. 'There's a good artist in Gisela's group. He did a stand-out piece today.'

'Don't change the subject.' Julia lent over and topped up her glass. 'How much do you need? No questions asked.'

Rachel ran a finger round the rim of her glass. '£75,000 … Just a loan.' Rachel took a gulp of wine. 'In cash.'

Julia threw back her head. 'What the hell? Look, you can have the money. No problem. I can arrange it. But what sort of trouble are you in?'

Rachel looked to the side and then down at the flyer, which she was folding into ever decreasing squares. 'It's not me in trouble. But … a friend of mine is, and I need the cash urgently. I can't explain further, Julia. I hope it will be a loan. But there are no guarantees.'

Julia got up and ran a hand through her hair. 'I'll need to make some calls. How soon do you need the cash?'

'Tomorrow. Tonight. As soon as possible, Julia. Thank you. I hate burdening you with this.'

Julia shrugged. 'It's you that concerns me, Rachel. This isn't right. What aren't you telling me?'

The door creaked open, and Chelsea stood in its frame, the portrait of Oliver behind her.

29

Brandon

'So, what have we got?' Brandon put down his takeaway coffee and turned to the incident board.

'Not an awful lot, Boss,' Jo said. 'There were some witness reports on the B3304 to Porthleven. A local shopkeeper saw a blue Renault van parked around 5pm on March 1. It was gone when he travelled home later that evening. I've put out a description of the van – on the road and to the patrols.'

'Any vehicles reported stolen?'

'We're looking into it,' Jo said. 'I'm going out that way myself tomorrow.'

'Oh yeah?' Brandon was watching her intently.

'I'm going to pick up the yacht with Jason.' Jo hesitated. 'If that's okay?'

'Depends on how long your sea voyage will take, Jo.' Brandon rocked back in his chair. 'We need all hands on deck. Here.'

'Okay. I understand. But it just seems—' Jo looked at her hands, 'interesting that the van was in the same vicinity as that Ford Ranger that rammed you into a hedge a few nights back. That was stolen too. For a quiet spot, it's becoming lively.'

Brandon nodded. 'But if you could postpone your ... trip until we've got a handle on the Kane situation.'

'Of course, but it is a waiting game and I'm itching for action.'

Brandon looked at her and smiled. 'I can see that, Jo.'

Jo blushed and it was, Brandon thought, nice to see. 'Just a few days, DS Menhenrick.'

Brandon's phone pinged. He tapped on the screen and enlarged the WhatsApp image.

'What is it?'

Brandon passed his phone over. 'More markings? On a leg this time and not a tree trunk. Rachel should go into forensics.'

Jo passed his phone back. 'Maybe, but I can't see her in a white space suit somehow.'

Another message came in. 'It's the leg of one of her student's. Jethro,' Brandon said.

'No surname?'

'No. Rachel said it's a course policy. But it will be easy to find out.'

'I'm on it,' Jo said.

'It could save you a trip to the wise woman of The Lizard. Give Gisela von what's her name a call.'

'Okay, Boss. Don't have to rub it in. But Rowena may know what they mean.'

'And so would Jethro. Jo, what is it with you?'

'Nothing, Boss. Just short of ideas. But couldn't Rachel ask him? We wouldn't wish to alert him.'

She was right, of course. And so, he nodded affirmation. But this fixation she had with Jason was unsettling.

30

Rachel

Rachel passed her sketch of his leg to Jethro.

'You can draw,' he said, studying it carefully.

'That's what they pay me for.'

'Will you sign it?'

'If you tell me what your tattoo means?'

'If you don't know, then you don't deserve to.' He handed her sketch back.

'Rude!' Chelsea joined them. She peered at the drawing. 'Aren't those Cornish independence symbols?'

'Go to the top of the class.'

'Still rude,' Chelsea said. 'Naughty chair for him, Miss. I mean, Rachel.'

'Sadly, I think he'd enjoy that.'

Jethro smiled.

'What did I miss yesterday!'

'Look around, Chelsea – all captured on canvas,' Jethro said, spreading his wiry arms.

Chelsea huddled close to Rachel. 'Shall we have a look?'

'Sure. And then maybe a coffee outside? The weather's brightening.'

Chelsea squeezed her hand. 'Have you sorted things?' she whispered.

'Sort of ... now what have we here?' Duncan had painted Magda, centre stage in the foreground of his canvas. Instead of the sofa she'd posed on, he'd placed her on a sedan chair at the edge of the sea, flanked by Summer. Bea was paddling in the shallows, while the Jethro crucifix hung from a rock in the middle distance.

'Awesome!' Chelsea exclaimed. 'Double Awesome. You must show Julia Trenowden – she could sell this.'

For 250k? Rachel thought ruefully. But Chelsea was right. It was a stunning piece.

'You like it, *Miss*?' Duncan said, serious eyes, belying the banter.

'Very much. Why don't you take it to The Arthouse Gallery for an opinion?'

'We can do better than that.' Gisela had emerged. 'I'll ask Julia to come in for a private view on graduation next week.'

'Graduation?' Duncan looked puzzled.

'Yes. A fun episode to round things off.'

Chelsea gave Rachel a knowing look and nudged her in the ribs. 'Can we go for that coffee now?'

* * * * *

Rachel waited until they'd reached the gate at the bottom of the garden before speaking.

'I have £75,000 in cash.'

'How?'

'Don't ask.'

'And the rest?' Chelsea looked over her shoulder.

'I think we'll get there by the end of the week. Anyone watching?'

'No. Not that I can see. But only a matter of time before Gisela turns up!'

'You needed some fresh air. *That's all.*' Rachel gave her a meaningful look. 'Don't we all. I can't concentrate in there. Too much going on in here.' She tapped her head.

'I'm sorry, Rachel. Dragging you into this.'

'You didn't, Chelsea.'

Chelsea took another look over her shoulder. 'Uh?'

'So many connections with … my family and friends.'

Rachel's phone began to ring, and she fumbled for it.

'Hurry,' Chelsea urged.

Rachel swiped the screen. 'Yes?'

'Got the cash?' Same electronic voice.

'£75,000.'

'Not good enough.'

'I can get the rest by Friday.'

'Leave it in a rucksack in Penberth Cove at 4pm today.'

'I …' The line went dead. 30 seconds. 'I was going to say it would be difficult to get there as I'm working. Could lose my job. But, hey, what's the loss of a few hundred pounds in the great scheme of things.'

'Here comes Gisela,' Chelsea said.

Chelsea hunched over the gate and gazed into the bay. The tide was in, gentle waves lapping the rocks. 'Dad will get the money back. I know he will. But he can't know right now.'

'Ladies!' Gisela was striding towards them.

'Dad's going to kill us when he finds out we kept this from him,' Chelsea said, giving Rachel a sideways glance.

'If we're not dead already.

* * * * *

The others followed Gisela out into the garden, lumbering their easels for some plein air. The sun was struggling to cut through the clouds – any colour would have to come from spring flowers and Jackie and Gisela's clothing.

Jackie, flushed with success from her nude debut, was

wearing a flimsy, abstract kaftan. The chiffon glanced over her curves. Gisela was wearing a daffodil yellow catsuit, her long thick hair swung as she walked.

Magda was wearing beige. And Jethro his jacket. Duncan was also wearing a jacket, cream linen with cream chinos.

'Very Hopkirk,' Bea said, wiggling the feet of her easel into the grass next to him. Noting his quizzical look she added: 'The dead one from Randall and Hopkirk. They're playing the repeats on *Great* TV.'

Rachel had seen the programme. Wished she could vanish like Hopkirk and pop up by Damien's side and solve the mystery.

Chelsea set up her easel by Jethro. Rachel hoped she wasn't developing a crush. She was admiring his jacket, stroking the badges.

'Are you a member of the Cornish Liberation Army?' Chelsea said.

'No.'

'Why the badges. The symbolism?'

'Why do you wear a smiley face on your T-Shirt when you're torn up inside?'

Chelsea's face fell and Rachel had to stop herself rushing to her defence.

'Because—' Chelsea faltered. 'Because that's my default. I like to be happy.'

'The impossible dream,' Jethro said.

Chelsea turned away. 'Not for me.'

'Does anyone need anything – brushes, *expensive oils*, paper?' Rachel was in the centre of the lawn, her phone burning a hole in her pocket. She needed to get things moving and plan her early escape to Penberth Cove. It didn't have a car-park and would be hell to reach.

'I'll have some oils.' Magda was setting up the other side of Jethro, her back to Rachel as she spoke.

'Any particular ones?' She already had a wide selection.

'Black. And white.' Magda turned, her small dark eyes shards of slate.

'Right,' Rachel said, heading off to the house, a drop of rain glancing off her hand.

* * * * *

It was belting down when Rachel left for Penberth Cove at three. She was cutting it fine – particularly as the school day would be ending soon – but it had been difficult to escape.

The drop-off destination was inspired. No CCTV. Just the small hamlet of Treen in the middle of nowhere. The thought made her heart race. Next Christmas she'd put a taser on her wish list. She comforted herself with the thought this was a down payment. They wanted more. Needed her alive.

Rachel parked the Fiat in the Logan's Inn car park at 3.40pm and picked up the weighty rucksack of cash Julia had given her at lunchtime. She hadn't been able to meet Julia's eye. She'd hoped the search parties would have found something by now. Penwith wasn't exactly huge.

She took some shots of the cars in the car park and pinged them over to Brandon, with a cock and ball story about seeing some lurkers. A white lie, but they had to be watching. She heaved the rucksack over her shoulders and strode out of the car park and across the fields to the narrow woodland path which led to Penberth Cove. The tree branches formed a long thin tunnel, which slanted down towards the sea. She was alone – with no escape, and the thought made her accelerate and stumble over the rocks and tree roots on the path.

Her heart was pumping. The sky darkening. A gull cried above, calling time on the day. Keep walking, and watching, she told herself as she descended, one hand gripping the straps of her rucksack, the other brushing away stray twigs and branches, as she turned right towards the cove. In the near distance, the sea shimmered like liquid mercury. The big flat rocks, which formed the cove floor, as hard and grey as tungsten. The bay was deserted. As it would be on a bleak day in early March. But her skin crept under the watch of unseen eyes.

She'd keep going until she came to a spot where she could place the bag. Somewhere obvious.

There was a loud rumble. Thunder?

Rachel looked around and saw two figures rushing towards her, hurtling stones, one striking her hard on the cheek. She started to run, slipping on the wet ground, heart thumping, another volley hitting her back, making her fall. They were closing in like hounds, and she leapt up, shrugged the bag off her back and slung it at the first one, catching him on the legs, making him yelp and fall. He wasn't down for long, and Rachel raced to the shore, leaping over the flat stones and into the shallows. Tugging off her trainers and coat she waded in to her waist and began to swim, hard and fast.

She could hear shouts from the beach as she pulled herself through the waves, her legs kicking furiously, eyes searching for landmarks as she turned her head to breathe. A small green rowing boat bobbed up in front of her as she turned the corner of the cove. Their getaway vessel? Was there another way for them to reach it? Her oar skills were limited. But so were her options. She figured she was a better rower than they were swimmers and dragged herself into the boat, catching her knee on one of the wooden benches, two oars stowed beneath them. Rachel looked behind her. They were heading back to the woodland path. She took up the oars and rested them in their oarlocks, pulled up the anchor and started to row east, the lights of Mousehole harbour in her sights. Rachel had never liked rowing at the best of times. But she was grateful. So grateful for those early morning sessions now, where most of her attention was on the Adonis of an instructor. But she'd learnt enough, and the knowledge was moving her in the right direction. It was still drizzling, and the light fading, and she'd have been shivering with cold if not for the physical exertion.

She looked over her shoulder and saw Lamorna. Mousehole was still a way off; its lights a colourful abstract yet to shift fully into focus. But Penberth cove was diminishing oar stroke, by stroke, the rhythm allowing her mind to wander. *Shit.* Was the first word it landed on. She'd left her iPhone in the rucksack. She'd only got it back that morning. Would they notice? The burner was in her pocket sodding wet and useless. The realisation put her off her stroke and she veered left towards the rocks, righting the boat just in time. She needed to keep away from the land. They were out there somewhere. Could be watching from the clifftop, waiting for her to moor.

Chelsea would have called her by now to check. Would she put out an alert? She glanced back at Lamorna. It was more defined. She could see some fishing boats and further out a trawler heading for Mousehole harbour. Concentrate. Strong steady strokes. Keep alert. Rachel wiped her hair away from her eyes with her right arm, careful not to lose the oar, as she rowed on, the wind whipping up the waves, and sapping her strength, as she battled through them.

31

Brandon

Brandon rushed into Penberth Cove. It was a tiny place, and he didn't expect to see Rachel in it. Or the rucksack with £75K. His low expectations were met.

Jo joined him. 'Do you think they have her too?'

'Fuck knows!' Brandon said, wiping his hand across his mouth. 'What the fuck made her decide to go it alone!'

Jo touched his arm. 'Chelsea. You know that.'

Brandon swung around to face her, eyes blazing. 'Yes. But Chelsea is a child. If …' The old saying 'if she told you to jump off a cliff' sprung to mind. But he left it there. 'Thank God, Rachel had the good sense to send those photos.'

'It was a massive hint,' Jo agreed. 'And Chelsea came good phoning us.'

Brandon shook his head lightly. 'Okay. Let's look around.'

Brandon strode to the waterfront, while Jo veered off to the left.

The light was fading. Brandon turned on his phone torch and cast it around the shore and shallows, catching something floating a little way out; something else by the edge of the cove.

He kicked off his shoes and socks, rolled up his trousers and waded in.

'Rachel's trainer!' he yelled, waving it above his head. 'And—' He turned left towards the rocks at the edge of the cove. 'Rachel's coat.' He brandished them above his head as he returned to the shore.

'What do you think?' Jo said.

'I think she swam away.' Brandon looked to the ocean. 'They were probably following her, and she saw it as her best option.'

Jo nodded. 'I can see Rachel doing that. And they have her phone. So, she couldn't call us.'

'Had her phone. Chelsea called and someone picked up. Now it's dead. No way of knowing where they are now. But they were here.' Brandon tilted his head and looked at Jo. 'Get on to Jason See if he can't get a RIB out there. I'll phone the RNLI too.'

Jo nodded and keyed his number. 'Jason. A friend of ours is missing at sea. Rachel Matthews. We think she went swimming off Penberth Cove around 30-45 minutes ago.'

'More than likely heading for Lamorna or Mousehole,' Brandon cut in.

'Heading east towards Lamorna and Mousehole. Thank you.' Jo clicked off.

'How long?' Brandon said, his eyes on her. 'How long before he launches the RIB?'

'Ten Minutes.'

'I'm getting on the boat. And if not that one. The next.' Brandon picked up his shoes and started to run. Jo waited a beat, before chasing after him.

32

Rachel

Cold gnawed at her, but she struggled on, the waves rising, the dark deepening. It made her think of that time all those years ago when Oliver was at the mercy of the sea. He was just nine years old. How long did he fight, before he gave up and let the sea claim him? She was older and stronger, and there was another boy who needed her. Not anyone to replace Oliver, but a boy too young to die. She yanked the oars, got back into the rhythm, and sang. It's what you did when it was bitterly cold, your strength ebbing, spirit dying. 'Row, row, row your boat gently down the stream. Merrily, merrily, merrily, merrily, life is but a dream. Row, row, row your boat, gently down the stream. If you see a ... crocodile.' A splash of sea water slapped her in the face. She spat it out. 'Don't forget to scream!'

Rachel was scowling at the heavens, just as a shaft of light hit the water, making her jump and drop an oar.

'No,' she sobbed, as it slid from its oarlock into the sea, sending her scrambling over the side for it, the boat rocking dangerously as it drifted away.

'Shit. Shit. Shit.' Rachel thumped her forehead with her right hand, the left gripping onto the other oar.

The beam of light was traversing the waves now. She looked up; eyes narrowed. Headlights. And torches. A torch procession – coming down the cliff towards her. She must be just outside of Lamorna.

This could be a good thing. But the way her luck was

running, likely not. She placed the lone oar in its cradle and started to pull away from the cliff. But, frustratingly, circled back.

'Didn't you learn anything at Sea Scouts?' yelled a deep, familiar voice.

'It was rowing club!!' Rachel yelled back. 'And not a lot. *We learned more from a three-minute record than we ever learned at school!*'

'Yep,' Brandon said. 'And I admire your ability to quote Bruce Springsteen in an emergency.' He'd clambered down to the bottom of the cliff, and stood three metres or so from the boat. 'Here,' he said, tossing over a blanket, the fringe trailing the water, as she grabbed hold of it.

'Thank you!!'

Brandon was giving her a disapproving look. She knew she was going to get it in the neck. But hoped her effort, and the incredible expense, wouldn't be wasted.

The sound of a motorboat made her start.

'Your lift home, Rachel,' Brandon said. 'Jason Pascoe is going to tow you in. Where the hell did you get the boat?'

'It was moored around the other side of Penberth Cove. It must have been theirs? How else were they going to get away after the drop off?'

'Good thinking. We'll run the boat through forensics.'

Rachel was huddled in the blanket, shuddering uncontrollably. 'They chased me. I didn't want to hang around to find out why."

Brandon nodded. 'You're safe now. I'll get Stew to drive you home from Penzance.' He stood watching over her as the RIB came alongside her boat. 'I need to run through things at the station. See if we can't hunt these guys down. Did you get a good look at them?'

Rachel spoke through chattering teeth. 'They wore covid masks and dark jeans and outdoor wear jackets, hoods up. Oh, and one of them was wearing a grey bobble hat. Have I messed things up?'

'In your own weird and wonderful way, you've set the cockroaches scuttling.'

She'd take that as a compliment. Rachel hugged the blanket closer as Jason attached ropes to her boat and one of his crew helped her board the RIB.

33

Brandon

An enormous sense of relief flooded over him. Rachel was safe. And, possibly, they had a trail to Damien. But that didn't stop him being darn annoyed that she hadn't told him about the ransom. It almost got her killed and now he was going to have to move mountains to get the money back. Passing on Rachel's descriptions to the patrols was his first move. They were already on the look-out for one, maybe more suspects, last believed to have been on the Treen bus heading for St Ives. That's when the mobile phone trail went cold. Chelsea had phoned to check on Rachel within 15 minutes of the drop off. An admirable thing. But, in the circumstances, unfortunate because that connection had been cut immediately. They'd have to rely on eyewitnesses and bus CCTV to find out where they got off.

Jo was waiting for him at the top of the cliff.

'You solved the case on your ascent?' Jo was smiling lightly.

'It's amazing how a blast of cold sea air can make you think clearly.' He took Jo's hand as she helped him up the last step. 'But not quite yet. We're going to have to go through the CCTV. They'll show up somewhere.'

'They've found the rucksack, already,' Jo said, as they walked towards the BMW. 'In Sennen.'

'Empty?'

Jo grimaced. 'Not even a fiver tip.'

Brandon laughed, despite himself. 'The mind boggles thinking where they stashed it. In a local hidey hole? Up their jumpers? In a couple of carrier bags? Maybe they'll leave a paper trail.'

They'd arrived at the car and Brandon rested a hand on the roof, eyes on the souvenir shops over the road. 'They wouldn't have expected this. It won't have been easy getting back to base, unobserved, rustling with pound notes.'

34

Brandon

Brandon stood on the steps of Penzance Station, cameras rolling and snapping. Jodi Kane, Damien's mother, was next to him, her skin sallow, bags under her eyes.

'This is an emergency appeal to the people holding Damien Kane captive. This is a young man in a critical medical condition, only just taken off life support when abducted from Truro Hospital. Make no mistake, his life is in grave danger. Please notify us of Damien's location. I cannot stress how important it is for him to be returned to care. His mother is here to make a personal appeal for the life of her son.' Brandon gestured to Jodi and stood aside.

'I beg you as a mother to release my boy. He is my only son. Whatever he has done to you, it cannot ...' She fumbled for the words.

'Justify,' Brandon said quietly.

'Be justice for you to kill him. It can't. I love him. And I blame myself for not lookin' after him proper. Don't take it out on him. I beg you. Leave my child and go. Please.' She sniffed, but her eyes were dry. Her slight body as brittle as a gull's bone baked in the sun.

Brandon touched her shoulder lightly, and she stepped down from the steps, the press barking questions.

'Please respect Ms Kane's privacy. I'll take questions from the press now.'

'How did Damien Kane get taken from the hospital? Didn't he have a police guard?' a young woman from *The*

Cornishman asked.

'There was a police presence at the hospital. We are investigating how this was compromised.'

'Can you contradict rumours that the policeman on guard was bogus. One of the gang?'

Brandon hesitated before replying. 'The policeman on duty was on secondment. That is all I can say right now, while the investigation continues. Next question.'

'Kirsten Lovejoy, *BBC Cornwall*. You've given full details of sightings of the suspects this evening. How soon can we expect their capture?'

'We are only as good as the information we receive. So, I appeal to the public to send us any observations, no matter how small or seemingly inconsequential. The man with his hand up at the back.'

'Graham Highsmith, *The Times*. You say that the captors visited Penberth Cove today to pick up a ransom. The rucksack used was discarded in Sennen.

Brandon nodded in agreement.

'Does this not contravene police guidelines?'

'The money was delivered by a civilian concerned about the welfare of Damien. Next question. The lady in the beret at the back.'

'You've asked for people to look out for stray notes. Are you being serious?'

'Deadly. The accomplices were carrying a large amount of cash on them. It's highly likely that some will have dropped, particularly if they were rushing. This could give us a paper trail.'

'An unusual one?'

'But significant. People don't tend to drop twenty-pound notes in the street.'

'And people don't tend to hand them in,' the woman replied.

Brandon smiled softly. 'A young man is captive, his life in mortal danger, I look to the milk of human kindness.'

35

Rachel

It was getting late. Rachel sat on Julia's sofa, knees to her chest, arms wrapped around them, feet cocooned in woolly socks. Brandon sat opposite, arms resting on splayed legs. He reached for the bottle of Jack Daniels he'd brought with him and poured Rachel a large one. And himself one even larger.

'I want to apologise.' Rachel reached for the tumbler. 'I just didn't—'

'What's done is done. I understand your ... reasoning. And the emotional pressure.'

Rachel took a sip of whisky. 'Thanks, Brandon. God, I wanted to tell you. But I know the guidelines and I was careful.'

Brandon raised an eyebrow. 'Well, you did give us a hint, with the photos.'

'Did you ... know, straight away?'

Brandon looked to the side. 'Pretty much. And we came out as soon as we got them. Probably missed the bastards by minutes. But we have their DNA now. We've already had a few sightings and we're waiting for people to hand in any stray notes. I'm not holding my breath on that.'

'I don't know. You made it plain – anyone seeing a random £20 note might have their conscience nudged. I mean, even if they pocketed it – they could take a photo and send it in?' Rachel ran a finger around the rim of her tumbler, considering her theory.

'You're overthinking things, gal.' He was looking at her

from under his fringe in that old way. She bit her bottom lip and went back to circling the rim.

'I'm concerned about Lizzie,' she said lifting her eyes to his. 'She's understandably worried about Piers and their close connection has got to unnerve her. It could trigger a psychotic episode?'

'That I can understand.' Brandon shifted towards the edge of the sofa. 'I ... *advised,* Piers Jardine to leave town.'

'Oh, it was you?' Rachel held his gaze.

'Yes. I mean, he was concerned – unsurprisingly – about his own safety, after the murder on the yacht.'

'Of course.' Rachel moved forward on her sofa, mirroring him. 'I – *advised* – Mum to go with him. God, we're tangled up in this. Piers' friend is murdered, the bogus collector wanted Dad's paintings – I get the ransom call ...'

It felt so right sitting there, going over things with Brandon. Despite the circumstances, he induced a sense of calm. When she looked up, he was studying her.

He averted his gaze, picked up the bottle and poured them both a small one.

'I need a clear head tomorrow. And you?'

'Not really. The job's tame – now that I've got past the nude room challenge.'

'What?'

'Gisela has turned the attic into a French brothel.' She caught his startled expression. 'No need for a raid!'

'As if we needed any more drama,' Brandon said, swirling the whisky.

'Well, that's what it is, really – a stage for our "actors" to perform.'

Brandon relaxed back into the sofa. 'Phonies?'

Rachel grimaced. 'I wouldn't say so. Just people trying

different things to make sense of themselves. Or merely trying different things.'

'Are they paying you to spout that guff?'

Rachel burst out laughing. 'Of course!'

'Any interesting characters?'

'Have you got an hour?'

Brandon looked at his phone. 'If you think they would help my inquiries.'

'Why don't you come along ... in disguise. I mean who would recognise you with your clothes off.' Rachel was smiling broadly.

Brandon put down his glass and tilted his head to look at her. 'I have my own artist's attic studio. Remember?'

Rachel studied her glass. Of course she did. They had got extremely close that winter of 2018. 'I do. Is my painting still—'

'It's still there.'

'I'll finish it one day.'

'I know you will. Be sure and give me a head's up on the timing.'

The silence hung heavy between them.

'You two hungry?' They hadn't noticed Julia at the door. 'I was going to make some cheese on toast.'

Brandon smiled widely at Rachel and then turned to Julia. 'That would be awesome, Julia. Can't thank you enough.'

'Can't think of anything better, after a day like today. Do you want me to help?' Rachel said, going to get up.

'No, not after the day you've had.'

'Tha—' Rachel jumped when her burner phone started to ring. Brandon was at her side in seconds, his shoulder touching hers as she took the call.

'Mum?'

'Hello! Hello! Can you hear me? That old phone of yours has such a terrible connection!' Lizzie shouted.

Brandon moved back.

'Yes, I can hear you loud and clear!'

Rachel got up and started pacing the room, holding the phone away from her ear, as she listened to Lizzie's breathless account.

'Okay,' Rachel said, as Lizzie paused for breath. 'Just a second—' She turned to Brandon. 'Lizzie just opened a jiffy bag which she found on the mat just now. It contained a photo of Damien looking terrified.' Rachel took a breath, before continuing. 'And a bloody toenail.'

Brandon took the phone from her. 'Lizzie, I'm sending a car round to you now. Do not, in any circumstances, open the door until I call you again to say who's out there. Put the … letter and item somewhere safe. Try not to touch anything, as we'll need them for forensics.' Brandon ran a hand across his chin. 'Was there a note in the envelope?'

Rachel could hear Lizzie fussing around. 'There's a piece of paper wedged in the bottom.'

'Remove it with gloves or tweezers.'

The line went quiet. The smell of bubbling cheese on toast drifted from the kitchen.

'They want the rest by tomorrow … the letter is smeared with blood,' Lizzie could be heard saying.

'Here's something to cheer you two up.' Julia walked into the room, carrying a tray laden with Welsh rarebit. 'Whatever's the matter?'

36

March 4, 2022

Rachel

Rachel forced herself to get out of bed and dressed. The alarm had snoozed beyond its remit, and she was going to have to catch a coffee and something to eat at work. Her mind was spinning, as if she was still on that boat paddling around in a circle, going nowhere. And now she had to fake it for the day, leaving Brandon and Jo and the search parties to find Damien before it was too late. If it wasn't already.

The drive to St Ives was easy enough, the roads clear, no need to cram the Fiat against a hedgerow to allow a four by four or bus to pass. She caught herself searching the road and hedges for random bank notes. Had to stop herself laughing at the madness of it all. Rachel turned on the radio, to see if there'd been any news. *Pirate* was playing *I can't get no satisfaction*. Too true, she thought, taking the right towards Carbis Bay and the arts centre.

'Rachel!' Gisla announced, as she crept in through the bi-folds. 'I'm surprised you came in after yesterday.' All eyes were on her as she headed for the coffee machine. Surely Lizzie hadn't told her?

'I'm good,' Rachel said, sorting through the pods for a cappuccino. They were running low.

'Something you ate?'

So, Lizzie had covered for her. 'Yes. But I'm fine now.'

Cup in hand, Rachel surveyed the room. The usual suspects were there, but people were missing. She did a mental head count. Three out today. Four including Chelsea who had joined a search party. Magda and Fryda were missing and one other. She felt Duncan's eyes on her from his usual place at the back of the room. Bea wasn't by his side.

'Numbers down today?' Rachel said as she started to prepare the materials by the sink.

'Two of the group – Magda and Fryda – decided to do some spontaneous sunrise sketching. They'll be along later,' Gisela said.

'And Bea?'

'Dentist Appointment.'

'Now, everybody if we could just start,' Gisela said.

They were standing awkwardly by their easels, in need of direction. Free spirit was running as low as coffee pods.

'Why don't we—' Rachel stopped when she saw Chelsea scurry in through the door.

'Yes?' Gisela questioned.

'Why don't we do some spontaneous seascape sketching,'

Gisela cupped her chin with a fist. 'Hmm.'

'There's not so many of us and it's a ... glorious day. Why waste it.'

'Couldn't agree more,' Duncan said resting an arm on the top of his easel.

'Jethro?' Gisela asked, as if he were an artistic arbiter.

He took his time answering. 'Yes.'

'Yes, what,' Jackie said. 'I was hoping to finish my life study.'

'We're not joined at the hip, Jackie. You stay.'

'Agreed.' Gisela walked to the centre of the kitchen. 'The group is splintering. Which is perfectly normal and healthy at this stage in the process. You are finding your feet. Whether that is standing your ground – or exploring higher plains. I will stay here and everyone who wants to grab a sketch book and join Jethro, Duncan and—'

'Me. I'll go with Rachel and the ... others.' Chelsea zipped up her puffer jacket and strolled over to Rachel. 'Such a good idea. I can't keep still, right now.'

'What happened with the search party?' Rachel said quietly.

Chelsea rolled her eyes. 'Like a Ramblers Society walk. Chatting away. I couldn't concentrate.' She tugged at the elasticated cuffs of her jacket. 'They've got it covered though.'

'Any more news?' Rachel said, sliding a palate knife through the Sellotape of a cardboard box.

'Yes.' Chelsea turned to face the garden, resting her back against a work surface.

Rachel ripped open the top of the box and thrust in a hand, picking out a few sketchpads. 'And?'

'The bus CCTV caught two people, dark clothes, wearing hoodies and carrying two Co-op plastic bags – each.'

'Unusual?'

'Textbook, Dad said. Similar clothes, and same bags of a similar size. You know, as if they'd divvied out—' Chelsea lowered her voice. 'Wads of cash.'

'Wow!'

'Gets better,' Chelsea said, helping Rachel with the sketchpads. 'They were filmed in the St Just Co-op, buying the bags.'

'With the cash?' Rachel took out the last sketchpad.

'Duh! They're not that dumb. Well, I don't think so. Coins.'

Rachel's heart leapt. 'This is looking good, Chelsea.'

'But it worries me.' She hid her face behind a sketchpad.

Rachel silently agreed. The vision of Damien's frightened

face flashed before her. People do rash things when they're cornered.

* * * * *

Jethro joined Rachel and Chelsea as they crossed the garden to the gate. He was a man of few words, so it was surprising when he broke the silence.

'How's it going with the case?'

Chelsea stopped walking and stared at him.

He walked on for a few paces and then stopped and turned. 'Did I say something wrong?'

Chelsea shrugged her shoulders. 'You know who my father is?'

'Of course.'

'Well let's keep the conversation light, shall we?'

Jethro smiled. 'Fancy a drink after class?'

Chelsea's mouth fell open and she stomped past him to Rachel. 'No sensitivity,' she hissed.

'He is a stone,' Rachel replied, opening the gate.

'A rock,' she heard him say softly as he followed them down the cliff steps. Rachel questioned the 'my rock' cliché. Rocks could be lethal. By the time they'd reached the cove at the bottom of the steps, Jethro and Chelsea were walking side by side, their heads cast down in hushed conversation.

37

Brandon

Brandon and Jo were seated in the BMW over the road from scrubland on the outskirts of St Erth. CCTV had seen the suspects, thought to be male, get off a bus in Marazion. Street cameras had traced them to the area. The neglected farmland – a few ramshackle pre-fabs and a barn – was a likely hide-out.

Brandon was waiting for firearm back-up before making an approach. The place had an eerie feel – not so much a ghost town as a place ghosts avoided. A poor haunt. He felt invisible fingers on the back of his neck and rolled his shoulders involuntarily. No sounds of sirens yet, just the whistle of wind in a lonely place. Brandon stroked the megaphone in his lap, waiting for the performance to begin, uneasy about the reception.

Jo's phone buzzed. Brandon caught the name. Jason Pascoe. He wasn't sure about the nature of their relationship, although he had a good idea. He wasn't sure whether it was a good idea, either. But Jo was a grown woman. A sensible one at that.

They sat in silence. Jo reading and tapping her phone, Brandon watching the prefab, until they heard tyres on uneven ground. Brandon and Jo got out of the car and walked towards the one storey build, a megaphone in Brandon's left hand, taser in his right, car doors opening and slamming as the others joined them.

Brandon stepped forward and put the megaphone to his lips.

'Come out of the building. Hands above your head.'

The words drifted in the dead space.

He tried again: 'Out of the building. Now. Hands above your head.' He gave sideward glances to the Specialist Firearms Officers (SFOs), who were togged up in helmets and protective clothing, Glocks, and rifles at the ready.

Brandon tensed when he heard a noise coming from the prefab, exhaling sharply when he saw a cat dash past chasing a moth.

He took a few steps towards the prefab, two of the SFOs close behind, two others veering off to the left and right to cover the back entrance.

His gut told him that this wouldn't be a shootout. The perps hadn't used firearms before, although £75k richer, they might have bought some shooters.

Bang! A stun grenade lit up the entrance as the six-person team charged in.

It took around a minute before the leader, Bob Graham, came out.

'We need an ambulance.'

'Jo,' Brandon said, watching her reach for her phone. 'I'm going in.'

The door was swaying on its hinges as two SFOs rushed out. Two others were crouched on the floor by an object. It was murky in there, curtains drawn against the grim outside, but Brandon knew what was on the ground. Recognised the scuffed trainers and odd socks. He sucked in a breath and walked over, the two SFOs moving aside for him.

Damien was tied to the chair; blood ran from fresh wounds to his arms and head. His eyes were closed, his face white.

'Get me a blanket,' Brandon said, leaning down and feeling the boy's pulse. 'And help me get him off this.'

As one of the SFOs started to cut through the ropes, Brandon lay down beside Damien and gave him mouth to mouth resuscitation, moving to chest pumps, pushing life back into the boy, hoping they'd got there in time. He increased the pressure, thumping the boy's puny chest. On and on he pressed until he felt a small movement against his hand – and then a sigh and the flutter of eyelashes.

'Thank God,' Brandon yelled, above the sound of sirens.

A paramedic rushed in with breathing apparatus. Another two with a stretcher. 'We'll get him comfortable. Stop that bleeding,' said a young guy with a shock of red hair.

'Just don't lose him this time,' Brandon said under his breath, as he stood up feeling for his phone and making a call to Al Chapman. 'We're going to need you at the crime scene,' he told Al, 'There's a lot for you to ponder.'

'A body?'

'Sorry to disappoint you. I think we have a survivor here. But no perps –they left in a hurry.'

'Did they leave the cash?'

Brandon looked. It wasn't hanging around like loose change, that's for sure. 'I'll leave that for you to find out.'

He clicked off and walked to the back of the room and through to a small kitchen. There was breakfast debris on the worksurface. A cup of cold tea, bowl of congealing porridge. The back door was ajar – he pushed it open, almost tripping over an upturned potted geranium. The gravel was scuffed up as if someone had left in a hurry.

Jo was standing outside by a blue Renault van talking into her mobile. She clicked off when Brandon approached. 'I've just called for a patrol to look out for the two suspects on foot.'

'They won't have got far,' Brandon said, looking past the

scrubland to the industrial and housing estates beyond. 'But, and here's the thing, we have no idea what they look like.'

'Yet,' Jo added, looking back at the prefab. 'Damien should be able to help there.'

Brandon sighed. 'If he fully recovers. They left him for dead, Jo. He would have been if we'd arrived five, maybe ten, minutes later.'

'Poor love,' Jo said.

Brandon grimaced, thinking of how much blood the little guy had spilt. 'We're going to have to go easy on him until he pulls through.'

'Agreed,' Jo said, turning to look at him. 'And we'll tighten security.' She paused. 'Even if I have to sit at the end of his bed.'

Brandon smiled and rested a hand on her shoulder. 'All's well that ends well.'

'That Shakespeare Treasury is still serving you well, Boss,' Jo said, smiling. 'But we have a way to go yet.'

'True.' A dead Frenchman in the morgue; an English gent fleeing the country in fear for his life, this drama is only in the second act.

38

Rachel

A cool breeze was rustling the pages of the group's sketch books. Chelsea was sitting on a rock pinning down a sheet of paper with her elbow. 'Whose bright idea was this?' she said looking over her shoulder at Rachel and then grinning brightly.

'I am not the custodian of Penwith weather! Be grateful your pastels don't turn to water colours.' She was joking, but rain clouds were gathering.

Chelsea's phone started to ring, and she answered, allowing her paper to blow away. 'Oh my God! Oh My God!!! How is he!' She flicked a look at Rachel. 'It's Dad. Damien's alive. They found him!'

Rachel felt a massive surge of relief. The extent of which made her legs quake, and she slumped down on the rock beside Chelsea. 'Thank God.'

Chelsea ended her call. 'Dad had to go. Just wanted me to know. Damien's in a terrible state though.' Her brow crinkled. 'But he'll survive. I just know it.'

'Hey, what's the big deal?' Jethro was standing over them.

'Nothing important,' Rachel said.

He looked at Chelsea.

'My hamster, they found him.'

'You have a hamster?'

'Of course.'

'I forget you're barely out of school.'

Rachel gave him a sharp look. He was a good ten years

164

older than Chelsea, although he still had the aura of a teen rebel without a cause.

He opened his sketchpad, did a quick drawing, and passed it to her.

'Looks nothing like … Hamilton. He *does not* have buck teeth!' She passed the sketch of a hamster, shrugging its shoulders and flat up against a rock to Rachel. Chelsea was trying to suppress a giggle.

'I don't know,' Rachel said.

'No, you don't,' Chelsea said, snatching back the pad and giving it to Jethro, her face breaking into a big grin as she turned to Rachel. 'No offence! I'm just so happy.'

It was lovely to see. Rachel wanted to preserve her sunshine yellow mood in a bottle, like coloured sand. She got up and walked over to the other sketchers, a happier person. Duncan had been joined by Bea on an elevated flat stone a few yards away. Beyond them Summer was sitting hunched on a wooden groyne looking out to sea. In the distance dog walkers ambled and a couple walked towards them – one tall, the other short and rotund. As they got closer, Rachel recognised Magda's purposeful stride and Fryda's loping one, her arms swinging free.

'Hi,' Rachel said as they drew close. 'How did the sunrise sketching go?'

'Good,' Magda said.

Rachel looked at the large leather bag she was carrying. 'Can I have a look?'

'If you like.' Magda pulled out a piece of paper with a few crayon smudges on it.

'Mine was even worse,' Fryda said. 'So, I binned it.'

'Weather turned,' Magda said, slipping the sheet back into the bag and fastening it. 'We'll go to the house.'

She watched the unlikely couple walk past the others, giving the briefest of salutations, and up the steps to the gate.

The sun was putting on a brave show, thrusting bolts of light through the thick blanket of grey. But it was a fading performance, and the class responded by chatting idly. Every now and then Chelsea broke into giggles at something Jethro said; they were as odd a couple as the two walking up to the house. And Duncan and Bea, for that matter. Rachel sat down on a rock and started to sketch them; her energy restored by the news. But it was merely one bolt of light in an otherwise bleak world. She wanted to discuss it all with Brandon. Hear his thoughts and theories. See what identikit sketches they had produced of the suspects. Just be in his reassuring company. Not this strange environment where even Chelsea was drifting away, enthralled by a pretentious kidult, taking advantage of her vulnerability.

Rachel's sketches were no more than doodles when a shadow fell over her.

'So not quite as inspirational out here as you anticipated.' Gisela was wearing a smug smile. 'I think we need to rally the troops and give them something to get the blood pumping through their veins again.'

Rachel guessed what was coming.

'I have opened the louvres in the attic – these dramatic shafts of light will create the perfect atmosphere. We only have the use of this place for a few more days. We need to make the most of it.'

This was news to Rachel. She closed her sketch pad and got up. 'Do you have any more courses planned for the coming weeks.'

'No,' Gisela said firmly, 'I have decided to go back to

Germany. I have been offered a position at one of the local art schools. It will be perfect for me!'

Perfect for everyone, really. 'Congratulations.'

'Thank you. Perhaps you could take over the course, here?'

'I don't think so, but thanks for suggesting it.'

Gisela looked her up and down. 'You are probably right. Not really you, Rachel. Maybe Julia Trenowden?'

'She's not a therapist.'

Gisela waved a hand. 'There are courses. With her experience of trauma and her knowledge of art, she would walk them.'

'If she wanted to.' Rachel nodded towards the others. 'Shall we make a move.'

Gisela clapped her hands and boomed. 'Pack up your things, we're going back to the house.'

* * * * *

The attic reeked of patchouli oil. A hookah pipe was bubbling away on a brass topped occasional table. 'For relaxation,' Gisela said, drawing on the mouthpiece. She held the smoke in her mouth for a good while, before puffing it out in short bursts.

'You should try it,' she said, passing the mouthpiece to Rachel.

'God no.' Rachel pushed it away. I gave up smoking after Art School. I really don't want to get into the habit again.'

Gisela was scrutinising her. 'I hear you were a wild child at Art School. What happened?'

The inversion of the usual phrase made Rachel smile. 'Life.'

'Here!' Gisela thrust the pipe at her.

Chelsea came to her rescue. 'Let me try. Although nicotine

usually makes me barf!'

Gisela withdrew. 'We wouldn't want that, Chelsea. If any-one else wants a puff. It is here. With some sweetmeats.'

'Turkish Delight has the same effect on me,' Chelsea whispered to Rachel, who laughed.

'I know what you mean.'

Gisela supped on the pipe, holding the smoke in her lungs before releasing it in a dramatic blast. 'Right,' she said. 'To business. Who wants to model today?'

Jethro went to speak.

'Who hasn't modelled before.' Gisela looked around the room. 'Fryda?'

Fryda was lurking in the shadows under the eaves. 'I'd rather not.'

'Duncan?'

'Ditto. I didn't pack my jockstrap.'

Bea laughed and looked about to volunteer when Chelsea piped up.

'I'll do it.'

Rachel shot her a look.

'Oh, come on, Rachel. I am 18 and it would be cool to have a few nudes to take home.'

She was right, of course. Rachel was reminded of the young Pre-Raphaelite muses. She had to get over this maternal fretting. Chelsea wasn't her child. And she was an adult by ... Rachel studied her, not a whisker an eyelash. She had taken to wearing the false, thick, mannequin lashes all the kids were wearing.

'Anyone else?'

'I will.' Summer had sidled up to Chelsea. 'But not butt naked.'

Chelsea gave her a bashful smile.

'You can change behind the screen ... ladies.' Gisela had moved away from the hookah and was handing out A3 paper. 'Do your best, students. Julia Trenowden will be visiting in two days and the most – promising – will be exhibited at The Arthouse.'

She handed Rachel a sheet. 'Thanks, Gisela. I think I will sketch today.'

Rachel pinned the paper to an easel and lifted it to a corner near the entrance. It gave her the best view of the room. She wanted to capture them all.

Chelsea and Summer snuck out from behind the screen like Victorian bathing belles. Chelsea had kept her bra and pants on. Summer was wearing a vest and shorts. They wore less on the beach. No Fanny Cornforths here. Summer reclined awkwardly on the chaise longue, draping a throw over her legs. Chelsea rested her head against them, and lay prostrate, her eyes on the skylight. It was a pretty scene, the light falling on their skin and the folds of the crimson velvet, a Rossetti composition.

Rachel drew them first, before turning her attention to the others, who were all scribbling. Apart from Magda. As soon as Rachel started to draw her, she glanced over.

Jethro was working furiously in charcoal. Duncan leisurely applying pencil to paper. Jackie darted backwards and forwards making grand sweeps with her brush. The hour passed quickly, and Chelsea had to be woken when the class was over.

'How was it for you?' Rachel heard Jethro say as Chelsea wandered over to look at his work, still in her undies.

'Awesome. I managed to get some kip. Which wasn't really the intention. But did I need it! Let's have a look then?' Chelsea went around to his side of the easel. 'What?'

Rachel walked over to see and was amazed at his interpretation. He'd transformed Chelsea into a damsel, the velvet throw a medieval gown; Summer stood before her in a suit of armour like a young Joan of Arc.

'I have another one.' He flipped the first over to reveal it.

Chelsea squinted. It was a truer life study – the two young women as they were; the sleeping Chelsea, her lips parted, her eyes closed to the world, Summer emerging from the throw.

'I prefer the first one,' Summer said, joining them.

'Me too! You can put a red sticker on it,' Chelsea said.

'You don't know the price yet.' Jethro was looking at her intently.

Chelsea shrugged. 'I can take it or leave it.'

'Here,' he said, unpegging the sheet. 'I'd like Summer to have it.'

Chelsea stomped off in a huff to join Rachel.

She bent over Rachel's canvas like a connoisseur. 'Wow. I barely get a look in. Love your portrait of Jethro. He does purse his lips just like that when he's concentrating!'

'On a bitchy remark or his subject?'

'Both!'

'He works so hard at being the *enfant terrible*. Don't let him wind you up, Chelsea.'

'Too right. And nothing can get to me today. Damien's out of danger. I dreamt of him, and he told me not to worry, Rachel.' She paused and fiddled with her bra strap. 'I really ought to put some clothes back on.' She glanced over her shoulder at Jethro and Summer, who was wearing the throw like a toga.

'You can have this picture if you like,' Rachel said.

'Really? That's awesome ... and if Dad sees it, he will have no idea who is lounging on that sofa. Right?'

Rachel burst out laughing. 'That wasn't the intention … not consciously. I'll colour it in a little and bring it along to the exhibition.'

'With my red sticker on it?' Chelsea was grinning at her, one false eyelash threatening to fall off.

'Yes. I'll pinch one from Julia's collection.'

* * * * *

Rachel was staring at the painting at Julia's kitchen table when Brandon walked in around 7pm.

'Been working hard?' he said, leaning over her shoulder to look. 'That is very good.' He plonked a bottle of red on the table and took a closer look. 'Is that fine young lady conked out on the sofa my own lovin' daughter?'

'Ah, so I did get the likeness.'

'And the essence.' He continued to scan the painting. 'Great composition. But don't you usually concentrate on the actual models?'

'The course is coming to an end, and I wanted to capture them all. We're having an end of term exhibition on Friday. Julia's coming along – you're welcome to join us.'

Brandon was still scanning the picture and gave a distracted answer. 'If I get time … who's the squat one second on the left?'

'Magda. Why?'

'Similar build to our identikit.'

Rachel swung around. 'What?'

'Yes. A little Laurel and Hardy – if you know what I mean. One short and rotund. The other tall and slight.'

'Like the one in the far corner?'

Brandon stroked his chin. 'Yes. Do you recognise them from Penberth Cove?'

'I only glanced back once. And they were fully clothed, with masks. I couldn't say.' Rachel paused. 'The person up front was quite tall, I remember.'

'This is a real long shot. And they were at the centre this morning with you, so had an alibi.'

'Not until later. They pitched up around 11.30. Said they'd been doing some independent sketches of the sunrise.'

Brandon cocked his head. 'You would have missed that sunrise in the blink of an eye. Rachel, do you know where they live.'

'No. Both monosyllabic.'

Brandon sucked in his top lip. 'Perhaps it's time to get them talking.'

39

'Who's the other guy?' Jo was looking at a framed photograph among the collection of knickknacks on the bookshelf in Rowena Pascoe's living room.

'My bro,' Jason said, picking up the photograph and dusting it with a napkin.

'I didn't know you had a brother?'

'You didn't ask.' Jason put the frame down as his mother came back into the room with a tray.

'Lemon Drizzle cake today,' Rowena said, standing over the coffee table, waiting for Jason to shift some things to make space for the tray.

'My favourite,' Jo said, smiling.

'I know, my lover.' Rowena returned her smile with a full wattage one.

'I won't ask how,' Jo replied, averting her eyes, before glancing quickly up at Jason.

He was grinning. 'I told her. Word of mouth, rather than the tea leaves.'

Rowena gave him a playful slap with a napkin. 'Don't know anyone that don't like Lemon Drizzle cake – not round these parts, anyway.'

They sat in silence while Rowena cut and shared slices of cake. Jo was allowed two bites, before Rowena spoke.

'They found that wee lad, then? How goes the boy? Is he talkin' yet?'

Jo dabbed her lips with her napkin. 'I'm not at liberty to say.'

Although her eyes were on her plate, Jo could feel Rowena's powerful gaze.

'Of course you can't, my lover.' She picked up her cake, 'But a few crumbs, eh? For a ma concerned for the child.' Rowena took a bite.

'He's still in a critical condition. Or was when we set out for The Lizard this morning. That's all I know.'

Jo's phone beeped and Rowena glanced over. 'Take it my lover. It could be important.'

'It's not,' Jo replied, slipping the phone into her bag. 'I didn't know Jason had a brother.' She nodded towards the bookshelf.

'He does indeed. Our young-un.'

Jo took a small bite of cake and waited for more information.

It didn't come. 'Is he local too?'

Jason shifted on the small sofa he shared with Jo. 'Helston.'

'Not a fisherman then?' Jo said.

'No – a life on the ocean wave wasn't for him. He's a salesman.'

'What does he ...'

Jason sprung up from the sofa and walked to the bookshelf. 'He sells art.'

'Is he an artist too?' Jo said, following him with her eyes.

'Likes to think he is.' Jason picked up a small, framed watercolour. 'This is one of his.' He walked back to Jo and handed it to her.

It was a miniature biblical scene, resplendent in opulent colours. A tangle of semi-naked men lay on the ground, arms stretching upwards to a Christlike figure on a cliff. Jo recognised the rock formations of The Lizard.

'It's pretty good,' Jo said, returning the frame to Jason. 'Are

174

his paintings on sale anywhere?'

'He don't like to sell them, my lover,' Rowena said. 'Too precious, he says.'

'How …'

'I can see why you're a detective, my lover.' Rowena heaved herself up from her chair. 'He's a rum sort, my Jethro. But he means no harm. Can I take your plate, my lover?'

Jo picked up the last morsel of cake and handed the plate to her. 'That was delicious. Thank you.'

'Pleasure is all mine,' Rowena said, beaming down at her.

'We oughta be making a move, while the tide is high,' Jason said, clearing the table.

Jo was about to get up when Rowena held out a palm. 'Not before I read Josephine's tea leaves.'

Jo studied the mess of leaves at the bottom of her cup. She had one stuck between her teeth, which she'd been too polite to remove during the tea party. Jo didn't believe in fortune telling. Intuition, yes. And observation. She figured, best to get it over with. Brandon had given her leave to come here to pick up the boat and pick up any other sundries. But she had to get back. She wanted to get back, could feel Jason's leg pressing against hers as he sunk into the sofa, the sensation rippling through her.

Rowena lent across the table and turned her cup upside down on its saucer. She tapped it a few times, before removing it with a flourish, like a waiter revealing a dish of haute cuisine.

To Jo's untrained eye it looked like a central blob with wet trails of leaves running from it.

Rowena inhaled deeply and threw back her mass of frizzy salt and pepper hair. 'Your world is exploding! All those threads – some broken, others running away with themselves, all disconnected, all …' She paused for breath; one hand pressed against her chest. 'All in disarray. But—' Rowena paused again, her fingers tracing the edge of the saucer. 'The centre is strong. The core is stable. Be careful, my lover, as you follow those strands.'

'Ma!' Jason said, giving her a little salute. 'Great reading – if it hasn't scared the pants off Jo.'

'On the contrary. It's … it's given me confidence.'

Rowena was smiling at her benevolently. 'And you have the imp.'

'Yes,' Jo said, feeling in her bag. She'd made a point of bringing the little fellow along out of politeness. She placed the imp on the table by the framed watercolour and the trio observed them in silence.

* * * * *

Jo and Jason walked back through the fields to Polpeor Cove holding hands and admiring the seascape that stretched before them, distinctive Shag Rock jutting from the deep. It was a reminder of how rocky it was around the cove, and the expertise needed to navigate the obstacles, some hard and some soft like the undercurrents. If anyone could do it, Jason could. Jo had never felt as safe in anyone else's hands. Not her father's, who was weak and selfish and had left her and her sister when they were five and seven. Not her mother's, who taught her early on to look after herself. Brandon had, for some time, filled the role of protector. But he could never be her partner. She could see that and – this was the glorious thing – she didn't want him to be now.

They came to a stile, and Jo climbed up, Jason's hands on her thighs, giving her support, and that sensation she'd felt earlier. She rested back against him, and he put his arms around her, pulling her close, his head burrowed in her back, small kisses moistening her shirt. Jo moved away and stepped from the stile; Jason vaulted it, took her in his arms, and pulled her to the ground.

* * * * *

Afterwards, they lay on the grass verge, bodies close, hands held, looking up at the sky and the gulls, listening to the muted sounds of the country. Her phone buzzed and Jo left it, wanting the warmth and beauty of the moment to last.

Jason turned onto his side and brushed away her hair to look at her. 'I wish I could paint you. Capture your radiance. But that's my bro's line.'

Jo turned on her side to face him. 'You could ask him?'

Jason fell back and gave a short laugh. 'I could try. He's a law unto himself.' He pulled himself up into a seating position and gazed across the fields. 'I suspect he would like to paint you ... who wouldn't?' Jason said turning to look at her, his face softening, a hand reaching out to stroke her cheek. She rubbed her cheek against his hand, and he dropped back down to lie beside her.

In the end, it was Jo that made the move to leave, her common-sense clicking in. 'I guess we'd better get going?'

'Aye aye, skipper,' Jason said, taking her hands and pulling her to her feet, planting a firm kiss on her lips.

It was still early – around 2pm – but the clouds were scurrying and grouping and that often spelt trouble. Jo tugged on her waterproof jacket and Jason zipped it up to the neck.

'Come on,' he said, 'that sea won't thank us for dawdling.'

40

Brandon

Rachel was back using her old iPhone, which had been found discarded in a litter bin in Sennen. Brandon was looking from the snaps of Magda and Fryda she'd sent him in the morning, to the identikits and trying to form a strategy. He couldn't exactly call the two in for questioning, as they weren't suspects … yet. But he didn't want them to leave the area before he'd grilled them. He called Stew.

Stew ambled into the room clutching a takeaway coffee. 'Would have got you one, Boss. If I'd known we were having a crisis meeting.'

Brandon grimaced and gestured for him to join him at the incident room table. 'No crisis, just caution. I need you to do a bit of surveillance in Carbis Bay.'

'At that wacko artist's retreat?'

'That would be the place.'

'You're not expecting me to sign up for a course?'

Brandon laughed. 'Stew, I do know your limitations. I just want you to keep an eye on two of the students. Magda and Fryda.' Brandon passed over the photos and the identikits.

'Surnames?'

Brandon shook his head lightly. 'They don't do surnames at *The Art of Living* and I don't want to alert anyone by asking for them.' Brandon rested his arms on the table and fixed Stew with a steady gaze. 'We need to tread carefully. I may be wrong about Laurel and Hardy.'

Stew shot him a look. 'You what, Boss?'

'Google them ... But out of all the images we've had through these doors, these two fit the descriptions best. And the pair are reticent. Rachel knows nothing about them, despite teaching them for nearly a week.'

Stew took a slurp of coffee and smacked his empty carton down on the desk. 'The art course would make a perfect cover for anyone with dodgy intentions.' He grabbed hold of the photos. 'They rock up in town, cause untold mischief and idle away the days behind an easel. But why?'

'Beats me. What's the motive? I mean, money, clearly with the ransom. But it seems well thought out. Rachel teaching on the course, Damien a former student of hers – my daughter's ... boyfriend.' Brandon had never admitted that before, but circumstances change. 'And let's not forget the murder on the boat – Alain Boucher an art dealer friend of Piers Jardine, custodian of Lawrence Matthews' paintings.' Brandon blew out and shook his head lightly.

'I best get my coat, Boss.' Stew got up from the table. 'We don't want Hardy and Laurel slipping out of Penzance on the GWR.'

No, thought, Brandon remembering those other two lurkers who had derailed the train just a week ago. He glanced at the clock. Jo still wasn't back from her sailing trip. Her presence was missed. It was making him edgy. Too much to do on too tenuous links. Where to start? The hospital was on strict instructions to call him when Damien so much as coughed. Security was rock hard, so no worries on that score. But Damien's witness account and descriptions held the key to at least one chapter of this sorry story.

Roberta Bevan remained as enigmatic as the Scarlet Pimpernel. They had nothing on her. She could have slipped out of the country, for all he knew. Brandon slammed back into his chair and started rapping the table with his fingers.

'Missing me?'

Brandon turned sharply to see Jo at the door. Her sweet, concerned smile, broadened into a grin.

'I brought you a present from The Lizard.'

'A reptilian felon?'

Jo laughed. 'I wish! Next best thing.'

'Jo, get on with it. I have enough mysteries to solve.'

'It's what you signed up for ... as you are often fond of telling us.'

Brandon cocked his head. 'Stew sometimes needs reminding. I can usually rely on you.'

Jo pulled out a package from her bag and unwrapped it. 'Lemon Drizzle cake. Homemade Lemon Drizzle cake.'

'A pleasant surprise. Thank you, Jo.' He took the generous slice, the linen wrapping fell open releasing an aroma of the sea.

'Did you bring anything else back from your sea voyage?'

Jo looked past him to the metal cabinet at the back of the room. 'A fortune telling. A ceramic imp. A hunch.'

Brandon took a baffled sigh. 'I take it you had an audience with Rowena the sorcerous?'

'A tea party and a tea leaf reading.' Jo hesitated. 'I picked up the imp on my last visit.' She placed it on the table.

'Will it be needed for DNA analysis?' Brandon was smiling up at her, his hands cradling his face.

'Not one for Al, Brandon. Maybe a wise owl?'

Brandon was smiling broadly. 'You are in a good mood.'

Jo blushed. 'Possibly better than yours. Sorry to leave you here on your lonesome.'

Brandon stroked his top lip. 'Don't worry I won't be playing the blues any time soon. But I am getting frustrated. Now,

DS Menhendrick, what did you pick up on your travels? Apart from the imp. And the cake.' He picked up the slice and took a bite before fixing his eyes on her.

She sat down opposite him. 'I'll cut to the chase. Rowena Pascoe saw a big, solid blob in my tea leaves, with lots of strands running away from it.'

Brandon studied the slice in his hand. 'Aha?'

Jo smiled. 'She implied it was a solid central core, like a sun, I suppose, but emitting chaotic rays. Or a poached egg in a pan of boiling water with those straggling bits.' Jo was still in a kittenish mood.

'Or a blob of tea leaves with some trailing off in liquid.' Brandon frowned. 'The hunch, Jo. You said you had a hunch.' Brandon glanced at the clock.

She looked to the side. 'More of an observation.'

Jo hunched her shoulders and placed clasped hands on the table.

'Jason's got a brother.' She gave Brandon a quick look, before continuing to stare at her hands.

'And you didn't know?'

'No. But I haven't been ... seeing him long.'

'So, what's the issue?'

'I get the feeling the brothers don't get on, that's all.'

'A common complaint, sibling rivalry.'

'True.' Jo gave a gentle thump on the table and looked up at him. 'He lives in Helston. And he's an artist.'

'Not uncommon.' Brandon lifted his eyes to hers. 'What's his name?'

'Jethro.'

Brandon rocked back in his chair. 'No wonder you got a vibe.'

'Why?'

'There's a guy at The Art Therapy Centre called Jethro. Chelsea has been nattering on about him. Rachel has done a few sketches of him – he's the one with the Celtic words on his calf. She also drew him in the art studio. He'd be about thirty.' Brandon reached over for Rachel's painting and slid it across the table to Jo. Ring any bells?'

Jo narrowed her eyes. 'That's him, I'm sure.'

Brandon leapt up from his chair and began to pace the room. 'I've sent Stew to the centre in Carbis Bay to do some surveillance. There are a couple of other dodgy guys in the class. I know these sort of courses are meant for people looking to find themselves. But, and here's my hunch, DS Menhenrick, maybe it's us that should be looking to find them?'

'You want me to join Stew, Boss?'

'Unless you want to join me rapping fingers on the desk, Jo.'

'I'll keep you posted,' she said, heading for the door.

41

Rachel

Brandon's text came through just as Rachel was standing over Duncan's work, admiring his craftsmanship. The first line read: 'Find a quiet spot to read this.'

She made her excuses to Duncan, who smiled absentmindedly, intent on getting back to his exhibition piece.

Rachel went downstairs to the loo, bolted the door, and leaned against it.

She read: 'Don't be alarmed if you see a few people lurking outside. Jo and Stew are doing a bit of surveillance on Fryda, Magda and Jethro. I'll explain later. Didn't want to alarm you or anyone else!'

Rachel sent back a thumbs up, before flushing the chain, washing her hands, and blasting them with the dryer – just in case someone was listening outside. Paranoia? If the course wasn't finishing on Saturday, Rachel would have handed in her notice anyway. Rather than being a place of enlightenment and freedom of expression, The Art Therapy Centre had the oppressive air of a prison. An open prison, but one where you couldn't take a step out of line without being noticed. She could hear someone outside the door right then. Rachel pressed the dryer, turned the bolt and flung the door open, nearly hitting Magda in the face. A face which flickered, before returning to its inscrutable resting expression.

'Be careful,' Magda said, as she stepped back and then into the toilet.

Rachel muttered an apology and then silently reprimanded

herself. She'd done nothing wrong. So, she loitered by the kitchen door and timed Magda, before sauntering through to the breakfast bar when the handle moved.

From her safe space behind the Nespresso machine she watched Magda march across the foyer and up the stairs. She switched on the machine and composed herself, turning to the view through the garden doors. Two of the class were wandering towards the gate. She recognised Chelsea's jaunty step and Jethro's narrow stride. The class were meant to be finishing off their artwork for the exhibition, so they were effectively bunking off. Bunking off. A phrase with several connotations. She couldn't suppress her nagging duty of care where Chelsea was concerned. So, she went out into the gardens and down to the gate. The early spring weather had been kind to the wildflowers, which dotted the lawn and climbed the weathered woodwork of the gate. The pair were already on the beach, Chelsea chasing across the sand towards the sea, her summer dress puffing up around her thighs, Jethro trailing behind. When she got to the water's edge, Chelsea tucked her dress into her knickers and waded in. Jethro stood perfectly still apart from one hand which was sketching her on his pad.

'A pretty sight.'

Rachel spun around to see Duncan, just feet away.

'I didn't hear you coming,' Rachel said.

'I tiptoed through the daisies and a few wild tulips too,' he said, joining her at the gate. He rested his forearms on the wood and studied the couple below.

'Have you finished your painting?' Rachel asked, following his gaze.

'I think so. If I apply any more touches of light, I could ruin it.'

'Overworking a piece is a temptation best avoided.'

'Overworking in general.' Duncan gave her a sidewards glance.

'What do you do when you're not trying to achieve *The Art of Living*?'

Duncan sighed. 'I work myself into the ground.'

Rachel made a sympathetic sniff.

'Hayfever?' Duncan said, glancing her way again.

'No, just lost for words. What is it that you do that grinds you down?'

'The law.'

'Ah, it all makes sense now,' Rachel said giving him the side eye.

'Do I look like a dry old stick that pores over papers to find precedents, loopholes and caveats?'

'No. But you don't look like a man happy in his linen jacket and chinos. I can't speak from experience, of course, but the law bores me rigid. And it also strikes me as a high-pressure game – this art of advocacy.'

'You're not far wrong.'

'Not like it is in the movies?'

'Worse. Late nights putting together corporate takeover deals. And no sex. Everyone is too knackered and wired for anything but a takeout.'

Down below, Chelsea was draping herself over a boulder like a siren, Jethro standing over her with his sketchpad like a celebrity photographer with a Nikon.

'What are you going to do about it?' Rachel said.

'Plan my escape.' Duncan paused, before continuing. 'Sell a painting. And then another. Buy an air ticket to somewhere where the natives aren't constantly suing each other.'

Rachel smiled, her eyes still on the beach. 'They could be

doing something a lot worse.'

'I'm not sure that's possible.'

Rachel turned to see him clearly for the first time. The amused air replaced by a look of desperation. He really did want escape.

'I'll look at your painting when we go back. Tell you if you need any more *touches of light*.'

'Thanks, Rachel,' he said, turning to rest his back against the gate.

'I'll see you back in class. I just want to check out my two plein air students,' Rachel said.

Duncan straightened his back and stepped away from the gate. 'Of course.'

'By the way,' Rachel said, her hand on the gate bolt, 'Where do you live? Where's your practice? London?'

'Truro. I'm local, I am.' His eyes were twinkling again, although his mouth was set.

* * * * *

They didn't stir as Rachel walked towards them – Chelsea still lying on the boulder, Jethro sketching, the waves tickling the tips of his Birkenstocks. Further along the coast Rachel spotted another couple and a dog. She wondered if it was Stew and Jo and looked away so as not to draw attention to them.

'What do you think, Miss?' Jethro said as she came alongside, passing her the sketchpad, his eyes on his muse.

'Beautiful,' Rachel said, taking in the elegant lines of the body and the rock and the infinite backdrop of sea and sky.

'That is quite a compliment, coming from you Rachel Matthews.'

Chelsea waved a hand from her prostrate position. 'Rachel

is not as scary as she looks! As harmless as my … hamster.'

'Perhaps you'll introduce me to your beloved furry companion one day.'

'In your dreams,' Chelsea said, 'Can I get up yet?'

'Just finishing off your toes – the grains of sand between them are many.'

Chelsea shook one foot and then the other. 'And irritating. How long must I suffer for your art!'

'Not long now,' Jethro said, dabbing dots on the page with a fine tip pencil.

Rachel watched him draw, observing the others on the beach from the corner of her eye. They were heading the other way, presumably with little to report.

'Finished,' Jethro said, reaching down to give Chelsea a hand.

'Thanks,' she said, letting him pull her up. She massaged the back of her neck and shook her shoulders. 'Let's have a look?'

Chelsea cupped her chin with a fist. 'Awesome. I just love the way you find the hidden Goddess in me.'

'Hidden,' he said taking the sketchpad back. 'You are too modest.'

Chelsea put her nose in the air and did a twirl. 'I guess we better get back to reality.'

Reality simmered in the downlights of the garden room, just visible from the beach.

'Will you include your sketch of Chelsea in your exhibition work?' Rachel said, as they passed through the gate to the gardens.

'That's up to Chelsea.'

Chelsea was looking ahead at the others in the room, packing up their things, filing out, Summer standing alone, her rucksack on her back. 'Put it in. Nothing to lose,' she said, edging open one bifold door and squeezing through.

Magda and Fryda had already left, and Rachel visualised two people and a dog trailing them home. The others looked like they were waiting for something, a low energy flowed through the room, ready to flare.

42

Jo was sitting in the passenger seat of Stew's Mazda MF-5 convertible on the main St Ives Road which skirted the avenue to The Arts Centre. His rescue dog Greta, a cute as pie little Shih Tzu, was sitting in her basket at Jo's feet, cradling her toy slipper. They were waiting for Magda and Fryda to come out on foot, and, more than likely, catch a bus. There had only been four cars on the centre's forecourt – Rachel's Fiat 500, a Mini Cooper, a BMW, and Gisela's Suzuki Vitara.

The Mini Cooper came out first, driven by a grey-haired woman, she turned right towards St Ives. Five minutes later Rachel came out with Chelsea in the Fiat. She glanced at them as she turned left towards the A30; Gisela was one car behind, and Jethro, Fryda and Magda on foot.

Jethro parted company with the women at the end of the avenue, Fryda and Magda walking towards the bus stop for Marazion, Jethro making off in the opposite direction towards St Ives.

Jo had her hand on the car handle when the BMW sped to the end of the avenue, turned left and slowed to a halt at the bus stop. The driver, a man in his late forties with greying hair, lent across to open the passenger door and Magda and then Fryda got in.

Jo gave Stew a look 'Shall we part company now? I'll follow Jethro.'

Stew turned on the ignition. 'You'd better get a move on.' Jethro was striding down the street.

'I'll see you back at the ranch,' she said, hopping out of the car.

Jo looked back to see Stew move away from the kerb 20 seconds or so after the BMW. She easily caught up Jethro and had to dawdle in doorways to keep her distance. He was heading into St Ives town – a good way from his hometown of Helston. But it was still only 4.30, and there was no reason why he'd want to return home.

They reached St Ives town within 10 minutes. The place was out of season empty, the shops and cafés open, but quiet. Jethro followed the cobbled streets into the centre, and the cut through to Porthmeor Beach and The Tate. The ascent up through the narrow lanes, slowed his pace, and Jo fell back, tying her laces and fumbling in her bag a few times. She felt the hard leather of her Ray Bans case, snapped it open and put on her Wayfarers. He didn't know who the hell she was, but it didn't do to be too careful.

When she reached the top of the lane, she stopped to admire the view. Over the roof of The Tate she could see waves crashing onto the surfers' beach below, a few hardy souls riding them. Jethro was at the bottom of the steps which wound round to the gallery and Jo hurried down so as not to lose him. There were three places he was likely going – The Tate, The Porthmeor Beach Café, or the beach itself ... although, she reckoned he'd done the beach already that morning with Chelsea.

When she turned right at the bottom of the steps, she almost bumped into him standing outside the entrance tapping into his phone.

'Sorry,' he said, moving back and giving her an appreciative look. The look of an artist which studied every sinew. Her hair was down, deliberately so, and she hid behind it as she walked up the impressive, tiled steps to the entrance. It was annoying that she'd been wrong-footed, but she didn't think he suspected her. There was an exhibition on – so she wasted a few minutes queuing to buy a ticket, watching and waiting for him. He walked by and up the stairs to the galleries as she pressed her credit card on the machine.

She snatched the ticket and hurried up the stairs to the first-floor galleries, rushing through the permanent exhibitions and on to the one showcasing Vietnamese artist Thao Nguyen Phan. Jethro wasn't there. Or in the gift shop. Unless he'd given her the slip he had to be in the scenic café at the top of the building. She took the stairs two at a time, and entered the bright white space, her phone in her hand as a prop, her eyes scanning the tables. He wasn't in the main room, so she walked towards the door that led out onto the terrace, catching sight of his tousled hair, and the arm of his leather jacket.

Jo returned to the food counter, which gave a better view of the terrace, and saw him sitting opposite someone. She moved forward for a better look, but jutted back when she saw Jason, his shoulders hunched, head lowered in conversation. Her heartbeat quickened and she gripped the tray rail. Putting on her sunglasses with shaky hands, she watched them in the reflection of the mirrored glass behind the counter.

'Can I help you,' the young guy serving said.

'No. Sorry, no, I forgot something.' She backed off, studying the reflections in the mirror one last time.

* * * * *

Jo walked over to the Porthmeor Beach Café opposite The Tate, took a seat and texted Stew. 'Have you got anything?'

'Can you talk?'

'Quietly.' Jo looked up as the waitress came over. 'An Americano, please.'

'Anything else I can get you?' The cheerful young woman asked the obligatory question.

'No thank you.' Jo watched her return to the kitchen station, before calling Stew.'

'Where are you,' she said, guessing he was in the car.

'Just coming back from Truro. The silver fox lives in a nice apartment in town.' Stew paused. Jo heard him blast the horn. 'Idiot in a Range Rover just cut across me. Anyways, Hardy and Laurel.'

'Laurel and Hardy,' Jo corrected.

'They live in less salubrious dwellings. A guesthouse, on the outskirts of Marazion.'

'Both of them.'

'Yeah. Are they a couple?'

'I don't know. Maybe. Did Silver Fox go in there with them?'

'No. He parked up for a little while. And then they got out. I'm heading back there now unless the Boss tells me otherwise.'

'Hopefully, they won't have left town.'

Stew made a hissing sound. 'I can't be in two places at once.'

'It wasn't a dig, Stew.'

'Not your style, my lover.'

Jo cringed but accepted the Cornish term of affection for what it was. 'I'm at The Tate, by the way.' She smiled up at the waitress who'd come over with her Americano.

'Not an unusual setting for an arty farty.'

'Agreed. Keep in touch, Stew.'

'Ditto.'

The line went dead, and Jo scrolled down her messages. Nothing from Brandon. The investigations were slow. Nothing from Jason. She took a deep breath. There was no reason why he shouldn't see his brother. Absolutely none. She took a restorative sip of coffee, her eyes all the while on The Tate entrance. So why had it rattled her? Because his presence nearly caught her out? Nearly. She felt sure he hadn't seen her. He would have come over. Or maybe not if he'd worked out why an on-duty cop was in the same café as his 'law onto himself' brother. That description had lodged itself in her brain.

Her body tensed when she saw Jethro coming down the stairs of The Tate, Jason by his side. Jo bolted the last of her coffee, took a fiver out of her purse, her eyes trained on them. She watched them say something in parting before going their separate ways, Jason turning left up the steps towards the car park, Jethro crossing the road towards her. She put her sunglasses back on and took an imaginary sip of coffee. From her peripheral vision she saw him hesitate at the entrance. He took his phone out of his pocket, maybe to check the time, and walked in.

Jo braced herself. He'd forced her hand, there was no way she could charge out and follow Jason, although that would have been a duff idea. Jason was innocent. A RNLI hero. The Law Unto Himself, Jethro, was at the entrance talking to the waitress, who led him to a table next to hers.

'Americano,' he said, resting back into his chair, his jacket squeaking against the plastic.

'Would you like anything else?' The waitress had turned to her, her eyes on the fiver by the bill.

'An Americano,' Jo said, quietly.

'I can see we have a few things in common.' Jethro was watching her. 'I saw you at The Tate.'

'Yeah. Did you see the exhibition?'

Was he going to lie?

'No. Just meeting someone. Was it any good?'

'Yes.' Jo had no idea; the collection of watercolours a blur.

'Are you an artist?' He looked up when the waitress came over with two coffees, placing one before him and the other on Jo's table.

'No, just interested in art.' Jo moved swiftly on. 'And you?'

He was watching the waitress as she sashayed away. 'I have an eye.'

He returned his attention to Jo. 'You caught mine. Your hair ... it's pre-Raphaelite. Do you model?'

Jo grimaced. 'I don't even like my photograph taken. So, no.'

'That's a shame. What do you do?'

Jo picked up a satchel of sugar as she decided how much to impart.

'Routine stuff ... and you?'

'Routine stuff.' He lounged back into his chair, watching her all the while.

'Where do you do your routine stuff,' Jo said, smiling gently. She felt she'd dodged a bullet.

'In Hell's Stone. Do you know it?'

Jo smiled. 'Been to Hell and back a few times ... but never stoned.'

Jethro gave a short laugh. The man was so cool it must have cost him to crack his face. He placed his cup in his saucer and stood up. 'Gotta go.' Reaching into his pocket he pulled out a card and handed it to her. 'My gallery. If you're in Hell ... ston any time soon, pay me a visit.'

43

Brandon

Brandon was sitting by Damien's hospital bed; a nurse stood the other side replacing a bottle of fluid attached by a tube to his arm. Every now and then Damien's eyes opened, and he flexed his left hand, as if trying to find the strength to move.

Brandon had been in these circumstances before and knew it was a waiting game. And a sensitive one at that. The boy, although he was 18, Brandon still categorised him as a boy, needed time, to avoid a relapse. With his skinny, short frame and delicate features he could pass for a 15-year-old. Right there in that bed he was as vulnerable as a child.

Brandon looked down at his phone to view a text from Jo. 'Followed Jethro to The Tate. We got chatting. He invited me to visit his gallery in Helston!'

Brandon smiled. 'Complicated. But you know you have to go,' he typed.

'Do I?'

'Just take the car, not a boat. An hour of your time – to waste or otherwise,' he replied.

'DI Hammett?'

Brandon's head shot up from his phone when he heard Damien's quiet voice. 'Yes, son,' he said, putting his mobile away.

Damien went to raise his head, but it fell back. Brandon got up and adjusted his pillows to give support.

'Do you want to talk a little … about what happened?'

Damien nodded, his eyes widening, salvia trickling from

the side of his mouth, his left hand trying to make a fist. It was like watching a chick breaking out of a shell.

'In your own time, Damien.'

Brandon returned to his seat and reached into his briefcase for the photos he'd brought of Fryda and Magda.

'Do you recognise these people?' Brandon said, holding the photos up for Damien.

Damien blinked and then narrowed his eyes. 'Shapes. The shapes.' He was looking agitated and struggled to say more.

Brandon put the photos aside on the bed. 'Shapes? The shapes of the people who held you captive, Damien?'

'In the shadows. Shapes.'

Brandon clasped his hands together and leaned forward. 'Did you see your captors? Would you recognise them if you saw them again?'

Damien went to speak, but the effort was too much, and he collapsed against his pillows, his eyes closed, lashes quivering.

'I think that's enough for now, Detective Inspector.' The nurse who'd been fussing with the fluid bottle had reappeared. She had a trolley of medicines, and it looked like it was feeding time.

Brandon studied Damien's pale, tired face, and gathered his things together. He sighed as he heaved himself up from the chair.

'I'll be in the café,' he told the nurse as he walked towards the door. He paused for a moment outside to have a word with the officer on duty. He recognised him as DC Wentworth from the Newquay Firearms squad.

'When does your shift end?' Brandon said.

'7pm.'

'Who's replacing you?'

'Not sure yet. Someone from the Firearms Unit.'

'Be sure and let me know.'

DC Wentworth nodded. No explanations needed.

44

Rachel

There was a febrile edge to the gathering around The Hall dining table. Julia had made a special fish stew and had invited them into the dining room, rather than kitchen for supper. There were six of them: Rachel, Brandon, Julia, Nick, Chelsea and Lizzie. Gisela had been invited, but couldn't make it, despite the Fish Stew Supper being a farewell one, and a prelude to the End of Course Exhibition.

'So why couldn't she make it?' Rachel asked, ladling some stew onto Lizzie's plate.

'Too busy.' Lizzie raised a palm when Rachel went to ladle a second helping.

'Packing?'

'Oh, she's done all that. Not much to take really.'

'Then what? The exhibition is sorted. Plane tickets?'

'Questions, questions!' Lizzie took a nibble of focaccia. 'Surely it's better she's not here.' Lizzie widened her eyes and looked around the table. 'She irritated the hell out of you, darling. Aren't you glad to see the back of her?'

'I didn't say that,' Rachel said, reddening – through anger rather than embarrassment.

'You didn't need to, darling. Written all over your face.'

Rachel rolled her eyes at Julia and helped herself to some food, passing the ladle to Brandon.

Brandon smiled at her. 'I'd like to come along to the exhibition if that's all right?'

'Why yes,' Rachel said, 'In a professional capacity?'

'In a parental one.' Brandon tilted his head towards Chelsea.

'Dad,' Chelsea whinged. 'Really!'

'Yes, darlin'. I wouldn't miss it for the world.'

'But won't you be busy?' Julia said, taking the tureen and passing it to Nick.

'Yes.'

'Killing two birds?' Rachel said, catching his eye.

He gave her a look which spelt, zip it. 'I believe my fine young daughter has been an inspiration on the course – with her own work and as a muse. Now—' Brandon picked up his napkin and dabbed the sides of his mouth. 'This is just delicious, Julia—'

'How's the young lad doing?' Lizzie said, idly pushing a piece of squid around her plate.

Chelsea jumped in. 'He's getting better, Lizzie. But they can't rush him.' She glanced at Brandon, who put his finger to his mouth.

'Can't they give him something to … rejuvenate him. Vitamin D? Speed!' Lizzie's eyes widened. 'He knows who they are for … goodness' sake. We're all in danger while his attackers are out there.'

'It's not that simple,' Rachel said.

Lizzie jolted her chair back, the legs screeching as they scraped the parquet.

'We're doing our best with the information we have,' Brandon said politely. 'Tell me, Lizzie, where is Gisela going? What university?'

'God knows! She tells me nothing.'

'You live with her, Mum, surely you talk about things.'

'All psychobabble with Gisela. Mindful this, express yourself that. Never any details. And she's out most nights. She would have been better at the Premier Inn. And so would I! She hasn't paid me a penny yet.' Lizzie looked at her plate forlornly. 'Cost of Living Crisis – not sure she's heard of it. It's all pie in the sky with her.' She pushed her barely touched plate away.

'Would you like me to put that in a container for you, Lizzie,' Julia said, looking concerned.

'That would be very kind of you. You are lovely, Julia. Rachel's lucky to have you as a landlady.'

Julia burst out laughing. 'She does pay her dues ... so I'm not complaining.'

'I've signed up for a Ukrainian,' Lizzie said, looking smug.

'Good for you,' Julia replied, giving Rachel a look. 'My spare room is yours as long as you need it, Rachel.'

Rachel sighed. 'I am a refugee from that faraway and foreign land Londinium and very grateful for your patronage.' And she meant it. Tomorrow she would be out of a job as well.

Julia read her thoughts. 'We need someone at The Arthouse. Curating the exhibitions ... including the one tomorrow if it's the right standard.'

'It is!' Chelsea cut in. 'There is some awesome stuff.'

'And your work too, Chelsea?' Julia asked.

Chelsea contemplated the piece of haddock on her fork. 'I haven't done much. Been preoccupied. But I've been inspired. Deffo.'

Chelsea looked like she was trying to convince herself. She looked as inspired as the flaking haddock which dangled before her. Gisela's promise for them all to pull themselves together had been hit and miss. It had missed Chelsea. And it had missed Rachel, who cast a jaundiced eye around the room. There was energy, but it had a feverish quality.

Everyone looked like they needed their brows mopped, before being tucked up in bed with a cocoa.

When the others went through to the drawing room, Rachel made for the kitchen to upload the dishwasher. As she began to stack, she could hear Lizzie's staccato outbursts duelling with Chelsea's excitable chatter, through two walls and two closed doors. Rachel turned on Pirate FM for some light relief and didn't hear Brandon come into the kitchen.

'Rachel, how goes it?'

Rachel spun around clutching a wooden spoon. 'You gave me a fright!'

'That isn't in my job description … unless you're a perp.'

'Wouldn't want to get on the wrong side of the law, then.'

Brandon's face softened and he looked at the floor, before raising his eyes to her. 'You could never get on the wrong side of me.'

The words rested there, among the dirty plates and empty wine glasses, waiting to be picked up. Rachel left them and returned to stacking the dishwasher.

Brandon came alongside. 'We've got to stop meeting like this.'

Rachel kept her eyes on the dishwasher. 'That is so corny.'

'The best lines often are.' He grabbed a handful of knives and forks and slotted them randomly in the cutlery tray. 'What happened in London? Why did you come back? You never did say.'

'That's too big to go in there,' Rachel said, taking a carving knife from him.

'You never did say.'

'That's because I didn't – don't – want to.' She placed the knife carefully on the top shelf between the cups and glasses.

'Why not?'

'Because it's over and I don't want to revisit it all, just yet.'

'Just yet?'

Rachel went over to the island to fetch some wine glasses. 'It's still raw,' she murmured over her shoulder.

'Do you want to get back with him?'

Rachel was clutching the stems of two wine glasses when she returned to the dishwasher. 'No. It didn't work. And it was best for me to leave. Believe me I wanted to.' She looked up at Brandon, the one tear she couldn't help producing hovering in her eye, waiting to spill.

'You'll break those,' he said, softly touching one of her hands. 'With your kinetic energy.'

Rachel flashed him a look. 'Detective Inspector Hammett, you never cease to amaze me with your ...' The look in his eye, sent a different sort of energy pulsing through her.

'My housekeeping skills?' Brandon smiled at her and took one glass and then the other and stowed them safely in the dishwasher.

'Yep, that was it,' Rachel said, smiling back at him, the moment stashed away. When Julia popped her head around the door they were chatting amiably. *As befitted their platonic relationship.* Rachel couldn't believe she'd just said that to herself, while smiling passively and passing dirty crockery between them.

'Your daughter needs you!' Julia said as she bustled into the room, a glass of wine in her hand, an empty bottle in the other. 'Lizzie is driving her scatty with her theories about Damien and Piers and any other subject that might raise its opportunistic head.'

'I'll drive her home now. Chelsea, I'm sure, is giving as good as she gets ... Before I go.' Brandon beckoned Julia over. 'I will be at the exhibition tomorrow morning in a parental capacity, of course. But a cop is always on duty.'

He looked from one to the other.

'What are you saying?' Julia said, her ready frown forming.

'There are some interesting people at the arts centre, by all accounts.'

'People of interest? To the—' Julia replied.

Brandon looked to the door as Chelsea bounded in. 'Maybe,' he said, walking towards her, his phone ringing.

'DC Wentworth at the hospital,' Brandon advised.

Rachel could hear his booming voice.

'Shift change. Officer in charge is Brody MacKenzie – a Scot with attitude. No one is going to get past him. Good night, Detective Inspector,' Wentworth said.

'Before you hang up, DC Wentworth, how's the boy? Any change?'

'He's got some colour. Said a few words, I believe. The doctors are optimistic,' Wentworth replied.

Brandon sucked his top lip and gave the thumbs up to Chelsea, who was listening in. 'Fit enough to look at a screen?'

'Eh?' Wentworth said.

'I may have something I want him to view tomorrow morning.' Brandon said the words quietly, but Rachel heard. She didn't expect Damien to be viewing art.

45

The delicious aroma of pan-fried lemon sole, cooked in wine, garlic and herbs filled Jason's small apartment. He'd caught the fish himself that morning and was showing off his culinary skills to Jo.

'Don't get up,' he said, as he came into the dining area of the living room carrying two plates. He put them down and rushed back for a bowl of beans and sprouting broccoli and another with baby new potatoes, glistening in mint infused butter.

Jo unfolded a paper napkin with a sunflower design. 'This looks delicious. Thank you.'

'Hope it tastes as good as it looks,' Jason said, sitting down opposite her at the small round table. It overlooked a louvre window which had a narrow view of the harbour at the end of his road. The setting sun was melting into a calm sea.

Jason followed her eye. 'I ironed the waves specially for you.'

Jo smiled appreciatively. 'I can see.' She cut a piece of lemon sole and raised it to her mouth. It tasted of brine and delicate seasoning. He was watching for her response. 'Divine.'

Jason rested back in his chair. 'Phew! I passed another boyfriend test.'

Jo smiled obligatory. But the words rankled. Test? Why was he trying to win her over? The curse of being a detective was that Jo could see hidden motives everywhere. And the curse of having a cheating father that deserted you is you couldn't ever really believe that another man, in another guise, wouldn't do the same again. She was waiting to broach the Jethro question. Hoping, possibly, that he would mention their meeting.

'You're quiet tonight,' Jason said, putting his knife and fork aside and looking up at her.

'Just enjoying your cooking. It deserves my full attention. Utterly delicious.'

Jason reached over to touch her hand. 'Thank you. But the food takes most of the credit. We are spoilt living here. I've been to other places – London, for example – and the fish is defrosted from Icelandic cargoes. It doesn't taste fresh and it isn't. You might as well buy Bird's Eye.'

Jo smiled. 'I've never been to London. Bristol's about as far as I've been.'

Jason squeezed her hand. 'Stick with me and I'll show you the world. We'll sail to the Med. Sail anywhere you want.'

'And be crew cook too?'

'While you sun yourself on the deck? You got it.'

Jo cut into a potato. 'So, what have you been up to today, apart from fishing and food shopping?'

'Hardly food shopping.' Jason helped himself to the last of the potatoes and a piece of broccoli.'

'Did you buy the food and wine at the Co-op?'

'You caught me out, I didn't get as far as a farmer's market.' He forked the remains of his meal, took one last bite, and placed his cutlery neatly on his plate. 'Would you like a coffee?'

Jo finished her mouthful before answering. 'That would be lovely. It's been a busy day.'

'Have you finished?' Jason said, noting the small pile of vegetables on her plate.

Jo nodded. 'Thank you. That was such a treat.'

Jason gathered up the plates and took them to the kitchen. 'So, what were you busy doing?' he said, over his shoulder.

'Just following up a few leads.'

'Oh, yes? Sounds interesting.' He turned on the tap and raised his voice. 'Making progress then?'

Jo hesitated before answering. When the words came, they sounded cold. 'Not exactly. But I got to spend some time in St Ives.'

She saw his back tense as he stood over the sink. He reached for the kettle and filled it with running water. 'Could be worse places to spend time in the line of duty. Black, or white?'

'Black no sugar,' she said, all the while considering her next move, her gut churning with disappointment.

'You okay,' Jason said, coming over to the table with two cups of coffee.

'Bit tired, that's all.'

'I'm glad I cooked then. You work so damn hard, my love. You need that sea voyage.'

'More than likely. I am married to the job, though.'

'Me too, so that's another thing we have in common.' Jason edged forward in his chair. 'In fact, I was in St Ives today too.'

Jo took a sip of coffee, all the while watching him. 'Business or pleasure?'

'Neither,' he said. 'A duty call. Why don't I walk you home? It's a lovely night, stars out, my girl by my side. You make me so happy, Jo.'

She let him take her hands but couldn't look him in the eye. Even though he'd passed – scraped – another boyfriend test.

46

Brandon

Brandon parked the BMW out front and strode over to the front door of the arts centre, which Rachel opened with a knowing look and a glance over her shoulder. She was looking pale, but her eyes were clear and bright. Sometimes she looked like she carried the world's problems on her shoulders. A look he recognised in his own mirror.

'Come through,' said a commanding woman with a helmet of brown hair. 'I'm Gisela von Schoenburg.'

'I'm—'

'I know who you are Detective Inspector Hammett. So pleased you could find time to see your daughter's work. All the class's work. We are family here.'

Brandon gave a small, polite nod and followed her through to the garden room studio.

'This is where the exhibition begins,' Gisela said, throwing out an arm. 'Their early work. They were such timid things. Frightened of their own shadows. You will see how they have advanced.'

'In less than a week? Very impressive.'

'Judge for yourself, Brandon.' She feigned a look of indecision. 'Sorry, is it okay to call you Brandon?'

'I'm off duty. So yes, Gisela.'

'I'll get you a drink then,' she said, snapping her fingers at Rachel, who bristled. Brandon had seen that response often enough, but only on rare occasions directed at him. Generally, he liked to avoid the bristle. It was darn prickly.

Rachel came over and gave him a small curtesy. 'What can I get you, kind Sir,' she said in a Cornish wench accent.

It was 11am. Why not. 'A Doom Bar?'

'A Doom Bar, without ale, but with prosecco in a flute glass?' Rachel said, the colour returning to her face.

'*Okay,*' Brandon said walking over to the counter with her, leaving Gisela stony-faced.

'Fasten your safety belt this is going to be a bumpy tour,' Rachel said under her breath as she topped up a flute for him.

'Steady on,' Brandon said, smiling as she ignored him. 'I am on duty ... really.'

'This is just a prop for your under-cover surveillance.' Rachel put the flute in his hand. 'I'm so glad you're here.' She poured herself some fizz and took a large swig.

Brandon had surveyed the room when he'd entered it, as he always did, and had managed to take a few photos. They were a strange mix – all shapes, sizes, and ages. Chelsea was hanging at the back with Jethro. He needed no introduction. Neither did Magda and Fryda; although their photos weren't pinned to the incident board ... yet ... they were pinned to his memory.

There was a ring at the door and Gisela glided towards it.

'My apologies for being late.' He could hear Julia's pleasant voice.

'We can forgive two minutes, Julia,' Gisela said brightly. 'We're just so grateful that you could spare the time to see our little exhibition.'

Rachel whispered in his ear. 'We're only just taking off and I need a sick bag.'

Brandon frowned at her. 'You gettin' demob happy, gal?'

'What if I am,' Rachel said, taking another gulp of prosecco.

'It feels like party-time having you in here among the –' she looked around the room. 'Exhibits.'

Julia swept over to them, a secretive smile on her face. Rachel poured her a glass of prosecco which she took gladly. 'This should be fun,' she said, taking a sip, her eyes inspecting the artists standing to attention by their easels.

'They haven't permission to put their work on the walls, despite Gisela's best efforts and heated exchanges with the letting agency,' Rachel said quietly.

'No matter,' Julia said, 'Who's the guy in the far corner?'

'Duncan – a lawyer based in Truro. He's pretty good.'

'You never mentioned him?'

'He's normal. No real reason to.'

The two friends exchanged looks, as Gisela took to the floor.

'I am delighted to introduce you to Julia Trenowden, owner of The Arthouse gallery which, you may be aware, is at the forefront of promoting local and new talent. You have all impressed me with your work this past week. I hope you agree that your experience here, at *The Art of Living* has allowed you to blossom as artists. And as humans. Feel free to ask Julia questions. And enjoy yourselves.'

Brandon hung back with Rachel as Julia went forth, making a beeline for Duncan.

'Let's go and see Chelsea's work first and then you could introduce me to Laurel and Hardy.' They didn't look too comfortable. Magda was skulking behind her easel. Fryda had her back to him as she fussed with a canvas. They looked ready to scarper any time. With Jo out front and Stew lurking in the garden, it would make his job easier if they incriminated themselves by legging it.

'Hi, Dad,' Chelsea said, struggling to suppress a gleeful

smirk. 'Meet Jethro. He thinks he's a better artist than me. I'm not so sure.'

Jethro raised an eyebrow. 'I don't think that statement would hold up in a court of law.'

A wise guy. Brandon gave him an appraising look and went over to Chelsea's work. It looked murky and depressing, nothing like the bright paintings she did a few years ago at school.

'You don't like my painting, Dad?'

'Art's not my thing, darlin'. I can't really offer an opinion. Rachel?' He gave her a pleading look.

'It's a powerful piece. It really is, Chelsea. Your dad knows nothing about art. But he has other qualities.' She smiled at him, and her warmth travelled.

'I'll put him on a course!' Chelsea said, her eyes shining. She was so easily mollified. It broke his heart.

'Save your money, darlin'. My interest in art doesn't extend much further than identikits.'

Chelsea looked at Jethro. 'He plays a mean fiddle. You should come along to one of his gigs.'

'Are you asking me out on a date?'

Jethro was beginning to irk him. Brandon had to stop himself picking him up by the collar of his leather jacket and putting him firmly in his place.

'Moving on,' Rachel said, doing her art critic thing, squinting and curling her fingers around her chin to critique Jethro's work. 'I hate to say it, but it is very good.'

'Why do you hate to say it, Miss?'

Brandon wanted to clock him. It was a big mistake calling Rachel, Miss. Brandon reckoned he was a kidult around his own age.

'Turn of phrase.' Rachel pulled out her phone and started filming him. 'For the website.' He struck a pose, before moving aside as Julia joined them.

'This piece does have something. I like the layering of different images – biblical in parts,' Julia said.

'Jethro has a God complex,' Chelsea chipped in.

Brandon loved it when Chelsea gave as good as she got. Maybe he didn't have to worry too much about her after all?

'Shall we move on?' Brandon gave Rachel a nudge and looked towards Magda and Fryda, who were looking right back at them.

'I'll film them on my phone,' Rachel whispered. 'It will look better coming from me – I can say that it's for the course website.

'The website's down,' Brandon said, 'Although, that hardly matters in this case.'

'No, but odd?'

'Indeed,' Brandon said, trotting along beside her as she worked the room, filming the others and passing comments.

As they approached Magda, she slipped on a mask. Fryda did the same. 'We're vulnerable.'

'You weren't vulnerable yesterday,' Rachel said.

'More people today – it's still government guidelines to wear masks in crowded indoor spaces.'

'And I don't like being filmed. The company didn't say anything about filming us in their paperwork,' Fryda added.

'Are you sure,' Rachel said. 'I was filmed in the garden on my very first day.'

Rachel kept the video running as they debated the legality.

'Well, it weren't me filming you. I wasn't there the first day.'

'Me neither,' Magda said. 'So, you can put that away now.' There was a mean look in the eyes which peered over her mask.

Rachel clicked off the camera. Job done. She gave a

cursory look at their work, as did Brandon. He didn't know much about art, as he'd made clear, but these two were surely taking the piss.

Rachel sighed, not bothering to be diplomatic. 'I'll get Gisela over for her expert assessment. And Julia,' she added, seeing her making departing remarks to Jethro.

'I don't know what they've been doing for the past week, but it hasn't involved a pencil, crayon or paintbrush,' Rachel murmured to Julia as they passed in the centre of the room.

'Duncan's work is hot,' Julia said, 'I love it.'

Rachel smiled. 'Book him then.'

'I have. And Jethro and Chelsea. Both promising artists.'

Brandon came alongside Rachel, and she handed him her phone as Julia, unwittingly, shielded them from Fryda and Magda. 'I've got everyone on the video.'

'Well done, my trusty accomplice. I'll be in the foyer.' Investigations involving Rachel always took a circuitous route.

'Leaving already?' Gisela said, as he headed towards the door.

'Going to the John,' he said, bustling past and into the foyer.

* * * * *

'DC Wentworth?' It had taken a few exchanges and minutes before the call went through to Damien's ward.

'Yep,' came the reply. Brandon switched to FaceTime to make sure it was the right copper this time. He recognised his foxy face, ginger sideburns peeping out from below his helmet.

'Is the patient awake?' Brandon looked up as Duncan came through the garden room door and made for the toilet.

'I'll just check,' DC Wentworth said. Brandon heard him open the ward door. 'He's awake. They'll giving him meds.'

'I'm going to send you a video of people at an exhibition,' Brandon said.

'Huh?'

'I want you to show Damien the video. He may recognise one or more of the people in the room. Don't steer him. Call me when he's ready. I want to hear exactly what he says.'

Brandon went out of the front door and lit a cigarette. He took a drag and rested against the wall, the bricks pressing into his back. Just beyond the drive he could see the tip of Jo's shadow on the tarmac. He pulled on his cigarette, tapped the ash on the gravel, and held the smoke in his lungs, before exhaling slowly. Cigarettes were both his medication and meditation. His doctor might not thank him in a year or two, but he couldn't get his head around new age mindfulness. He hoped it was just a passing fad for Chelsea. She was too forthright for affectations. And yet she seemed to like Jethro, with all his airs. He couldn't be more different from the prickly, wiry boy in the hospital ward. Brandon's phone was in his shirt pocket and the sudden vibrations of an incoming call made his heart miss a beat. He took a long, steadying drag, pulled out his phone and clicked receive.

'I'm passing the phone to Damien now, Detective Inspector,' DC Wentworth said,

Brandon saw a flicker of ginger sideburns before Damien's pale face appeared on the screen.

'How you doin' son?' Brandon said, noting his tired expression.

'K,' Damien muttered.

'DC Wentworth is going to play a video for you on his iPad.'

Damien's face tensed and he pulled away.

'It's nothing to be alarmed about. Just people at an art exhibition. Ordinarily, something you would find boring, I'm sure.'

Damien's expression was impassive.

'I just want you to say – or indicate – if you recognise anyone in the group? That's all. If you don't, fine. If you do, then tell me. In your own time.'

DC Wentworth's white hand, with its light ginger down, appeared as he held an iPad up for Damien to see. 'Ready?'

Damien nodded. He was biting down hard on his top lip. His left hand was flexing and unflexing. Brandon was wondering if his other hand was functioning yet when he heard a whinnying sound from the phone. Not a sigh, but a small exhalation between clenched teeth. 'Shapes. The same shapes.'

'What shapes, Damien?' Brandon said, holding back his phone, so Damien could see him properly. But Damien wasn't looking at him. His eyes were on the iPad.

'At the back. Thin. Man. And the woman?'

'Not the two in masks?'

Damien side-eyed him, before returning his attention to the iPad. 'No. The thin man by … Chelsea. Same shape. And the girl.'

'What girl, Damien?'

'By the … by the …' He was struggling to find the words and Brandon clicked on the video on his phone. Summer was standing by the coffee machine wearing a black hoodie with tattoo type roses on one sleeve.

'Coffee machine?'

'Not Summer. Not Summer.' Damien was getting distressed, slapping the duvet with his left hand. 'By the glass doors.'

Brandon hadn't noticed her there. She wasn't a girl, exactly.

A small woman. He started walking around the side of the building towards the back garden, one eye on his phone.

'A small woman?'

Damien nodded. 'She wasn't around …. Much. Didn't say much. But small. Yeah.'

Bea was saying her goodbyes to the group as Brandon arrived at the bifolds. She had one hand on the handle and her arm circling a large cardboard tube, presumably containing her artwork. But Brandon didn't like to presume anything. She still had her eyes on the group as she went to turn the handle. Brandon obligingly saved her the trouble.

'Let me help you with that,' he said, taking the tube away from her.

Bea didn't resist. Her eyes swept the garden, but she made no attempt to run. And why would she?

'Did you enjoy the exhibition, Brandon?' Bea was looking up at him with bright round eyes, encircled in black-rimmed glasses.

'I'd say so. My gal's getting her work exhibited at The Arthouse.'

'You have a lovely daughter, Brandon.'

Brandon smiled. 'And did—'

Bea helped him out of his discomfort. 'Yes. My work was chosen too. In fact, everyone's was. Julia is very kind.' Bea paused and tapped the tube. 'I'm taking it home with me to work on. 'It's not as good as it could be in my humble opinion.'

Standing a good foot below him, Bea was doing a good impression of looking humble. But was she? Damien had singled her out. And that required some careful questioning, at the very least.

'Ms?'

'Bea.'

Brandon looked to the side and wiped a hand across his mouth. How best to put this? 'And your surname, Bea?'

Bea smacked her lips in disbelief. 'Well, aren't you hen ffasiwn? Or do you want to speak to me in a professional capacity, Detective Inspector Hammett?'

'Now you come to mention it,' Brandon tilted his head and looked at her. There was something intimidating about small women, he'd often found.

'Do you think I've got a Glock in there? Or a portable broomstick?' She flicked the side of the tube.

'In my job, few things surprise me.' Brandon looked away before meeting her eye. 'You will be aware of the on-going investigations concerning the body on the yacht and the abduction of Damien Kane.'

'Of course.'

'There has been a new development, and I would like to ask you?'

Bea remained tight-lipped.

'Invite you to the station to answer a few questions.'

'Oh,' Bea said, looking at her hands. 'Now?'

'As good a time as any? Just to clear up a few things.'

'Things?'

Brandon held her gaze. 'It would be helpful.'

Brandon needed to have a similar conversation with Jethro but didn't want to give Bea the opportunity to buzz off.

'Can you come to the house, Stew.' Brandon tapped the words into his phone.

The garden gate opened, and a small, blonde bundle of hair bounded onto the grass, wagging her tail. Brandon couldn't help smiling at the sight of Greta, who was delighted to see him and was pawing his trousers before he'd had the chance

216

to signal to Stew.

'Do you know each other?' Bea said, a look of wonderment on her face.

'You could say that. A long story, best kept for another day.'

Stew scooped up Greta and gave her a small kiss on her head.

'You going soft? Brandon said.

'Nah. Well, only for Greta. I have a weakness for blondes.'

'Can you … introduce Greta to Bea while I go inside for a moment?'

'Sure thing, Boss,' Stew said, giving him a not too discreet wink.

* * * * *

The class were packing up their things when Brandon entered the room, Julia chatting to Duncan and Gisela at the counter, Rachel washing brushes at the sink with Chelsea.

Damien's identification was tenuous. It made the whole exercise tense and highly sensitive. The percentage of public relations and diplomacy in police work took up a lot of time but went largely unnoticed. He walked over to Jethro, who had his back to the room as he dabbed some paint on his canvas.

Jethro took his time before turning to face him. 'I didn't think you liked art, Detective Inspector.'

Brandon shrugged. 'I can take it or leave it, Mr Pascoe.'

Jethro looked momentarily shaken by the use of his surname. But he soon regained his cool. 'So, we're on second name terms now?'

Brandon didn't answer. 'I'd like to ask you to come to the

station for questioning. Nothing serious. Just procedural.'

'Has there been a development? In your inquiries?'

Brandon scratched the side of his neck. 'It's best if we have our conversation at the station. As I said, nothing to be concerned about.'

Jethro swung his rucksack onto his chair in a petulant manner. It didn't endear him to Brandon. He fussed around in the bag for a while, his back to Brandon. 'Now?'

'Now,' Brandon said, getting out his phone and warning Jo that her lover's brother was paying them a visit.

47

'Do you mind if I sit out of this interview?' Jo said as Brandon briefed her in the interview room.

'Probably for the best.' Brandon gave her a quick glance, before returning to his papers. 'Although I will miss your subtle touches. Stew lacks your soft power.'

'Greta not doing her job properly then?'

Brandon laughed. 'She's working on it.' Brandon was still looking down, fiddling with a paperclip. 'Why don't you check on Jason? See if he has anything to say about this. If he's been told, of course.'

'*Okay.*' Jo put the top back on her takeout cup. She bit back a feeling of … she wasn't sure exactly. It was a mess of feelings – apprehension, offence at being sent off, when she could have watched proceedings in the viewing room, and fear. Fear of what Jason would or would not disclose. The blob of tea leaves with the straggle of strands flashed into her mind. She still had the imp in her bag … but could even that be trusted to be on her side. Paranoia. She added that to her list of incoherent feelings.

'You okay?' Brandon was looking at her with his kind, questioning eyes and it made her want to cry. But she never cried in front of people. Not even Brandon.

'Yes. But you know how I hate not to be involved.' She fussed in her bag, her hand skimming the smooth surface of the imp.

'I know,' Brandon said carefully. 'But I want to keep you as a trump card for later. You still have that open invitation to visit Jethro.' He'd remembered.

'Of course, I almost forgot. I'll get a date in my diary.'

'That's my gal.' Jo knew some people who would bristle at these terms of affection. But Jo took them in good spirit. She was his 'gal', his partner, his friend … and she wouldn't have it any other way.

'I'm off then,' she said.

Brandon rose from the table and reached out to touch her arm. 'Be careful, Jo. I know I don't need to tell you that. But, sometimes, it's good to state the frigging obvious.'

* * * * *

Jason was on the cobbled slip of Newlyn Harbour, rigging out his boat. She'd called him earlier, and he'd suggested a short sail. The wind was south-easterly, the clouds light, the forecast reasonable.

Jo bent down to help him fix the mast and he took his chance to kiss her softly on the mouth.

'Looking forward to this,' he said, brushing her shoulder as he turned, her body responding to his touch.

'Yes,' is all she could say.

'And later?' he added, stroking her face, leaning in for another kiss.

'Hey, Pascoe!' someone shouted from the Fish Market.

He held out a palm. 'Just jealous … but I best not get distracted. Yet—'

Jo was already distracted. But a lot could wait for later. Including questions about Jethro. How much easier it would be to ask nothing.

'Take a seat.' Jason helped her into the stern of the boat

and started to push it down the slip, before jumping in and paddling until they'd got into deeper water. He knew the winds like his own breath, and used them to power the vessel out of the harbour.

'Here, look what I laid on for you this evening.' Jason stood up, his arms flung wide as he marvelled at the magnificent coastline, a riot of sunrays slashing the canopy of clouds. To the left was the promenade to Penzance, leading to the iconic Art Deco Lido, flags fluttering before it; across the bay loomed the unmistakable silhouette of St Michael's Mount. 'I never get tired of this. This view. This life.'

'I thought you wanted to take me away on a trip around the world?'

'That's doable,' he laughed and sat down beside her. 'With the right crew mate by my side.' He passed her some ropes. 'You are still on trial, you know.'

Jo took hold of the ropes, her brow creased in concentration. She tugged to the left, and they slipped under the boom, settling on the other side of the boat as it tacked.

'You've got the job!' Jason said, looking at her appreciatively.

'If I decide to take it,' Jo said, smiling, pushing her hair back over her shoulders.

'You will,' he said, cupping her face with his hands. 'I have a few more incentives for you.'

He kissed her hard on the mouth, his hand travelling down.

'Jason, I—' The boat was rocking violently.

'Okay,' he said, pulling away, one hand curling the hair behind her ears. 'I have other ways of wooing a lady. Dover Sole tonight, a cold white and I've booked the gulls to serenade us. Any other requests?'

'No,' Jo said, smiling gently.

48

Brandon

The unrolled painting on the interview room table gently mocked him. Dorothea Llewellyn (Bea) was sitting opposite, a small smile on her face, a finger on one corner of the curling paper. She'd placed two flimsy coasters on two others, and Brandon had weighted down his corner with a coffee mug. Dorothea's portrait of a Queen Bee on her throne of nectar, was hardly the pirate's map he'd hoped for. Stew took some photos of it to show willing.

'Why am I here, Detective Inspector Hammett?' Dorothea said,

'You have been identified as a possible accomplice in the abduction of Damien Kane.'

Stew gave him a surprise side eye. But he had to be open with her. Why else would she have been brought in. A predilection for art wasn't enough.

'I would have thought a lot of people look like me?'

'Don't be modest, Ms Llewellyn. Although you show a strong resemblance to members in your family.'

Dorothea quivered, as if invisible wings had been ruffled. 'So, you googled me?' She looked to the side and shook her head lightly. 'Am I to be told who *identified* me?'

'You were singled out by a witness on a video recording. We would like to do a formal investigation parade.'

Dorothea was flapping again, and it wasn't clear whether it was due to fear or indignation. Brandon picked up his coffee mug and drained the cold remains.

'Can I refuse to attend?' Dorothea said, regaining some composure.

'Yes. But it's not advisable. There is every chance this is a case of mistaken identity. We can then move on to find the right culprit.'

'I see,' she said. 'Can I go now? I want to work on the piece of art your coffee cup has left a nasty ring on.'

Brandon whipped up his mug. 'My apologies. But I'd like to ask a few more questions. It won't take long.'

Dorothea remained silent.

'What attracted you to the art therapy course?'

'Is that relevant?'

'I'm not making conversation.'

'I am a doctor, as you will know. The last few years have been stressful, and I went on the course to regain my mental equilibrium.'

Good answer. Brandon glanced down at the curling corner but let it alone. 'There are a lot of artists in your family. But you chose a different career.'

'We can't all slosh around the family pile, doing little more than checking our privilege. I wanted to make a difference.'

'I can see you have.' Brandon was referring to her work as a surgeon in A&E. She was also on the ICUs during the pandemic. 'Have you ever worked overseas?'

'Is that relevant?'

'I don't do small chat, Ms Llewelyn. I thought I'd made that clear.' Brandon rested back in his chair and watched her closely.

'I worked in France for a short time.'

'In the medical profession?'

'No. I went to the *dark side*.'

Brandon edged forward. 'Dark Side?'

'The family business. I took some time out before the pandemic to help a family member sell some stuff. The chateaus in Brittany are crying out for English shabby chic antiques and art. My family has plenty of it.'

Brandon's neck prickled, as if tiny wings were tickling it. 'Did you come across Alain Boucher?'

'The dead art dealer?'

Brandon nodded.

'No. I think he spent most of his time in Marlow … according to the papers.' Dorothea looked pleased with her answer.

'Did you have any art selling contacts out there?'

Dorothea ran a finger along the edge of the painting. 'I had my contacts.'

'And would you like to name them?'

'Piers Jardine. He is the go-to art dealer. For us.'

Brandon leaned in. 'For us?'

'The Cornish. The true Cornish.'

Brandon scribbled something on his notepad and looked up to catch Dorothea's hard stare. 'Where did you sell most of your artwork?'

'Piers took it all. I am quite lazy, you see. I just enjoyed a few days at his villa and let him pick and choose from the family silver.'

'Are you still on good terms with Mr Jardine.'

'I didn't try to murder him if that's what you're suggesting.'

'Just a simple question. You didn't regret the sales.'

'Yes and No.'

Brandon tilted his head and waited for her to elaborate.

'Yes, we are still on talking terms. No, I didn't regret the sales. They helped bail out some of my less productive siblings.'

'Llewellyn Manor is up for sale.'

'And has been for years. That money didn't pay for much more than a fresh lick of paint and my brother's bar bills.' Dorothea picked up two coasters holding her painting down and looked Brandon in the eye. 'If there isn't anything else I'd like to leave now?'

Brandon moved away the final coaster and let the paper roll up, revealing a few Celtic inscriptions on the back.

'May I?' he said, taking out his camera and photographing them.

'Just good luck charms,' Dorothea said, rising from her chair to her full five foot.

'And you will make yourself available for the identity parade.'

Dorothea sighed. 'Of course.'

49

Rachel

Rachel was in Brandon's attic studio with Chelsea when they heard the key turn in the front door below. Chelsea's head shot up from behind her easel. Rachel put aside the brush she was mixing oils with.

'Early for Brandon?' Rachel said, in little more than a whisper.

'Yes.' Chelsea moved to Rachel's side. 'Hope everything's all right?'

'Call him.'

Chelsea fluttered some nods and tapped his number. It rang and rang and Rachel's heart beat in tandem.

'Hello?' came Brandon's clear voice.

'You in the house?' Chelsea said in a breathless whisper.

'Yes. That a problem?'

Chelsea wiped her brow in a mock phew. 'You were creeping around down there. Thought you might be an intruder!'

'No one's going to break into Brandon Hammett's house, darlin'.'

Chelsea gave Rachel an ironic look. 'Apart from you, Dad. Why are you back so early?'

'It's gone five. I've been up since five. Give me some slack, gal. And I could be paying your fella a visit at the hospital later.' They could hear Brandon coming up the stairs. 'Who've you got there with you?'

Rachel beamed at him as he opened the door. 'Just helping Chelsea with some finessing.'

'Like the old days,' Brandon said, gazing at her, his eyes as blue as ever, the shadows darkening below.

Rachel glanced away. Sometimes the intensity of that look was too much.

'So, how's it been left at the centre?' Brandon walked over to his armchair and collapsed into it.

'I helped Gisela tidy up. She's sorting the removal of some of the attic furniture.'

'How was she?' Brandon was watching her carefully.

'Distracted. She wasn't keen on your conversations with her students.'

'She said that?'

'She didn't need to.' Rachel pulled up a wooden chair.

'Damien's taking calls, by the way,' Brandon said to Chelsea, who was back at her easel applying paint.

'I know! I called him earlier. But, you know, I may just call him again. Limber him up for …' Chelsea dropped her brush in a jug of turps. 'I'll make the call downstairs.' She gave Rachel a knowing look before skipping out of the room.

Rachel looked over at Brandon who yawned and stretched like a big cat. She'd read that cats do this when they're nervous. Was he? They used to be so easy around each other. What had changed? It was like now there were no obstacles between them, they had to invent some.

'What are you thinking about?' Brandon was scrutinising her, hands behind his head.

She wasn't going to tell him. 'How did the interview with Bea go?'

Did he look relieved? 'It was interesting. I did some rough research beforehand. I had no idea she was a Llewellyn.'

'Me neither. Gisela kept all the surnames secret to encourage us to develop as *individuals*.'

Brandon stroked his chin. 'I'm going to interview them all tomorrow. Jethro … again.'

'You didn't get much out of him?'

'No. But he, like Dorothea Llewelyn, has agreed to a formal identify parade.'

'Little choice?'

'It's not in their interest to throw too many spanners in the works. In fact, if they're innocent they should welcome the parade.'

'And Magda and Fryda?'

Brandon sucked in his top lip. 'They're not off the hook. I'll ask them to attend the identify parade, along with the whole class. So, no one feels excluded.' He tilted his head at Rachel.

'Me too?'

Brandon rocked forward so his knees grazed hers. 'No favouritism here … but I reckon Damien would have identified you as his assailant by now.'

They were marooned in that sea of silence again, knees touching, neither wanting to break the connection.

'Dad!' Chelsea was bounding up the stairs.

Rachel edged back her chair a little and turned to the door.

'Damien's much better. I think they could discharge him. Or transfer him to a rehabilitation centre. Shall we go and see him tonight?' Chelsea's eyes washed over them. 'You on for this, Dad?'

'Didn't I say the very same on the phone five minutes ago?' He heaved himself out of his chair.

'Shall I come too?' Rachel looked up at him.

He rested a hand on her shoulder. 'No, Rachel. You get something to eat.'

Rachel looked away and nodded. 'I might pick up some food and drop in on Lizzie?'

Brandon flashed her a look. 'Excellent idea. And ask after Piers Jardine.'

* * * * *

A blue and yellow Ukrainian flag hung limp from the top window of Seabird Cottage. It looked like Lizzie had attached it in a hurry and it was clinging on before a gust of wind blew it away.

Lizzie opened the door with a Ukrainian flag daubed on each cheek.

'I see you're getting into the spirit for your new guests.' Rachel looked over Lizzie's shoulder. 'They haven't arrived yet, have they?'

'Tomorrow, darling.'

'Gisela hasn't left yet?'

'Gone, darling. With the wind. Barely a kiss on the cheek. She had a plane to catch.'

Rachel stood in stunned silence. 'Where to?'

'God knows, darling. But when one door shuts another opens. I went straight down to the Ukrainian Support Centre and they had a few poor souls unable to find a home. Paperwork hadn't worked out for them. Or something yarda yarda. It was like Battersea Dogs Home, Rachel, in the old days when Lawrence and I had that teeny attic flat in Chelsea. We took an ancient Great Dane.'

'Whatever happened to that dog? I remember Dad talking about him. Killed a deer in Richmond Park?'

'He ran off into the night. Last seen bounding towards Battersea Park. Larry searched the streets for him – howling his name. Went on *another* bender to get over it.'

Lizzie gave a sheepish smile. 'I'll take better care of Anastasia and Dmytro. In fact, Anastasia is an elite athlete. It will be like having my own bodyguard in the house. And her son —' Lizzie's voice faltered, and she cleared her throat. '.... reminds me of Oliver. Same age when Ollie died. Same aura of innocence.'

Rachel was overcome, as she always was, when someone mentioned her son in glowing terms. And there wasn't any other way to describe him. She gave Lizzie a hug, spilling tears into her mother's nest of hair. When she pulled away, Lizzie's cheek flags were smudged.

'Your—' Rachel pointed at Lizzie's face.

'No matter, darling. They're just a bit of nonsense, designed to fade. Unlike tattoos.'

'Don't even go there!' Rachel said. She wouldn't put it past Lizzie, although, there was wisdom not far below the surface.

They hadn't got further than the small, cluttered porch and both made awkward moves to go inside.

'Tea, darling?' Lizzie said at the kitchen door.

'Please.'

Rachel looked around the place. It was if Gisela had never been. A Germanic Mary Poppins who blew into town and then out after she'd transformed her charges' lives. Except Gisela hadn't transformed them for the better, as promised. Bea, Magda, Fryda and Jethro were Brandon's 'Unusual Suspects'. And the rest of the class, Duncan, Jackie and Summer were being dragged into it. One day a promising exhibition. The next an identity parade.

'Take a pew.' Lizzie had returned with a tray of tea and biscuits. Rachel took a mug and a plate and sat down on the sofa. It was a sad and saggy piece of furniture, and the one place Gisela had left a cavernous imprint.

Lizzie read her mind. 'They're refugees from a war zone, darling, they won't be expecting Designer Guild.'

Rachel bit into her biscuit. A Ginger Nut. It made her smile. You didn't often get them these days, and they reminded her of her childhood, which was mostly bohemian, but not without its home comforts. She remembered her leonine father dipping one into a mug of turps, taking a bite and roaring with discomfort and then laughter.

Rachel took another bite. 'Don't you think it's odd, Mum, that Gisela took off so abruptly. With all her belongings too? She could have had them sent on.

Lizzie waved a hand. 'She didn't have much. One suitcase. A hat box and a leather bag/come briefcase which she kept her papers and passport in.'

'Oh?' Rachel took a sip of tea, watching Lizzie over the rim. 'I never saw that bag. She came to the arts centre with a big portfolio, carrying art paper and inspirational stuff.'

'That's gone too,' Lizzie said, picking up and putting down a biscuit. 'It wasn't with her when the taxi came. I think she must have dumped it. It's not here. I checked the garage and studio.'

'Gone without a trace?'

'Not quite.' Lizzie got up from her chair and walked over to a small bureau. She pushed open the lid and took out an envelope. Be careful as you open it,' she said, walking back to Rachel.

Rachel took the envelope from Lizzie's trembling hand. The flap was already open, and a small square fell out and floated down to the Persian rug.

'A passport photo?' Rachel said, kneeling to look at it.

'Yes. I never saw her passport. She must have always kept it with her. But I found this sellotaped to the outside back of the bedside drawer in her room.'

'You were snooping, Mum?'

'Of course! I am a defenceless senior citizen. Knowledge is power.'

'Do you have any tweezers?'

'You are becoming so CSI, Rachel. I worry about the company you keep.' Lizzie was smiling when she went out of the room. She was back in minutes with her manicure set. 'Here you are, darling,' she said, passing it to Rachel. 'And I'll turn the lights on, so you can actually see.'

Lizzie switched on her reading lamp and shone it on the photo. Rachel picked it up with Lizzie's tweezers. It wasn't the Gisela Rachel knew, although she recognised her prominent brow, and strong jawline. It was a woman with long blonde hair and no make-up, apart from thick dark eyebrows, which looked tinted. The face looked familiar. Rachel gasped as she made the connection. 'It's that woman they're looking for in connection with Alain Boucher's murder. Roberta—'

'Bevan?' Lizzie said, clutching her throat. 'I only found it half an hour ago. I need to call Piers.'

'I need to call Brandon,' Rachel said, slipping the photograph back in its envelope.

50

Brandon

Brandon put down his fork and took the call at the hospital café table. 'Rachel?'

'Brandon, there's been what could be a major development.'

He pushed his plate away and strode towards the main doors, which swished open for him. 'Okay.'

He could hear the tension in her voice. 'Lizzie found a passport photograph in the bedside table drawer Gisela was using. It was taped to its back – so you wouldn't see it.'

'But Lizzie saw it?'

'Lizzie was doing a snoop after Gisela left … the photo must have caught the back of the cupboard and poked up a bit. But that's semantics.' Rachel paused. 'The thing is. Why was she hiding a photo at the back of her drawer?'

'And why did she leave it?'

'Forgot in her hurry to leave?'

'And maybe she didn't need it anymore? So not at the forefront of her mind.' Brandon ran a hand through his hair. 'Who was in the photo?'

'Gisela. But done up to look like—' Rachel took a deep breath. 'Roberta Bevan. Same long blonde hair – thick dark eyebrows.'

Brandon was pacing up and down when Chelsea rushed out of the doors to join him. He put a finger to his mouth. 'I suppose it's too much to ask where Gisela/Roberta or, probably, someone with a completely different ID, was going?'

'Yes.' Rachel sounded deflated but immediately rallied. 'But it's likely to be Europe.'

Brandon wasn't so sure; it could be Timbuktu. His mind was racing. He needed the photo to send to MCIT for face recognition and to be distributed at the airports and seaports. It was probably too late ... unless she hadn't left yet. Which was a possibility. 'Send me the photo.'

'It's on its way.'

'Brandon?'

'Yes,' he replied.

'Lizzie's worried about Piers. She's calling him now.'

Brandon put out a palm as Chelsea tried to interrupt. 'Tell me what he has to say. Call me as soon as she's off. Thanks, Rachel.' He ended the call and turned to Chelsea.

'Damien's been going through the video again on my phone. He is wondering about some of the others. He didn't see much when he was captive, but he thinks he'll get a better idea at the parade.'

'What others?' An ambulance siren sounded, and Brandon strained to hear her.

Chelsea raised her voice. 'Magda and Fryda. It seems there were a few people in the shack. They all wore masks and kept him blindfold for most of the time. But he could see a little bit when he put his head back through the bottom of the blindfold. Dad, we need to get him in front of that parade.'

'You go and say your goodbyes, darlin'. Tell Damien to rest up. I'm going to organise something for tomorrow ... Is DC Wentworth still on duty?'

'Yes. But he goes off soon.'

'Okay.' Brandon made a mental note to call him and ensure security was tight for tonight and the following day. 'I'll see you at the car,' he said and stood there as she hurried back

234

through the doors to Damien. So many loose strands. It was hard to choose which to follow first.

'Jo,' he said, his ear to his mobile as he beeped the BMW open and eased himself into the driving seat.

'Yes, Boss,' came her reassuring reply.

'Are you alone?'

'I can be.'

'I need you to organise a identity parade with art students for tomorrow. Morning, if possible.'

'Give me a minute.'

He could hear her making her excuses to someone – probably Jason Pascoe. A door opened and then Jo was back. 'I'll call them asap.'

'Great—' A call was coming through from Rachel. 'Jo, I need to take a call.'

He switched to Rachel, who didn't wait for him to speak. 'Lizzie can't get through to Piers. She's fretting.'

'Odd that he isn't picking up. Maybe the broadband isn't great in Provence now? The Mistral?'

'Could be. She'll keep trying. Thought I'd let you know.'

'Thanks,' he said, switching back to Jo. 'Piers Jardine has gone AWOL. And, get this, Gisela von Schoenburg has too.'

'What!'

'Indeed. Good news is she was in Cornwall at least an hour ago.' Brandon paused while he opened the door for Chelsea. 'I know I don't have to ask you but keep this all to yourself.'

'Of course, Brandon.'

He switched on the ignition as Chelsea snapped on her seat belt.

'Are we off?'

'We're out of the blocks, darlin',' he said, putting his foot on the accelerator.

51

'You're going to leave me again, aren't you?' Jason was lounging on the sofa, his arm stretched along its back, when she came into the room.

Jo sighed. 'Yes. I have so much on.'

'Come here and explain yourself properly.'

Jo stood stock still. 'Jason don't tempt me. You know I can't.'

He got off the sofa and walked towards her, his hand reached for the back of her neck, his head bent to kiss her lightly. 'I understand. But don't expect me to like it.'

'I don't,' she said, letting him pull her close. A wave of warmth washed over her, and she teetered on the edge of abandonment.

He pushed her gently away. 'I'm sorry, darling. I shouldn't tease you. I know you have to work. And it's such an important case. I wish you could share with me.'

'I can't.'

'Then I give you my blind devotion and support. Maybe there will be a time when we can tell each other everything.'

Jo went to him and rested her head against his chest, letting him stroke her hair. 'I hope there is. Believe me.'

'Will I see you tomorrow?' he said as she made a move to leave.

'I hope so.'

'You don't look happy, Jo.'

She didn't feel happy. Her body ached under the strain of

so much expectation. As if the solid core that Rowena had described was, in fact, a boulder on her back. 'Not right now – too much to think about.'

'When this is all over, I'm going to sail you to Hawaii. Put some flowers in your hair and a cocktail in your hand.'

Jo pulled the strap off her shoulder and put her bag down. He took her in his arms, and they nestled together, neither wanting to say goodbye.

* * * * *

Jo went through the phone list of the students on her walk home along the promenade. She'd left her car at home, anticipating a few glasses of wine. In the event, there'd only been one. But she was grateful for her abstinence – something told her she needed her every brain cell to be sharp.

The earlier sea breeze was strengthening, and Jo's hair was flying in her face as she made the calls. But she was making progress. Jackie was the only one not to pick up. And Jackie wasn't a likely suspect.

She'd left Jethro to last. Her breath quickened when she heard his cold, questioning voice. 'Hello?'

'DS Menhenrick here. Just calling to let you know about the arrangements for the Identity Parade.'

Silence.

'Are you there?'

'I'm here.'

'10.30am tomorrow morning, Penzance Police Station. Check in at the desk.'

'Will you be there?'

Jo faltered. 'No. My colleague DC Bland will be supporting DI Hammett.'

'Shame. I like the sound of your voice.'

He was a pathological flirt. Or maybe he recognised her voice? She didn't think it was particularly distinctive, but you never know what people pick up – what senses work best for them. Visual, Audible, Smell ... The Sixth Sense. He was the son of a witch, after all.

'I am just the goffer,' she added, disguising her voice a little.

'As I said, shame. I can't say I'm looking forward to meeting Bland. Hammett, I can take or leave.'

'Good evening, Mr Pascoe.'

'Ciao,' he said, clicking off the phone.

Her job was done, and she stepped over the low wall that separated the pavement from the promenade and sat down on one of the new post pandemic aluminium benches. She'd preferred the wooden ones, even though they had to work that much harder against the elements. Just outside Penzance harbour wall she could see a small yacht buffeted by the strengthening wind, the sails flapping as the sailor tacked.

It was still early – not yet 8pm – and she thought about returning to Jason's. She was halfway between his place and hers. There would be little time tomorrow, she reasoned. And she didn't want to disappoint him. The thought of him leaving her now, filled her with a visceral sadness and memories of a grief buried in time and rarely visited.

Jo swung her bag strap over her shoulder and turned back to Newlyn. His curtains were closed, and the place in darkness when she arrived. But she rang his bell and waited. Rang again and waited five minutes before calling him. It went straight to voicemail. Jo's stomach lurched. Was he sulking? She thought they'd left things in a good place. Maybe he was having a drink at Newlyn Harbour?

She called in at The Star, but he wasn't there and so she

wandered down to the small mooring where he kept his boat. Gone. He'd only moored it five hours ago. Jo looked out at the sea, the waves were choppy, but a breeze for a sailor like Jason Pascoe. Was he out there right now? A crescent moon peeped at her from behind a puff of cloud. He had to be.

52

March 6, 2022

Brandon

Damien was seated in a wheelchair behind the two-way mirror in the investigations room annexe. Brandon could feel his nervous energy. That was a good sign after the ordeal he'd been through. The boy was as wired and alert as ever.

Jo was beside him, Brandon a few feet behind, watching as the students filed into the room behind the mirror.

Jethro was first, then Duncan, Fryda, Magda, Jackie, Summer and Dorothea.

Damien gave a small jerk, his left hand gripping the side of the chair, his neck pushed forward.

Brandon took tentative steps towards him, like he was treading on the proverbial eggshells. There was something so delicate about Damien, even when he was in the best of health, which was rare. He could never understand why his healthy, wholesome daughter had taken up with him.

Damien was rocking, almost imperceptibly. Brandon put a hand on the back of his chair and bent down to speak. 'Take your time. They're going nowhere.'

Damien blew out and gave Brandon a side look. 'There's something familiar about a few of them. Not the one on the end. Or the big woman with the frizz hair.'

Damien returned his gaze to the mirror. The rocking continued, but he was calmer, almost looked like he was enjoying the experience.

'You singled out the man at the end of the video, Damien.

Jethro Pascoe.'

Damien shot him a look. 'But now I see him in the flesh …
I'm not so sure. There was a man in … there. Similar build.
But stockier. I didn't see their faces. Just their shapes and,
sometimes, their hair, their feet. And their smell.'

Brandon looked at Jo over his head and widened his eyes.
Just how feasible was it to allow Damien in to sniff around
them. Was there a precedent?

'Do you have any definites in there, Damien? Anyone that
you feel sure about.'

Damien stared ahead. 'The small woman. I got quite a good
look at her when she gave me the meds. She didn't speak.
She wore a white coat and surgical mask. Her body rubbed
against me a few times. Fleshy.'

'Are you sure, son?'

'As sure as I can be, sitting here, looking at people I only
got a glimpse of under my blindfold. But … the fuckers who
brought me down were fit. One was a bloke, that's for sure –
strong, stocky, quite tall.' Damien glanced at Brandon. 'Not
as tall as you. The other could have been the tall woman,
third from left. I thought it was a bloke at the time but could
have been her. She smashed me with an oar.'

'An oar?' Jo said.

'Yeah.' Damien turned to the screen. 'I know what an oar
is … and what it feels like.'

'What about the man, second on the left, by Jethro?'

Damien shook his head. 'Nowt familiar about him. He
looks like a suit. There were just the three of them, holding
me. The small woman, keeping me ticking on meds, and two
others – one could have been Fryda, the other Jethro. Not
sure.' He shrugged.

Brandon gave Jo a look. 'Damien, I'm just going to have

a word with DS Menhenrick outside. DC Bland will come in to join you.'

'Don't need him. No one's going to crash through this mirror to get me.'

Damien was regaining his old swagger. It would be hard to have him as a son-in-law … but right now he'd take swagger.

Jo followed Brandon out of the door and into the corridor. 'What you thinking, Boss?'

'I'm thinking we wheel him in, with a blindfold on … with a little gap below so he has partial vision.'

'Different!'

'We can remove the blindfold after a while. But it will give Damien an opportunity to *smell* the suspects and view them through the aperture he had at the shack.'

'Inspired, Boss, and it could unnerve the line-up.'

'Indeed. I'll be watching their faces.'

'You think he's strong enough, Brandon?' Jo was looking concerned. 'And is it ethical?

'You've just seen how he's coped in there. He's getting stronger by the minute. Enjoying the theatre. We can always get him out if things go wrong.' Brandon paused and looked down the long corridor to the foyer. 'There's an ambulance outside and a medic on call.'

'I'm backing you, Boss.'

Brandon nodded. 'If all goes to plan, I'd like them to put on masks for a second wheel-by.'

'Good thinking.'

Brandon went to leave but stopped in his tracks. 'Jo?'

'Yes?'

'What do you make of his hesitancy over Jethro?'

'I don't know.' She glanced at the floor. 'Maybe he'll have a better idea when he goes in close. Re-enacts his captivity.'

'Here's hoping,' Brandon said, opening the annexe door.

*****

There was a collective intake of breath when Stew wheeled Damien in. Jo was at his side, but Brandon had opted to watch from behind the mirrored wall. They were on strict instructions to wheel in close to the line-up, so he could use his sense of smell. Stew was pushing him nice and slow, stopping at each one, and turning the chair so Damien could get his partial view. The boy was giving nothing away. He never ceased to amaze Brandon with his street smarts.

The suspects displayed a variety of micro responses. Fryda looked edgy, Magda affronted, Dorothea maintained a haughty cool, Duncan was impassive, Summer was trying to climb into her hoodie, and tugged repetitively on the overlong arms, Jethro was as still as a stone. Chelsea said he painted one on the course as a self-portrait. How art imitates life.

Damien had got to the end of the line and Stew was wheeling him around to make a second journey, while Jo handed out masks. Jethro was making a thing of putting his on. Duncan slipped his on unobtrusively. Fryda and Magda fussed with theirs, while Dorothea pulled hers up high over her nose with practiced surgeon's hands. Brandon noticed that she was keeping those hands largely hidden in the folds of her skirt.

He texted Jo. 'Can you ask Dorothea Llewellyn to ensure her hands are on show.'

He saw Dorothea respond to Jo's command and then discreetly tuck them away as Damien was wheeled back down the line.

'Have a quiet word with her as Damien approaches,' Brandon texted.

Damien still had his blindfold on as he passed down the line a second time, this time even closer to them. When he got to Dorothea at the end, Damien looked up at Jo and she lent down to listen. Jo had a quick word with Stew, and Damien was wheeled to the centre of the wall mirror. Stew turned the chair to face the suspects, who were around six feet away. Jo went around to the back of the chair and untied Damien's blindfold. It was deathly quiet in there now without the sounds of wheels and footsteps.

Summer broke the silence. 'I'm having a panic attack. I am not a criminal. This is emotional abuse.' Her little sobs and moans punctuated the quiet.

Damien was sitting up, his head moving slightly as his sharp black eyes travelled up and down the line.

It seemed an eternity before he spoke. 'I've seen enough,' he said, looking up at Stew, who wheeled him to the door.

'Can we go now!' Summer shouted at the mirror, her words echoing around the room.

* * * * *

Brandon sat drumming his fingers on the interview room table, waiting for Damien to make his entrance. The line-up were being given some TLC in a safe room down the corridor and Damien was being checked out by the medic. Brandon was scrolling his messages when Stew wheeled him in. Brandon directed him to the top of the table. The chairman's seat. He wanted to give Damien the confidence to give his verdicts.

'When you're ready, Damien,' Brandon said, addressing him from the other end of the table, Jo on his right, Stew on his left.

'The small woman, I'm sure, gave me the meds.'

'How are you sure?' Brandon said, his arms outstretched on the table, hands clasped.

Damien glanced at Brandon's hands. 'Her hands. She wore gloves when she gave me stuff. But I recognised her short, stubby fingers. And a ring. On the small finger of her left hand, I saw the shape through the plastic.'

Brandon nodded at Jo. And then turned swiftly to Stew. 'You are recording this?'

Stew nodded. He hadn't said. But Stew often didn't.

'Anyone else?' Brandon returned his steady gaze to Damien.

'Not Summer. I know Summer, and she weren't there.'

'Okay,' Brandon said, sighing inwardly with relief. He also knew Summer, through Chelsea. She was a fragile girl, with a history of self-harming. He didn't think she was faking the panic attack.

'Not the thin guy. He has a tattoo on his left leg. There was someone in there with a tattoo on his … maybe her … right leg.'

'What sort of tattoo?' Jo asked, carefully.

'Scribble. Small symbols, just peeking out of the bottom of their jeans.'

Jo turned away, pulled a notepad out of her bag, put it back in again.

Brandon continued the questioning. 'You're doing very well, Damien. Anyone you can't discount. Anyone you believe attacked you and held you captive?'

'The tall woman. When she put on the mask, it confirmed it for me. And her boots. The Doc Martens with the roses.'

'Okay,' Brandon said, shooting Jo a look. 'Any smells you recognised?' Brandon rested back in his chair and waited.

'The doc who gave me the meds mostly smelt of sanitiser, so I wouldn't be able to identify her through smell. But I'm sure it was her.'

'The guy with the grey hair. He was wearing a nice after-shave.'

Brandon sat up straight. 'Oh yeah. Is that relevant?'

'Could be,' Damien said, meeting his eye. 'There was one time when I heard talk behind the door, and I smelt after-shave. That was unusual in there. Could have been his brand. I don't know them. Not something Ma puts in my Christmas stocking.' Damien gave a small smirk.

'You say it was just the one time?' Brandon said.

'Yes.'

'Do you remember when? Early on in your captivity? Or later.'

'I remember. It was the last day, and they were panicky. It was just before they tried to finish me off. When I think about it now, he could have told them to do just that.'

Brandon rocked back in his chair and blew out. 'Anything, or anyone else, Damien?'

'Nah. Over to you cops now,' Damien said, a thin smile cracking his face.

53

Jo was at Lena's Café down the road getting some coffee and cake to sustain Brandon for his next round of questioning.

'The usual?' Lena said.

'And a Swiss Bun too.'

Lena smiled. 'For Stew?'

Jo rolled her eyes. 'He can't get enough of them.'

'But he keeps his figure,' Lena said, smiling.

'Well, yes.' Jo gave her a quick look. So, Stew had an admirer. Why should that surprise her?

She shrugged off the thought, took out her phone and checked her messages as Lena made the coffees. Jason hadn't returned her texts. It was 11.30am. He'd been gone for over twelve hours. She felt a surge of dread.

'You okay,' Lena said, putting the takeaway tops on three cups and placing them in a cardboard tray.

'Yeah,' Jo said, managing a small smile. 'Time of the month.' Time of the day, more like it. Where was he? Her stomach tightened.

'Shall I put the cakes in a box?' Lena said.

'A bag will do.'

Jo snatched up the bag and picked up the cardboard tray. She put the tray down sharp, her hands trembling.

'Are you sure you're okay?' Lena came out from behind the counter.

'I'm fine. My hand glanced one of the hot cups.'

Lena looked concerned.

'But all good, now.' Jo swooped up the tray and made for the door.

When the morning was over, Jo would go to Jason's. She knew where he kept his key. Why wasn't he returning calls and messages. He was all over her the day before. Something was up.

*****

Brandon and Stew pounced on the tray and bag of cakes when she placed them on the incident room table. They were like hungry dogs and oblivious to her mood.

Or so she thought.

'You not having anything?' Stew said through a mouthful of Swiss Bun. He dabbed the side of his mouth and licked a bit of icing off his finger.

'In a minute.' They were both looking at her over their cake and coffee. Maybe she didn't give them enough credit for emotional intelligence. She picked up a flapjack and they relaxed.

After a few minutes Brandon pushed aside his cup and got up from the table. 'Are we ready? Dorothea first and then Fryda and, possibly Magda. They are a duo, after all. There must be something they have in common, and it could be crime.'

'Are you letting the others go now?' Jo said.

'Yes. With a request that they make themselves available for further questioning. I can't see that Jackie or Summer will be back. I'm either losing my intuitive touch, or they're darn fine actors.'

'Jethro?' Jo said.

'He's not off the hook … but, without Damien's identification, we haven't got much to go on.'

'There's not much to go on, as far as motive is concerned anyway, is there, Boss?' Stew said.

'No. Let's hope we can wring something out of these two. You ready?'

Brandon stopped short when his phone pinged.

'What is it?' Jo said, turning to him.

'MCIT. Nothing on Roberta Bevan or Gisela von Schoenburg. Or anyone with the passport photo we're circulating.'

Brandon's phone pinged again.

'And?' Jo said.

'Nothing on Piers Jardine. Lizzie can't get in touch with him.' Brandon ran a hand through his hair. 'Worrying.' He paused. 'Jo, can you take this on, while Stew and I do the interviews. Something is running away from us here. Speak to Lizzie. Find out where Piers is staying and get the local gendarme round to check on him.'

'I'm on it.' Jo felt a rush of relief. She couldn't handle the interviews right now. She had nothing to contribute. They were in Brandon's safe hands and Stew was getting good. Bloody good. He'd be after her job next. Although he had that soft side. She could almost call him a friend.

She got her jacket and bag and checked out of the station. The first thing she did when she got into the Skoda was check her messages. Nothing from Jason. Was he ghosting her? In the rear-view mirror she saw Jethro coming out of the main entrance, car keys in his hand. She ducked down and let him pass. It was an instinctive reaction. It didn't matter if he saw her. It looked like he was off the hook. But she still had that invitation to his gallery waiting to be taken up. She'd make her calls, give him time to get back to his gallery, if that's where he was going, and then question him on another line of inquiry. Jason.

54

Jo clicked off her call to Lizzie and texted Piers Jardine's villa details to MCIT. They had the muscle to get things moving in Provence. She hoped. Her schoolgirl French wouldn't cut the Dijon and nor would her credentials. It was a waiting game now. As it often was. But Jo was getting impatient. She tapped in the postcode for Jethro's gallery in her sat nav and got on the road to Helston. The traffic was clear at this time of day and the eta was 20 minutes. Jo unscrewed a bottle of Evian with her left hand. France. And the luscious landscape of Provence. Who would have thought this mash-up of a case would take an excursion through the lavender fields of Grasse. She didn't rest much confidence in the Gendarmerie coming up with anything conclusive. But what choice did they have right now?

Jo took a swig of water as the line of traffic slowed at the first roundabout out of Penzance. The sea was hidden behind the road and railway tracks, but she could almost feel its swell. Visualise that small boat heading out of the harbour. Where was its destination?

Jason still hadn't called. She'd stopped checking her phone every five minutes. Increased the time to ten. It wasn't until she was on the A394 towards Helston that she allowed herself to think about that insignia on the right leg that Damien had spotted. There had to be an explanation. So many people had tattoos on their ankles and legs. Jason was a fisherman – they were trade logos. And he was a proud Cornishman

– why wouldn't he have a Celtic emblem on his leg? And how reliable was Damien as a witness anyway? He'd been blind-folded the whole time, treated badly, probably dehydrated. Brandon might believe he had the low cunning and instincts of a feral creature. Perhaps he was just a rat.

Jo moved the gears up to fifth and put her foot down. Why, she asked herself, would Jethro have the answers?

* * * * *

Jo parked the Skoda in a public car park and walked the short distance to Coinagehall street. Jethro's gallery was on the cor-ner of Church Street, which led to the Museum of Cornish Life. It was a small glass-fronted box, with a window display featuring a few of his biblical miniatures. She could see him at the back of the empty room reading his phone. It didn't look like the sort of place that got a lot of visitors. His head shot up as she approached the glass door, and he rose to greet her.

'I'd like to say I was expecting you, like a James Bond vil-lain. But let's settle for the truth. To what do I owe this plea-sure?'

Jo had yet to decide how much truth to impart. 'I was on my way back from The Lizard. Your card was burning a hole in my pocket. Thought I'd pop in and say hi.'

'Hi,' he said, looking over her shoulder as an elderly cou-ple came in, emboldened by her presence. 'Excuse me for a moment.'

Jethro walked over to them, giving Jo a chance to formu-late her line of questioning. He seemed ordinary in this set-ting. A young gallery owner hungry for a sale. A more direct approach could work. And she had witnesses now. To what? Jo tensed at the thought, and pressed her bag, with its taser, close to her thigh. She pulled her mobile from her pocket and checked her messages. Nothing from Jason. A curt reply from MCIT. They were on the case.

'Pale sunset is my personal favourite. I'm not even sure I could bear to sell it,' Jethro was saying to the couple.

'It is beautiful,' the woman said, looking like she meant it. Jo was largely unmoved by art – preferred real sunsets, which were aplenty in Penzance.

'Can we just think about it? Have a coffee and get back to you,' her husband said, his stomach protruding over the belt of his light blue slacks.

'Of course.' Jethro forced a genial smile and returned to Jo. 'Now, what can I do for you?'

Jo looked him straight in the eye. He was a little taller than Jason, but there was a strong family resemblance. 'I'm looking for Jason.'

'Oh?' He stepped back and appraised her. 'Why?'

Jo looked down, before raising her eyes to meet his. 'I'm a friend ... and—'

'And?'

She clasped her hands together to stop them shaking. Her heart was beating fast, and she struggled to get the words out. 'He's not returning my calls.'

Jethro walked around her to the back of the sales counter and pulled out a chair.

'Please sit down,' he said, placing it behind her. 'Would you like a glass of water?'

Jo nodded. 'Thank you.'

She watched him disappear through a door behind the counter and took a deep breath. His solicitude had thrown her. And her inability to control her feelings hadn't helped either. It was like when something bad happens and someone asks if you're okay, and it all comes out. Like the morning she went into school after her dad had left. She bit down hard on her bottom lip, swiped a tissue from a box on the counter and dabbed her face.

Jethro came out with a glass of water in one hand and another chair in the other.

'Here,' he said, handing her the glass and sitting himself down in front of her. Right then, as he lent forward his long hair hanging either side of his face, he did look a bit like Jesus.

Jo took a few sips of water and drew herself up straight.

'Better,' he said.

She nodded.

'So why are you so concerned about Jason?'

Jo gave her rehearsed answer. 'I've been seeing him, and I thought it was going well. He seemed to like me and then I hear nothing.'

Jethro gave her a reassuring look. 'He's at my ma's. She's been poorly and he went to her.'

Jo edged forward on her seat and met his eye. 'When did he go to your mother's?'

'Last night. I was ... busy. So, he went.'

This didn't explain the radio silence. 'Is he there now?'

Jethro picked up his phone and put in the call. It went straight to voicemail. 'Maybe he left his phone at home.'

Jo frowned. 'Could you try your ma?'

Jethro put his phone away. 'I don't want to disturb her. She was taken ill and ...'

'And?' Jo couldn't read his face ... was he wary about sending his brother's "stalker" girlfriend to his mother's house? Or was there something more sinister at play? Jo could feel the iron hardening in her veins and got up from the chair.

'Thanks for your help,' she said turning to him as he rose

to walk her to the door.

'You have been a great disappointment to me,' he said, one hand on the doorframe.

Jo tilted her head. 'Sorry?'

'I had hoped you'd come here to see me. And now I find that it's my brother that you seek.'

Jo looked to the side. 'If you hear from him, please give me a call.' She stopped herself handing over one of the police cards she kept in her top pocket. 'Do you have a pen and paper?'

'Just say the numbers and I'll remember,' he said, watching her closely.

'Are you sure?'

'I have a good memory. For numbers—'

'07931 348892.'

'And faces,' he said, as he opened the door for her.

* * * * *

Jason's yacht was in the mooring at Polpeor Cove, rocking on the incoming tide. The ropes were secure, but the knots were scrappy. Jo had been practising hers and she could recognise a rushed job. But he was here. It all made sense. He would have rushed off – maybe without his charger – to his ma's. He wouldn't have memorised her number … like Jethro … if she was to believe his photographic memory story. She trudged back up the cobbled slip towards the Old Lightboat Station and Lizard Point. Stood watching the waves roll in and out, lashing the rocks below, the endless sky festooned with candy-coloured clouds. It was a short walk through the fields to Lizard town, so she left her car in the car park and walked through the narrow path, hedgerows alive with the first signs of spring. When she reached the Witch Ball pub on the outskirts of town, she forced herself to focus on what lay ahead, quickening her pace as she passed the pretty pink and lilac painted cottages to Rowena Pascoe's cottage. The white wooden gate was open wide, and she walked through, turning to close it, before giving a polite rap on the door. A tiny picket fence extended either side, bordering a tangle of flowers, ceramic pots and figurines. She felt in her pocket for the imp Rowena had given her. She still carried it around, although she wondered why.

Rowena took her time to come to the door and looked surprised to see her. 'Jo?'

'Sorry to disturb you ... Rowena.'

Rowena gathered herself and leaned forward to peck Jo on the cheek. 'Lovely to see you, my child.'

Jo could see Jason's wet boots just inside the door and his cagoule on the coat rack.

'He's here,' Rowena said, following her eyes. 'Just taking a shower.'

Jo stood on the doorstep waiting to be invited in.

'The place is in a pickle,' Rowena said, taking a step back, 'But do come in. He won't be long.'

'Thank you,' Jo said, comparing the cool welcome to the warm one last time. The first thing she noticed on the hallway shelf was Jason's phone in its Cornish flag case. A part of her wanted to run out of the door, but another part, the one that controlled most of her actions, told her to stay firm and observe. She didn't need a crystal ball to see things weren't what they seemed just days ago.

Jason came down the narrow staircase, rubbing his hair with a towel. He didn't look surprised to see her.

55

Brandon

'Do you fancy a trip to Provence?' Brandon had Jo on the phone after receiving a call from MCIT.

'The Gendarme haven't found Jardine?' Jo was practically whispering.

'Quelle surprise. Can you talk?'

'Not really. I'm—'

Brandon's phone pinged and a message came through from Jo. 'I'm pursuing another line of inquiry right now. But sure. Do you want me to book a flight?'

'I'm sending Stew with you,' Brandon said. 'He'll make the bookings. Fill me in asap on this other *line of inquiry*.'

'Everything okay, Boss?' Stew looked up from his iPad.

'Yes,' Brandon said, turning to face the window.

'Jo's coming?'

'Of course,' Brandon said, his back to the room. 'First flight tomorrow morning.'

'Any directions, once we're at the village?' Stew said as Brandon breezed past, shrugging on his jacket.

'Use your imagination, Stew. You're holidaymakers – maybe honeymooners, and you're wining and dining your gal. You're visiting her Uncle Piers, but he's not at the villa. Does anyone know him and where he might have gone …' Brandon stood at the door watching Stew scribble down notes. 'Do you have an imagination, Stew?'

'Non,' he said, continuing to write. 'But I speak fluent French.'

Brandon exhaled sharply. 'Why didn't you say?'

'You never asked.' Stew put down his pen and looked up at him. 'Contrary to rumours I did go to school. And I spent some time in France in my misspent youth.'

'You're full of surprises, DC Bland.'

'Maybe. Boss—'

Brandon turned slowly to face him, one foot out of the door.

'Can you look after Gigi, my dog, while I'm away.'

'Sure,' Brandon said, a ghost of a smile on his face as he left the room.

56

'Work?' Jason said as Jo ended the call.

'Yes.' Jo lowered her voice. 'And you? Where've you been for the past 24 hours? I've been worried sick.'

'Sorry, love.'

'Jethro said you'd come here to look after your ma?'

'You've been talking to my brother?'

'I was worried about you.'

'Why don't we take a stroll. Get some air. I can't really talk around here.' He nodded towards the kitchen where Rowena was filling the kettle. 'Ma, don't worry about tea – we're going out for a bit.'

'Fancy a drink?' Jason said when they turned at the end of the lane.

'I'm on duty.'

Jason's eyes hardened. 'I'm not. Let's go to the Witch Ball. You can read me my fortune or my rights.'

When they arrived at the pub, he steered her to a small nook in the far corner of the bar, away from the restaurant. She sat watching tourists eating fish and chips and moules when he went to the bar.

'I asked for a coke,' Jo said as he put a glass of white in front of her.

'You look like you need a drink. I certainly do. It's been, as they say, a journey.'

'Or, in your case, a sea voyage?'

Jason laughed and picked up his glass. 'Very good!' he said

clinking her glass. 'Jo, lighten up. I'm alive. We both are. And I'm a little richer.'

Jo pushed her glass away. 'What have you done?'

'I took a fare.'

'A fare?'

'To Brest.'

'Brittany?'

'Yes.'

Jo's hand reached for her glass, but she left it lingering on the base. 'Who was the passenger?' Her forefinger traced the glass rim. Her eyes didn't leave his face.

Jason took a gulp of beer and stared into his tankard. 'I don't know. I was just told she wanted to get to France that night.' He looked up at her. 'Just take a bloody sip, please. You're not sailing to France – one glass of wine isn't going to push any limits.'

Jo forced a small smile, pulled out her phone and tapped on photos. 'Was this the woman?' She held up the passport image of Gisela.'

Jason squinted. 'Could well be,' he said. 'She was togged out in waterproofs and was wearing massive, tinted glasses.'

'Sunglasses?'

'It was dark, so probably those transition specs. Her hair was covered under a snood.'

'Did she speak.'

'A little.'

'Any accent?'

Jason looked over his glass towards the bar and swilled his dregs.

'Did she have an accent?'

'Maybe. Could have been Eastern European. Just a tinge. She was well-spoken. Like those types who try and get your accent as well as your lingo.'

'But she wasn't English?'

Jason shot up from the table. 'Do you want another wine?'

She hadn't touched hers. 'For fuck's sake, Jason. Did you ferry Gisela von Schoenburg to France in your boat so she could evade port checks!'

'She didn't give me her name.'

'And you didn't ask?'

'No.' He looked at his hands. 'I took a brown envelope.'

Jo slumped back in her chair.

'We've got enough dosh to go anywhere we want in the summer. You and me. No passengers.'

'It's not good enough, Jason, to take money and not ask questions.' She lowered her voice. 'You could be done for aiding and abetting. Or worse. Von Schoenburg is wanted for questioning for both murder and abduction and attempted murder and GBH.'

'If I'd known that I wouldn't have taken the fare.' He sat back down and reached across the table to hold her hands. 'You're shaking.'

'That's the least of my problems, Jason.'

'I don't want to be your problem. I can walk out of that door and never see you again.'

Jo swallowed hard. She fought back the tears. As she always did. 'I'm a cop, Jason. I can't let you walk away.'

He let go of her hands and sat back in his chair. 'One final beer for the condemned man?' His eyes were imploring her. 'I promise not to do a runner.'

'I'd catch you,' she said, looking away.

'Race you to Lizard Point.'

'Another time, perhaps.'

Jason got up to go to the bar. 'I didn't know it was von

260

Schoenburg. It doesn't pay to ask questions. You do believe me?'

'You don't read the papers?'

'Not much.'

'Would you have sailed her to Brest if you'd known?'

'No. I saw the corpse on the boat. If she'd done that to a man, she could have done the same to me. I was in it for the money. Pure and simple. For you and me.'

'Jason,' she said as he moved away from the table. 'You'll have to accompany me to the station.'

'And if I say no?'

'They'll hunt you down. You just need to tell the DI what you've told me and give him all the details you can.'

Jason leant over the table, spreading his arms wide and pushing his face close to hers. 'I can do better than that,' he said. 'I can tell you right now where she was heading. I took a leak before the return journey, and I heard her on her mobile. She was heading south to Nante.'

57

Brandon

Al Chapman had taken the time to deliver his forensics report on the suspects DNA at Penzance Station. 'I was in town, Brandon. No biggie. But I wanted to confirm the evidence, as soon as possible. And explain a little bit too.' He cocked his head. 'Mind if I take a seat. Too much leaning over and bending the knees in this job.'

Brandon smiled. 'Sure.' He pulled out a chair and joined Al at his office table.

'It might be easier to eliminate those not at the shack first.'

Brandon rested his arms on his legs. 'I'm all ears.'

'Summer Jenkins wasn't there. Neither was Jethro Pascoe. Obviously not your daughter.'

Brandon nodded.

'Nor Gisela von Schoenburg, Duncan Littleton or Jackie Nixon.

'You said it might be easier?'

'I'm narrowing it down.'

'You're that convinced?'

'As far as DNA is concerned.'

'Damien Kane thought he might recognise the aftershave Duncan was wearing.'

Al paused. 'Possibly. But his DNA isn't at the place. Or on Damien's clothing.'

'He could have been careful. Only there a short while?'

'More questioning. Your department, Brandon.'

'Duncan Littleton, Summer Jenkins, Jethro Pascoe, and

Jackie Nixon have already been released on the condition they will be available for further questioning. Magda Pethick, Dorothea Llewellyn and Fryda Chegwin are still being held,' Brandon said, adding: 'You said you wanted to explain further.'

'Only that the DNA deposits were scrappy. The captors had made efforts to clean up. I think we got lucky when you caught them unawares. I found a few blue gloves smothered in DNA – Llewellyn's and Pethick's. Chegwin's DNA was largely around the kitchen area. Maybe she liked to snack. Or was the cook?'

'Thanks, Al. Really useful—' Brandon cut Al short when a call came through from Jo. He looked up to see Al already on his feet, his palm raised in acceptance.

'I'll be off,' Al said, picking up his bag. 'Littleton's aftershave. Might be worth taking some sniffer dogs to the shack and then his place.'

Brandon nodded, but his attention was on what Jo had to say. 'Bring Jason in,' he said, watching Al leave the room. 'Now.'

*****

Jason Pascoe walked into the interview room first, Jo a few strides behind, her face flushed, hair escaping from her ponytail.

'Take a seat.' Brandon was sitting at the table facing the door, a pen and notepad in front of him. Props. They'd have to record the interview, no matter how awkward it was for Jo. This was more than a routine chat.

Jo hesitated before coming around to his side of the table.

'I'll do the honours,' Brandon said, clicking on the recorder.

'6pm, 6 March, 2022.'

Pascoe looked miserable – labouring under the same fug of melancholia he bore as he steered *The Seagull* into harbour eight days ago.

'So, what can you tell me about Gisela von Schoenburg?' Brandon wasn't expecting a long answer.

He didn't get one.

'I don't know her. I sailed a woman over to Brest yesterday evening. She could have been Gisela von Schoenburg. She looked to be in her mid-forties. Had a light European accent. But said very little.'

'You heard her say she was going to Nante?'

'Yeah. I was just coming out of the port lav and she was five yards away, back to me, on her mobile.'

'Did you hear anything else?'

'No. She clicked off when she heard my steps.'

'Okay.' Brandon kept his eyes on Jason. He could feel the tension coming off Jo but couldn't bring himself to look at her. 'Who gave you the fare?'

This was always going to be a tricky one, but Jason was prepared. 'A Newlyn local.'

Brandon hid his surprise. 'Name?'

'Ivan Roskilly. He said a woman had come down to the harbour asking around.'

'How do you know Roskilly?'

'Everyone knows everyone in Newlyn, DI Hammett. You know that?'

'But he thought you'd be prepared to sail all the way over to Brest late at night.'

'It wasn't so late when we set sail. And the waters were sailable.'

'They were choppy last night, Jason.'

'Sailable for me.'

'What did Roskilly get out of it?'

'The satisfaction of helping a damsel in distress.' Jason gave an ironic smile. 'And a quarter of the booking fee. Before you ask: £250.'

'That little?'

'That much, for the likes of me. We don't make much fishing these days. It was a nice earner. Fuel extra.'

'And you didn't question why she wanted to get out of town so quick.'

'No. I let the money do the talking.' Jason looked to the side. 'I figured marital problems.'

'How romantic,' Brandon said, his eyes still fixed on him.

'I am that.' Jason glanced over at Jo, but she didn't move a muscle.

'You didn't think she might be running from the law.'

'I try not to overthink things.'

Brandon rested back in his chair and looked at Jo. She was sitting ramrod. Looked like she might snap. 'Anything to add DS Menhenrick?'

'Why do you have a Celtic insignia above your ankle on your right leg?'

Jason flinched. 'I'm a celt. Like you. Why not?'

Brandon was stunned by the question. He'd heard Damien mention the tattoo and yet Jo had kept this under wraps, only revealing her suspicions now.

Jason looked lost for words; his sad eyes widened. 'Good time to bring up the subject, DS Menhenrick,' he said shooting her a look. 'As it happens the tattoo was a present from my ma. She got it done on my 18th birthday.'

'Jethro's too?'

Jason's eyes were tearing into Jo. 'Yep. A rite of passage. I got the right ankle, my younger bro, the left.'

'But you can't tell right from wrong?' Jo said. Her voice breaking.

'Whoah! What have I done to deserve that?'

'I don't know, you tell me?' Jo said.

Brandon was beginning to feel like a relationships counsellor, but a scrap might shake out some truth.

'You wouldn't understand,' Jason said, dropping his head.

'Try me?' Jo said, her voice stony.

'We were brought up to believe in our heritage. Our country – Kernow.'

'Country?' Jo said. 'You're part of the CRA?'

Jason threw back his head and gave a mirthless laugh. 'No. No. There's nothing jingoistic about the Pascoes. Quite the opposite. You see what I do?' He looked up at Jo with his soulful eyes.

'Yes,' she said, her voice softening. 'If you mean your work for the RNLI?'

'We don't ask for identification papers when we pull people out of the deep.'

Brandon bit his tongue, waiting for Jo to ask the question on it.

Her telepathy was uncanny. 'So, what do the inscriptions mean?'

'Protect our beloved land of Cornwall. At all costs.' Jason glanced at Brandon.

Brandon waited a beat before pulling out some photos in the folder on the table. 'Do you recognise these people?' He pushed across Rachel's photos of the two characters on the side of the rail track when the GWR train crashed.

'I was occupied, remember.'

Brandon did remember. Jason was on the RNLI RIB

hauling in *The Seagull.*

'But I do know who they are.'

Jo started but remained silent.

'Enlighten us.' The remark had also surprised Brandon, but he wasn't going to let it show.

'Looks very much like Fryda Chegwin and Summer Jenkins.'

'In what way?'

'Their stance. Size. Their mode operandi. Talk in town.'

'Talk in town and you didn't think to share your concerns?'

'Fryda is a known CRA sympathiser. Summer a lost soul clutching on to a cause. The log had militant Cornish slogans on it. People were going to gossip. The photos aren't the best quality. But it could well be them.'

Brandon put down the pen he was fiddling with. 'Do you know them?'

'Not intimately.' He glanced at Jo. 'They're not my type.'

'What do you mean?'

'Militant women. Militant anyone. I'm a peace-loving guy.'

Jo made a move to get up. 'Any other revelations? Or can we wrap this up now?'

Brandon watched him draw a deep breath and throw back his shoulders.

'Nothing to add, DS Menhenrick and DI Hammett.'

'Interview terminated at 6.10pm, 6 March, 2022.' Brandon clicked off the recorder.

'Can I go now?' Pascoe looked up from studying his hands.

'We'll need to take some swabs.'

'Whoah!' Jason shook his head. 'This is getting heavy.'

'Nothing heavy if everything is above board.'

'Sure.' Jason leapt to his feet.

'And, as you've done us the favour of a visit. I'd like to tick you off one more list.'

Jason swung his head around, his eyes blazing.

Brandon put in a call to Stew. 'Can you organise an identity parade asap ... working around Damien and the medics.' Brandon waited for the answer. 'Yep, just Pascoe. He's making himself available.'

'From hero to zero?' Jason said, his eyes on the pair of them.

'I'm sorry if that's your assessment. You did a fine job on *The Seagull* but Alain Boucher is still dead. We still don't have a killer or motive. An identity parade could well get you off the hook.'

Jason jolted at the word hook, and Brandon wondered whether he could have chosen his words more carefully. *Fuck it*. Pascoe might not be a killer, but he was a chancer.

Brandon got up when he saw Stew at the door. 'I won't be a minute,' he said walking over and shutting the door behind him.

'What the hell?' Stew looked gobsmacked to see Pascoe.

'He's been up to some fishy business.'

'Nice one, Boss.'

'He sailed von Schoenburg over to Brest last night – for 1,000 notes. Swears blind he didn't know who she was and—' Brandon walked a few more feet from the door. 'Jo asked him about a tattoo on his right leg, just above the ankle. Something Damien mentioned earlier.'

Stew whistled lightly. 'First you'd heard of this?'

'Yes.' Brandon gave Stew a quick glance. 'Did she mention anything to you?'

'As if ... maybe she wanted to check with Pascoe first.'

Brandon nodded lightly. 'Of course. Now if you can get hold of Damien Kane and ask him to do another IP.' Brandon looked at the clock. 'Tomorrow will have to do. And bring in Summer Jenkins for further questioning.'

Stew glanced at the clock and felt for his car keys. 'I thought Summer was clean?'

'Pascoe claims to recognise Summer and Fryda from the crash photos.'

'Fryda? She gets around.'

'Not so much now. I take it she's still down the corridor?'

'Yep. Just waiting for her transfer to the Newquay holding cell.'

'Let her stew a little longer. I'll speak to Summer first.'

'Tonight?'

Brandon sighed. 'It's gonna be a long one. You've booked your flights for the morning.'

'Yep … although all the action looks like it'll be happening here.'

* * * * *

The night wasn't so long. Summer had a meltdown in the interview room and confessed to her part in the log sabotage, despite her legal aid's efforts to shut her up with a box of tissues. Talking through a stream of snot and sobs, Summer shifted the blame to Fryda and gave a colourful account of scrambling down onto the tracks to move the log when the storm broke. Fryda had been less loquacious. Her day will come in court when she's tried for a litany of charges, including GBH, abduction, sabotage and possibly arson and attempted murder. Brandon was still smarting from the warehouse debacle. And although Fryda hadn't admitted to the arson and attempted murder, she fitted Damien's description of one of his attackers that day. The smoking gun was the note left by his would-be assassin – Fryda's handwriting didn't match it. However, further examination could suggest otherwise.

Brandon checked the time. Maybe he'd make supper with Rachel after all. He needed to get out of the station. He needed the company of somebody who wasn't telling him a pack of lies. He needed Rachel.

58

Rachel

Rachel was sitting with Brandon at Julia's kitchen table eating spag bol. Julia was at a fund-raising event and Chelsea was at her grandma's.

Brandon poured some red wine into her glass. 'Is Lizzie okay?'

'She's hyper. Worried sick about Piers.'

'And for herself?'

'No.' Rachel took a sip of wine. 'She has Anastasia and Dmytro. They are both strapping! And very good company.'

'That's a relief. One less worry.'

'Is it getting to you, Brandy?'

Brandon's head shot up. 'Where did that come from?'

'Your old nickname from school.'

Brandon grimaced. 'Thanks for reminding me.'

'Could have been worse. Randy?'

Brandon burst out laughing. 'Never did have much luck with the gals.'

'Back then.'

'Not the ones I wanted to have *luck* with.'

'More wine?' Rachel reached for the bottle.

'I best not. Big day tomorrow?'

'Oh?'

'I can't talk about it, obviously.'

'Could you mime some scenarios?'

Brandon laughed. 'Rachel, it might be easier if we ...'

'If we?'

'Got married. Then you wouldn't be short of police pillow talk.'

Rachel put down her glass, spilling wine onto the table. 'That is the most original proposal ever.' She picked up the paper towel she was using as a napkin and wiped away the spillage. 'You are kidding?'

'Of course,' Brandon said, watching her closely. 'Just a case of ... I could tell you but then I'd have to marry you.'

Rachel burst out laughing.

'As you managed to shake out a few suspects, I can tell you that they've been questioned and ... I'm making progress.'

'Has Gisela been found yet?'

'Fancy a trip to Penzance Registry Office?'

It took a moment for Rachel to get the joke. 'Very good! But I'm beginning to read between the lines. Maybe we can postpone the wedding.'

Brandon's eyes widened. It would be so easy to get lost in them. Images of little Brandys flitted through her mind.

'Well, I best say no more, for now,' he said, stroking the stem of his glass.

'Be sure to let me know just as soon as you can. Penzance is a tinderbox. I just want to put it all to rest.'

'Me too, Rachel. Me too. Then we can chat more freely.'

Rachel felt something stirring within; a warmth which was more than friendship. She'd always loved Brandon. As a friend. It was during lockdown that she realised how much she missed him and wondered why. Was there more to their relationship? He always seemed to think so. Time had raced on, but it was if the clock had paused and was offering a unique opportunity. She was single. So was he. He'd let the tentative connection he had with Julia fade, and she seemed happy to let it. And there was another factor. Motherhood.

She'd lost her beautiful Oliver – didn't think anyone could replace him. And they couldn't. But maybe, just maybe this could be the time to try for another child.

'What you thinking, gal?' Brandon was looking at her from below his fringe. He wasn't touching her, but she could feel his energy.

'If I tell you … I'd have to kiss you,' she said quietly, so quietly he couldn't have heard and got up to take the plates over to the dishwasher. They'd hardly touched their meal.

'Let me help,' Brandon said. And they stood together, saying nothing, scraping pasta and Bolognese sauce into the waste disposal, casually brushing against each other, setting off sparks.

59

Jo poured the remains of her black coffee into a travel mug and took the handle of her small suitcase. She'd packed light. Didn't expect to be long in France. Didn't want to go. The journey seemed pointless. As everything did since Jason's stunning revelations. She'd trusted him and yet he had kept so much from her. She glanced at herself in the mirror. Her appearance hadn't changed despite the feelings which raged within. How easy it was to conceal the truth. It was a blessing to have Stew as her partner in this investigation. She was the senior investigator, and his work would be cut out proving himself, not judging her.

The hesitant knock at her door made her heart leap. Dragging the suitcase behind her she looked through the spy hole and saw Stew smarming down his hair. He looked as twitchy as she felt.

'Hi,' he said, standing there in his holiday best. 'What side of the bed do you want?' He paused for his punch line. 'We're going as Mr and Mrs.'

Jo raised an eyebrow. 'The one on the other side of the wall to you.'

Stew burst out laughing. 'Good to see you haven't lost your sense of humour.'

Jo bristled. 'Why would I?' So much for expecting Stew to keep his attention on the job.

'Let me take that for you, darling,' Stew said picking up

her suitcase.

'Tickets, Euros, Passport ... dear?' Jo snapped back a smile creeping onto her face.

'Don't look too happy,' Stew said through the side of his mouth. 'We want people to *believe* we're a married couple!'

'Where did you get your delightful view of marriage from?'

'France, as it happens ... I'll save the story for a balmy night over one or two Pernods.'

* * * * *

The heat hit Jo as she came down the plane steps in Nice, and it was a glorious feeling. Penzance, for all its charms, didn't do Mediterranean hot. Stew hopped off before her, flinging his arms open, his duty-free swinging from one hand, his suitcase from the other. 'Bonjour Tristesse!'

'Er,' Jo said stepping down to join him.

'I'm just reminding myself that I'm here on business. Likely sad business. It would be easy to forget,' he said, his palms still raised his eyes surveying his surroundings. Heat rose from the tarmac to greet him.

'You've read the book?'

'Bonjour Tristesse by Françoise Sagan. Yep. And I enjoyed it, funnily enough.'

'You are full of surprises.'

'I would like to think so.' Stew threw his rucksack over his shoulder and took hold of Jo's suitcase. 'Allez maintenant,' he said, pointing at the transfer minibus.

* * * * *

It was a good hour and a half before they arrived at La Croix-Valmer – a holiday village 12km southwest of St Tropez.

They went straight to the local gendarme to pick up the cleaner's keys to Pier Jardine's hillside villa *Les Hirondelles*. The desk sergeant was short, and surly and only looked up briefly from his online poker when they came in the door. Stew pulled out his card and placed it on the desk, accompanied by a full fat camembert grin. 'Bonjour Monsieur l'agent. Avez-vous clés to the villa qui appartiennent Monsieur Jardine?'

'Ze Englander?'

'Oui.'

'He was known around these parts?' Jo cut in, wanting to test his English.

'Bien sûr!' monsieur said.

'Populaire?' Jo resorted to her schoolgirl French.

'La bon viveur! Tres bon.'

'Le clés, s'il vous plaît.' Stew was doing his forceful, let's be having you smile. It largely worked in Penzance. Less so in Provence.

The gendarme looked Stew up and down, took out a Gauloise and lit it, before offering Stew one. Stew waved a hand, causing the smoke to spiral.

The gendarme puffed out a stack of smoke rings and studied them.

'Le clés?' Stew's cheesy smile had congealed, and a bead of sweat had appeared above the bridge of his nose. Jo stepped forward.

The gendarme gave her an appreciative look and edged his chair back from his desk. Resting his cigarette in an appropriate, if unimaginative, Gauloise ash tray, he went to the back of the room to a table lined with metal trays, piled with paper. He picked up a sheet and handed it to Stew.

'Le stylo?' Stew's face clouded when he saw the length of the form he had to fill out for a bunch of keys. He hated formalities.

The gendarme settled himself back at his desk and opened a drawer. He pushed a black biro across to Stew and took a drag from his cigarette, before lighting the tip of another. 'Voilà.'

Jo pulled up a chair opposite and took the pen from Stew, whose eyes were watering from the smoke. 'Let me,' she said sitting down and filling in the details.

* * * * *

'That was as much fun as queueing up to replace a hire car with a flat battery in a one-horse town.'

'I can see you're playing the part of grouchy spouse to perfection,' Jo said, climbing into their own hire car – a bright blue Peugeot 3008.

Stew switched on the ignition and air con. 'The guy was useless. The gendarme have been in there – nothing to report. He waved the wad of paper he was carrying and flung it in the back. Monsieur l'agent had given them a five-page ticking the boxes report on *Les Hirondelles*. They'd concluded that Monsieur Jardine had left voluntarily. The place showed no signs of forced entry. The smaller, of a nest of suitcases was absent and so was Jardine's car and driving licence. He'd left of his own volition. The air con was ruffling Jo's hair and she had a sudden vision of Joan Fontaine in Rebecca, laughing gaily under a silk scarf, in a convertible against an old black and white film reel. She caught Stew's eye in the rear-view mirror – an unlikely Max de Winter, but he was a good driver. Jo was happy to let him take the wheel, while her own batteries recharged.

They wound up the hillside road, a precipice one side, a pine forest on the other; every so often a villa would punctuate the green like a rare flower. A gentle man like Piers Jardine would be vulnerable in such a setting. How much force would anyone need to abduct him? Wandering in his garden. Drinking on his terrace. Strolling back from the village after a few drinks.

Jo glanced at Stew, and he caught her eye. 'Do you buy this sanitised story,' he said, changing down the gears as they took a steep incline. The drop was vertiginous, the sea below a swirl of indigo and teal, foaming on sharp rocks. But she wasn't scared. It took a lot to frighten her. And she'd already faced her worst fears.

'I don't know. Just been going through the scenarios.'

'Ditto. Let's see if we can find anything more telling than a missing suitcase.'

'A phone would be good,' Jo said, rolling down the window and resting her elbow on the frame.

'Too right. Why would he go off grid?'

Jo stretched out a palm like a child and let the air rush through her fingers. 'It's not usually a good sign.'

'Agreed,' Stew said as he took another bend. 'Jardine's place is up here on the right.' He slowed to take the turning.

The lane was narrow and ended at an imposing wooden gate.

'Encouraging,' Stew said, slowing to a halt outside. He reached out of the window and tapped in a passcode that the gendarme had given him, and the gates edged back for them. The villa wasn't huge. It wouldn't take long for them to get a feel for it. Stew was out of the car and at the door with the keys in seconds. What he sometimes lacked in finesse he made up for in enthusiasm and energy.

Jo pulled on some gloves and followed him in. The place had a gentle charm – art adorned the entrance and most of the walls, an eclectic mix of life studies and landscapes. Jo opened a door into the downstairs living area – it was furnished with two comfy, worn sofas and a heavy oak coffee table. Standard lamps were stationed nearby – Jardine was a man of advanced years; he'd need the light for reading. She walked to the bookshelf – it had a selection of well-thumbed thrillers and historical fiction – nothing surprising.

Stew poked his head around the door. 'I'll take a look upstairs in his lord's chamber.'

Jo made her way to the small kitchen and opened the country style wooden cupboards. Everything was neatly displayed. The surfaces clean. On the window ledge was a row of cookbooks. They looked well-read. Particularly the James Martin. It was poking out of the line, as if Jardine had recently used it. She picked it out and flicked through the pages until she came to some at the back stuck together, maybe from oil and grease. Jo took a butter knife out of the top drawer and began to gently prise them open. Small rolls of glue attached themselves to the blade, revealing the pages had been glued together. Jo persevered, working her way down the line of adhesive, until she could see the postcard secreted within.

Stew bounded into the room making Jo drop the knife. 'No great secrets upstairs. Shame. I thought Jardine would have some interesting parlour games.' He paused when he saw Jo's face. 'What have you found?'

'Let's find out,' Jo said, easing out the postcard with the pair of tweezers she kept in her bag.

Stew was behind her, breathing down her neck. 'An old love letter?'

'It's in French.'

'Well give it here, then.'

She passed him her tweezers with the postcard of a donkey

in a field of poppies.

'Cheesy!' Stew said, before scrutinising the almost illegible text. 'You know where to come if the shit hits the fan,' Stew said in a faux French accent.

'Charming. Does it say where?'

'Yes,' Stew said, 'And it's not a million miles from here.'

60

Brandon

Damien Kane was wheeled into the interview annexe by DC Rathbone to identify Jason Pascoe. Pascoe was already in the adjoining room, together with a couple of guys of similar build they'd pulled in. His shoulders were hunched, forehead knitted, fists in pockets. He'd have to bring those out. Kane had an eye for digits. Brandon recalled his description of Bea's stubby fingers. The boy was wearing his default sulk, as if he had better things to do than identify the man who had near as dammit given him a free pass to hell.

Brandon texted the uniform in the room and told him to prepare the line-up. Shoulders back, hands free. He watched as they shuffled into place, Pascoe reluctantly playing ball.

'When you're ready, son.' Brandon took the handles of the chair and wheeled him right up to the mirror.

Damien glanced up at him, a flicker of emotion lighting up his small black eyes. And then he edged forward and stared through the glass. 'Can I go down … Sir?'

Brandon was disarmed by the curtesy. Damien was a prickly ball of resentment and pain. This latest brutal attack could only have made him more bitter. But the boy's instincts were right. Brandon was on his side.

'I'll take you down myself, Damien.'

'Thank you,' Damien said, glancing at Brandon before looking down at his hands. They were covered in ink. Rachel had mentioned Damien's propensity to fiddle with pens when she taught him at St Pirin's. She suspected he used them to self-harm – he had a history of nose bleeds.

Pascoe did a micro flinch when Brandon wheeled Damien into the room. The others stood impassive. Damien gave Brandon a side eye and he wheeled him to the top of the line and then slowly down it. Damien sat like a young emperor inspecting his gladiators, deciding which one would get the thumbs down.

'Can you ask them to roll up their trousers,' Damien said quietly.

It was unclear if Jason had heard, he stood emotionless, his eyes on the mirror.

Brandon had received sillier suggestions, but all the same Damien's demands were pushing it. 'If you could just—' Brandon coughed lightly and ran a palm across his mouth. 'Roll up your trouser legs.'

'The right ones,' Damien whispered, a smirk slashing his pale face.

'The right legs.'

Pascoe was the first to bend down and pull up his jeans.

'And his sock.' Damien was looking up at Brandon. 'Tell him to roll down his sock.'

'I heard the kid,' Pascoe said, leaning down again and shoving his sock below his ankle, to reveal a black and white stamp. It looked like something you'd see on a Ming vase.

Damien's hands gripped the sides of his chair. He turned to Brandon and then back at the line. 'It's him.'

'Who?' Brandon said watching him closely.

'The guy in the middle with the tattoo.' Damien paused and looked back up at Brandon. 'And he has another, a little further down.' He pointed at Pascoe. 'You can see the tip just poking out of his sock.'

'Roll the sock further, Mr Pascoe,' Brandon said.

'Is this really necessary?' Pascoe shook his head in disbelief and raised his hands in protest.

'Yes.'

They watched in silence as he removed his shoe and sock and a roughly etched tattoo of a chough– the Cornish bird – emerged.

Damien's face clouded. 'Can I have a closer look?'

Brandon wheeled him over, his hands ready to pull him back if Pascoe took a kick.

'Your memory not as clear as you thought, Kane?' Pascoe was sneering at him from above.

Damien glanced up at Brandon. 'I've seen enough.'

'Can you elaborate, son?' Brandon said when they were back in the annexe.

'Yeah. That bird is new. The ink is barely dry.' Damien looked at his own hands, covered in biro.

Brandon pulled up a chair and moved closer to him. 'Can you prove that?'

Damien shrugged. 'Maybe. I know a few tattooists.'

Brandon wondered if he'd been *inked* himself. But there was nothing on show. Damien wore his clothes like a zipped-up body bag. He wasn't likely to 'tear open his shirt and show Rosie on his chest', like Dion's Wanderer.

'And wouldn't that forensic pal of yours be able to tell if it was new? If it covered another tattoo?'

Brandon nodded his head lightly. 'Maybe'. It would be a departure for Chapman, but, hell, nothing was straightforward in this case.

'But you think it's him, son?'

'Yes. I'm pretty sure. Same build. Same smell.'

And there was Jo, of course, she'd know when the chough landed.

61

Jo's phone had been vibrating on and off for ten minutes as Stew drove her through the lush countryside to the small village of Saint-Paul-en-Forêt. It was the address on the postcard Jardine had glued inside his cookery book. How had the gendarme missed that, she thought, watching Jason Pascoe's name disappear from her phone screen only to pop up again.

'Why don't you pick it up?' Stew said, taking a wine gum from the side compartment and popping it in his mouth. 'Can't wait to have some liquid wine. It would be easy to forget we're on assignment, Madame Bland.' Stew tossed over the bag of wine gums to Jo. She took one and put the bag in her pocket.

'I wouldn't want you to develop a tummy, hubby.'

Stew burst out laughing. 'Don't make me choke!'

'Not while you're driving,' Jo added, smiling into the rear-view mirror.

'Joking aside, Menhenrick, you need to answer his call. It could be important.' Stew caught her eye in the mirror. 'Not for him. For the inquiry. This isn't about …'

'About my feelings?' Jo flashed him a look. 'I'm aware of that.'

'You don't want to talk to him with me in the car?'

Jo took a while to answer. 'No. It's not that. I'm dreading what he—'

Her phone started to vibrate again, and she picked up the call. 'Hello.'

'Hi. How are you? Where are you? I've been trying to get hold of you for ages.'

The call wasn't on speaker, but Stew could hear him. Jo felt sure of that.

'I'm fine. What's the urgency?'

Jason sighed heavily. 'What's not the urgency. I need your help, Jo.'

Stew was concentrating on the road but listening hard; he'd turned down the air con and stopping sucking his gum.

'How?' Jo said, staring into her phone. Jason wasn't on FaceTime, but she was avoiding Stew's eye.

'The tattoo. Well, who'd have thought it. But it's become an issue.'

'How so?'

The … boy. Kane is questioning it.'

'Why? He was the one who first mentioned it?'

'Yeah, well, he's getting all confused and can't remember what it looked like! Can you credit it.'

Jo remained silent.

'Jo, you remember the celtic emblem my ma gave me for my eighteenth? Hey, remember the lucky imp she gave you? You still carrying it around?'

It was in an evidence bag in her locker at the station.

'Do you remember the chough bird on my ankle. I got it done for you – for us – to remember Cornwall when we fly to foreign climes.' She'd never heard him pile on the patter so liberally. It turned her stomach. Chilled her heart.

'You never mentioned the chough?'

'Sure, I did. I kept it covered up the last few times we were – under the covers!' He gave a fake laugh.

'Well, can't wait for the big reveal when I see you.'

'Don't be long, girl. I miss you. Love you.'

'Goodbye Jason.'

'Just for now,' she heard him say.

'For now.' They would meet again, that was certain. But not in the best of circumstances.

She sat silent, head down, staring into her lap.

'Do you want to talk about it,' Stew said his eyes still on the road ahead.

'I have to talk about it.'

Jo put a call through to Brandon. 'We're making progress. On route to a place where we might well meet Piers Jardine. St Paul en Forêt in the Provence countryside. But don't set the gendarme on this ... yet.'

'Anything else to report?'

Jo took a deep breath. 'Jason Pascoe called me. He was trying to convince me that he had a chough bird tattoo on his leg. Does that make sense to you?'

'Totally.' Brandon paused. 'Are you saying that he didn't?'

'Not the last time I ... saw his leg. Just two nights ago. There was an emblem with markings and an inscription below.'

'You can vouch for that, Jo?'

'I have a photograph of it.'

Stew's head jolted and Brandon did a force 9 exhalation.

'God, you're good.'

'Good at some things,' she said, biting her top lip and catching Stew's sympathetic eyes in the mirror. But even that bit of evidence was a fluke. They'd been using Jo's phone to take a selfie on his boat, when it rocked, and the camera caught the deck and their feet. But she hadn't deleted the photo. So, something was working for her on a subconscious level.

62

Brandon

Brandon studied the photo Jo had pinged over to him. It was a blurred, diagonal shot of the bow of a boat, Pascoe's right leg bent from the knee revealed his ankle and lower calf, Jo's left leg in waterproofs.

Brandon printed the photo out and pinned it to the incident board.

It was going to be another lengthy day of interviews. He reckoned they'd got enough on Pascoe to make him sing like a chough, so he could sweat in the holding cell for a while longer. It was time to have another chat with Dorothea Llewellyn, Magda Pethick and Fryda Chegwin. He was just waiting on reinforcements from MCIT – DI Tamsyn Maguire was going to join him. He could hear her motorbike drawing up outside. She was a feisty cop, and he could do with her fire brand this afternoon. Last night was on his mind. What would have happened with Rachel if Nick and Chelsea hadn't bounded through the door with Gigi? Cursed dog. He'd have to call out for coffees to sharpen up.

* * * * *

'Come in.' Brandon was surprised to see Lena from the café at the door with two takeaway coffees. She was immaculately turned out, as usual.

'So, no DS Bland, today?' she said, sashaying to the table and placing down the cardboard tray.

Brandon smiled up at her. 'Thanks for bringing them over,

Lena. Much appreciated.'

'I brought a bag of muffins too,' she said, producing a paper bag from the strapped holdall that crossed her ample bosom.

'You have me sussed.'

Lena smiled. 'You and the guys are my best customers. Glad to help.'

Brandon felt in his pocket for his wallet.

'No ... this is on me today. My pleasure.'

'Well thanks, Lena. Just what we need, eh?' Brandon looked over at DI Maguire, who was staring at the clock.

'Very thoughtful,' Tamsyn said, taking a coffee, but declining a muffin. 'If you could excuse us,' she said, with a smile so forceful it almost blew Lena out of the door.

'Same tomorrow?' Lena said, as she went to leave.

'I'd like to say, yes. The muffins are darn good for the soul – less so for the waistline.'

'You don't have to worry about your figure,' Lena said, her hand on the doorknob.

Brandon stroked his left eyebrow and raised his coffee cup. 'Thanks, Lena. Sure, kind of you to bring these in.'

As the door closed behind her, Tamsyn rolled her eyes and took a gulp of coffee. 'You'd think Ms Deliveroo would hop it when we have important business to do.'

Brandon grimaced. 'There's always time for pleasantries, don't you think?'

'If you say so.' Tamsyn took another slurp of coffee and started to go through her notes. 'Looks like you had a pretty good chat with Dorothea Llewellyn last time?'

Brandon leaned back in his chair. 'It was a revelation. Her current *persona* belies her past. But she has a lot more to give. I feel we've only seen a small piece of Ms Llewellyn. Let's bring her in.'

* * * * *

Dorothea, a diminutive figure, looked to have shrunk further. She perched on the edge of her chair like a child on the naughty step. Or a witch that had taken a vanishing potion. Brandon didn't know whether to be encouraged or not. Particularly as the glacial lawyer Jemima Rattison was at her side. Llewelyn clearly had the funds to afford expensive defence.

'Fourteen hundred hours and ten minutes, March 7, 2022,' Tamsyn announced in her strong, confident voice. Brandon was thankful for it today. The ground was shifting beneath him. It was like the train crash had derailed his equilibrium. He had to wrap this case up before it got the better of him.

'Ms Llewellyn, you have been identified as the medic who attended to Damien Kane in captivity. Your DNA has been found at the premises. You are being charged with the abduction of Damien Kane and the unlawful administration of drugs, you do not have to say anything, but if you do it will be noted and may be used as evidence.'

Jemina Rattison lent in to have a word, but Dorothea brushed her aside. 'I have been advised to say nothing.'

Rattison bristled.

'However, I can't see how that is going to accomplish anything. As you know, I'm a doctor and have an understanding nature.'

Tamsyn yawned. 'Let us be the judge of that, Ms Llewellyn. So far, your actions have spoken louder than your words.'

Dorothea ignored her and turned her attention to Brandon, who was in the enviable position of playing good cop. 'DI Hammett knows my history.'

'Part of it,' Brandon said.

'Part of it.'

Tamsyn went to speak but Brandon leaned forward and cut in. 'Would you care to tell us the whole story?'

Dorothea sighed and fiddled with the ring on her finger. 'It would take too long. But I can give you the abridged version.'

'The unedited version,' Tamsyn said.

Rattison leaned in again but met the same stony response from her client. Brandon wondered why she had employed her and not Jimmy Moyle the legal aid lawyer, who made a nice living out of saying nothing on the public purse?

'The truth.'

'Your truth?' Tamsyn said.

Brandon raised his voice slightly. 'I want to hear what you have to say. But can we start with Piers Jardine. He's gone missing in Provence, and I need to know why. You said he was your friend.'

Dorothea shifted in her chair. 'I have many friends. Or so-called friends.'

'He let you down, Ms Llewellyn?'

'He let a lot of people down,' Dorothea said her eyes glistening.

'In what way? You said previously that he did you a favour buying your artwork and selling it for you. It bailed out one of your relatives, you suggested.'

Jemina bent over to speak to her client, but Dorothea edged away.

'I'll tell you when I want legal advice, Ms Rattison.' Dorothea looked Brandon in the eye. 'I believe he sold on the artwork for much more than he told me at the time. Made a killing. And, as I mentioned to you previously, the sums I received were a drop in the ocean of family debt. We are still drowning in it.'

'This is a murder and abduction investigation, Ms

Llewellyn. Do you expect us to sympathise with your financial mismanagement. You didn't do due diligence, and you got screwed. It happens all the time,' Tasmyn said.

Dorothea glared at her. 'Thank you for your council, DI Maguire. DI Hammett, I didn't intend to kill Piers Jardine or be part of a plot to do so. In many respects I agree with your colleague. Like a fool I rushed in. Money has never been my … passion.'

'What is your passion, Ms Llewellyn?' Brandon said, his eyes on her.

Dorothea sighed again and fiddled with the ring. 'Helping people, I suppose. I'm a doctor.'

'You worked in a prison? Why?'

'To serve society. I have – in the main – lived a privileged life.'

'Did you feel you helped?'

Dorothea clasped her hands. 'I thought I was helping. Making a difference. But now … Now I know differently.'

Tasmyn went to speak, but Brandon shot her a look. 'Please explain. What do you know now that you didn't originally?'

'That I am a fool. An old fool. And I allowed myself to be used and I'm now paying the price.'

'I object to this line of questioning,' Rattison raised a palm, the gleam of a platinum ring and chunky chain bracelet catching the light.

'Objection overruled,' Dorothea said, a small smile on her face. It was contagious and Brandon smiled back.

'If I can continue,' Dorothea said, and turned, once again, to Brandon. 'DI Hammett, I don't know whether you've ever visited prisons in your time in the force.' Brandon nodded. 'But those visits were likely fleeting. As a medic you spend more time with inmates. You get to know them.'

Brandon's eyes widened. 'I can imagine.'

Dorothea looked to the side, tears glistening in her eyes. 'I fell in love. And I ... allowed my emotions to control me. Dictate my actions.'

Brandon was relieved Stew wasn't with him. His favourite exclamation *Fuckadoodledandy* flashed through his mind. Brandon bit his top lip and nodded. 'You fell in love, Ms Llewellyn. With an inmate?'

'Yes.'

'Is this relevant to our inquiries.' Rattison looked rattled.

'Very.' The words looked like they were banking up against Dorothea's lips ready to spill.

'Who did you fall in love with?'

'Magda Pethick. She was there at the time.'

Brandon looked down briefly at his notes, although he remembered her details. Pethick was in Eastwood Park Women's Prison for six months for handling stolen goods and fraud. He hadn't had time to go through the notes thoroughly. That was Jo's job. She should have made the connection – even though Llewellyn and Pethick's paths had only crossed for a short time.

'Did you hatch up this ... scheme ... while you were in prison, or after?'

'Much later. There was lockdown, of course, but we kept in contact via Zoom and really got to know each other. It wasn't until early this year that we became involved in what you've described as the scheme.'

Rattison was tapping her manicured nails on the back of her iPhone 13. 'Ms Llewellyn. This is not a court of law. You are under no obligation to say more.'

'I want to. And it may even save a life.'

'Piers Jardine's?' Brandon said.

'Yes. He doesn't deserve to die for being a shrewd business-man.'

'Why would Magda want to see him dead?'

'You will have to ask her. But I now know, money is her motivation.'

'I still don't understand why him? What had he done to her – and how did she stand to benefit.'

'A contract had been put on his head. He'd ruffled more feathers than mine. This was an act of revenge, pure and simple.'

'And you went along with this?' Brandon was leaning forward, his brow creased.

Dorothea sighed. 'I wasn't given all the details. In fact, I was given very few. I was just back-up, really. They said they wanted me to sedate him. The idea was to get money with menaces. Of course, it all went horribly wrong.'

'Too right!' Tasmyn had seized her chance to speak, while Brandon rubbed his forehead like a baffled bear. 'Not only did you sedate the wrong man, but your accomplices also finished him off with an industrial fishhook. How, in dear God, did that happen?'

'It went wrong when Gisela got involved.'

'Except she's not Gisela is she?'

'That, I can't help you with.'

'Really?' Tasmyn said, her eyes widening.

'Can Pethick?'

'Maybe. But we were links in a chain. No one had the full picture. Gisela was running things from The Wellbeing Centre.'

Tasmyn scoffed. 'The irony of it.'

'I've told you everything I know, DI Hammett.' Dorothea put a finger to her eye and wiped away a tear.

'If you're withholding information, then that will stand against you in court.' Brandon paused, waiting for her to speak. But she didn't.

'Damien. Why did they go for him?'

'Revenge. He'd upset Gisela, or whatever her name is.'

'How?'

'They didn't go into detail. I was brought in as the medic. And, as events unfolded, I thought it would best suit me not to ask questions.'

'Shame,' Tasmyn said, her finger hovering over the recorder.

'Anything else to add, Ms Llewellyn?' Brandon said, his eyes softening as he spoke.

'I'm sorry.'

* * * * *

Brandon put through a call to Jo as he waited for Magda Pethick to be brought in. He leaned back in his chair and felt for the bag of muffins in the table drawer.

'Can I tempt you,' he said, offering Tamsyn the bag.

'Thanks,' she said, dipping in a hand. 'How's Jo doing?' she said through a mouthful of muffin.

'She's … making progress.'

'As we are.' Tamsyn took another bite. The gal was ravenous. 'Well, we were … what are they doing out there?'

'Changing of the guard,' Brandon said. Jimmy Moyle, the legal aid lawyer, was evidently late. He was always chasing from one assignment to another.

'It can't be easy for Jo and Stew? Looking for a needle in a … vineyard.' Tamsyn looked pleased with her wordplay.

'They have a lead. But—' Brandon shook his head and studied the half-eaten muffin in his hand. 'I wish I was there.'

'Well, you can write that on a postcard and send it to me!' The sugar in the muffin seemed to be firing the woman.

'I'm worried. Worried they could be walking into a trap.'

'They have reinforcements?'

'The gendarme has been less than helpful so far.'

'Tasers?'

'Thankfully, yes.' Brandon put his muffin back in its wrapper.

'Not hungry?'

Brandon shook his head and then looked out of the window. He could hear people outside – recognised Jimmy's low-pitched whine.

'You heard what Llewellyn said. Piers is a marked man. Jo and Stew won't be the only ones looking for him.'

There was a light knock on the door.

'Come in.' Brandon rose to his feet as DC Rathbone brought in a sullen Magda Pethick. She had her hands behind her back as if she was already cuffed and waiting to be incarcerated.

'Take a seat Ms Pethick,' Brandon said, gesturing to the one opposite him and Tasmyn.

Tasmyn clicked on the recorder. 'Fourteen hundred hours and 45 minutes, March 7, 2022.'

Brandon raised weary eyes to the interviewee. 'Magda Pethick, you are being charged with collusion in the murder of Alain Boucher and abduction, GBH and attempted murder of Damien Kane. You have the right to remain silent, anything you do say can be used against you as evidence in a court of law.'

Pethick didn't bat an eye. Her rotund, solid body hit the seat of her chair with a thud, the only sound she omitted.

'Your DNA was found on the premises where Damien

Kane was kept captive. Mr Kane has identified you as one of his captors. CCTV images of you on the day you picked up the ransom have been identified. There is an image of you asking me a question in the press briefing on that same day. What do you have to say for yourself.'

'No comment.'

'Dorothea Llewellyn has named you as one of the accomplices in the plot to abduct Piers Jardine and Damien Kane. Do you deny this charge?'

'Yes.'

'Do you deny that you became lovers after meeting her at Eastwood Park Prison.'

'Yes.'

'You continued your relationship via Zoom and phone during the lockdown.'

'No comment.'

'It will be easy to trace this communication. Think again before you speak.' Brandon looked at Jimmy for assistance. But Jimmy shrugged. His life wasn't so hard, but you wouldn't know it by his pissed off expression.

'Ms Llewellyn said you were links in a chain. You both only knew so much. How much did you know? The life of a man depends on your answer.'

'No comment.'

'A beret was found on *The Seagull*. I believe it belonged to you.' He believed nothing of the sort – but Pethick was wearing a beret when she questioned him at the press briefing. It was worth a try. Sometimes you had to toss a grenade.

Pethick didn't explode but her face went puce. He could see her brain ticking, scrambling to remember when she'd worn the beret. If she'd been photographed in it.

'Anything on that boat wouldn't have a lick of DNA on it.

Just salt water.' Her face was like thunder, her cheeks puffed out, small eyes burning.

'You'd be surprised. It's at the lab right now. We're waiting for the results ... due any time.'

In truth, the beret was not the first specimen to be analysed, and Chapman had his doubts about recovering any DNA. But he'd rattled Pethick.

He tossed another grenade. I am in possession of a written note left for me after I was locked in a burning warehouse on the day Damien Kane was attacked in Newlyn. We will need to take an example of your handwriting to see if it matches.

Pethick looked set to explode. That would do. For now.

63

The waiter put down their drinks at the table outside Paul's Bar in Saint-Paul-en-Forêt. A lager for Stew and a glass of white burgundy for Jo. Jo wouldn't ordinarily have drunk on the job, but they were undercover, masquerading as a holidaying couple. Stew reached out a hand to touch hers and she snatched it away.

He laughed and picked up his glass. 'Cool. The French do know how to pour a cold Kronenbourg.'

'Don't get too relaxed.' Jo pulled out a map and spread it across the small table. She could have used her phone, but the map would do a better job of flagging their tourist credentials. The rustling had already pricked up the ears of two old men sitting to their left playing dominos. 'According to the postcard, the place is around here.' Jo pointed to an area on the edge of town.

Stew lowered his voice. 'Looks like ... a caravan site?'

'Not very Piers Jardine?'

'No. Unless that card is very old or we're heading entirely in the wrong direction. Let me ask one of the old timers.' Stew got up from the table with the map. 'You relax my dear. I'll just ask the kind gentlemen if they can help us.'

Jo had rarely felt less relaxed. The sun was shining, and they were in a cute rustic setting – a small bar in a small square. But the surrounding hills were closing in on her, creating a creeping unease. She took a sip of wine and watched Stew doing his thing with the locals. They seemed to understand him and were making a lot of fuss around the map, arms waving, exclamations spouting. At one point the map knocked off a stack of dominoes and Stew scrambled on the pavement to retrieve them.

'Zut alors,' Stew murmured, returning with the crumpled map, under the watchful eyes of the old men. 'Drink up.' He left a 20 on the table and rattled his car keys.

'So just where are we going?' Jo said, once they had crossed the square to the Peugeot.

'Not the St Pauls Ritz.'

Jo gave him an incredulous look. 'Spit it out. I have enough suspense to deal with right now.'

'A run-down caravan site en forêt. It used to house Algerian immigrants back in the day, according to Jules et Jim over there.'

'And now?'

'All sorts. Odds and sods. A transient crowd which don't go down so well with the locals.'

'Quite a cover for Jardine then?'

'If he's there. Jo, he could be anywhere. This postcard you found … it's not a GPS tracker.'

'You're saying I'm losing it?' Jo had her hands on her hips.

'Of course not. It was a hunch. A good one. And we have nothing else.'

'True. Or maybe not.' Jo was looking over his shoulder at the bar. A man was staring at them. He was standing by one of the old men who was pointing at them. The man started to run towards them yelling at the top of his voice.

64

Rachel

'Is this really necessary!' Lizzie Matthews had her arms folded proprietorially, as a group of SOCOS filed past into Seabird Cottage.

'Mum, you did find the photograph of Roberta Bevan in Gisela's drawer. There could be more evidence.'

'If you say so, darling. But it is causing such a kerfuffle. And just when I am trying to *settle* Anastasia and Dmytro. They've just escaped a war zone and now they're in another.'

'Hardly.' Rachel spied Brandon's car at the end of the lane. Her stomach did a flip. What was the matter with her. It was Brandon. Good old Brandy. But now, possibly, Randy. He was getting out of the car. Rachel spun around to face Lizzie.

'What's the matter with you?' Lizzie had an annoying knack of reading her. 'Ah, Brandon has arrived. Perhaps he can establish some order.'

Brandon was striding down the lane, which was jammed with parked cars, his mobile clamped to his ear. Business, as usual, thought Rachel, until she caught his eye. Things would never be the same between them, she realised. They hadn't done anything. But they nearly had. If Nick hadn't walked through the kitchen door when he did with Stew's dog.

Brandon addressed Lizzie first. 'I'm real sorry about the inconvenience, Lizzie. They shouldn't take too long.'

Lizzie was charmed. 'No trouble at all, Brandon. You must do what you must do. Rachel and I will take Anastasia and Dmytro on the bus to Land's End.'

Brandon glanced at Rachel and the amusement in his eyes broke the ice. 'Look out for any spare £20 notes that may have slipped between the seats.'

The joke was lost on Lizzie, but not on Rachel. Had it only been six days since ransom money was central to the investigation? No one had handed in any loose notes. The thought made her smile and Brandon caught it.

'How's things,' he said looking at her in that way. It was an old look, but it was like he'd turned up the dial. Warmth flooded through her.

'Good. Yep, good,' Rachel said, idly kicking some gravel.

Brandon looked like he was going to say something else but was interrupted by one of the SOCOs. It was the main one, Al Chapman, his sharp eyes studying them.

'I'll leave you,' Rachel said, glancing at Al.

'I'll call you later. What's a good time?'

'Er, when you're done with business?'

Brandon smiled. 'That wasn't the right answer. I'm not gonna be done with business for a while yet. Days. 8pm?'

'Sure.' Rachel's voice quaked a little and she hated that. Brandon liked Rachel Matthews not a tongue-tied, quivering schoolgirl. She had too much time on her hands, she figured as she watched him huddled with Al Chapman, probably talking about DNA or bones.

Lizzie snuck up beside her. 'They've got oodles of Gisela's DNA. Hair out of the bathroom sink. Ugg!' Lizzie tutted. 'You'd have thought she would have been more careful … and hygienic!'

'How do you know?'

'I have my spies—' Lizzie nodded towards Dmytro. 'He speaks much better English than his mother and he understands it. Such a sweetheart … What were you saying to

Brandon?'

'Nothing.' Rachel's cheeks were burning.

Lizzie gave a knowing smile. 'Hopefully you will both have some time to spend together once this case is closed. If Brandon is still alive, that is!'

'Mum!'

'He has a dangerous job, darling. Something, of course, to take into consideration.'

Lizzie's brow creased. 'I am so worried about darling Piers. They still haven't found him, and he hasn't called me.'

'He'll be fine. Piers is a survivor.'

Lizzie nodded and threw back her shoulders. 'He dodged that … fishhook a few days back. But what happens when his luck runs out. And who's out to get him?'

Brandon gave them a side glance.

'Interpol are looking for him.' And, Rachel suspected, so was Jo. Brandon hadn't said anything … they weren't married yet! … but Jo hadn't been around. It seemed likely she was trying to track him down in France. Her thoughts were interrupted as one of the SOCOs rushed out carrying a tea caddy which she handed to Al Chapman.

'That's my—' Lizzie was silenced by the unfolding scene.

Brandon approached and asked them to back off a little. 'Just while we … deal with this.'

'What?' Lizzie said, 'Or am I, as owner of this house, not allowed to know what nefarious goods you've found in it.'

Brandon grimaced and Rachel touched Lizzie's arm. 'Not now, Mum. It's clearly not a bomb, but—' Rachel's voice faltered when she saw a single £20 note float from the tin on a gust of wind.

'Who would have thought?' Lizzie said, watching it land at her feet.

65

'My name is Fared Zidane,' said the middle-aged man sitting at the table in front of them. Jo and Stew were back at Paul's bar, this time in a backroom that the owner had given them access to.

'I'm a friend of Piers Jardine. A very old friend.'

'Why are you telling us this?' Jo said.

'Because you are gendarme. British cops.'

'Pourquoi penseriez-vous que,' Stew said.

'Because your French is … no, offence, not the best … and you have police written all over you.'

'Really,' Jo said, raising an eyebrow.

'And—' Fared lowered his voice. 'The locals knew immediately. The gendarme network is like pigeon post around here.'

Stew was eyeballing him, stung by the bad French jibe.

'L'agent Gideon Martin in La Croix-Valmer is the cousin of our gendarme here.'

'I see,' Stew said.

'Where is Monsieur Jardine?' Fared said, looking from Jo to Stew.

'We rather thought you might tell us that, Monsieur Zidane.' Jo glanced at Stew.

Fared reached over to a decanter of Pernod on the table and poured into three shot glasses. Stew took his in one. Fared smiled and poured him another.

Jo raised a hand. 'I'll drive.'

'No need.' Stew put down his glass.

'I will.'

'Okay, Fared. Can I call you Fared?' Stew turned his attention to his bartender.

Fared shrugged. 'Sure.' His English was perfect. And it kept Jo in the loop as her French was at best patchy.

'Are you here looking for Piers?' Fared took a sip of Pernod.

Jo nodded. 'Yes.'

Fared smiled. 'Me too.'

'Well, can you take us to him?'

'No.' Fared topped up his glass and Stew's.

'No?' Stew said, taking a gulp.

'No. He's gone.'

'Where?'

'I don't know. We were in this bar, and he said he was going to Croix to buy a phone. He wanted to make some calls. And then poof!' Fared waved his arms. 'Nothing.'

'He didn't call you from it?' Jo said.

'One call. He sounded odd.'

'In what way?' Jo moved to the edge of her chair.

'Distant. Said he was going back to the villa after all. That he had blown things out of … how you say, proportion.'

'When did he make that call?' Jo was watching him closely.

'Yesterday.'

Stew and Jo exchanged looks.

'You were at the villa today?' Fared said, his small brown eyes tearing into them.

'Your sources are good, Monsieur.'

'Not as good as I'd like, right now.'

'Was there anything else you noticed about the call.' Jo edged closer to the table. 'Did he say anything that might suggest he was scared, or that someone was with him?'

304

Fared poured himself another shot. 'He did. We have a code. We've had it since we were boys playing round here – Piers' family had a house in the village. I lived on the local caravan site. I still do, some of the time.'

'What was the code?' Jo was leaning in, so close she could smell the Pernod on his breath.

'They've run out of cheese. It means danger. Running out of time.'

'Okay, so he was last seen in Croix-Valmer yesterday afternoon. I don't know what your CCTV is like around there?' Stew said.

'Do you have any CCTV?' Jo said.

'Un petit peu.'

Stew got up from the table abruptly. 'I think we need to check the town's partial vision asap.'

Jo scrambled her things together and joined him at the door.

'Interesting that he reverts to French when he admits to the region's shortcomings,' Stew hissed in her ear.

'We need to keep him on board,' Jo said quietly and turned back to Fared and gave him a contact card. 'What's your mobile?'

* * * * *

Jo sat in the passenger seat of the Peugeot while Stew made some calls. The first to Gideon Martin in La Croix-Valmer. Her eyes were on the bar. As she thought, Fared left it a suitable five minutes before he came out.

'I'm going to follow him.' Jo felt for her taser and mobile in her bag.

'On your own!' Stew put his hand over the mouthpiece of his phone.

'I'll be careful. Track me and join me when you've finished your calls.' She handed him a GPS tracker.

Stew didn't look assured.

Jo hopped out of the car before he had further chance to protest. Fared was out of the square but not out of sight. She paced herself to his steady gait. It didn't help that the streets were empty, but, with the distance between them, he wouldn't be able to hear her. Besides he had his earphones in. And was talking to someone. A blessing for a stalker, but it only served to pique her curiosity. It wasn't that she didn't buy Fared's charming tale of a childhood friendship, it was the narrative he was keeping to himself.

He was at the bottom of the cobbled street of small stone cottages that led out of the village and onto the main – the only – road out of town. According to the map, the caravan site was beyond the rise on the left. Fared stopped dead in his tracks at the end of the street and tapped something into his phone. Jo backed against a garden wall; her slim frame hidden by a Christmas camelia. He didn't look back and she waited a beat before continuing to follow him.

Jo kept close to the hedgerow – ready to leap into it if Fared turned. The wind was getting stronger. She'd heard about the region's Mistral and wondered if she was walking into a tempest. A Coke can blew into the street from what could only be the caravan site. Fared kicked it out of the way and flicked a look over his shoulder before turning left. Jo was a way back and didn't think he'd spotted her. Her heart was pounding as she walked up the road; the gradient was steep, but it wasn't the climb which was taking its toll. She was out of her depth. Brandon would never have let her do this. But she was senior to Stew, and he had no choice. It was her decision and her challenge. The taser nudged her hip as she walked. She had that. And the element of surprise. She looked up – no cameras on this street.

Jo slowed as she approached the site entrance. There was no gate ... just a gap in the hedgerow which led to a scattering of caravans, trailers, tents and makeshift dwellings. It looked like a refugee camp. People were sitting or loitering outside their places, some on old chairs or upturned boxes – a supermarket trolley was piled with rubbish. Beaten up cars and trucks were parked randomly. Eyes followed her as she walked into the heart of the camp, her own gaze on Fared who had stopped by a trailer, a black Mercedes parked outside. The car was a diamond in the rough. A two-year reg, clean bodywork, wheels with tread.

'Looking for someone?' She turned around to see an old man sitting on a rocker outside a rusting campervan.

'Fared Zidane,' Jo said. Fared was standing outside the trailer – palatial compared to the neighbouring dives. He'd knocked already. Where were his keys?

The old man shook his head. 'He's not there.'

Jo studied him. Tanned skin, sunken, wary eyes that met hers fleetingly.

'That's Fared Zidane?' Jo said watching as he entered the home.

The man slumped back in his rocker. 'Non. You best go Mademoiselle.'

His words chilled her, but she held her nerve. 'Who's that man?'

'A stranger. Go,' he said.

Jo pulled out her mobile and took some shots of the car and place. She'd missed a call from Stew and another from Brandon, was going to call Stew back when she felt a hand on her shoulder.

66

Brandon

They'd had to bash the door down to let in the sniffer dogs at Duncan Littleton's place, a modest two up two down terrace house on the outskirts of Truro. He billed himself as a corporate lawyer on LinkedIn, but there were no visible signs of wealth on the street he lived.

Tasmyn had got her team to do some research on the art-loving lawyer and found a sketchy history of conveyancing, short stints at some London firms and a little legal aid work. Nothing to set the world on fire. As yet, Littleton wasn't returning calls and that smelt stronger than the aftershave the dogs were scenting.

Brandon was having a crafty cigarette outside the door when Al Chapman sidled up. Brandon knew better than to offer Chapman a smoke: he was a clean-living man. Left the dirty work at the lab.

Brandon took a long drag, blew it out of the side of his mouth and stubbed out his fag end on the brick wall, before depositing it in a tissue.

Chapman smiled. 'Just as well most of our perps aren't as fastidious about litter. We'd lose a lot of debris DNA.'

'Talking of which. Any news on the beret?'

'Funny you should mention it,' Al said, unable to suppress his glee. 'Magda Pethick's crowning glory. The splashes of sea water and contaminate fish traces weren't nearly enough to eradicate her DNA. She was wearing that hat around the time Alain Boucher copped it.'

'Well done, Al. Magda will have a hard time denying that DNA evidence in court.'

'Indeed. She's nailed, I would have thought. They're dropping like flies, eh Brandon.'

'Or tiddlers.' Brandon pushed himself away from the wall. Reached for his packet of cigarettes, but remembered he was with a non-smoker.

'Don't mind me.' Al tapped him on his shoulder. 'I come into contact with many contaminates. I know how to avoid them.' He slipped on a blue mask. 'You were saying. Or going to say.'

Brandon lit up. 'It's like we're reeling in the small fry, but there's a shark swimming just below the surface. We see the ripples, but he – or she – evades us.' He took a drag and exhaled to his left.

Al moved back against the wall, although, Brandon noticed, he wasn't quite touching it with his white coat. Their styles, so different, but so complementary. He took another drag and waited for Al to speak.

'I don't usually work off feelings, but there is something off with this case. There does seem to be a shark ... a power ... below the surface,' Al said.

Brandon blew out, the smoke wafting over to Al on a gust of wind. 'Dorothea Llewellyn said they were all just links in a chain. Each with a role but only knowing so much.'

'We're linking them together. That's the important thing.' Al moved discreetly away from the smoke.

'Sorry, pal,' Brandon said pushing away from the wall. 'Caught up in my darn thoughts. But the chain is building, and we'll soon be able to yank it in. By the way, I'd like you to examine the written note I was left on the day I escaped from the burning warehouse. I have a feeling it could have

Pethick's paws on it.'

'You could well be right,' Al said, 'It may reveal her DNA – but, also, pass me an example of her handwriting.'

Their conversation was interrupted by the sound of hounds barking and an outburst of excitable chatter in the house.

'Looks like the dogs have found something,' Brandon said, rushing in through the front door and up the stairs, Al trailing him. The bathroom door was wide open, two dogs were barking at the sink, their handlers pulling them back before they knocked down the bottle of *Eau Sauvage* on it.

They'd picked up the scent at the shack. Another link in the chain. But Littleton hadn't hung around to explain it.

Damien had first noticed the scent on the day he escaped death by a whisker. He'd suggested that whoever was wearing it had signed his death warrant. He'd never smelt the aftershave before or after, until the identity parade. That would explain why none of Littleton's DNA was found in the shack. But it didn't explain why he'd want to get involved in a plot to take out a list of people loosely connected to Piers Jardine.

'What you thinking?' Al said, coming up close. He smelt of soap and disinfectant.

'I'm wondering just who's on the hit list? And why?'

'Jardine seems pivotal. It should have been him on the boat … unless that was a, excuse the pun, red herring. And it was Boucher they were after all the time?'

Brandon shook his head. 'Boucher has no connection with any of the suspects. Llewellyn did business with Jardine … which turned ugly. And why target Damien and myself? And, quite possibly, Rachel Matthews.' Just saying her name felt good.

'Rachel Matthews?'

'Rachel was on the train that crashed. We now know a log

was thrown on the track … despite Summer Jenkins' bullshit about trying to remove it.'

Al scratched his ear. 'And they got her involved in the ransom. Which nearly killed her. And would have stung financially.'

Brandon pushed back his fringe. 'So nearly. If they hadn't finished her off themselves the sea could have claimed her.' She'd been struggling out there when they pulled her in. Jason Pascoe had piloted the RIB. He was a mystery, that was for sure. One part saint, the other knave. Maybe his mom had a Tarot Card with his two faces on it.

Brandon pulled out his phone and showed Al the photo of Pasco's ankle that Jo had sent over.

'May I?' Al separated his thumb from his forefinger, miming enlargement.

Brandon passed him the phone.

'You want me to take a look at the tattoo? I could easily check how fresh?'

'Could be helpful, Al. Or just the suggestion might spook Pascoe. But we already have Jo's account.'

'They're, eh?'

'An item. Yep.'

'Still?'

Brandon shrugged and took back his phone, noting Jo had yet to return his call.

67

'What the hell!' Jo swung around, fists flying.

'Whoah!' Stew leapt back, just missing a left hook.

Jo's eyes were blazing. 'What the hell do you think you're doing!'

'Coming to support you.' Stew reached out and pulled her away as a truck hurtled down the dirt track. 'The Merc will be next, dontcha think?'

Jo turned to see four figures coming out of the trailer Zidane had entered – the truck had given them a welcome dust screen. 'I take it the Peugeot's on the roadside?' Jo said, still shaking with shock and rage.

'I'd say, motor running ... but not worth the chance around here.'

The old man was grinning at them from his rocker.

'Tell them, we went thata way,' Stew said, throwing the old man a 20 note.

'You reckon that's going to wash?' Jo said hurrying along beside him out of the camp.

'Nah ... but I've always wanted to do what they do in the movies.'

'For chrissake!' Jo said when they got out onto the road. Two boys with spanners were kneeling by the front wheels of the Peugeot about to lever them off. They looked up briefly when Jo and Stew strolled over and then carried on.

'Where's that roll of cash when you need it,' Jo said in exasperation.

'Don't need it.' Stew towered over them. 'Allez maintenant!'

And they did. Stew knelt to check the wheels. 'Oi – chuck us a spanner!'

The smaller boy gave him the finger and ran off laughing into the camp with his friend.

'Merde!' Stew said, crouched by the car, his head in his hands.

'Pourquoi?' Jo kicked over the spanner the other kid had dropped.

Stew put his hands together in prayer, before grabbing the tool and tightening the bolts.

'Anything happening at the homestead?' Stew said over his shoulder.

'There's a big black limo coming this way right now. Hurry, Stew!'

Stew gave the right wheel bolts a last tighten. 'Done. Get in.'

Jo had barely got her foot in the door before the Mercedes flashed past, turning left out of the site. They were doing a good speed. Stew had his foot on the accelerator before Jo had shut the door.

'Is Fared in there?' Stew said, the speedometer touching 80kph

'That's not Fared!' Jo said, struggling to get her seat belt on.

'What!' Stew gave her a look in the rear-view mirror.

'The old man said it wasn't Fared Zidane.'

'What old man?'

'The one you bunged!'

'And you believe him?'

Jo turned her head to the window. The hedgerows were

flashing by. 'As much as I believe the *Fared Zidane* in the back of that car … watch out!'

The Mercedes narrowly avoided a red truck coming in the opposite direction, Stew swerved to the left as the truck came at them. 'Jesus! Do they not teach these people how to drive!'

'It's got a GB reg plate,' Jo said, as it rattled down the road.

'Full marks for observation.' Stew went into overdrive. 'So, the guy who introduced himself as Fared Zidane is in the car.'

'Yes,' Jo said, her eyes on the road, alert to more hazards. 'And someone who could be Piers Jardine and two others, including the driver.'

'You reckon they spotted us?' Stew said, taking a U-bend as the road climbed higher into the hills.

Jo gave an exasperated grunt.

'Just kidding!'

'This is not the time for jokes, DC Blunt. Period.'

'Where did you get the period from?'

'Cut it! Or you'll get us both killed.'

'Ye of little faith,' Stew said taking another bend at 60kph. 'You forget that I was raised in this neck of the forêt.'

'You were going to give me your backstory over a Pernod. If we get to the end of this road in one piece – my round. But for now, concentrate. Like your – my – life depends on it.'

Stew was a good driver – but his adrenaline rush needed to be controlled. And they needed backup. God knows what waited for them at journey's end. Jo got out her phone. Two more missed calls from Brandon. She tapped in his number.

'Where are you?' Brandon said picking up immediately.

'The D559 just outside Freju. Following a black Mercedes reg EQ-854-CS carrying, possibly, Piers Jardine, his child-hood buddy Fared Zidane, another passenger and the driver.'

'Any descriptions of the two unknowns?'

'No. I couldn't get a good enough look.'

'I'll get onto Interpol. Keep me up to date. Don't do anything rash. Let me rephrase that, don't let Stew do anything rash. You have back-up now. Just track them and fill me in when you can.'

'I have a GPS tracker with me. Can you pick that up.'

'Darn right I can. Keep it charged. And Jo, don't do anything risky. We have this now. Good work. Both of you.'

* * * * *

The Merc was doing its best to shake them off, but Stew was hanging in there, they were on the outskirts of Frejus now and the traffic was building.

'I wish I'd packed my portable siren.'

'Is it bilingual?'

'That is a valid point, DS Menhenrick. The locals might not recognise its Cornish accent.'

'Christ what's that!' Jo could see a massive queue ahead.

A loud trumpeting filled the air.

Stew slammed on the brakes. 'That's some siren!'

'I think …' Jo had her head out of the window. 'I think it's an elephant. I can see its trunk!'

'A travelling circus? Well, how is Zidane and co going to navigate that—' As he spoke, the doors of the Merc flung open and the four of them got out and made off in two different directions.

'This has taken an unexpected turn,' Stew said, reaching to the back seat for his taser.

Jo had her taser out already, door open. 'I'll take kerbside you the road.'

Stew nodded, leapt out of the car, and started chasing along the line of cars, swiftly overtaking the back carriage with the elephants, their trunks waving between the bars.

'I didn't know they allowed this anymore,' Stew yelled over the vehicle roofs.

'We don't have time to book 'em,' Jo shouted. She was ahead of Stew and catching up with Zidane, who was dragging a man along with him. He turned and waved a gun in her direction.

'Police! Drop your weapon now!' Jo yelled.

Zidane replied with a bullet, which whizzed past her head and hit a carriage. A mighty roar shook the vehicle.

'Fuck-a-doodle-dandy,' yelled Stew. 'I have a pathological fear of being eaten by lions!'

Zidane used the distraction to make some headway. But it was a fruitless task, dragging a reluctant other, most likely Jardine. The other two were getting away, though.

'Stew keep going, I'll deal with Fared.'

'Good luck!' she heard him shout above the racket of the animals.

'Drop the gun!' Jo commanded, scrambling up onto the towbar between two carriages to take cover. 'Reinforcements are on the way. You can't escape.'

'Who says?' Fared had a gun to the hooded head of the man next to him. He pulled off the hood and jammed his pistol into the side of Piers Jardine's head. 'He gets it unless you back off,' he said dragging him away backwards, his gun trained on Jo.

'Listen to him Detective. He's ruthless. He killed Fared Zidane.'

Phoney Fared pistol-whipped Piers. 'Shut it! Next time the bullet will be for you.'

Jo could see Stew in the distance chasing the others. She

faced a dangerous criminal who had no intention of backing down. The circus carriages rolled on relentlessly; curious, chattering chimpanzee faces crammed up against the window of the carriage door behind her. She felt the handle on the carriage door. It was bolted but not locked. Jo tugged the bolt along, with one hand behind her back. 'Come on guys, freedom!' she said opening the door and jumping off the towbar, chimps leaping down after her.

'Where you going!' she yelled at the Algerian's departing back. 'Reinforcements!' Jo ran after him, felt in her pocket, grabbed a handful of wine gums and flung them at him. The chimps chased after them excitedly. She threw more – emptying the packet, the chimps climbing all over the man to get them, making him drop the gun, Piers kicking it out of his way.

'Merde!' he yelled, six chimps hanging off him and Piers.' Enlevez-les de moi.'

The carriages stopped abruptly, and voices could be heard yelling from the front. A rotund man in circus gear came rushing at her, spouting expletives.

Jo pulled out her badge. The man considered it, doffed his hat and turned his attention to the two on the ground and the remaining chimps. Most had headed into the hills.

'Parlez-vous Anglais,' Jo said, cursing her poor French.

'Mais oui, Detective Menhenrick,' the man said.

'I'm sorry about the chimps.' Jo looked down at one of the two remaining ones which was sitting on Piers' lap. The other was ruffling the perp's thinning hair with one hand and toying with a wine gum in his other.

The circus man smiled. 'I am Monsieur Loyal, the Ringmaster. They are my family. I expect them back by teatime. A chimp cannot exist on wine gums alone.'

Jo returned his smile. 'No,' she said, thinking of Stew and wondering how he was getting on.

'Just let me deal with monsieur here,' Jo said, walking over to Piers. 'Who is?'

'*They*,' Piers' voice was trembling. 'Refer to this ... thug ... as Said.' Piers looked up at the Ringmaster. 'Do you have any snakes in your entourage that I can strangle this piece of filth with.'

'As it 'appens.'

Said recoiled.

'I think handcuffs will do for now,' Jo said, coming forward.

Piers raised an eyebrow.

'To restrain your assailant.' Jo unclipped the ones at her waist, and cuffed Said's hands behind his back.

'Can I detain him for you? Give him a ride into town?' said the Ringmaster. 'In the Snake carriage, peut tre?'

Jo's phone started ringing. She gave a thumbs up to the Ringmaster. 'We have him, Stew,' she said into her phone. 'I can join you now.'

'Gisela's given me the slip. The other guy went in the opposite direction towards the cliff, and I could never resist a cliff-hanger,' said a breathless Stew.

Jo cringed. 'Can you never be serious?'

'I'll tell you over a Pernod, tonight.'

'In the meantime, DC Bland, can you bring in our mystery man. Gisela – or whoever she is – can run but she won't be able to hide for too long. Too many people know her real identity.'

Piers was nodding vigorously.

'What are you going to do with Fared?' Stew said.

'The Ringmaster is going to look after him in a *holding*

carriage until the gendarme pick him up.'

'Cool,' Stew said.

'I'm going back for the car, where did you say you were?'

'On the clifftop at Kokonut plage. I'll flag you down.'

* * * * *

Jo drew up alongside Stew five minutes later. The suspect was standing a little way back on the cliff edge.

'I'm not going to prison! You tell him, DS Menhenrick. I will jump off this cliff if you attempt to take me in.'

'Who says you're going to prison?' Jo walked towards him, but he backed away, dangling a foot over the side. There was something familiar about him.

'I will go to prison and my life will be over.'

'What have you done that's so wrong?'

He scoffed. 'You aren't much of a detective if you haven't worked that out. Oh, I see, you've been out of the country for a few days – on your hols. That's not unreasonable.'

Jo moved a little closer and he dangled his other foot over the cliff, which made him wobble. 'Let's just find somewhere – where we can talk this all through,' Jo reasoned.

'The poste de police. No merci. They aren't particularly friendly, I'm led to believe. I'd say DI Hammett is a pussy cat in comparison.'

Jo scrutinised him. So, he knows Brandon. Their paths had been diverging of late, so she lacked important details. There'd been a stack of interviews – all of which she'd missed, apart from Jason's. Her mind went through the notes she'd made for Brandon. There'd been one other man, other than Jethro Pascoe, and latterly Jason, under suspicion. She studied him. Caught the look of realisation in his pale blue eyes. Duncan

Littleton. His house had been raided today – the sniffer dogs had identified his aftershave.

'Has the euro dropped, Josephine. May I, as a condemned man, call you Josephine?'

'I'd prefer DS Menhenrick. But if it calms you to call me Josephine, then do so.'

'I am a wretched man. Nothing and no one can calm me now.'

Stew stepped forward. 'Did you kill Alain Boucher?'

'No.' Duncan Littleton rose onto the balls of his feet.

'Who did, then?' Jo moved a little closer, but Stew touched her lightly on the arm.

'That I won't tell you.'

Duncan outstretched his arms and raised them above his head and walked to the very edge of the cliff, springing up onto the balls of his feet.

'No!' Jo cried, rushing forward to grab him as he performed a perfect swallow dive.

68

Brandon

Brandon sat opposite Jason Pascoe in the interview room, Tasmyn Maguire to his right. The recorder was whirling quietly in the well of silence.

Pascoe looked like a condemned man. His face had a greasy film, like he was looking at them through dirty glass.

Brandon placed clasped hands on the table. The move made Pascoe jump. Brandon wondered if he was using.

'Mr Pascoe, would you care to explain yourself?'

Before he'd had a chance to answer the door opened and Jimmy Moyle, Pascoe's lawyer, sauntered back into the room. He'd taken a convenience break, even though the interview had barely started.

Jimmy gave Brandon a brief nod and sat down beside Jason. 'Did I miss anything?'

'Nothing whatsoever,' Tasmyn said, mirroring Brandon by clasping her hands and resting them on the table.

'Mr Pascoe, can you explain why you covered up an incriminating tattoo? One which the victim Damien Kane remembered seeing?'

Pascoe sighed. 'He identified my ma's birthday tattoo, but not the chough.'

'He didn't remember the chough, Mr Pascoe, because it's new.'

Pascoe looked at his hands and then back up at Brandon. 'It's *newer*. I had it inked for … a friend.'

'Your girlfriend. Jo Menhenrick?'

'Sure. For Jo.'

Brandon opened the manila file on the table and pulled out a print of the photo Jo had sent over. He pushed it to Jason.

Jason glanced at it and pushed it away. 'Okay. So, what are you accusing me of? Covering up an old tat, with a new one? People do it all the time.'

Brandon grimaced. 'I don't have all night, Mr Pascoe. Damien Kane recognised your original tattoo – the one with the Celtic wording – as being on the ankle of one of his assailants. He said it was unforgettable because it was the last thing he remembered before the boot it was displayed above kicked him in the head. Jo Menhenrick, your girlfriend, took the photo of the same tattoo just days ago. The chough is a new tattoo. I can get it analysed by the forensics if you fancy putting your feet up in the lab for a few hours. Or we can take a tour of the local Tattoo Parlours and check their records. Or you can tell me the truth.'

Jason rocked back in his chair and sighed deeply. Jimmy went to say something, but he silenced him.

'Guilty. Guilty of tampering with the evidence.' Jason let out a low laugh. 'I kicked the kid. Just the once. The brief had been rough him up. Pay him back. He had enemies.' Jason fell back forward, both hands splayed on the table. 'I'm a poor fisherman and a paid hand. I run errands. I do people's dirty work. But I'm not a murderer. The boy reeled back when I kicked him and hit his head on the harbour wall. That's what knocked him out.'

'So, say you.' Brandon pulled himself up straight. 'But someone pushed him down the steps and left him for dead on the shingle.'

Jason looked to the side. 'It was only a matter of time before he was found. Newlyn harbour is a busy place. And …

I saw him call someone. We panicked and got out of there.'

'We?'

'Fryda and I.' Jason paused. 'I took my orders from her.'

'And Fryda. Who does she take her orders from?

Jason shook his head. 'I don't know.'

'I think you do.' Brandon leaned forward. 'Look at me when I'm talking to you, Pascoe.'

Pascoe looked up, his eyes full of hatred. 'Of course, *boss*.'

'The person Fryda was taking instructions from is the person who you ferried across to Brest two days ago. The person who is on the run in Provence right now.' Brandon's phone pinged with a message from the French gendarme. 'In fact, the person who the gendarme has just this minute pulled in. Ursula Chabrol.'

Jason put his fist to his mouth and sucked hard.

'Does the name Ursula Chabrol mean anything to you, Pascoe?'

Jason scribbled a note and passed it to Jimmy.

'We'd like to adjourn the meeting for a convenience break.'

Brandon looked from Jimmy to Pascoe. 'Not convenient for me. Answer the question, Pascoe.'

'I may have heard the name, briefly. But not for some time.'

'Go on.'

'There was a ... Chabrol a few years back. Not a woman, a man. A contact.'

'Fishing?'

'No—' Pascoe sighed. 'Smuggling.' He answered Brandon's intense look. 'Art.'

Brandon threw back his head. He remembered the case. It had been messy and had involved a lot of the local community. Fishermen, dealers – friends, even. They'd rounded up the local culprits and interpol had dealt with the French

Connection. A Henri Chabrol had been involved and was now behind bars, as far as he was aware.

'Ursula is his wife?'

'Same name – could be his sister, I suppose, or daughter. I don't know how old Chabrol is.' Pascoe looked at Brandon with his sorrowful eyes. He'd seen sadder sights, and they didn't wash with him. 'I was small fry back then – doing rides, shifting cargo – and I haven't been promoted. Neither would I wish to be. You won't find any DNA at that shack they kept the kid at. I didn't go anywhere near it. The harbour is my manor. I didn't mean the kid any great harm.'

'Who did?' Brandon said, his eyes boring into Pascoe's.

Pascoe wiped a hand over his mouth. 'Chabrol, I guess. Damien messed up a good business with his prying eyes. And prison. Not much fun, eh, for someone used to the high life.' Pascoe faced Brandon head on. 'You said earlier that you didn't want to waste time. Well, I can tell you now, I've got nothing else to say. Apart from, I guess, I'm sorry that I got involved. Even though it meant I got to meet Jo … But then I got to lose her.' Pascoe went to get up.

'Just one other thing, Pascoe.' Brandon raised a palm, gesturing for him to remain seated. 'Who killed Alain Boucher?'

'That I cannot tell you.'

'Really?' Brandon spoke into a hushed room. 'The beret on the boat belongs to Magda Pethick. Were you briefed to get rid of it?'

'Yes.' Pascoe hung his head. 'No Roll of Honour MBE for me.'

'So, Magda Pethick was involved that night?'

'I should imagine so – if the hat fits, and all that. DI Hammett that is really all I can help you with right now. Go get some rest.'

Brandon shook his head in disbelief. 'Thank you for your concern.' He glanced at Tasmyn and she terminated the interview.

'What next?' Tasmyn said when Jason Pascoe had been escorted out of the room.

'Well, I won't be booking a night ferry to Brittany. Jo and Stew can handle the Chabrol interview.' Brandon glanced up at Tasmyn. 'They'll be fully briefed. This is a team effort.'

'Yep,' Tasmyn said, packing up her things. 'Looks like we're beating the opposition.'

'Some of them, yes,' Brandon said, following Tasmyn to the door and turning off the lights.

69

Jo and Stew were sitting outside Paul's bar in Saint-Paul-en-Forêt waiting for the gendarme to show up so they could escort them to the caravan site.

'Ursula must have been a looker in her day,' Stew said pouring Jo a glass of burgundy.

'Still is,' Jo said, taking the glass. 'But not much of a talker.'

'No. But she didn't need to be. Zaid did that for us.' Stew sighed heavily. 'What a day, Menhenrick.' He took a long draft of wine. 'Two confessions at the poste de police, a suicide and a trip past the Circus. I should be bushed, but I'm buzzing.'

Jo frowned. 'I wish we'd been able to save Littleton.'

'Nothing more we could have done. He was convinced he'd go down. As a lawyer he will have been aware of the evidence stacked against him.'

'Of course, but he didn't kill Boucher. That was likely Pethick, according to Brandon.' He'd called them to fill them in. 'They have the beret and … Jason Pascoe's statement.' Jo took a quick sip of wine and averted her eyes.

'Hey, Menhenrick. He was a bad'un. Don't waste any tears on him.'

Jo looked up at him. 'Easy to say.' She was doing her upmost to stay sane. It had felt like love. Perhaps it was, but she couldn't forgive Jason.

Stew got up and walked around to her side of the table and put a hand on her shoulder. Jo looked up at him and the tears fell fast and furious.

Stew crouched and took her face in his hands. 'Jo, it's all right. We've got your back. You've got me.' Jo tensed and Stew slowly rose to his feet. 'You've got your pal Stew as back-up. As always.' He called over the waiter. 'Je voudrais la carafe Pernod.'

'Are you trying to get me drunk?'

'Oui,' Stew said, pushing aside his wine glass. 'I promised to tell you a story over a glass of Pernod if you remember?'

'I do remember, but that was an age ago.'

'11am this morning. You can't wiggle out of it, Menhenrick.' He grinned and poured her a stiff one. 'God knows we deserve a drink after today. I was almost eaten by a lion!'

Jo burst out laughing. 'I guess that's another story you'll be storing up for a Pernod sess.'

'Don't happen every day,' he said pouring himself a drink and taking a slurp. 'Where is Brandon when you need him?' Stew looked around the joint.

'Eh?' Jo said taking a sip of Pernod. She wrinkled her nose.

'To play the fiddle. Dun dun dun, de dun dun dun. Here's my story, it's sad but true. About a guy whose name is Stew.'

'You are on fire tonight!'

'I have just had a near death experience. You don't like your Pernod?'

'An acquired taste.'

'Well, I'll keep my story short.' Stew poured himself another glass. 'I came to live here when I was seven with my dad. My mum had left us …'

'Oh, Stew.' She reached out and touched his hand.

'Explains a lot, don't it. Well, Dad met a French woman – Estelle – and we came over to live here. My old man was a builder, so his skills were transferrable.'

'That's how you learnt French?' Jo took a companionable sip of Pernod.

'You don't have to drink it to be *nice*.'

'It's *okay*,' Jo said, 'Go on.'

'To cut a long story short, Estelle was a strict mama, and I was very much under the cosh with her. But I got to learn French and to love this country ... almost as much as I love Penzance.'

'Phew!' Jo said, wiping her brow theatrically. 'I think Brandon would miss you if I carelessly left you behind.'

'He'd miss you more.'

Jo looked away quickly. Felt her cheeks reddening.

'I'm not suggesting anything, Menhenrick. You've got a guy – well you had one.'

Jo flashed him a look. 'Brandon and I have always been nothing more than colleagues and friends.'

'And that suited you?'

'Hey, Bland. I thought we were meant to be talking about your past.'

'Yep. Well, you know all there is to know about mine, really. I am your ordinary Joe.'

She glanced up at him. 'I wouldn't say that Stew.'

'So not quite so ... Bland, then?'

'Ha ha!'

'Do you mind if—' Jo looked down at her glass of Pernod.

'You've paid your dues.' Stew took the glass and poured its contents into his own. 'You have to be a local to really appreciate this.'

Jo frowned. 'You were seven when you came here.'

'Formative years, Menhenrick. Formative years.'

Jo picked up her wine glass. 'Thanks, Stew.'

He gave her a quizzical look. 'Pourquoi?'

'For being ace, today. For being a great partner. For being a friend.'

Stew gave her a straight look. 'I wouldn't do anything else, Menhenrick. You deserve the best – well the best I can give.'

Jo stretched her hand across the table and rested it gently on his. It was a balmy evening – warm for the time of year and Jo felt herself easing into the moment. But something, a memory, a premonition, snuck up on her.

'What is it?' Stew said, his hand still beneath hers.

'It's all too pat. Something. Someone is hiding something.'

'Maybe,' Stew said. 'But can it wait 'til tomorrow?'

70

March 8, 2022

Brandon

It was gone midnight and Brandon was going over his notes in his kitchen diner. Through the French windows, he could see moonbeams dancing on the old wood table. He picked up his papers, pushed open the French windows and went out, breathing in the cool Cornish air. So fresh he almost didn't light up a cigarette – but this was no time for abstinence.

He lit up and sat down. So, Ursula Chabrol was avenging the incarceration of her husband Henri. Piers Jardine had been a small, but integral part of the uncovering of those stolen artworks back in 2017. As had Damien Kane, who'd provided video evidence of the smuggling ops. The Brits involved had both been killed – a local woman, Valerie Mason, charged and imprisoned, although there had been numerous appeals. Her case had become a cause célèbre for some. Including one besotted lawyer. Brandon was looking into the face of Duncan Littleton, thought he recognised an underlying tension or intensity in that confident smile, those beguiling cool blue eyes.

He had the self-portraits which Rachel had passed him, including the one of Duncan Littleton, who depicted himself as a small figure poised to dive off a clifftop. What drives you to such madness?

His phone pinged. 'Goodnight. Hope it all went well today? Rachelx.'

Okay, so they weren't married. And they weren't sharing

the same bed – so not strictly pillow talk – but he had to share his thoughts. And Rachel, more than anyone, would understand them.

He called her. 'You okay to talk right now?' He spoke quietly, not wishing to disturb his sleeping daughter.

'Yes.'

'Talk shop?'

'Whatever else?'

Brandon smiled. He was glad he hadn't got into the habit of FaceTime, it was nice to shield his feelings from time to time. 'Just wanted you to go over that conversation you had with Duncan Littleton when he opened up to you.'

'Is anything wrong?'

They hadn't found the body yet. But it only had to be a matter of time, surely? 'Duncan was part of the gang who were cornered in France. He dived off a cliff to escape.'

Rachel gasped. 'Is he alive?'

'Unlikely, the gendarme says. But it can take weeks to find bodies. Or never.'

'I am sorry. He was nice. I find it hard to believe he was caught up in all this.'

'A crime passionnel. And a cause célèbre.'

'Gisela?'

'No. Gisela – Ursula Chabrol, as we now know her – was acting out of revenge. Littleton's motives seem more complicated. I'm going through the papers they found at his place right now.'

'Do you want me to come over?'

More than anything. 'Yes.'

'Want me to bring some snacks?'

Brandon smiled. 'Sure. It could be a long night.'

* * * * *

Rachel was at the door in her green duffle coat, a Co-op bag in one hand, car keys in the other. 'Cheese and biscuits. And a bottle of red wine.'

He smiled and took the bag from her. 'Perfect.' She went to take off her coat, but Brandon rested a hand on the sleeve. 'Leave it on for now, let's go outside and enjoy the night.'

She followed him into the garden, her hair swaying in the breeze, her cheeks flushed.

'I feel I've got special dispensation with this midnight meeting.'

'You have that,' he said, looking into her eyes until she glanced away. 'I'll get some plates,' he said, leaving her at the table with the file of papers.

'You didn't rifle through them,' Brandon said, when he came back with a tray.

'I was sorely tempted. But I did have another look at his painting. God, how prescient was that?'

'You couldn't make it up. Lizzie okay, by the way?'

'Absolutely, Anastasia and Dmytro have been a real comfort to her. The whole thing has bonded them. And, of course, she is so relieved about Piers. Oh Brandon ...' Rachel let her face drop, before looking back up at him. 'I really thought he wouldn't survive this. And, you know, he's been a friend of the family for many years. I wouldn't say like a father. Lawrence was irreplaceable, but like a fun uncle. I am so pleased he's okay.'

'I shared your concerns. We have Jo and Stew to thank for saving him. I'm not sure he had much more time – I'll find out why they didn't kill him immediately later. Possibly a case of raiding his finances.'

'Are you allowed to tell me all this? Isn't it confidential information.'

'Come here, I need your brain.' And body, he thought as she sat down beside him, her leg brushing against his thigh.

They sat shoulders barely an inch apart, heads down, eyes on the papers, Brandon's heart beating hard. So hard he wondered if she could hear it or feel it. His hand touched hers as he went through the papers, and she snatched her fingers back as if scolded by fire. So, they continued the task in forced silence, taking a few papers each with gloved hands and discarding them on two small piles.

Brandon was the first to speak. 'This looks interesting.' He'd come across a stash of letters tied together in a blue ribbon. He untied the bow and lifted out the first one.

Rachel pulled herself up straight and brushed her hair back behind her ears. 'You read them.'

Brandon took a deep breath. 'My Love,' he read, pleased his voice was steady and deep. Not the shaky squeak he feared would betray his emotions.

'It won't be long before your release. I am working on your defence constantly and rallying together support. There is nothing – absolutely nothing – but insubstantial evidence linking you to the case. Keep strong, my Love, and always keep with you my undying devotion. My eternal love.'

Rachel dropped the knife she was spreading butter with. 'The man was besotted. With Ursula?'

'No. It's addressed to HMP Bronzefield, Ashford, Surrey. I'm so pleased he kept copies – of his own letters and hers.'

'That's a lawyer for you,' Rachel said, cutting a bit of cheese and putting it on a cracker. 'Hungry work,' she said, meeting Brandon's eye.

'Let's see if we can't find some names, other than My Love, or Honey Bunny, or whatever.' Brandon went through the pile, Rachel watching. 'No names. Littleton was careful. But

I think we will be able to piece this together ... So, My Love, moved from Bronzefield to Eastwood Park.'

'When?' Rachel had put down her cracker and was leaning in close. 'And is that significant?'

'Sure is, there was quite a thriving community there – Magda Pethick, Fryda Chegwin, Dorothea Llewellyn as medic. And, it would seem, Duncan Littleton was offering his legal services. Looks like the last few weeks have been a cracking reunion.'

'Are you going there?'

'Yes, it has to be her, doesn't it? The woman wasn't ever going to be happy simply weaving baskets.'

'If you're talking about Meghan – Valerie Mason as we now know her – I agree. Although she always had an artistic bent.'

'Bent being the operative word, Rachel.'' He tidied up the papers. 'I think that's a wrap.'

'When will you go to ... Eastwood Park?'

'As soon as possible. Some more interviews tomorrow, but I sense this could be important.'

Brandon put the papers back in their file and took off his gloves. He turned to face her, saw that she was shivering, didn't know whether it was the cold or the memories of that time four years back now when Valerie Mason brought Penzance to its knees.

'Hey,' he said, reaching over and pulling her coat around her. 'Shall we go inside. Take the wine up to the attic, watch the stars from there.'

'Yes,' Rachel said, resting against him, letting him pull her close, feel her silken hair.

71

It was pitch black when the gendarme descended on the Saint-Paul-en-Forêt campsite. Jo and Stew led the police in, past the trailers and caravans and the old man's campervan, his chair rocking as bodies bumped against it in the dark.

'Merde!' yelped one officer, who barged right into it. He grabbed hold of the rocker and threw it out of the way.

'Oú est le caravane de Zidane?' said the detective leading the investigation.

'Voilà.' Stew pointed to the trailer which the perps had left in a cloud of dust that afternoon.

The place exploded into light when the gendarme ranged their torches on it. Shadows slunk down the walls as the officers approached four abreast, waving pistols and making threatening noises.

Stew hung back with Jo. 'Reckon they'll find Zidane?'

Jo felt for her taser, but let it rest in her holster. 'Dead or alive?'

There was an almighty bang as the gendarme made their entrance. Lights flicked on throughout the campsite.

'Ew!' exclaimed one of their number, backing out with his hand over his mouth.

'Does that answer your question?' Jo said, glancing at Stew. 'Yep.'

They watched as the gendarme moved into mop-up mode, calling for an ambulance, pegging out Crime Scene tape.

'Stew, I think our work is done here. Can you let the

Inspector know that we'll be staying at the Hôtel La Rotonde in La Croix-Valmer, before joining them in Nice for interviews tomorrow.'

Stew smiled. 'Nice to be of service, Boss.'

It was nice to have someone of service. Stew had been a real support – his language skills, good humour, courage. She watched as he chatted amiably with the gendarme, beckoning them away from the trailer which stunk. The stench was carrying on the breeze and Jo moved back to stop herself from heaving. Zidane's body must have been there a while.

'Sorted,' Stew said joining her, and switching on his phone torch. 'I'll drive you back.'

Jo nodded and followed him along the dirt track, saw the old man dragging his rocking chair back onto his makeshift porch, noticed the other shadowy figures lurking.

They walked out of the site just as an ambulance turned up, lights flashing.

'Why don't you take a snooze while I get us to the hotel,' Stew said, opening the passenger door for her.

'That is very gallant of you, Monsieur Bland,' Jo said, getting in, glad that she could relax at last. It didn't take more than a few minutes before the dark enveloped her and she let her eyes close and mind drift. She didn't wake until she felt the gentle touch on her shoulder.

'Stew? We're here?'

'Yeah.'

'How long have I been asleep?'

'Nearly an hour.'

'What! Where are we?'

'Nice. No point doubling back to La Crois – and it means we can have a leisurely breakfast.'

Jo rubbed her eyes and looked out of the window at the

majestic beach-fronted hotel.

'And you got this on expenses?'

'Copains rates. The gendarme insisted. Besides, we're out of season.'

'I'm not arguing,' Jo said, rubbing the back of her neck. 'Our luggage?'

'Never left the boot of the Peugeot. I got this covered Menhenrick.'

Jo gave a weary smile.

'Okay, you could look a little more impressed, Mademoiselle.'

A doorman rushed out and offered to take their things.

'Not even a brownie point?'

'I'll buy you a night cap if you've the energy.'

'Oh, I have the energy.'

Jo looked him in the eye. 'How did I ever doubt.'

* * * * *

The waiter came onto the terrace with a gin and tonic for Jo and a Pernod for Stew.

'You sure you don't want one of these to warm you up?' Stew said, passing her the Pernod.

Jo shook her head, and Stew asked the waiter to turn on the outside heaters for them.

'Just like Penzance in August,' Stew said settling down beside her as she looked out across the boulevard to the stretch of water which separated the two countries.

'I think I've run out of stories to regale you with, Menhenrick. Your turn.'

'I'm happy to admire the view,' Jo said, and she meant it. The pedestrians had thinned out, but there were still the night owls, and beyond them the rolling waves, which spoke the same language the world over.

'You thinking about that fisherman friend of yours?' Stew said into her silence.

'No, as it happens.'

Stew relaxed back into his chair. 'That's good to hear.' He clinked their glasses. 'Santé.'

72

A croissant in a paper napkin was peeping out of Stew's pocket shedding crumbs on the Nice police station floor. They were waiting to be taken into the main interview room.

Jo scowled at him. 'Have you smuggled out the saucisson and cheeses too?'

'What do you take me for – a perp? Although I did help myself to a few miniature Bonne Mannan jams. I'm going to need all my energy to help conduct these interviews – if I'm to be translator too.'

Jo spoke quietly out of the side of her mouth. 'Brandon has requested the Ursula Chabrol interview takes place in English.'

Stew looked disappointed.

'The French team conducted the interview in French yesterday, rapelles toi?'

'Aw, you're getting better Menhenrick. Maybe you should give Brandon some French lessons.'

Jo rolled her eyes. 'Ursula Chabrol is a German who speaks perfect English. Besides, it will make it so much easier for me to understand her.'

'Sorry, Boss,' Stew said, tearing off the top of his croissant and popping it in his mouth. 'I bow to your – and Brandon's – greater knowledge and experience.'

Jo nodded towards an opening door at the far end of the room. 'We're on.'

They were escorted into a grand room with high windows and a very long table; a table Vladimer Putin would likely approve of. On one side were four chairs. On the other two. TV screens faced each other on the surrounding walls. Jo and Stew took their seats in the row of four while the two French detectives briefed each other in the corner.

The clicking of heels on the tiled floor signalled the entrance of Ursula Chabrol, and she swept into the room followed by her lawyer. Jo was surprised to see Jemina Rattison.

'She gets around,' Stew whispered under his breath. 'Reckon Jimmy Moyle would have set his alarm for this gig.'

Jo tidied her notes and prepared herself for what could be an epic conversation. Both women were notoriously sharp and confident – they'd have to be with the evidence flashing guilty as accused. As they settled themselves at the table Jo caught Brandon entering the Penzance interview room on the screen. She felt a rush of affection, for him and the place she called home.

'Bonjour mesdames et messieurs,' Brandon said in his deep southern drawl, and the words touched her. But he looked distant. As if it was more than the screen that was separating them. A softening of expression. An undefinable emotion radiated. He gave her a smile from the screen, but it didn't reach his eyes, and she wondered what was preoccupying him.

'Ahem,' Stew said. 'Allez maintenant.'

'Ms Chabrol, you must be exhausted after the events of the past two weeks. And all the planning too. And no chance to *paint yourself a better person*,' Brandon said from the screens above.

Stew spluttered into his glass of water.

'I don't think this is a time for cheap shots,' Rattison said, her eyebrows arching.

Brandon continued. 'So, whatever made you devise this convoluting plan which has seen the death of an innocent art dealer, the abduction and near death of a young man, my own near demise, and the extortion of £75,000 which endangered the life of Rachel Matthews?'

'Alain Boucher was unlucky, granted,' Ursula said, smoothing a loose lock of hair behind one ear. She was sporting a severe pixie cut, quite a departure from her thick brown mane and the wigs she wore incognito.

'The man was …' Brandon paused. 'Brutally murdered and his body displayed in the manner of a ritual killing. And you say unlucky?'

Ursula sat perfectly still. 'Yes. It was a mistake – P-thick by name, V-thick by nature.'

'So, you're saying Magda Pethick killed Alain Boucher by mistake?'

'Yes,' Ursula said, staring at the screen.

'And it should have been?'

'Join up the dots, Detective Inspector.'

'You join them up for me, Madame Chabrol.'

'Piers Jardine.' She rolled her eyes.

'And you abducted him to finish off the job.'

'That's not my style.'

'Something for your henchman. Said Hamza. He said you killed Fared Zidane.'

Ursula threw back her shorn head and laughed. 'His DNA is all over the corpse.'

The two French detectives looked at each other and started muttering.

'These two Clouseaus have yet to have the DNA analysed, but I can tell them now – Hamza's grubby hands did the deed. He didn't even bother to hide the evidence.' She rolled her eyes again. 'Stoned. We found Zidane only minutes before those two turned up.' She jerked her head at Jo and Stew.

Stew made a small grunt and said under his breath. 'Madame Chabrol is going for an Oscar.'

'Thank you for your expert opinion,' Brandon said, his face barely concealing his amusement. 'But why, on earth, would you wish to kill Piers Jardine?'

Ursula played with the Hermes scarf at her throat. 'I didn't particularly.'

Brandon's face hardened. 'Particularly? Just didn't take your immediate fancy?'

'I got … persuaded … to take a harsher line.' She looked down and then back up at Brandon.

'By who?'

'My husband, Henri, is wasting his time in prison because of Piers Jardine and his *expert* knowledge of the art world.' Ursula spat out the words.

'He put a hit on Jardine?'

'It wasn't like that.'

'What was it like?' Brandon was leaning forward, his full attention on Chabrol.

'A collaboration. A critical mass of people coming together at the same time with grievances.'

'List them.'

Ursula gave a theatrical sigh. 'Pethick was working with Dorothea Llewellyn, who had been cheated by Jardine – or so she said. I was unhappy too. My lifestyle and reputation were destroyed overnight, and I was forced to work in arts therapy, to pay the solicitors' fees and buy food.'

'Our hearts bleed for you,' Stew chipped in.

Brandon gave him a sharp look from the screen, before turning back to Chabrol. 'And that was enough to kill

Jardine?'

'Money, revenge, sure. That's motive enough.'

'Why was Damien Kane targeted?'

'I wondered when you were going to get to that.'

Brandon gave his cold stare.

'There was a list of people that needed to be punished. You must understand that we were hurting badly. Dorothea, myself, Henri and Valerie and Duncan.'

'Valerie Mason? The woman that took the wrap for the smuggling heist in 2018?'

'Yes, but there is still doubt isn't there?'

'Duncan Littleton seems to think so.'

Rattison, who had been uncharacteristically reticent so far went to speak.

'Let me finish, Jemima!' Ursula scolded.

'Duncan was beguiled by her, like all the rest. Including my husband. I've never forgiven her for dragging him down with her. So, I have no qualms but to lay all the blame for this *project* at her feet.'

'Why did you go along with it, then?' Brandon said, his eyes tearing into Chabrol's.

'Because it suited me. And I thought – I still think – this will be the final nail in that witch's coffin.'

'You also stood to make a packet,' Jo said, glancing up at Brandon. He nodded at her to continue. *The Art of Living* was being used to launder money. The company's coffers made a huge profit from your short course in St Ives. £500,000 to be exact. How do you square that sum, Madame Chabrol?'

Rattison turned to face Chabrol her mouth poised to speak, until her client shut her down with a withering look.

'A debt owed,' Chabrol said. 'My course was … forced to close because of unseen circumstances. The finances were a cash flow loan, to keep the business viable until business could resume.'

'Nicely put,' Brandon said. 'But we've done a check on your cashflow – and your courses in Germany hardly broke even.'

Ursula shrugged. 'They paid the rent.'

'But that was never enough for you, was it Madame Chabrol,' Jo said, 'You wanted more. You wanted your old lifestyle back.'

Ursula shrugged again, although her shoulders were trembling. 'I am only human. I seized an opportunity to rebuild my life and settle a few scores.'

'Okay, I'm counting the scores. Piers Jardine, who was an unwitting agent in your downfall. Valerie Mason, who seduced your husband and dragged him into her schemes. Damien Kane, whose video evidence was pivotal. Any others?'

Ursula turned to Rattison.

'She has no comment.'

'Why did you stay at Lizzie Matthews? Because of her connection with Piers Jardine? Why did you employ Rachel Matthews to work for you? Did you seek to punish them too?'

'My client has no comment to make,' Rattison said.

Ursula sighed heavily and turned two weary eyes to Brandon. 'I was taking paid orders. I didn't compile the list. You may wish to know that you were on it, DI Hammett.'

Thoughts of the warehouse fire flashed through his mind. That was ugly. He was lucky to have survived.

'Who compiled the list, Madame Chabrol? Who was paying you?'

'Our cause célèbre in East Park Prison and her gimp, Duncan Littleton.' Ursula waved a tired hand at Rattison.

'My client has no more to say.' Jemina Rattison looked at the French detectives and rose from her seat. Ursula sat there, her head in her hands, until escorted out of the room.

Stew went to say something, but Jo shushed him.

'Do we have enough?' Jo said to Brandon.

'Yes. From all but the two at the top of the triangle. Valerie Mason, who has a firm alibi sitting in her cell, and Duncan Littleton who is likely at the bottom of the deep blue med.'

'The body hasn't surfaced yet, Boss,' Stew said.

'Maybe he perfected that dive then?' Brandon replied.

'What dive?' Stew said.

Jo grimaced. 'I'll explain later.' A gendarme was holding the door open for them, and Jo got her things together.

'See you later, Boss,' she spoke to the screen and caught Brandon's hazy smile before his finger ended the video call.

'This croissant is burning a hole in my pocket,' Stew said once they were outside the station. 'Shall we take a wander down to the front before check in?'

'Cool,' Jo said, adding, 'Do you have another one of those in your pocket.'

'Or am I just happy to see you?' Stew said smiling broadly. 'Voilà!' he said flourishing another.

73

Rachel

'I bought us some Chinese,' Brandon plonked two carriers down on his kitchen table.

'That looks like a banquet,' Rachel said crossing the floor with two glasses.

'Chelsea and Damien can tuck in later – we may well be fast asleep by then. They're going to a gig.'

Rachel felt a flutter in the pit of her stomach at the suggestion of another night alone with Brandon. It had been beautiful last night, so easy and right. She looked at him and he returned her gaze with his dark blue eyes, the colour of the night sky.

'Come here,' he said, and she walked over and let him pull her close and lift her up onto the table.

'Hey,' Rachel said, 'Why'd you do that?'

'Because I can.'

'Have you got written consent?'

'Matthews, don't mess with a lawman.' He cupped her face with his hands and kissed her lightly on the lips. 'Particularly not one who is intent on enjoying his banquet.'

Rachel blushed and Brandon stepped away and pulled out a prawn cracker. He waved it at her. 'I left you in charge of the drinks, gal.'

'You did indeed.' Rachel hopped off the table and went over to the kitchenette to get a bottle of red and a small bottle of whiskey.

'That's mighty thoughtful of you,' Brandon said, studying

her from under his fringe. 'It's been a long time since ...'

Rachel unscrewed the wine bottle top and poured him a glass. 'Since?'

He let her take a sip of wine and then kissed her softly on the lips and then harder.

'The food will go cold,' Rachel said, as she moved against him.

'What food,' he murmured.

* * * * *

They lay together in Brandon's big iron bed, the sheets kicked on the floor, a patchwork quilt flung over the ornate foot stand.

'This bed is impressive – did you ship it over from Texas?'

'You kiddin? Dreams.co.uk. This is no heirloom – yet.' He turned on his side and looked at her.

Rachel snuggled up close. Sometimes those eyes were too much to bear. 'Have I won the right for some pillow talk?'

Brandon kissed her lightly on the head. 'I am putty in your hands, darlin'.'

'That's a start!' Rachel pulled back and looked at him.

Brandon rolled onto his back like a sated bear. 'We got the answers, we got the evidence, we got the perps in holding cells in Penzance and Nice.'

'So, a satisfactory conclusion?' Rachel propped herself up on her elbow.

'I've always said you should join the force. You always ask *that* question.'

'I need to make a prison visit tomorrow to see one Valerie Mason. Fingers are pointing at her, but no firm evidence.'

'Clever woman.'

'No doubting that.'

'And Duncan. Have they found him?'

Brandon sat up and reached for his packet of cigarettes, but fell back.

'Have one,' Rachel said.

'You sure? I'm giving up, you know.'

'I know. But it's been quite a time, for us all.'

Brandon lit up and blew the smoke out of the side of his mouth. 'They haven't found Littleton's body. But it's so rocky around there. He can't have survived.'

'Do you think any of those letters will implicate Valerie?'

'Unlikely. He never named her as such and there were never any implicit instructions.'

'The money though? That he laundered?'

'We're looking into it. But overseas bank accounts are as tight as a clam and easily transferrable. We may never find the link. As we may never find his body. But we got the killers and the gang that abducted Damien. Hey, is that his dulcet tones I hear in the kitchen right now?'

Rachel scrambled for her clothes on the floor, much to Brandon's amusement.

'You two want some supper!' Chelsea shouted up the stairs.

'Yes,' Brandon called back.

'Just finishing up in the attic,' Rachel called down, reddening.

Brandon spun her around. 'There's no foolin' my gal Chelsea. But she's cool. You know she loves you.' He looked away and then back at Rachel. 'We love you.'

Rachel touched his arm. Wanted to say, 'How love me? Like a Lover? A Friend with benefits but left it there. Sometimes you can't get all the answers … at once.

Her phoned pinged a message from Julia.

Rachel picked up her phone.

'How's it going with Brandon?'

Rachel bit her top lip. She wondered just how far Julia and Brandon's relationship had developed while she was in London. But Julia had reassured her that nothing had happened, and Rachel should follow her heart. She was practically pushing them together, with her convenient 'Events' nights. But a nagging guilt prevailed. Julia was her best friend, and her happiness was paramount.

She looked over her shoulder and saw Brandon buckling his belt.

'We did it.' Rachel texted.

'Again?'

'Yes *embarassed face*.'

'At last. Now I can let out my room to a handsome stranger!'

'I have a tendency to *boomerang*.'

'Not anymore, Rachel. This feels right. *face with hearts*.'

'You coming down, darlin'?' Brandon came over and wrapped his arms around her.

'Just saying bye to Julia.'

'Thank you. *red heart*.'

'Love you,' Julia replied.

'Ditto.' Rachel sent the text and pulled on her blouse and trousers.

'Julia okay?' Brandon said.

'Yes. She truly is.'

'She's quite a woman, your best friend,' Brandon said reaching over to give her a hug.

'The best sister I never had,' Rachel said, resting against his arm.

74

Brandon

'You're saying she's left?' Brandon was on the phone to Eastwood Park Prison.

'This morning. She's served her time DI Hammett.' Brandon thought he recognised reproof in the prison deputy governor's tone. Mason's Fanclub knew no bounds.

'But she was sentenced to six years.'

'Valerie Mason won a succession of appeals.'

'But not all. She was caught red-handed absconding with stolen goods.'

'Ms Mason was an exemplary inmate. Her sentence was reduced for good behaviour.'

'I'm surprised she isn't up for an MBE.'

The woman hissed down the line. 'If I can be of any further assistance.'

'You can. Where can I contact her?'

'I am not at liberty to say.'

'It is part of a major investigation.'

'Ms Mason has been in prison for four years. How could that be?'

'Don't be so naïve.'

'On the contrary, it is you being naïve if you think we can give out forwarding addresses without going through the proper channels.'

Brandon slumped back in his chair. She was right, of course, but he hadn't expected Mason to take her leave the very day he wanted to pay her a visit. Surely the woman's tendrils hadn't wrapped their way around Her Majesty's Prison Service. He tapped the packet of cigarettes in his pocket and gave a rueful grin. She had skedaddled and there wasn't much he could do about it right now. He wasn't even certain they had enough to bring her in for questioning. It was all 'she said, he said'. Nothing in writing. No DNA. Or CCTV. The smoking gun was the laundered money – but a team of investigative journalists doing a Panorama special would have trouble tracing the origins. From what he could gather, Littleton handled that side of the business. And he was dead. Or as good as.

'Euro for them?' Stew was at the door with a bag of muffins and croissants.

'Call me back if you can be of any help.' Brandon put down the receiver, wasn't even sure if the woman on the other end was still there.

'The returning heroes,' Brandon said, getting up to greet Jo and Stew.

Stew looked momentarily taken aback. 'We did alright – me and the boss lady.'

'You sure did. You've closed down a nasty sect. I mean, set of criminals. But they were, in many ways, like a sect with their warped vengeful ideology.'

Jo moved forward quietly. 'Anyone left in the cells here.'

Brandon tilted his head to look at her. She'd been through the mill and now she had to face the final interview. Or did she?

'Jason Pascoe is still here.'

'Aha,' Jo said.

'The questions now are pretty routine. We've been through Pascoe's role with him already. Just need to determine if there is any more information he can give us to … mitigate his—'

'Sentence,' Jo said. 'Brandon, don't worry, I've processed all this. I'm good.'

Brandon had his hands on his hips, lips parted. 'You processed all this while chasing down an armed perp, with a hostage. And … the rest.'

'Wasn't all work, no play,' Stew chipped in. 'We chewed the fat a bit over a few Pernods and Vinos.'

'Yes, I heard about the stay at the Grande!'

'Nicegate!' Stew said his joke easing the tension. 'The gendarme insisted. Very gallant of them. Reckon they fancied Jo.'

Jo rolled her eyes but blushed all the same.

'In all seriousness, Jo, you don't have to come into this interview. In fact, it would probably be more appropriate if you don't.'

'Boss, for once in my life can I be inappropriate?'

* * * * *

Jason jolted upright when Jo followed Brandon into the interview room. Maybe it wasn't such a bad idea bringing her along. From what he could gather Pascoe had a real affection for Jo – she was way out of his league, so who could blame him. Perhaps she could draw a few last strands that could tie the case firmly together.

'Interview commenced, 11 am, March 10, 2022,' Jo said, her voice steady, although her hands shook when she turned on the recorder.

'Mr Pascoe, how well do you know Valerie Mason?' Brandon said.

'I—' Pascoe looked like he was going to deny knowing her but had a change of heart. 'A few years. She was involved in the smuggling back then. She's in the cooler, in't she?'

Brandon let out a small sigh. 'Doing time for her sins. As you will be soon, Mr Pascoe.'

'Am already.' He spread his arms.

'To cut to the chase, Pascoe, we have enough conclusive evidence to jail everyone involved in your party games. But fingers have been pointing to Mason as the ringleader. She appears to have been organising events from prison. What say you?'

Pascoe frowned. 'It wouldn't surprise me. She was a bossy moo. But, let me make this clear, this is the first I've heard of her … in a long time. My line manager was Fryda.'

'Jason.' Jo's quiet voice startled the men. 'Is there anything – anything at all – you can add now to help our inquiries?'

Jason looked like a man in torment.

'We believe Mason was laundering money through Ursula Chabrol's arts therapy course in St Ives. Do you have any recollection of this being discussed? Did you overhear anything?'

Jason ran a hand through his hair. 'There was a drop off in Newlyn Harbour 'bout this time last year. A box. I ferried it over to Brest.'

Brandon edged forward. 'How big was the box? Was it heavy?'

'It was big and heavy. And quite dirty – as if it had been buried.'

'What was in it?' Jo said.

'It was bolted fast. But I can tell you this, it weren't fish.'

'Who picked up the box?'

'Some dudes in masks – and dark clothes. This was towards the end of lockdown in Europe. They didn't look out of place. And it was dark.'

'Did you think this was suspicious?' Jo said.

'Yes. But I was being paid well.'

'What do you think was in that box?'

'Artwork. Like before. Same careful packaging.'

'Was this the only drop off of this kind since 2018?'

'Yes.'

Brandon looked at Jo and then back at Jason. 'Thank you, Mr Pascoe. That information has been helpful.' And then under his breath to Jo. 'So, the money was being laundered through paintings. Mason must have stashed away a few masterpieces before she went down and has since cashed them in. They're going to be harder to trace than offshore bank deposits – probably lining the wall of a Sheik's yacht right now.'

'Interview terminated, 11.10 am, March 10, 2022,' Jo said.

'Glad to have been of service,' Jason said shaking his head lightly as a uniformed officer came up beside him.

Jason turned at the interview room door as he was being escorted back down to his cell. 'Jo, I'm sorry I misled you. I'm sorry I hurt you. I really did like you. More than anyone. Please believe that. Will you visit me? You don't have to. I'll understand.'

'Goodbye, Jason,' Jo said, and watched him leave.

75

Brandon

'Why don't you see him, Jo?' Brandon said, when they were alone.

'It hurts too much right now to even consider it.'

'I understand,' he said. 'But maybe later. He wasn't such a bad man. Better, in many respects than his pretentious brother!'

Jo gave a short laugh. 'Don't worry, I won't be transferring my affections.'

'And you, Brandon. Are you seeing anyone now?'

He took his time to answer. He was so happy, but sometimes that's not the best thing to be when you're faced with a friend's misfortune. 'Rachel. We've been seeing each other.'

Jo smiled. 'I had an inkling.'

'You wouldn't be the DS Menhenrick I know, if that weren't the case.'

'I'm so happy for you, Brandon. I really am.'

He put his hand on her shoulder. 'Come on, let's join Stew before he eats all the muffins.'

'And croissants,' added Jo, smiling.

'I want to know every detail of that jolly you two have been on,' Brandon said, opening the door for her.

The End

Acknowledgements

First and foremost, I must thank my friends and family for encouraging me to publish the third in the DI Brandon Hammett series. They expressed their desire for the next instalment and who was I to deny them? In many respects the book's characters feel like family and friends.

So, a rollcall for Yvonne Taylor, my sister and number one cheer leader, and Alex Buxton my son who gives me such clear-headed encouragement and advice, as well as my friends who gather at my launches and buy my books. Importantly, a shout out to my readers who enjoy my novels and write encouraging reviews that all writers need. And I cannot forget my writer friends from the UEA and from SCBWI. They've been there for me and given me heaps of support and inspiration.

I'd also like to single out Sophie Brownlow for her professional, meticulous and constructive editing. Sophie is new to the series and gave a welcome fresh perspective. All the books are standalone as well as part of a series, so it was invaluable to hear from a new reader.

Furthermore, a big thank you to Penzance artist Janine Wing who produced another amazing cover. And not forgetting designer Cavan Convery who makes it all hang together and sing.

Last, but not least, I want to acknowledge my parents – Alec and Maureen Taylor – who I have dedicated this book to. It wouldn't have happened without them, for too many reasons to mention.